The Jarrods: Inheritance

MAXINE SULLIVAN
EMILIE ROSE
HEIDI BETTS

MILLS &
BOON

Published in Great Britain 2015
by Mills & Boon, an imprint of Harlequin (UK) Limited,
Eton House, 18-24 Paradise Road, Richmond, Surrey, TW9 1SR

THE JARRODS: INHERITANCE © 2015 Harlequin Books S.A.

Taming Her Billionaire Boss, *Wedding His Takeover Target* and *Inheriting His Secret Christmas Baby* were first published in Great Britain by Harlequin (UK) Limited.

Taming Her Billionaire Boss © 2010 Harlequin Books S.A.
Wedding His Takeover Target © 2010 Harlequin Books S.A.
Inheriting His Secret Christmas Baby © 2010 Harlequin Books S.A.

Special thanks and acknowledgement to Maxine Sullivan, Emilie Rose and Heidi Betts for their contributions to the Dynasties: The Jarrods series.

ISBN: 978-0-263-25230-9
eBook ISBN: 978-1-474-00409-1

05-0915

Harlequin (UK) Limited's policy is to use papers that are natural, renewable and recyclable products and made from wood grown in sustainable forests. The logging and manufacturing processes conform to the legal environmental regulations of the country of origin.

Printed and bound in Spain
by CPI, Barcelona

TAMING HER BILLIONAIRE BOSS

BY
MAXINE SULLIVAN

With thanks to the fabulous Desire™ editors,
Krista Stroever and Charles Griemsman, who
worked so hard to make this series special.

And to friend and Harlequin American author
C.C. Coburn, for her helpful advice on
everything Aspen

Maxine Sullivan credits her mother for her lifelong love of romance novels, so it was a natural extension for Maxine to want to write her own romances. She thinks there's nothing better than being a writer and is thrilled to be one of the few Australians to write for the Desire™ line.

Maxine lives in Melbourne, Australia, but over the years has travelled to New Zealand, the UK and the USA. In her own backyard, her husband's job ensured they saw the diversity of the countryside, from the tropics to the Outback, country towns to the cities. She is married to Geoff, who has proven his hero status many times over the years. They have two handsome sons and an assortment of much-loved, previously abandoned animals.

Maxine would love to hear from you. She can be contacted through her website at www.maxinesullivan.com.

From the Last Will and Testament of Don Jarrod

…and to my beloved son Blake I leave the grand piano that was your mother's pride and joy. Some of my fondest memories are of you, lying beneath that piano, listening to your mother play. I hope you will find room in your home for this beautiful piece and enjoy not just the beautiful music it puts forth, but the true love it represents.

One

"What are you doing in here?"

Samantha Thompson almost dropped her pen as her head snapped up, the desk lamp shedding enough light for her to see the handsome man standing in the doorway. "Blake, you scared me!"

Her heart didn't settle down once she knew who it was, it only increased pace as she looked at him in a dinner suit that fitted his well-toned body flawlessly. His commanding presence was of a man born to lead. This was Blake Jarrod, owner of Blake Jarrod Enterprises' Las Vegas hotels, and now the new CEO of Jarrod Ridge, his family's renowned resort in Aspen, Colorado.

And as his assistant of two years there was nothing unusual about her being in his office at ten at night. Just because they were now in Aspen at the Jarrod Manor and she was using the desk in his late father's office didn't change a thing. She had her reasons for being here.

And they concerned her boss.

Or soon-to-be-ex boss.

"It's late," he said, cutting across her thoughts in the way he usually did.

She took a steadying breath and looked down at the letter in front of her, giving herself one last chance to change her mind. Then she remembered this evening. The final straw had been watching a famous blonde actress flirt outrageously with Blake, and him sitting there enjoying it, taking it as his due.

Samantha couldn't blame him for wanting to sample what was on offer if he so chose. It was just that *she* wanted a little taste of him herself. She usually dressed sedately in finely tailored clothes whether she was in Vegas with Blake or here in Aspen, but tonight she'd outdone herself. She'd worn this slinky cream evening dress designed to grab his attention, putting her long, brunette hair up in a chignon when she usually wore it pulled back at the nape with a barrette, but it was clear now that nothing was going to happen between her and Blake.

It was *never* going to happen.

She'd realized that when he'd caught her eye and she'd smiled for all she was worth, looked the best she could be, and he'd turned back to the actress without a second glance, rejecting her just like Carl had rejected her. Her moment of epiphany had been that simple. She'd come to a decision then. The right decision for her. The *only* one for her.

She lifted her gaze. "Yes, it's late, Blake."

Too late.

He walked toward the desk, almost as if he sensed

something wasn't quite right. "I thought you said you were going back to Pine Lodge."

That had been her intention. She'd even stood in the lobby of the manor, her coat resting on her shoulders, waiting beside the doorman for the valet to bring the SUV around. She'd been determined to go back to their private lodge at the resort—she in her own room and Blake in the master suite.

Then someone had entered the hotel and the doors had slid open, and the cold night breeze from a midfall wind had slapped her in the face and chilled her to the bone, reminding her that it didn't matter what she wore or what she did, her boss would never take any notice of her except as his assistant. She'd spun around and headed for the private elevator, coming up here to the office in the family section of the manor.

"I needed to do something first," she said now.

There was an alert look to his eyes. "It's Friday night. Work can wait until tomorrow."

They'd been working every Saturday, trying to keep on top of things until they moved here permanently. And now that wasn't going to happen. Not for her anyway. "This can't wait."

He paused, those blue eyes narrowing in on her. "What can't?"

She swallowed hard. "My resignation."

Shock flashed in his eyes then went out like it had never been. "What are you talking about?" he said, his voice quiet. In control. He was *always* in control, especially where she was concerned.

"It's time for me to move on, Blake. That's all."

"Why?"

The question shot at her like a pellet but she managed to shrug. "It just is."

He put his hands on the desk and leaned toward her. "What's this about, Samantha? What's the real reason you want to leave?"

She'd faced him down over business issues occasionally but this…*this* was personal. Cautiously, she pushed the leather chair back and rose on her stilettos, then went to look out the large arched window behind her.

The scene below at the luxurious resort was surprisingly charming in October. Tonight, pocketed in amongst the tall peaks, the sleepy hamlet twinkled like fairy lights in the alpine breeze, a tapestry of winding streets, lodges, and village square. To a southern California girl who now lived in Vegas, this place had something nowhere else seemed to have.

It had heart.

"It's time for me to go," she said, keeping her back to him.

"You're unhappy here?"

"No!" she blurted out, swinging around, then winced inwardly, knowing she sounded contradictory and that he'd have to wonder why.

To be truthful, she'd been feeling slightly down ever since Blake's sister Melissa had announced her pregnancy a few weeks ago. She'd been happy for Melissa, so why it had bothered her she didn't know. Yet since then she hadn't been able to shake a feeling of being slightly depressed.

He'd straightened away from the desk. "So what's the problem?"

You are.

I want you to notice me.

Dammit, I just want *you*.

But how did you say that to a man who didn't even notice you as a woman? She was his trusted assistant and that was about it. She'd never acted overtly female around him. She kept everything businesslike between them. Looking back, perhaps occasionally she should have let her feminine side show. If she had, then perhaps now she might not be in this predicament.

Yet it wasn't that she was in love with him either. She was intensely attracted to him. He was an exciting, charismatic man who effortlessly charmed women like they were going out of fashion, but he was still discerning in whom he took to his bed.

She wanted to be charmed by him.

She wanted to be in his bed and in his arms.

Oh, God, it truly was hitting home that she'd never be in his spotlight. Until now a glimmer of hope had kept her going, but after his subconscious rejection of her tonight, she'd realized that if he knew her feelings about wanting him, then everything would change. She'd be totally embarrassed and so would he. She couldn't work like that. She'd be humiliated just like she'd been with Carl. It was better to leave with some dignity.

"Samantha?"

Hearing her name on his lips struck her like never before. She tilted her head at him. "Do you know something, Blake? You've never called me Sam. Not once. It's always Samantha."

His brows drew together. "What's that got to do with it?"

Everything.

She wanted to be Sam once in a while. Sam the

woman who'd left her ordinary upbringing in Pasadena to embrace the excitement of Vegas after a one-sided love affair gone wrong. The woman who wanted to have a purely physical affair with a man she admired, without ever risking her heart again. Not Samantha the personal assistant who helped run his office and his life and who kept the whole lot in check for him, all nice and neat and tidy, just the way he liked it. She couldn't believe she'd actually thought she'd had a chance with him.

And he was waiting for an answer.

"I have my reasons for resigning and I think that's all you need to know."

"Is someone giving you a hard time?" he asked sharply. "Someone from my family? I'll talk to them if they are. Tell me."

She shook her head. "Your family's great. It's…" She hesitated, wishing she'd given herself time to come up with a suitable explanation. Needless to say, she hadn't expected to be here tonight writing out her resignation, or that he'd even come upon her. She'd assumed he'd probably go off nightclubbing with Miss Hollywood. "I simply want something more, okay? It's nothing against you or your family. This is about me."

One eyebrow rose. "You want something *more* than first-class travel and a world-class place to live?"

"Yes." She had to tread carefully. "Actually I'm thinking of going home to Pasadena for a little while," she fibbed, then realized that wasn't such a bad idea after all. "Just until I decide what I want to do next."

"And that will give you more of what you want? I seem to remember you saying you'd left Pasadena *because* you'd been looking for more excitement."

She'd definitely said that—and she *had* been looking

for more than weekly piano lessons and weekend shopping with her girlfriends—but it had been so much more four years ago. Having fallen in love with a young architect who'd gone off to travel the world after she'd told him she loved him, she'd decided to find her own excitement. Her job with Blake had provided that excitement without any emotional involvement. Until now. And even now it was about lust, not love.

His eyes pierced the distance between them. "You seemed happy enough before to move to Aspen."

"I was... I am... I mean..." Oh, heck. She was getting herself tied up in knots. When Blake said he was moving back home and she should come with him, she'd been delighted. His estranged father's will had stated all the Jarrod offspring had to return to Jarrod Ridge for a year or lose their inheritance. Blake, being the eldest—only by a few minutes ahead of his fraternal and more laidback twin, Guy—had taken up the challenge of running the resort.

She'd looked forward to it, too, and they'd been traveling back and forth between Aspen and Vegas a couple of times these past four months, getting everything sorted. Blake would keep his hotels but would spend most of his time in Aspen. She'd been very happy with that. Until tonight.

She cleared her throat. "All my family and friends are back in Pasadena. I miss them."

"I didn't know you *had* any friends."

She pulled a face. "Thanks very much."

There was a flicker of impatience. "You know what I mean. You're always working or traveling with me and rarely go home except for the holidays. Your friends have never been a priority before."

"I guess that's changed." Thankfully Carl had never returned and she'd heard he'd married an English girl. Of course, time and distance had only shown her that she hadn't really been in love with him at all. She'd been in love with the *idea* of being in love with a man who'd talked of adventure in far-off places. She'd thought they'd do that together. God, what was wrong with her that she kept wanting men who *didn't* want her?

He held her gaze. "What are you going to do after Pasadena, then?"

"I'm not sure. I'll find something. Perhaps even one of those rare friends of mine might help me get a job," she mocked. All she knew was that she wouldn't continue working for Blake, not in Aspen nor in Vegas. A clean break was needed.

He eyed her. "You have plenty of connections. You could use them."

All at once she had an ache in her throat. It sounded like he was beginning to accept her decision. And *that* more than anything showed he really didn't care about her. She was just another employee to him. Nothing more.

"I'm thinking I might get right away from this type of work."

"And do what?"

"I don't know." She took a breath. "In any case, I'd really like to leave Aspen as soon as possible, so that I can wrap up things in Vegas before going home. It shouldn't take more than a couple of days." She'd make sure it didn't.

He scanned her face. "You're not telling me every-thing," he said, sending her heart bumping against her ribs.

"There's nothing else to tell. I do have a life and a family away from you, Blake, as hard as that may be for you to believe." She couldn't take much more of this. Going over to the desk, she picked up the letter. "So I'd appreciate it if you would accept my resignation." She walked toward him. "Ideally I'd like to leave here as soon as possible. Tomorrow even." Reaching him, she held out the letter.

He didn't take it.

There was a measured silence, then, "No."

The breath stalled in her throat. "Wh-what?"

"No, I won't accept your letter of resignation and certainly not on such short notice. I need you here with me."

His words sent a jet of warmth through her until she remembered this evening. It had been torturous watching him and that actress flirt with each other. How could she stay and keep up the pretence that she didn't want Blake for herself?

She continued to hold the letter out to him. "I can't stay, Blake. I really need to leave."

Now.

Tomorrow.

Certainly no later than that.

He ignored the sheet of paper until she lowered her hand. "I'm the new CEO here, Samantha. It wouldn't be professional of you to leave me in the lurch like this."

She felt bad but it came down to emotional survival. "I know, but there are others quite capable of replacing me. Just contact a high-end employment agency. I'll even do it for you before I go. Someone else would love to work here in Jarrod Ridge. They could be here by Monday."

His mouth tightened. "No."

She lifted her chin. "I'm afraid you have no choice."

"I don't?" he said silkily, inching closer. "You can't quit without a month's notice. It's in your contract."

She sucked in a sharp breath. "Surely you could waive that for me? I've given you two years of my life, Blake, and I've done the job exceptionally well. I've been at your beck and call 24/7. I think you owe me this."

"If you insist on leaving before your contract is up then I'll see you in court." He gave a significant pause. "I don't think that would look good on your résumé, do you?"

"You wouldn't!"

"Wouldn't I?

"This is business," he continued. "Don't take it personally."

She almost choked then. That was the problem. Everything was business between them. *Nothing* was personal.

Her hands shook with anger as she began folding the letter in four. Then she leaned forward and tucked it into his jacket pocket. "Fine. You've got your month. Two weeks here and then two weeks back in Vegas to finish up. After that I'm leaving for Pasadena." She went to step past him.

In a flash he grabbed her arm and stopped her, looking down into her eyes. It was the first time he'd ever touched her *with meaning* and something passed between them. She saw his spark of surprise before he dropped her arm. It surprised her, too.

"I never take no for an answer, Samantha. Remember that."

"There's always the exception to every rule. And I'm it, *Mr. Jarrod.*"

* * *

She was still shaking when she got out of the SUV and back to her room at Pine Lodge. She was angry at Blake's refusal to let her go without giving a month's notice, and excited by the awareness in his eyes when he'd touched her. Was she crazy to look more into this than she should?

Her heartbeat stretched into a gallop at the thought that he was attracted to her. A split second was all it had taken and she'd known what it was like to have this man want her. Would he let himself take it further? Remembering the way he'd immediately dropped his hand and withdrawn, she knew he wouldn't.

Yet he'd wanted to, and that was the difference between him and Carl. Oh, she'd had a physical relationship many years ago as a teenager, but looking back, that had been so adolescent. Since then it had only been Carl, and he hadn't wanted her beyond a kiss or two.

But with Blake tonight, she'd known for a moment what it was like for a *man* to really desire her. And that gave her hope that with a bit of encouragement he might make her his. What did she have to lose now? If she went home without taking this opportunity to become Blake's lover she'd always wonder what it would have been like to be kissed by him, to be held by him, to have their bodies joined. And she'd always ache inside for what might have been.

She frowned. How could she capture his attention again and keep it? So far she'd tried everything and nothing had worked. She'd made herself as attractive as possible for him, to no avail. She'd even tried flirting over dinner earlier, but it had fallen faster than a lead balloon. Instead she'd ended up jealous of that actress's ability to flirt so naturally. If only *she* could act like…

Just then a thought clicked in her mind. She couldn't believe she hadn't thought of this before now, but if flirting with Blake hadn't made him sit up and take notice of her, maybe he needed to be stirred up. Maybe he needed an award-winning performance. And a little taste of jealousy.

Yet Blake wasn't the type of man who wanted things made easy for him. Making it appear at least a little difficult to catch her had to be the way to go. He wouldn't be interested otherwise.

And what better way to get his attention than letting him see that other men wanted her? Blake wouldn't be able to resist the challenge. This past week at least two good-looking men had asked her out to dinner but she'd turned them down. She hadn't wanted to be with any man but Blake. She still didn't, but he didn't need to know that.

Starting tomorrow, she'd let herself be wined and dined by men who desired her. She wasn't about to take it any further than that, but she wasn't going to sit around any longer and be uptight Samantha for the rest of her time here either. Sam Thompson was about to break out of her shell.

After Samantha left his office, Blake stood there for a minute, stunned by his encounter with his assistant, and not only because she'd wanted to resign. When he'd touched her he'd had the strongest urge to pull her into his arms and make love to her. She'd felt it, too. He'd seen an acknowledgement in her blue eyes she hadn't been able to hide. Strangely, it excited him. He wasn't used to beautiful women holding themselves back. Women usually *gave* themselves to him.

Clearly it had taken Samantha by surprise as much as it had him. Equally as clearly, she wasn't about to act on it. She probably didn't know *how* to act on it. Over the two years that she'd worked for him he'd rarely seen her date. She was a beautiful woman who socialized with grace and class at functions they both attended, but there had never seemed to be a permanent man in her life. Admittedly *he* kept her busy, but he'd often wondered if she'd had a bad relationship somewhere along the way.

None of that mattered right now, he told himself as he strode over to the window, catching sight of the SUV taking Samantha back the short distance to their private lodge. He waited until the car drove past the cabins and lodges then weaved around a corner and out of sight before letting his thoughts break free.

Damn her.

He didn't often feel thunderstruck, but she'd dropped a bombshell on him tonight. How could she think of leaving him at a time like this? She was his right-hand man. His assistant who made sure everything ran like clockwork. He couldn't do without her and certainly not after coming home to run the resort. He and his younger brother Gavin had already talked about building a new high-security bungalow for their most elite guests in a separate area of the resort.

So why, right when he needed her the most, did Samantha want to bail out on him? He'd expected better of her than desertion. Her excuse that she wanted to go home for a while hadn't made sense. She wasn't one to let her emotions get the best of her anyway and neither was he. That was what he'd liked about her from the start. Now his instincts told him she wasn't telling him the full truth.

Yet if she couldn't be truthful after working closely together, then something was definitely wrong. It just went to remind him to never trust anyone. A person thought they had everything, and in an instant it was gone. Hadn't that been the way since his mother had died from cancer when he was six and his father had withdrawn and blocked everyone out emotionally? It was like both his parents had died at the same time. He'd grown up determined to be totally independent from any emotional entanglements.

Okay, so Donald Jarrod had enough of himself left over to push his five children to be achievers, but at what cost? Four of Donald's offspring had departed years ago to make their mark in other parts of the country. Guy owned a famous French restaurant in Manhattan and ran another business venture. Gavin was a construction engineer. And Melissa was a licensed masseuse who had run a spa and massage-therapy retreat in L.A. Trevor was the only one who'd stayed in Aspen, but had chosen to have nothing to do with the resort, and instead built up his own successful marketing business.

Hell, Blake hadn't seen much of his four younger brothers and sister these past ten years. As his fraternal twin, he was closest to Guy, but he'd still kept a close eye on all his siblings. If they'd needed him, he would have been there. Of course his mind was still out on his half sister, Erica, who'd only recently shown up to become part of the family.

Unfortunately now he needed to rely on *all* of them to make sure the place continued to be a success. It wasn't a feeling he enjoyed. He didn't like relying on anyone, but he'd thought he could count on Samantha.

Obviously he couldn't.

Feeling restless, he looked out over the renowned ski resort that had always been the one place he called home. No matter how much he'd tried to forget it, Jarrod Ridge was in his blood.

He was now the CEO of Jarrod Ridge, for God's sake. His ancestor, Eli Jarrod, had started up the silver mine during the mining boom of 1879, and built himself one of the biggest houses in Colorado. Then "The Panic" of 1893 had closed many of Aspen's mines, and Eli had added to his house and made it bigger, turning it into a grand hotel that was now Jarrod Manor. This place had been through a lot, surviving right through to 1946 when the ski resort idea was born. Jarrod Ridge hadn't looked back since. It was a powerful feeling being in charge of all he surveyed.

And a big responsibility.

And dammit, he wasn't about to let Samantha walk out on him when he needed her most. Even in a month's time he would still need her by his side. It was important to the resort to make sure the changeover went as smoothly as possible, and only Samantha could help him do that. She was the best assistant he'd ever had and he wasn't about to lose her. He would find a way to make her stay, at least until the new bungalow was up and running.

He expelled a breath as he went over to his desk, where he sat down on the leather chair and took the resignation letter out from his jacket pocket. Under the lamplight, he read it, hoping to glean some hint on what was going on inside his assistant's mind. The letter was as professional as expected. No surprises there.

Frowning, he dropped the letter and picked up the pen, rolling it between his fingers as he tried to think. He didn't understand. Surprise appeared to be the name of the game with Samantha right now.

Why?

All at once the metal in his hand went from cool to warm in a matter of seconds, reminding him of his cool and remote assistant who'd soon warmed up at his touch. His heart took a sudden and extra beat. Would Samantha warm up for him if he touched her again? Remembering the electricity between them when he'd grabbed her arm, a surge of need raced through him. Samantha didn't seem to know what she wanted, but he *did* know women. She had wanted him. She had reacted to his touch.

And if that were the case, then perhaps he'd touch her some more and keep her around as long as necessary. He was sure he could persuade her to stay at least another six months. By then they'd both be ready to end the relationship. Sometime in the new year he'd more than likely be over needing her help anyway, and by then he would have someone to replace her, both in the office and the bedroom. No other woman had lasted longer than that. He wouldn't let them. Having affairs was the best he could offer.

As for Samantha, she was independent. She'd have no difficulty moving on when the time came. Hell, she'd probably even instigate it.

For now, it would be his pleasure to awaken the woman in her. Seducing Samantha was definitely going to be a priority task.

Two

Samantha felt more than a few moments of trepidation when she woke to the early morning light and remembered what she'd done. She'd actually handed Blake her resignation. She would be out of his life in a month's time. She tried to picture being apart from him for the rest of her life, but the thought brought silly tears to her eyes that she quickly blinked back.

Taking a shuddering breath, she tried to put all this in perspective. She'd moved on before, hadn't she? It wasn't so hard. Of course leaving Pasadena had been an adventure as much as an escape. It would be a long time before she escaped wanting Blake Jarrod.

Oh, God.

Then she remembered the plan she'd come up with last night. At the time she'd thought it was brilliant, but now she wasn't so sure she should go out with other men to try and make Blake jealous. It didn't seem right to manipulate the situation like that.

And that left her exactly…nowhere.

Remembering the sizzle of Blake's touch, she wondered if she really wanted to leave without giving them a chance. It was comforting to know that he would not want to get emotionally involved, but to become his lover, to be forever warmed by the memory of being in his arms, didn't she have to do this for herself?

She could do it. This was a goal that was achievable. She may not be a femme fatale but she was considered attractive and she knew how to flirt. And while it may not have worked with Blake at the dinner last night, she knew she could interest other men here in Aspen. Hopefully she'd grab his attention that way.

Tossing back the covers like she was tossing away her shackles, she jumped out of bed. She felt more lighthearted by the minute.

After her shower, Samantha figured it would be prudent to distance herself from Blake as much as possible from now on. She wouldn't capture any man's attention if she was with him all the time.

First things first.

Apart from the maids from the hotel who tidied up Pine Lodge each day, she and Blake had decided to be mostly self-sufficient. The refrigerator was usually stocked with food or they could eat at Jarrod Manor, the main lodge on the resort where some of the family chose to live.

Usually they ate a light breakfast together—surprisingly Blake hadn't brought any women back to the lodge while she'd been here—before they walked the short distance to his father's old office at the Manor. Anything to do with his hotels in Vegas was kept separate and done here in the office they'd set up in a corner of the large living room. That work was mostly done after dinner each evening. There was a lot to do with running both businesses, especially now that it was pre-ski season here. Samantha didn't mind keeping so busy. Besides, it kept Blake close.

But today was different. Fifteen minutes later, she quietly closed the lodge door behind her and left without waiting for him. The Colorado sun was making a shy return as she breathed in crystal air and walked the winding streets in picture-perfect surroundings. As she approached this grandest of hotels, a thrill went through her. With its main stone building complemented by guest wings on both sides, its peaked roofs and balconies with iron railings and its frosted windowpanes, it looked like an enchanted castle.

The doorman greeted her as she entered the hotel from under the stone arch leading off the driveway. She smiled and walked through the wide lobby dotted with tables and chairs. Being the off-season, it was quiet at this time of the morning with only a few guests up and about. A young couple stood viewing photographs of the mountains displayed along the wood walls. Older couples looked ready to go sightseeing the many popular tourist attractions, than pamper themselves in the spa.

It was no better in the casual eatery off the lobby, and Samantha sighed as she scooped scrambled eggs onto a plate from the buffet. Couldn't there have been one measly attractive man in sight this morning? So much for her plans to make Blake jealous. It wouldn't happen if she couldn't even find a man to flirt with.

She lifted her head and saw Blake's half sister, Erica Prentice, come out of the kitchen area and walk through the room with Joel Remy, the resort doctor. Joel was tall, blond and good-looking and he'd asked her out only last week and she'd refused, not giving it any consideration. Things had changed.

Erica saw her and blinked in surprise as she came over to her table. "Samantha, what are you doing here eating breakfast by yourself?"

Samantha liked Erica, who hadn't known she was a member of the Jarrod family until a few months ago. Since then, Erica had become engaged to the Jarrod family attorney, Christian Hanford, and everyone was happy about it. Everyone except Blake, that is, though Guy had taken a while to come round. Erica was a PR specialist who had thrown herself into the running of the resort, willingly giving a hand wherever it was needed, just like the other family members. Samantha didn't understand Blake's attitude toward her.

She smiled at the other woman. "I was up early so I thought I'd get a head start on the boss."

Erica laughed. "Yes, I think as Blake's assistant you'd need to do that occasionally."

Samantha let her eyes slide to the man beside Erica. "Good morning, Joel. You're here early, as well."

The doctor smiled. "One of the kitchen staff burned her hand, but thankfully it was only minor."

Samantha nodded, then, "Where are my manners? Would you like to join me for breakfast? Erica, you, too, of course."

As if she was getting a vibe, Erica glanced from one to the other and went to speak, but Joel got in before her. "I can't, I'm afraid, Sam," the doctor said. "I have to go out on another call. But how about I make it up to you? It's Saturday and my night off. If you're free I'd love to take you to dinner."

Samantha could have kissed him, but she managed to restrain herself. If Blake didn't get jealous over this, then at least she'd have some fun, right?

Thinking of Blake must have made him appear. He was at this moment striding through the lobby with a scowl on his face, heading for the private elevator. Her heart jumped in her throat when he glanced over toward them and saw her in the eatery. He changed direction and advanced toward her.

She turned back to Joel, waiting a few moments more for Blake to get closer. "Dinner tonight?" she said, raising her voice just a little. "Yes, I'd like that very much, Joel."

He grinned at her. "Great. How about I pick you up at seven-thirty?"

"Perfect."

Blake was almost at the table.

"I'd better go see my next patient," Joel said, then inclined his head as he passed by. "Good morning, Blake."

Blake nodded, then stopped at the table and practically glared down at Samantha. "You didn't wait for me."

She reminded herself how this man didn't like things made easy for him. "I slipped a note under your door. Besides, I do believe I start work at nine and until then my time is my own," she said, aware of Erica's speculative gaze.

Blake must have been, too. He darted an irritated look at his half sister, then away, jerking his head at Joel's retreating back. "What did the doctor want?"

Was he jealous already? She felt a thrill of excitement but before she could answer, Erica said, "Joel's taking Samantha out to dinner tonight."

Blake blinked in shock, but he recovered quickly, his blue eyes narrowing in on Samantha. "You can't go. I need you to work for a couple of hours tonight. I'm expecting an important call."

"I'm sorry, Blake, but I'm entitled to some time off."

He shook his head. "Not tonight, I'm afraid. I'd do it myself but as you know, I have a function to attend in town." He regarded her with a hint of smugness in his eyes. "That's why I pay you the big bucks."

Samantha's stomach started to churn. For all that she had wanted him jealous…for all that she anticipated him being difficult with the job…she still hadn't expected he would be quite so obstructive. It was obvious he was going to be exactly that from now on.

Well, she didn't like being told what to do, especially when it was out of spite. Oh, boy, she was going to really enjoy *not* making this easy for him now.

Her chin angled up at him. "Only for the next month," she pointed out smoothly, suddenly wanting to throttle him.

His mouth tightened. "Listen—"

"Blake," Erica's voice cut across him soothingly. "I really think you're being unfair here. If necessary, one of the staff can—"

"Mind your own business, Erica," he snapped, making both Samantha and Erica gasp. He grimaced, a pulse beating in his cheekbone. "Sorry. I shouldn't have said that." Then he looked at Samantha. "Go if you must," he said, then twisted on his heels and stormed off.

"Oh, my God, that was terrible, Erica," Samantha muttered. "I don't know what came over him."

Erica stood watching her half brother storm into the elevator. "I do."

Samantha sighed. "Yes, he seems to have a problem with you, doesn't he? I'm sure he'll be fine once he gets used to having a new sister."

"Half sister," Erica corrected with a wry smile, then sat down on the chair opposite. "Samantha, I don't think it's me who's upset him. What's going on between you two?"

Samantha was unsure how much she should confide in the other woman. When it came down to it, Erica was a Jarrod. Still, the others would have to know sometime. "I've given him my resignation. I finish up in a month's time."

"What! But why?" Erica cried. "I thought you loved your job." She reached across the table and squeezed Samantha's hand. "Please don't leave. I love you being here. You're part of the family."

Samantha felt her heart lift, then take a dive as fast. She'd only just begun to know Blake's family and now she had to leave. "It's time for me to make a change."

Erica gave her a penetrating look. "There's been something bothering you lately." She paused. "Blake needs you, Samantha."

For the job, that was all.

"Yes, he's made it quite clear that's why he's making me work out my contract for the next month." She couldn't stop her lips from twisting. "He told me it's nothing personal."

There was another pause, then, "I see."

Samantha realized she may have said too much. The other woman probably saw more than she should.

All at once Erica gave a disarming smile. "You know what I do when I'm feeling down? I go shopping. How about I take you into town after lunch and we buy you a new dress for tonight?"

Samantha knew Erica was trying to make her feel better. "It's a lovely thought, but I've already got enough dresses. And anyway, I have to work. Blake's going to make sure he gets his money's worth from me from now on."

Erica waved that aside. "I bet most of your clothes are suitable for Vegas, not here. And please…no woman ever has enough dresses," she teased, looking beautiful and happy but still slightly concerned. "Besides, I think it will do Blake good to do without you for a couple of hours." She winked. "He owes me now for being such a jerk."

Samantha appreciated it and she tried to smile but couldn't. "Erica, it's not a good idea." Despite being angry with Blake, she realized she'd probably pushed him a bit too much already today. She'd wanted to shock him into being jealous. Not give him a heart attack!

"Phooey! You want to look good for Joel tonight, don't you?"

Samantha thought about why she'd accepted the invitation to dinner with Joel in the first place. This was about making Blake jealous, she reminded herself, so she still had to keep trying. She couldn't give up after the first try.

She nodded. "Yes, I do."

"Then let's light a fire under him, honey, if that's what he needs."

Samantha did her best not to give anything away, but they both knew Erica was talking about Blake, not Joel. And seeing that this might be her one and only chance…

"Okay then, Erica. I'm in your hands. I have nothing to lose."

"Good girl! I'll come by the office after lunch." Erica got to her feet. "I'd better go and check on the staff member who burned her hand." She smiled and headed back the way she'd come.

As Erica left, Samantha sat for a few moments then looked down at the remains of her scrambled eggs. She just hoped she didn't end up like her breakfast—out in the cold and barely touched.

After lunch Blake's bad mood increased as he watched Erica leave his office, taking his assistant with her for the afternoon. They were going shopping, for Christ's sake! For a dress for Samantha's date tonight!

Damn Erica. His half sister was beautiful and smart, but, unlike his brothers and Melissa, he didn't totally trust her. After listening to her for the last five minutes, he hadn't changed his mind. She was unmistakably adroit at getting her own way, using his outburst this morning against him to make him feel guilty. It had worked like a charm, as she'd known it would.

But it was Samantha he really needed to fathom, he decided, leaning back in the leather chair. He'd woken up thinking he'd go after her with an enthusiasm he rarely felt for a woman these days.

And then it had all gone wrong. First, there had been the note slipped under his door that she'd already gone to breakfast and hadn't waited for him. She'd *never* done that before, not here in Aspen or anywhere else they'd stayed throughout the world.

Then he'd found her accepting a date with that gigolo doctor, Joel Remy. That was like going out with one of the ski instructors. Didn't Samantha know women were lined up to sleep with these guys? He'd seen it all his life.

Take a number, Samantha.

What the hell was going on here? She suddenly seemed a different person. It was like she'd decided to place being a woman first, his assistant second.

What had got into her? Was she trying to pay him back for not letting her walk out on the job early? Would she really *do* that? He grimaced. She was a woman, wasn't she? She'd probably decided to have a farewell fling just to rub his nose in it.

Thoughts of Samantha in bed with another man were suddenly anathema to him. He couldn't let her do it. He *knew* her and he knew she'd regret it.

And surely if she was going to make love to anyone, then she could damn well choose *him*. *He* was the one who'd worked closely with her for two years. *He* was the one who would appreciate her in bed. *He* was the one who had to save her from herself.

Three

As she descended the stairs that evening, carrying her clutch bag in one hand and her cashmere evening coat over her arm, Samantha's foot faltered on the next step. She'd been hoping to show herself off to Blake before he left for his business dinner, and now her heart began knocking against her ribs when she saw the man in question look up from the corner bar in their lodge and catch sight of her. His glass stopped halfway to his mouth and he stared…just stared…as she slowly came the rest of the way down.

Thanks to Erica, she knew she looked fantastic. She'd always taken pride in her appearance and in making sure she looked right for her position, but this long-sleeved dress—this piece of hot-pink knit material that stretched over her body like it had been lovingly cling-wrapped to every curve—made her feel a little naughty.

Without taking his eyes off her, Blake put his drink on

the bar and watched her walk toward him. "I'm stunned," he said in a deep, husky voice that held true admiration and sent her pulse skipping with delight. "I've never seen you look so…"

"Nice?" she gently teased as her confidence soared. She would forgive him anything right at this moment.

"Sexy."

The word took her breath away. She moistened her lips and saw his blue eyes dart to her mouth. "Thank you, Blake."

Then his gaze rolled down her, before slowly coming up again, his eyelids flicking briefly when he passed over her breasts both times. She had the feeling her nipples may have beaded with sexual excitement and one part of her wanted to hunch over and say "don't look," while another forced her to hold her shoulders back proudly.

His eyes—dark with a desire she'd never seen before—finally stopped at her head. "What have you done to your hair?"

She swallowed. It hadn't taken much to style the silky brown strands into bouncing curls around her shoulders. "I had a couple of inches cut off it."

"It looks terrific."

This was the reaction she'd been hoping for from him. "Thank you again."

He picked up his drink and took a sip. Then, "I have to ask you something."

Her heart took a leap. "What is it, Blake?"

"Are you sure you want to do this?"

She blinked. "Do what?"

Resign?

"Go out with Joel Remy."

His voice gave nothing away but her pulse started

to race even more. Dear God, could Blake be a little jealous? Had she actually managed to get through to him so quickly that she was a woman? A woman who needed him like she'd never needed any man before?

His eyes slammed into her. "He's not your style, Samantha."

Her heart almost burst through her chest. Blake *was* jealous. She tried to act nonchalant. She couldn't succumb and throw herself at him the minute he decided he wanted her for five minutes.

"How do you know *what* my style is, Blake?" she said, fluttering her eyelashes at him.

"I know what suits you and what doesn't and I know he's not the man for you."

No, this man in front of her was the man for her.

"Oh, so you're an expert on me now, are you?" she flirted, thrilled beyond her wildest dreams that he was finally noticing her. It was this dress. She had so much to thank Erica for. The other woman had…

"I'd like to think I know you very well, Samantha," he said, suddenly looking very superior, very arrogant. "You wouldn't be happy with Remy. Trust me."

Thud.

Clarity hit her like a bolt of lightning. What a fool she was in thinking anything had changed. This wasn't about Blake wanting her. This was about him being his usual conceited self. The man wasn't jealous. He was merely trying to stop her having a relationship with another man over the next two weeks so that she wouldn't inconvenience *him*. Frankly, she deserved better than this.

"That's your considered opinion, is it?" she said coolly now.

"Yes, it is." His eyes told her he'd noticed her change in tone. "Are you going to tell him you're leaving soon?"

She tried to think. She was *so* disappointed. "I'd prefer to keep that to myself for the time being. It's no one's business but my own."

"And mine, of course," he pointed out dryly. Then, "But you're probably right in not telling him. I doubt he's after a long-term relationship anyway."

"Neither am I," she said, taking pleasure in the way his face hardened. "In the meantime, I'm sure Joel and I will both manage to enjoy ourselves."

He looked all-knowing. "I doubt you'll have anything in common."

She raised one eyebrow. "Really? Don't forget I worked in a doctor's office before coming to work for you. And my family runs a medical transcription business, so I used to have quite a bit to do with doctors."

Blake's lips twisted. "So you'll talk about deciphering his handwriting? That'll be a laugh a minute."

Her fingers tightened on her clutch purse. He thought he was being clever, did he? She needed to wipe away that smirk. She gave him a sultry look. "Oh, I'm sure we'll have plenty of...*other things* in common."

The smirk fell off his face. "Dammit, Samantha, you shouldn't—"

The doorbell buzzed.

Samantha glanced over at the front door a few feet away and saw Joel through the glass panel. She tossed Blake an expressive look before going over to open it.

Joel stepped inside, his eyes sliding down, then up. "Wow! Don't you look like a million dollars." He grinned at Blake a few feet away. "I can't believe this beauty is going out with me."

"Neither can I," Blake muttered, then as quickly gave a smooth smile but Samantha heard him. "I mean, she's usually picky about who she goes out with."

She blinked. Was that still an insult? Joel had a puzzled look that said he might be thinking the same thing.

She hurriedly forced a smile. "Thanks for the compliment, Joel." She stood and looked him up and down, too. "For the record, you look like a *billion* dollars," she joked, then realized she'd overplayed her hand when Blake sniffed, though she suspected it was more of a snort. She turned her head slightly so Joel couldn't see her stabbing her boss with her eyes.

Blake ignored her. "So, where are you two dining tonight?"

Samantha was immediately suspicious. "Why do you want to know?"

He smiled. "No reason."

Joel then mentioned a restaurant in the center of Aspen. "It's only just opened and I know the owner. It'll be very hard to get a reservation in another month or so." He didn't sound like he was bragging, at least not to Samantha, but she saw a glint in Blake's eyes that told her he wasn't in agreement.

She smiled at Joel. "That sounds lovely."

He looked pleased. "And you, Blake? You're off to dinner, too, by the look of things."

Wearing a dark suit, Blake was the one who really did look like a billion dollars, Samantha had to admit, unable to stop herself from wishing she was going out with him instead of Joel, in spite of the fact that Blake was being an overbearing jerk.

"Just a business dinner in town." Blake looked at his

watch. "As a matter of fact, I'd better call a cab. I need to be on my way."

Joel frowned. "A cab? Don't you have a car?"

"I noticed it was leaking oil this afternoon so I thought I'd better not use it tonight."

Samantha sensed Blake was manipulating the situation for his own benefit again. Did he think she was stupid? He was doing this on purpose to try and keep her and Joel apart as much as possible to spoil her night.

She stared at him. "But you only bought the vehicle a few months ago and it's barely been used. How can a luxury Cadillac SUV have an oil leak already?"

He looked totally guileless. "I agree. It's the darnedest thing."

"We could give you a lift, if you like," Joel said, making Samantha want to rattle him.

"Oh, I'm sure Blake doesn't want to ride with us." She was determined not to give her boss any satisfaction. "The resort has a chauffeur service."

Joel frowned. "No, that's okay. I don't mind. We're going that way anyway."

She would have sounded mean-spirited to refuse. As Blake well knew, she decided, watching the satisfaction in his eyes. He was Joel's boss and he knew Joel wouldn't deny doing a favor for him.

She passed her coat to Joel. "Would you mind helping me on with this, please?"

"Of course." Joel held it open while she slipped into it, then he helped lift her hair out from under the collar so that it was once again bouncing around her shoulders. It was somewhat intimate and Samantha felt a little awkward at having a man touch her hair, but she soon felt better when she saw the steely look in Blake's eyes after he noted it, too.

"Thanks," she said, smiling brightly at her date, then deliberately linked her arm with his. She gave Blake a sweet smile as he put on his black evening coat, letting him know she didn't care that he wasn't pleased. Too bad!

"My car's out front," Joel said.

They left the lodge, then Samantha slipped onto the front passenger seat before Blake could take it himself. She wouldn't put it past him to try and make her sit in the back, and she wasn't about to let him play at being boss while she was on a date. This was *her* night out. Blake may have been the reason for it, but right now she wasn't about to give him an inch.

Soon they were driving off into the night.

"This is very good of you, Joel," Blake said, sounding grateful from the backseat, which didn't sound right to Samantha's ears. Blake *never* sounded grateful like other mere mortals.

"We don't mind, do we, Sam?" Joel said, shooting her a sideways smile.

"No, of course not. We have to keep the boss happy, don't we?" She smiled back at Joel, knowing Blake could see her from his diagonal viewpoint behind the driver's seat.

"By the way, *Samantha*," Blake said, placing the slightest emphasis on her name, making her realize that Joel had called her "Sam" again—the name Blake had never called her.

"Yes, Blake?" she said, keeping her tone idle.

There was a tiny pause before he spoke. "Don't worry about that very important phone call I was waiting for tonight. One of the resort staff will sit in the office and wait for it."

"Good." She took her job seriously, but Erica's suggestion had been a good one, so she wasn't about to feel guilty about it.

"But I did have to give them your cell phone number, as well. Just in case. I hope you don't mind. Someone has to take the call if by chance it's missed at the hotel, and I'll have to turn my cell phone off so it won't interrupt the guest speaker tonight."

She could feel herself stiffen. He was trying to take advantage of her good nature for his own purposes again. This wasn't about taking the call. He wanted to put a spoke between her and Joel's budding relationship, freeing up her time for the job.

She turned her head to face him. "Actually I *do* mind. This is my night off. I don't want to work tonight."

He raised an eyebrow, like he was surprised. "I'm sure Joel won't have a problem with it. He's a doctor. He's used to being on call. You understand, don't you, Joel?"

"Sure I do." Joel glanced at her and smiled. "Leave your cell phone on, Sam. I don't mind if you take the call."

Her mouth tightened but she didn't reply. Her cell phone was already off and she intended it to stay that way. And Blake knew this had nothing to do with Joel anyway. Blake was just trying to make sure the job was in her face tonight.

Joel must have sensed something amiss because he started talking about general things for the rest of the way. Samantha could feel Blake's eyes on her from the backseat but she ignored him as she responded to Joel, relieved when the car slid to a halt outside a restaurant.

"Thanks for the ride." Blake opened the back door then paused briefly. "And don't worry about how I'll get home. You two have a good time, okay?"

Samantha bit down on her irritation. His sincerity was so false. He was just trying to get a ride back to the lodge to make sure nothing sexual happened between her and Joel. Ooh, it would do him good to wonder and worry what she and Joel were getting up to later in the evening.

She smiled tightly. "We'll be very late, so you'd best get the car service. Good night, Blake."

His lips flattened and he shot her a dark look. "Good night." He waited a second, but when Joel said good night, he got out of the car and shut the door. The last Samantha saw was him striding into the restaurant.

Then they drove off and she looked ahead, hoping Joel wouldn't say anything. He didn't, at least not until they were seated at their table and the waitress had left with their order.

"Excuse me for asking, but don't you like Blake?" he said.

She smiled to soften her words. "Of course I do, but I've worked with Blake a couple of years now. Sometimes he thinks everyone is there purely for his benefit."

Joel grinned. "As a successful businessman, he's probably right."

She laughed. "Yes, that's true." Then she forced herself to relax against the back of her chair. "Now let's talk about something else. I really don't want to talk about the boss tonight."

Joel smiled. "I'm more than happy to oblige, Sam. Now tell me…"

They had a pleasant evening after that. As predicted, they talked about her family's business and her experience in transcribing, though Blake's earlier derogatory comment about deciphering handwriting spoiled the discussion for her. Did Blake always have to be there at the back of her mind?

Unfortunately by the time the evening was half over, Samantha knew Joel wasn't for her. He was handsome and he was a nice guy, but they really *didn't* have anything else in common, much to her disgust. Not like her and Blake. She grimaced. No, she and Blake had nothing in common either—except the job and an attraction that she hated to think was really only on her side. Shades of Carl came to mind.

"Sam?"

She pulled herself back from thoughts of the past. "Sorry, I remembered something I forgot to do," she fibbed, then she smiled. "But it can wait. Now, what were you saying?" She would have a good time if it killed her.

It nearly did.

Her social life and her work life were the same thing, so she'd never lacked for company at business dinners and parties. But she wasn't used to being on a date and having to tune in to one person for hours on end. It was very draining.

Unless of course that person was Blake. He never bored her. Every minute of every day he challenged her like no other person on earth. Life with Blake was the adventure she'd always been after. One she soon had to leave, she remembered, her heart constricting. She pushed the thought aside. She would get through this.

"We should do this again, Sam," Joel said, holding open his car door for her on their return to Pine Lodge.

It was strange, but for some reason an evening of being called "Sam" had started to get on her nerves. It wasn't Joel's fault at all, but it was as if the shortened version of her name was an issue between her and Blake and therefore belonged only to them now. And that was rather pathetic.

"I've got plans tomorrow night," Joel said, dragging her from her thoughts. "But I'm free after that. Would you like to go to a movie on Monday night?"

She hesitated, feeling a little bad in using him. She didn't want to go out with him again, yet if she didn't continue with her plan to try and make Blake jealous, then Blake would think he'd won. She wouldn't give him the satisfaction now.

She got out of the car, with Joel doing the gentlemanly thing and assisting her. "I'd like that, but let me get back to you tomorrow, if that's okay."

"That's fine."

All at once she felt his hand move from her elbow to her chin. It was a smooth move and said this guy knew what he was doing, so perhaps using him shouldn't really cause her concern after all.

"But first…" he murmured.

She didn't resist even though his kiss wasn't something she wanted, and not because he wasn't an attractive man. Despite still being angry with Blake for trying to manipulate the situation earlier this evening, she wanted it to be Blake's lips—and *only* Blake's lips—on hers.

Suddenly scared that she might never want another man to kiss her, she raised her mouth to Joel. Perhaps Blake's attraction for her was merely in her mind? Perhaps she needed to be kissed by another man just to remind her—

"Don't let me interrupt," a male voice muttered.

Blake.

Samantha jerked back guiltily and Joel stopped, and they watched their employer stride past them and go inside Pine Lodge. He'd been walking from the direction of Jarrod Manor, where he must have gone after dinner.

"That was good timing," Joel said, over her thudding heart. Unfortunately her heart's thud wasn't for her date. It was for another man.

"Now, where were we?" Joel murmured, lowering his head and placing his lips on hers, making her conscious of one thing. She'd have to stretch her neck higher if it was Blake kissing her.

Blake sat on the couch and tried to get the image of Samantha about to kiss another man out of his head. She'd been swaying toward the doctor like she'd needed a shot in the arm. If she didn't get inside here pretty damn quick he was going looking for her. On the pretext of her safety, of course.

And he *was* concerned for her safety. That and other things. She was clearly ready to jump into bed with the first man who looked twice at her, and all to get back at *him* for not letting her walk away from her job. Hell, if he'd agreed to that she would have already gone from his life. His gut twisted at the thought.

The front door opened right then and in she walked. His pulse began to race when he saw she was alone.

Good girl.

She seemed distracted as she headed for the stairs, undoing the buttons of her coat as she walked. Then she saw him sitting on the couch and her eyes flared with pleasure before she seemed to catch herself.

For a moment his breath stalled. She'd never shown any sort of emotion toward him before. They got on well together but it had always been business between them. He should be perturbed, yet he knew he could use it to his advantage.

Then her mouth tightened as she came toward him. "Are you waiting up for me?" she said, her tone less than friendly, making him question if it had been a trick of the light before. He mentally shook his head. No, he knew what he'd seen.

"Can't a man have a drink before bed?" he drawled, relaxing. She was home now…with him…and that's all that mattered.

Her top lip curled. "You certainly didn't have to worry about drinking and driving, did you?"

He pretended ignorance. "No, I didn't." He indicated another glass of brandy on the coffee table in front of him. "I poured a nightcap for you. Sit with me."

An odd look skimmed across her face. "Perhaps I'd prefer to go straight to bed."

If one of his dates had said that he would have taken it as a come-on. But Samantha was a challenge in a different way. Did she know what she was inviting in that dress? Did she have any idea what she actually did to a man's libido? All at once he was enjoying what he now suspected to be her sexual naïveté.

"One drink," he coaxed. "And you can tell me all about your evening."

She paused, then put down her evening purse and began undoing the rest of her coat buttons. Slowly she began taking it off in an unintentional striptease, exposing the sexy pink material beneath. How had he never before noticed what a stunner she was?

She sank down on the opposite chair and gracefully picked up the glass, indicating the already poured brandy. "You were so sure I wouldn't take Joel up to my room, were you?"

He hadn't been, no. "Yes."

She took a sip then considered him. "You certainly tried hard enough to make it *not* happen."

"Did I?" He was feeling rather proud of himself for putting obstacles in her way tonight. It must have worked or she wouldn't be here now. With him.

"You know you did, and I don't appreciate it. You're trying to make sure you get every last bit of work out of me before I leave."

Is that what she thought? "Maybe I was protecting you?"

She gave a short laugh. "From what? Having a good time?"

He looked over at her kissable lips that had recently been beneath another man's…and something became even more determined inside him. If she was going to have fun, she was going to have it with *him*.

He forced a shrug. "I just think you need to look at who you go out with in future."

Her lips twisted. "Thanks for the tip."

He'd never known her to be sarcastic, not like she was lately. It was…energizing, he admitted, watching as she eased back in her chair, the soft silk stockings making a swishing sound as she crossed her legs. He'd give anything to reach out and smooth those long legs with his hands. Or perhaps his lips…

Before he could put words to action, he told himself he had to slow it down. He didn't want to frighten the lady by going too quickly. Time was running out but he had to let her lead. Tonight, anyway. Tomorrow—when she was in a friendlier mood—was another day.

He took a sip of his brandy and let it soothe his throat. "So. Did you have a good time tonight?"

Her eyes darted away briefly. "Yes, I did. Very much."

She was lying. "I bet."

She arched one of her elegant eyebrows. "I hope you didn't put much money on that bet, Blake."

"I didn't have to." He knew women, both in the business world and out of it. She was lying. And he was intensely relieved.

A soft smile curved her lips. "Joel really knows how to treat a woman."

She was still lying. And he found that fascinating. "Sure he knows how to treat a woman. The guy's a womanizer."

"I suppose it's easy enough to recognize one's own sort."

He had to chuckle. She made him laugh. Then he saw a touch of real amusement in her eyes and something connected between them. She quickly looked down at her glass, hiding her eyes for a second.

He started to lean forward. "Samantha…"

Her head snapped up. "For your information, Joel's a

very nice man," she said, making it clear she was trying to ignore the sudden sexual tension in the room.

It was a wasted effort. "I'm sure he is. Ask *any* woman in Aspen."

She sent him a defiant look. "Don't think I wouldn't go to bed with him if I wanted to, Blake."

She was all talk, but his gut still knotted at her words. "Obviously you didn't want to, or you would be in bed with him this very minute. Am I right?"

"No, you're wrong. I mean, yes… I mean, mind your own business." Her lips pressed together. "I'll sleep with whoever I want *when* I want."

"You're being very contradictory tonight, Samantha. They'd eat you alive in the boardroom with that attitude," he mocked.

She stiffened. "Listen, Blake, I'll sleep with any man I want when I'm good and ready. Tonight I just wasn't ready. And in case you didn't notice, this isn't the boardroom."

No, but he did want to eat her alive right now. He wanted to kiss her and take away the imprint of another man's lips, his hands itching to slide up over her hot dress and lift that hair off her nape himself, exposing the soft skin beneath to his lips.

Adrenaline pumping through him, he knew it was time to take action. He'd had enough playing games tonight. He wasn't one to sit on the sidelines for long. He needed to know if her lips were as good as they looked, if her body would curve to his touch, if the skin at her nape was soft and sensitive.

Surging to his feet, he removed the brandy glass from her hand and put it on the table. He heard her intake of breath as he pulled her to her feet, but nothing would stop him now. Already he could feel a mutual shudder pass between them.

"Blake?" she said huskily as he brought her into the circle of his arms, leaving mere inches between them. He'd never been this close to her before. Not close enough to see the rush of desire in her blue eyes. It knocked the breath from his body.

And then a sudden flash of panic swept her face and before he knew it, she had pushed against him and spun away. Scurrying toward the stairs, she left him standing there, his arms never feeling as empty as they did right now.

As hard as it was, he let her go. He could follow her and she would take him as her lover, but he knew all he needed to know for the moment. She wanted him. And he wasn't giving up. His plans for seduction were still very much alive.

Samantha closed the door behind her and pressed herself back against it, willing her racing heart to slow down so that she could let herself think. She'd gone and panicked just now. Blake had finally reached for her and she'd blown it.

What was wrong with her! Being in Blake's arms and in his bed was what she wanted most, wasn't it? So why had she run away like a frightened deer? He must think her green when it came to relationships, which of course she was. One lover in high school, then falling in love in her mid-twenties, did not constitute experience. Not unless that included the pain of rejection, she decided, quickly pushing that thought away.

Then she knew.

Despite the spark of electricity when he'd grabbed her

arm last night, this evening she'd managed to convince herself that his meddling was actually about the job and nothing more. But just now the desire in his eyes had thrown her for a loop again. He really *did* feel passion for her, and when he'd touched her they'd both felt that zip of attraction. It had overwhelmed her, that's all.

Oh, Lord, what did she do now? Go back downstairs and beg him to make love to her? She couldn't. She'd reached the limit to her little seductress act tonight. She didn't have it in her to face him again so soon.

She took a steadying breath. Right, she'd messed this one up tonight, but something positive had come out of this. She now knew that Blake really *did* want to have sex with her. So if she wanted Blake, and he wanted her, then next time there should be no further problems.

She hoped.

Four

"Blake, did you get a chance to read those documents I gave you?"

Blake was in a good mood as he leaned back against the marble countertop. It was eight on Sunday morning and one of his younger brothers had come by Pine Lodge to discuss an upcoming project, but it was Samantha who was on his mind. Anticipation coursed through him as he remembered how sexy she had looked last night. Soon she would be *his*.

"Blake?"

Reluctantly he dragged his thoughts away from his assistant who was still upstairs sleeping in her room, to look at the man propped against the kitchen doorjamb. He hid a smile as he raised the coffee mug to his mouth. Gavin may look laidback but *he* knew it was all a facade. Taking on the job of building a new and exclusive high-security bungalow for Jarrod Ridge meant a lot to his brother.

"Yes. I've put them in the safe up at the Manor," he said, deliberately misunderstanding him.

"And?"

Blake chuckled and put him out of his misery. "And I think you've done an admirable job of running with this project."

Gavin began to smile with relief. "You do?"

"The intensive feasibility studies, as well as the building site and sustainability analysis reports you've put together, are impressive. But then, so were the ones you did for my Vegas hotels."

Gavin's grin widened. "It means a lot to hear you say that."

Blake indicated the coffeepot on the bench. "Grab yourself a coffee."

Gavin straightened away from the door and went to get a mug. "You know," he said, pouring himself a drink. "I've really welcomed this challenge."

"I can see that."

Gavin shrugged shoulders made impressive by many hours working with his crew on various construction sites. "It's nice to be home and together again as a family after so long, but I'm glad I don't have to pamper people on a daily basis. It really isn't my style."

Blake nodded. "You're a first-rate construction engineer, Gav, but I agree. There's nothing like doing something you love."

Gavin smiled, looking pleased. "You said it, brother."

"Seriously. I'm proud of you."

"You getting soft in your old age, Blake?" he teased.

"Probably." Blake was proud of all his brothers and sisters. Well, his half sister, Erica, was another matter.

All at once, Gavin's smile left him. "You realize Dad would never have said such a thing."

Blake grimaced. "I like to think I'm not quite as cold as the old man."

There was a moment's silence as they both remembered their father. Blake refused to feel anything for the passing of a man who had shunned his children's emotional well-being and so badly let them down. Donald Jarrod's legacy had been more than the Jarrod Ridge Resort. It had been a legacy that his children keep their emotions on ice, avoiding personal commitment. And while both Guy and Melissa had found true happiness with Avery and Shane, Blake couldn't see it happening for himself. Not at all. Nor for Gavin or Trevor either. That was just the way it was.

"That reminds me," Gavin said. "You're working out of Dad's old office now you're CEO, so wouldn't it be more convenient to be living at the Manor, as well? Why are you staying here at Pine Lodge instead?"

Blake shrugged. "Actually it's more convenient to be staying here. That way I can keep my hotel operations separate from the resort stuff." His hand tightened around the coffee mug. "Besides, even though Erica's moved into Christian's place, they both spend most of their time at the Manor during the day. I don't want to encroach on their territory. You know what newly engaged couples are like."

Gavin shot him a mocking smile. "Since when have

you ever taken a backseat to anyone, big brother? Or are you still scared of our new half sister?"

Blake knew Gavin was riling him, getting him back for stringing it out a few minutes ago. "I was never scared of Erica, as you well know."

"You're going to have to get over your dislike of her one day, buddy."

Blake felt an odd jolt. "I don't dislike her. I just don't totally trust her."

Gavin's eyes narrowed. "She really doesn't have to prove anything more to us, Blake." He paused. "But I guess it's all for the best that you stay here anyway. Your new assistant might not get on with the rest of the family as well as Samantha does." A speculative look entered his eyes. "Yeah, whoever is coming in as your new PA, it'll be much easier for them to keep the two businesses separate if you both stay here."

Blake's jaw clenched. He refused to even think about Samantha leaving, or someone coming in to replace her. And why was he surprised that word had gotten around the family? Samantha had said she didn't want anyone to know, but obviously she'd told one person at least. It had to have been Erica. No doubt the two had shared some girl talk yesterday while they'd been shopping together.

"Samantha is *not* leaving," he said tightly.

"That's not what I'm hearing."

"Shut up, Gav." He slammed down his half-empty coffee mug. "Now, if you'll excuse me, I have some work to do." He strode past his brother and out of the kitchen.

As he entered the living room, he heard a noise outside. He glanced through the picture window.

Samantha wasn't in bed asleep like he'd thought. She was standing on the bottom step of the lodge, dressed in warm clothes and a woolen hat, talking to a man who no doubt was one of the guests at the hotel. She must have gone up to the Manor to eat breakfast, probably with her doctor friend, and this guy must have followed her back like a lost puppy. No, make that a raccoon.

He heard her give a lilting laugh and his mouth flattened. The guy was in his forties and looked sleazy to Blake. And hell, Samantha looked like she was flirting with him. Didn't she have any sense when it came to men? The sooner he showed her what it was like to make love to *him,* the better.

"Look at that," Gavin murmured in his ear. "I think someone else may be working today…*on* Samantha."

Blake glared at him, then strode over and pulled open the front door in a rush. If she was going to flirt it would be with *him*.

"How about us going for a scenic drive?" the man was saying. "Maybe even do lunch in town? I know it's pretty quiet at this time of year, but we should be able to find somewhere to eat. What do you think?"

"I—"

"I think I need to speak to my assistant," Blake cut across her as he stepped out on the porch. They spun to look up at him. "Samantha, I need you to make some calls to Vegas for me."

She sent him an annoyed look, making it clear she didn't like the interruption. "Blake, it's Sunday and most of the offices are closed. It'll have to wait until tomorrow."

He had the urge to remind her that last night he could easily have taken her to his bed. She wouldn't have minded *that* interruption, he was sure. "Then I need you to help me with something else."

Her lips tightened. "So I'm not going to get any time off now until I leave?"

"No." He turned to go inside and waited but realized she wasn't behind him. "Coming, Samantha?"

Her chin tilted stubbornly. "I'll be there in a minute."

Blake saw Gavin's look of amusement as his brother pushed through the doorway then descended the stairs two at a time, calling out a greeting to the pair as he left.

Blake went back inside. He didn't hear her following. Counting to ten, he waited but he could see her still standing there chatting. At that moment something occurred to him. Wasn't it strange that she'd been jumpy with *him* last night, yet she seemed perfectly at ease with Mr. Sleazy down there? And what about last night with the doc? She hadn't seemed nervous around the guy.

So what did that tell him? That she was flirting with men she considered *safe?* Which meant she must feel nothing for them, he mused. Nothing at all. The thought filled him with relief.

As for what she was feeling for him...there was definitely something between them. Yeah, she knew they'd be explosive together in bed.

And that begged the question. Just how far was she prepared to go to fight her desire for him? More importantly right now, did she have any idea what she was inviting by leading those other two men on?

Making a decision, Blake pulled on his jacket and boots, grabbed his car keys and strode back out into the chilly air. "I need to go check on something," he said, going down the stairs, "and I want you to come with me, Samantha." He bared his teeth at the other man in the semblance of a smile. "Sorry, buddy, but I need my assistant."

"Blake—" she began.

"This is important." He cupped her elbow and began leading her toward the side of the lodge to the garage where he kept his black Cadillac SUV.

She glanced over her shoulder and called out to the other man. "I'll talk to you when I get back, Ralph."

Blake gave a snort as he clicked the remote to open the garage door.

"What was that for?" Samantha hissed, hurrying to keep up.

"I hope you're not thinking of dating *Ralph*. The guy's old enough to be your father. Hell, he's even got a name to match."

She hid her satisfaction. "Perhaps I'm attracted to older men?"

He sent her a knowing look. "Then you'd better not dress like you did last night. He doesn't look like his old ticker could handle a woman, let alone a sexy one like yourself."

Her own "ticker" jumped around inside her chest and she tried not to blush. She loved hearing that Blake thought her sexy, though she wasn't sure why he was looking so confident all of a sudden. Still, this time she wasn't going to run away from him if he made a move on her. No repeat of last night, she told herself firmly.

They entered the garage, but it was only after she slid onto the passenger seat of the SUV and was putting on her seat belt did she remember something. "Didn't you say this vehicle had an oil leak?"

Blake smirked at her. "Here's the thing. I took another look earlier and it wasn't leaking after all. The problem must have been with someone else's car."

"Now there's a surprise."

"It was to me, too," he drawled, starting the engine.

No wonder he looked pleased with himself, she decided. He'd orchestrated the "poor me" routine last night over the oil leak, and now he'd put a stop to her going out with Ralph. Not that Ralph was her type, though he seemed very nice, but he *was* a man and one she could flirt with for Blake's benefit.

Once the vehicle had warmed up, she took off her gloves as he reversed out of the garage.

"Where are we going?" she asked, when he started along the narrow road lined with thick trees, and it became clear they were heading for the main entrance to the resort.

"You'll see."

For a second she dared hope this might be about spending some time alone together away from everyone else. "Is this really about work?"

"What else?"

Disappointment wound its way through her. They were clearly still employer and employee. Had last night merely been an aberration on his part because of the late night and close proximity? Was this once again about Blake trying to stop her from leaving her job, rather than him actually wanting her?

Back to square one.

Soon Blake was driving past the two stone pillars with the brass Jarrod Ridge Resort sign, and turning the SUV onto the main road but in the other direction of town. At this time on a Sunday morning there wasn't much traffic and further along he took another turn onto a side road. She wondered where they were going as they drove through stunning natural scenery filled with golden fall colors that would soon disappear under winter-white, but it was no use asking him again. Blake only did what he wanted to do and he would tell her only what he wanted her to know.

Remembering Gavin had visited Pine Lodge this morning, she suspected then where they were going. Farther along, Blake pulled over onto a slot of land that looked out over the Roaring Fork River weaving its way through a lush green picturesque valley between towering snow-dabbled peaks. The Jarrod Ridge resort was nestled like a crown jewel amongst it all.

He stopped the vehicle and cut the engine.

He didn't speak at first, just stared straight ahead, so she had to ask the obvious. "Why did you bring me here?"

He nodded his dark head at the majestic mountain panorama before them. "I wanted to show you where the new private bungalow will be built."

"I see." Her suspicions were correct, but the way he spoke made her heart sink. It was as if he had acknowledged she was leaving now. Like he was showing it to her—while he still could.

"Let's take a closer look." He started to get out of the car then glanced back at her, his gaze going to the woolen hat on her head. "Put your gloves on first. There's no wind but it's chilly."

A couple of seconds later they were standing in front of the black SUV, looking at the breathtaking alpine backdrop in front of them.

He pointed to a wooded area near the bottom of the

mountain to the right of the resort. "See that over there? That's our silver mine where we used to play as kids. One of my ancestors started up the mine but it's been out of use for over a hundred years."

"How interesting," she said, meaning it.

"The bungalow will be farther up the mountain but not too close. We don't want to destroy the historical significance of the mine."

She'd briefly seen the documents Gavin had given Blake, and heard them discussing it at times, but Gavin was the one running with this project. He was keeping it very much between himself and Blake at this stage, though she knew they were keeping the rest of the Jarrods up to date.

"See that rocky outcropping?" Blake continued. "That's close to where we'll build the bungalow. It's going to be super luxurious with top-of-the-line security. There'll be iris-recognition scanners plus the usual cameras and motion detectors. Personal safety will be a must, as will our guests' privacy."

She could picture it in her mind. "I'm really impressed. It'll be great."

He nodded. "It's just what Jarrod Ridge needs to stand out above the rest," he said, a proud look about him as he appraised his family's empire.

An odd tenderness filled her as she glanced up at his familiar profile. There was something so attractive about a man confident with himself. An aura that pulled a woman close and made her want to get under it, to become a part of the man no one else knew.

All at once he turned toward her, his gaze fixing in on her. "Why are you looking at me like that?" he asked quietly.

Caught!

She cleared her throat. "I was thinking how much you enjoy a challenge. You're suited to these mountains."

He looked pleased. Then, "You could be a part of all this, too, you know."

Her heart stumbled. Had he brought her here for another reason? "Wh-what do you mean?"

"You love it here. You won't be happy anywhere else." He paused. "Think carefully before you walk away from your job, Samantha."

The job.

She groaned inwardly at her stupidity. Had she really thought this confirmed bachelor had been about to pop the marriage question to his personal assistant? What on earth was the matter with her? Hadn't she learned her lesson with Carl? The thin air must be making her imagine things that weren't and could never be. Not that she'd ever consider it anyway.

She took a shuddering breath before speaking. "I *have* thought about it, Blake." Very much so. She hadn't stopped.

He turned to face her. "Stay, Samantha."

"I…I can't." If it had been a plea, she might have considered it. As it was, she knew this was basically still about him being inconvenienced.

She went to turn away. She couldn't face him fully. The last thing she wanted was him seeing she'd mistakenly assumed he was talking marriage a minute ago. What a fool she was for even thinking it, let alone believing he might be thinking it, too. This wasn't about anything more than desire, she reminded herself.

His fingers slid around her arm and tugged her back. "Why are you being so obstructive?"

She couldn't feel the pressure of his fingers through her thick jacket but she knew they were there. "Obstructive to what?"

"To me being concerned for your well-being."

She ignored the thud of her heart. "Oh, so *that's* why you won't let me finish up my job early?" she scoffed, knowing this was the only way she could handle him. "You're *concerned* for me?"

He froze.

Silence surrounded them.

Then, he said quietly, "I am, actually."

She gasped midbreath. "Why, Blake? Why are you concerned for me?"

"Why wouldn't I be?" As he spoke she could feel his eyes almost pulling her toward him.

"Um…Blake…"

He drew her toward him and bent his head. He was kissing her before she knew what was happening, instantly destroying any defenses she may have drawn on, regardless that she wanted him so very much. Like an avalanche rolling down a mountain, she fell—and it was just as devastating.

Then he slid his tongue between her lips and she opened her mouth to him fully. Hearing his husky groan, she wound her arms around his neck and held on to him, trusting him, knowing where he took her she would follow.

Time blurred.

And then, amazingly, he was slowing things down, giving her back herself, letting her regain focus. Finally, he eased back and they stared at each other.

"Oh, my God!" she whispered, awed by the sheer

complexity of the kiss that should have been simple and wasn't. It left her trembling.

He was feeling something equally as powerful. She could see it deep in his eyes. He truly desired her. Her dream of being in his arms was finally becoming a reality.

His cell phone began to ring.

He remained still, not moving, and she knew why. Nothing could take away from the strength of this moment between them. Here in the mountains it was like they were the only two people alive.

Then as quickly as she thought that, he blinked and turned away, breaking the moment. She heard him answer it, but she couldn't seem to move. She understood why he had turned away. Why he had broken the moment. It had been too much for him. For her. For them both. Without him looking at her, she could take a breath again.

She did.

And then she found she could move. She swiveled to go get into the SUV, needing to sit down for a minute and feel something solid beneath her.

She took a few steps but as she went to reach for the door handle, her feet slipped from under her on a patch of ice and, with a small cry, she felt herself falling backward…backward….

She frantically made a grab for anything within reach, but there was only the air and she felt her legs going up and her body going down, her back hitting the grass, then her head on something harder. She literally saw stars….

The next thing she knew Blake was dropping to his knees beside her. "Thank God!" he muttered, when he saw her eyes were open.

"What happened?" she managed to say.

He glanced back to where she'd been walking. "You must have slipped on that ice back there."

She started to lift her head, then winced at the pain.

"Take it slowly." He put his hand under her shoulders to help her up. "Is your back sore or anything? Are you hurting anywhere?"

"No."

Then he swore. "You're bleeding."

"I am?"

His hand came away with some blood on it. "You've cut your head." He helped her to sit up, then he checked the back of her head. "It's only small but it's bleeding like the devil and might need a stitch. There's a lump starting where you hit it, too." Snatching up her woolen hat that must have come off during the fall, he placed it against the cut. "Hold that on it. It'll help stem the flow of blood. We need to get you to a doctor."

"Joel?" she said, without thinking, not meaning anything by it.

His mouth tightened. "Yes." He waited. "Do you think you can stand up? Are you dizzy or anything?"

"A little, but I'll be fine."

He helped her stand, then walked her the few feet to the car. Soon they were heading back to Jarrod Ridge.

"How do you feel now?" he said a few minutes later.

"Okay."

They drove a little farther. "Talk to me, Samantha."

"I don't really feel like talking," she said, calling herself an idiot for slipping. If only she'd looked where she was going, then—

"I want you to stay awake. You may have a slight concussion."

"Oh." She realized this was the correct procedure.

"Come on, you can do better than that," he said, a serious look in his eyes.

"Okay." She tried to think. "What do you want me to say?"

"I don't know. Anything. What's your favorite color?"

She didn't need to think about that. "Yellow."

His brow rose in surprise. "Yellow? Any particular reason?"

She winced a little as she adjusted the woolen hat against the injury. "Because it's bright and happy."

He glanced at her again, noting her wince, his mouth turning grim. "Okay, so what's your favorite flower?"

"Tulips."

Another look of surprise from him. "Why?"

"They're so beautiful."

There was a tiny pause. "Like you," he murmured, and her breath caught, then she moved her head and winced again. "Not long now," he assured her.

After that Blake drove straight up to the clinic at the spa lodge. The middle-aged nurse immediately took control, putting Samantha in an exam room. She checked her over, mentioning it wasn't too bad but that she'd need to call the doctor anyway.

"No need to get Joel if he's busy," Samantha said, feeling bad for interrupting his Sunday morning.

Blake nodded at the nurse. "Get him."

The nurse nodded in agreement then looked at her. "The doctor really should see you," she said, then went and picked up the wall telephone as Samantha glanced at Blake.

He gave a short shake of his head. "He's paid to do his job, Samantha. Let him."

Before too long, Joel strode into the exam room, nodding at Blake and giving her a chiding frown. "What have you done to yourself, Sam?"

Samantha didn't look at Blake, but she sensed he'd noted the shortening of her name. Joel was professional in his examination. She didn't need stitches but he tidied up the cut and it finally stopped bleeding. Thankfully he hadn't needed to cut any of her hair in the process.

"I don't think the lump on your head is anything to be concerned about," he assured her, "but we still need to keep an eye on it for any signs of concussion." He considered her. "If you like, I can come to Pine Lodge and check on you a couple of times throughout the day."

"I'll take care of her," Blake said firmly. "I know what signs to look for."

Joel glanced at Blake, held his gaze a moment, then nodded. "Fine. But I'll drop by the lodge and check on her this evening. Call me sooner if you have any doubts."

"I will."

Samantha looked from one to the other. "Do either of you mind if I have a say in this?"

Blake shot her an impatient look, but it was Joel who spoke. "Sam, this has to be taken very seriously. Your brain's had a knock, and sometimes things can develop later on. You need to rest up and you need to have someone keep a close eye on you for at least twenty-four hours."

She swallowed, not sure she liked hearing that, but before she could say anything the clinic door opened and someone called out for help, saying something about a twisted ankle. The nurse and Joel excused themselves to go check.

Blake came to stand in front of her. "I intend to look after you whether you like it or not."

"But—"

"It's my fault you were out there today," he cut across her, his eyes holding firm regret. "No arguments, Samantha. I owe you this."

She melted faster than snow under a heat lamp. "All right."

There was nothing in his eyes that said he remembered their kiss, and right now she was grateful for that. She would have plenty of time to go over it once she was alone.

He picked up her jacket. "Come on, then," he said gruffly. "Let's get this on you and get you back home."

Home?

Why did that sound so good to her?

Five

By the time Blake brought her back to Pine Lodge it was almost noon. Not that Samantha was hungry. She wasn't. She was glad now that he'd decided to stay close today. She wasn't feeling ill, but she was still a little shaky, so she was appreciative of him cupping her elbow as they walked.

That shakiness increased as they went up the staircase and he told her that tonight she was to sleep in the spare bedroom in his suite—a spare bedroom separated from his bedroom by only a connecting bathroom.

Her stomach dipped as they reached the top stair. "I'm only across the landing there, Blake. It seems silly not to stay in my own room."

"No. I want you near in case you need me."

She *did* need him, but not in the way he meant. He was being nothing more than caring right now, while she was still stunned by the impact of their kiss back on the mountain.

"Fine," she murmured, not up to arguing anyway. She was a bit of a mess. Her jacket had mud on it, her slacks were still slightly damp in places where she'd fallen on the wet grass, and parts of her brown hair felt like it was matted with blood. Yuk! She must look a wonderful sight.

"I need to change my clothes," she said, wrinkling her nose. "Actually I might have a shower. My hair feels sticky."

He shook his head. "Not a good idea. You might faint in there."

Her heart thudded and she could feel her face heat up as she pictured him coming in to rescue her. She looked away as they walked toward her room. "You're right," she said, then could have kicked herself. Any other woman would have used that to her advantage, but no, not her. What was the matter with her? Then she remembered. That's right, she'd had a bump on the head, she excused herself, wincing.

"Are you in pain?"

"A little."

He pushed open her bedroom door and led her inside. "Here. Sit on the chair and let me help you take off your jacket."

"Thanks." She did as he said.

"Your sweater's got dried blood down the back of it," he said, after he'd eased her out of the padded material. "I don't know how you're going to get it over your head without causing pain." A small pause. "I'll have to help you off with it."

She gulped. "You will?"

"Yes." His voice was nothing but neutral.

She tried to appear nonchalant, too. "Trust me to wear a tight-necked sweater today," she joked, feeling dizzy again but not from her injuries. It was the thought of him undressing her, even though it made sense to do it this way. She didn't think she'd be able to get the sweater off without him. She had a long-sleeved T-shirt underneath to cover herself, but that had a wide neck and she could easily take it off herself.

"Right. This won't take long." His voice sounded tight and she wondered… "Keep still now."

He slid her arms out of the sleeves, then she felt him touch the hem of her sweater, and almost like it was in slow motion he started to lift it upward. She could feel him move close…closer still as he inched it up higher and higher…. She could feel his breath change as he neared her breasts, though not once did he touch her in any intimate way.

"Okay, careful now," he said, as he reached her nape, his voice huskier. "This will be a little tricky." He moved closer…. "There. That's it. Now let me ease it over your head." He moved around to the front of her and eased the knit material gently up over her head, and suddenly it was off and she was sitting there, her gaze level with his belt buckle. And then she raised her eyes to his, saw him looking down at her, and she dropped her eyes to where her T-shirt had ridden up and was revealing her breasts cupped in her lacy blue bra.

She lifted her head again and their eyes locked together. Something dark flared in his, and in retaliation her breathing became practically nonexistent as she remembered their kiss. Until that moment back there on the mountain none of this had been purely about *them*.

Things had changed.

Now it was.

All at once he twisted jerkily toward the small table and placed the sweater on it, saying over his shoulder, "I'll leave you to do the rest, but I'll be back soon to check on you." His voice sounded rough as he headed for the door. "You should get into bed."

She realized he was trying to be a gentleman and keep it all under control because she was injured, but what if she wasn't injured? Would he take her?

The thought was moot, she told herself, swallowing hard and concentrating on what he'd said. "I'm not staying up here all day, Blake. I can sit on the couch downstairs and do some work." It didn't feel right to go to bed in the middle of the day. Not unless…

He stopped at the door, his eyes firm. "I won't let you work, but you can lie on the couch."

"Good of you," she joked, trying to ease the tension in the room.

He didn't smile. He had a hard flush on his face. "I think so," he muttered, then left her to it, shutting the door behind him and giving her some privacy.

Swallowing, she had to move or he might come back and decide to help her undress the rest of her clothes. And that wouldn't be such a bad thing on her part, but clearly he didn't want to right now. She appreciated that he was thinking of her, even as her body craved to be a part of his.

First, she went into her bathroom, groaning when she saw a streak of blood on her cheek and the mess of her hair. Carefully she lifted the T-shirt over her head.

Unable to stop herself, she stared at her lace-clad breasts, her cheeks reddening as she thought of Blake seeing the invitation of her body like this.

Filling the sink with warm water, she grabbed a washcloth and cleaned as much of the blood out of her hair as possible, then very gently combed it into place over the cut. She was pleased with the result. If she didn't know better, and if her head hadn't been sore, it would be hard to believe she'd just had an accident.

But if she was going to be an invalid today, she may as well be comfortable. She changed into denim jeans and a long-sleeve blouse that buttoned up so she didn't have to lift it over her head. Blake tapped on the door as she stepped into a pair of slides.

"Come in," she called out, half-surprised he'd knocked, considering he'd appeared to have taken charge of her welfare.

He pushed open the door then stood there, inspecting her from the face up. "You look much better."

"I feel better. Thanks."

Then his gaze traveled downward and a curious look passed over his face. "I don't remember seeing you in jeans before."

One glance from him and she could feel how much the jeans hugged her figure. Her stomach fluttered. "I usually only wear them at home." If they were staying at a hotel, Pine Lodge included, she wore stylish clothes even when going casual. She considered dressing right a part of her job.

"You should wear them more often," he said, his eyes blank but his voice tight again. He stepped back. "Come on. There's a couch waiting for you downstairs."

She avoided his gaze as she walked forward, then

went past him in the doorway, but she could feel his presence like a soft touch.

Thankfully soon she was lying on the couch with cushions behind her back and a throw over her body. Did she want a book to read, he asked. A movie on the DVD player? A magazine?

"Perhaps some magazines," she said, though she didn't actually feel like doing anything but lying there and being with Blake. "You don't have to do this," she said as he went to get them from the rack.

He came back with a selection, his mouth set. "I told you. It's my fault you were injured in the first place. I shouldn't have taken you with me."

"But you were only wanting to show me the bungalow location before I left Aspen," she said in a flood of words, then saw his mouth tighten further. She understood. She didn't want to be reminded that she was leaving soon either. "Anyway, what's done is done. I don't blame you but if you want to make it up to me, then I'd love a hot drink. A hot chocolate would be nice. With marshmallows."

"No."

She blinked. "Why not?"

"Because you shouldn't be drinking or eating for a few hours. It could make things worse."

She realized he was right, but, "I'm really thirsty, Blake, and I'm feeling fine now. How about some peppermint tea? That shouldn't hurt." She watched him consider that.

He nodded grudgingly. "Only a very weak one, then."

She smiled. "Thanks."

He set off for the kitchen and she could hear him

moving about in there. Her family used to cosset her like this at times, and she had to admit she liked being taken care of by Blake.

He soon returned with her hot drink, then he moved to the table in the corner where they'd set up the office. For a time it remained quiet as she flipped through the magazines and sipped at her tea. Then she began feeling sleepy. Eventually she finished her drink and made herself more comfortable, being careful with her sore head as she curled up on the couch. Her eyes closed and she found herself thinking about her and Blake back on the mountain. She could still remember the feel of his lips against...

The phone woke her with a start and she heard Blake swearing as he snatched it from the handset. She sat up and tidied herself, listening to his conversation, knowing someone in his family was inquiring about her. He soon ended the call.

"Sorry about that," he told her. "It was Guy checking to see how you were. He'd heard about the accident from Avery."

"Oh, that's nice of him."

The phone rang again and Blake reached for it. "Yes, she's fine, Gavin, but I'll be keeping an eye on her anyway." She saw Blake listen, then dart a look at her, before turning away. "You're a funny guy, Gav." Then he hung up.

Curious, she asked, "What did he say?"

"Nothing much."

Had Gavin made a brotherly comment about keeping an eye on her? Not that she minded. It might work in her favor. "That's good of your family to be checking on me."

"You're supposed to be resting. I don't want them interrupting that."

His comment warmed her as she glanced at the wall clock, surprised to see the time. "I must have been asleep a while."

"An hour."

So he'd been keeping an eye on her. "That long? I didn't realize."

"I did."

The phone rang again and he muttered something low. This time it was Trevor. No sooner had he hung up than they heard car doors slam shut and Blake strode over to look out the window.

"Who is it?" she asked.

"Melissa and Shane."

She watched him start toward the front door and quickly called his name. He stopped to look at her. "You *will* let them in, won't you?"

His mouth tightened. "For a short while."

"Be nice," she chided gently, and he shot her a look saying that was a given. "You know what I mean, Blake. I think it's wonderful of your family to be concerned for me."

His mouth softened a little. "Yeah, they're pretty good when they want to be."

Soon Blake's sister Melissa and her new fiancé, Shane McDermott, came into the lodge, bringing a breath of crisp, fresh air.

Melissa's long, wavy, blond hair flew behind her as she made a beeline for the couch. "Samantha! We heard you'd had an accident. Are you okay?"

Samantha was touched that they'd thought to drop by. "I'm fine, Melissa. Thank you for thinking of me."

"She's fine for the moment," Blake said, standing closest to the door, as if ready to open it in a moment's notice. "But she needs to rest as much as possible."

Shane stood beside him but he at least smiled at her, unlike Blake. "Good to see you, Samantha," he said, inclining his head in the cowboy way.

Samantha smiled back at the handsome man. Shane was the architect who'd designed the resort's riding stables. He might look urban and sophisticated, but he'd been raised on a nearby ranch and his cowboy status couldn't be disputed. "You, too, Shane."

Melissa sank down on one of the lounge chairs and frowned at Samantha. "You do look pale. So tell me. What happened?" Without giving her time to reply, she glanced at the men. "Blake, I'd love a hot chocolate so be a dear and make me one, won't you?" She darted a look at Samantha. "What about you, honey?"

Samantha wrinkled her nose. "Blake won't let me."

Melissa seemed to consider that, then darted a look at her brother before nodding at Samantha. "Yes, that's probably best." She looked at her fiancé. "Shane, darling, would you mind helping Blake in the kitchen? I'm not sure he knows his way around it," she teased.

Blake eased into his first smile since they'd arrived. "You'd be surprised, Melissa."

Melissa patted the small hump of her stomach on her slightly curvy figure. "You'd better hurry. This baby is getting hungry." She winked at Samantha.

Samantha smiled but as the men left them alone and she looked at Blake's sister, she felt a tug deep inside her chest. Melissa had a radiant glow about her. She'd only recently announced her pregnancy to Shane and they were soon to be married. They'd had a few ups and downs but now all was well.

Samantha was very happy for Melissa, and yet she felt sad for herself, with this inexplicable ache in the region of her heart. One day she wanted a baby and a family of her own, but she couldn't imagine any man she wanted to father them—except for maybe Blake. That would mean he would have to marry her, but he didn't believe in happily-ever-after, and she wasn't ready for that either.

Still, she couldn't shake off the thought of cuddling Blake's baby in her arms. It was natural for a woman to think about having children with the man she was attracted to, right? Strangely, she didn't ever remember thinking about having Carl's children. Her notion of being married to him had merely been about them traveling the world together. It hadn't progressed further than that. Thank the Lord!

"Are you okay, Samantha?"

She managed a smile. "Apart from a small headache, I'm fine."

Melissa's piercing blue eyes suddenly seemed so like Blake's. "I hear you're leaving us soon?"

This was why the other woman had got the men out of the way. Melissa wanted to question her.

Samantha tried to look at peace with her decision. "Yes, it's time to move on to new pastures."

"Blake will miss you."

"So everyone keeps telling me," Samantha said wryly, but was grateful that Shane came back in right then to ask Melissa a question about how hot she wanted her drink. Once he left again Samantha changed the conversation to the ranch where Shane had grown up. Melissa was more than happy to talk about her fiancé.

The other couple stayed for a while, until Blake shooed them out, reminding them that a certain person needed to rest up.

"Right," Blake said, once they'd gone. "I'll get some more work out of the way, then how does an omelet sound for dinner? I don't think you should eat anything too heavy, just in case. It's not a good thing to have a full stomach."

She looked at him in mild amusement. "Is this Doctor Jarrod speaking?"

He didn't seem to find that funny. "Yes, so take note."

"I would, only you won't let me work," she quipped.

"Funny," he muttered, then went back to his paperwork. She sighed. He was taking it all so seriously, and while that was sweet of him, it wasn't necessary.

After that, Samantha was itching to get up and move around but knew it was best she take things easy. For something to do while she was waiting for Blake to finish working, she popped a movie in the DVD and began watching it with earphones so that she didn't disturb him. It was a romantic comedy she hadn't seen before and it made her giggle. She didn't realize she'd been laughing loudly until suddenly she became aware of Blake standing near the couch.

She paused the movie and looked up at him as she pulled out her earbuds. "I'm sorry. Is this interrupting your work?"

"No." He went still. "It's good to hear you laugh. You don't do it often enough."

Her pulse was skipping beats. "The job isn't exactly a laugh a minute," she joked. Then realized how that might sound. "That came out wrong. I didn't mean—"

"I know what you meant," he said easily enough as he leaned over and pulled the earplug cord out of the television. Picking up the remote, he turned the movie back on, only instead of going back to his work he sat down on the other chair.

She blinked in mild surprise, then tried to concentrate as he began watching the movie with her. He'd only missed about fifteen minutes of the story, so they both watched it together. It was amusing enough that she could feel herself relax, and when it was finished even Blake looked relaxed. She was glad about that. He worked too hard at times, and took his responsibilities too seriously.

Later, in spite of him telling her to stay on the couch, she followed him into the kitchen where he was going to prepare dinner. "I need to walk. My legs are getting numb."

His brows immediately drew together on full medical alert. "They feel numb? Are you getting any pins and needles? Is it hard to walk or are—"

"Blake, I was merely trying to say I wanted to move around," she cut across him, somewhat bemused by his agitation.

He grimaced. "Okay, so that was a mild over-reaction."

"Mild?" she teased.

He gave a self-deprecating smile, then jerked his head toward the bench. "Go sit over there and take it easy."

She ignored that and turned toward the cupboard.

"I'll put out the place mats and cutlery first. We can eat in here."

He must have known it was a waste of time to argue because he nodded, then went back to preparing the omelet. It was a strange feeling watching him cook for her. It would be another memory to take away when she left.

Soon they were sitting down on the tall stools to eat and the next hour flew by as they chatted. As if they both didn't want to ruin the moment, neither of them spoke about her leaving.

Then he mentioned Donald Jarrod in passing, and that made her think. Blake had never spoken about his father while they were in Vegas, but now they were in Aspen she'd managed to put two and two together. "Your dad was pretty hard on you, wasn't he?"

He tensed even as he gave a light shrug. "After my mother died, he was hard on all his children."

She considered him. "But harder on you."

A flash of surprise crossed his face. "Yes. How did you know?"

"You were the eldest. He seems to have been a man who had set ideas about the order of things and didn't give an inch."

"He was. Very much so."

"Tell me more."

He paused and for a moment she didn't think he would tell her. Then, "Guy was only younger by a few minutes but it could have been years in my father's eyes. I was the oldest, so it was up to me to make sure I took responsibility for everything. None of us ever really got to play while growing up, but I suppose I got even less time than the rest."

The thought upset her. "That's sad."

He shrugged. "My father actually did us a favor. We grew up being very independent. We don't need anyone."

She could see that. And that was even sadder, but she didn't say so. She tilted her head. "It still would've been hard losing your mother like that when you were just a small boy. And then having your father distance himself would have made it far worse. Children don't understand why love has been withdrawn. They just know."

His expression suddenly bordered on mockery and she knew she'd touched a nerve. "And you understand the way a child's mind works when he loses a parent, do you?"

She pulled a face. He knew very well both her parents were alive. "Well, no, but—"

"I rest my case."

"Blake, I don't think it's too hard to comprehend what you must have gone through."

Anger flashed across his face. "Enough, Samantha. I don't want or need your sympathy for something that happened a long time ago."

"But—"

The telephone rang and he snatched it up from the wall beside him, almost barking into it. His mouth tightened. "Hang on, Erica. I'll put her on." He handed the phone over to Samantha.

"I see Blake's being his usual talkative self," Erica mused down the line. She didn't wait for Samantha to agree. "I heard about your accident and just wanted to see how you were doing."

Samantha appreciated her concern. "I'm fine, thanks,

Erica." She forced herself to sound cheery. "Blake and I just had dinner. He cooked me an omelet."

An eloquent silence came from Erica's end. "A man of many talents," she finally said. "I'd better let you go, then. I'll talk to you tomorrow." She hung up before Samantha could respond.

Samantha took her time placing the receiver back down, hiding her expression from him. She wouldn't tell Blake what Erica had been thinking. That his half sister was delighted the two of them were bonding, even if Blake did sound like a grouch. "That was really nice of her to call."

His lips twisted. "I wonder if I have any relatives left who might like to interrupt us tonight?"

Her brow creased with worry. "You really should give Erica a chance."

"To do what?"

Anger stirred the air, though she knew it wasn't directed at her. She tilted her head. "Do you blame Erica for your father's affair with her mother?" she said, coming right out and saying it.

He didn't look pleased by her comment. "I'm not blaming Erica for what my father did. I just don't want her coming in here and splitting up the family. I'm not convinced she'll stay in Aspen."

She didn't know how he could say that. Was he blind? "She and Christian are so in love. And she's in love with everyone here at Jarrod Ridge, too. Their hearts are here, Blake. They won't leave you."

He swore. "I don't give a rat's ass if they leave or not. This isn't about what *I* feel anyway. It's about her causing problems for the family and then walking away without a care in the world."

"I'm sure that won't happen. Erica isn't like that."

One eyebrow shot up. "You know her so well, do you?"

"Do you?"

A muscle began ticking along his jaw. "Thank you for your opinion, but I don't need it." He pushed to his feet and began collecting the plates, taking them over to the dishwasher. "Go into the living room. I'll bring in the coffee."

For a few moments she didn't move. She watched his rigid back and felt depressed by his remoteness and abruptness. She'd pushed him hard just now and she wasn't sure why, except that she somehow felt she was fighting not just for Erica's sake but for Blake's, as well. If she could at least get him to relent toward Erica then maybe when *she* left, her time here would have been of value. Maybe then something good would have come from all this. She sighed. Or was she simply looking for something to make herself feel good about leaving Blake?

And that brought her back to what she'd said before about Erica leaving him. Was that the crux of the matter? It occurred to her then that Blake may have abandonment issues with his mother dying, and now that made it difficult for him to get close to his half sister. Or to get close to anyone, including herself.

Someone rang the doorbell and Blake swore again.

"That'll be Joel," Samantha reminded him. "He said he would check on me."

"Stay there," he muttered and strode past her to let in the other man.

A couple of seconds later Joel breezed into the kitchen. She noticed he took in the homey scene, but he was all professional while he checked her over and announced he was pleased.

Then, "We have to get you better for tomorrow night," he teased, but she saw him dart a look at Blake and she suddenly had the feeling there was more to this. He seemed to be letting Blake know he was staking a claim.

"Tomorrow night?" Blake asked in a menacing voice.

Joel closed up his medical bag. "Samantha and I have a date for Monday night." He winked at her. "We're going to the movies."

Samantha wanted to say she hadn't actually accepted the invitation but the displeased look in Blake's eyes kept her quiet.

"Let's see how she feels first," Blake said grimly, then stepped back in clear indication that the doctor should precede him to the front door.

Joel hesitated, like he wasn't about to take orders, then he must have remembered that Blake was his boss. He inclined his head at Samantha. "I'll call you in the morning," he told her, picking up his bag.

He left the room and Blake saw him out, and Samantha couldn't help but wonder once again if Blake might be jealous of Joel. The thought made her heartbeat pick up speed. Blake had certainly *wanted* to kiss her back there on the mountain and surely that had to mean something.

Didn't it?

All at once she needed to know what he felt for her. "Joel finds me attractive, don't you think?" she said dreamily as Blake came back in the kitchen looking anything but relaxed.

His eyes filled with meaning. "Sure he does," he said cynically.

She couldn't let him get away with that. "What does that mean?"

"Just that any woman with the right equipment can attract a man. And believe me, you've got the right equipment," he drawled, slipping his hands into his trouser pockets, all at once looking very much in charge of himself, making her want to bring him down a peg or two.

"Thanks for the assumption that I'm only good for sex," she said with faint indignation.

His hands came out of his pockets and his complacency vanished. "I didn't say that," he retorted, then strode over to check on the coffee. He spun back around. "Dammit, what the hell are you doing with those men anyway? You don't need them. They're beneath you."

Startled, she gathered her wits about her. *This* was more like it. "Maybe I *want* them beneath me," she joked.

"Don't talk like that."

She hid a soft gasp. It *did* sound like he was jealous. She needed to push more. "I don't understand how you can say a doctor isn't good enough for me, Blake."

"That's because he's *not* good enough for you."

Her spirits soared. "What about Ralph? You don't even know what he does for a living."

"And you do?"

She did, then realized she'd set herself up here. She had to cough before she said, "He's a car salesman."

"Huh! That explains the slime rolling off him."

"Blake!" She hadn't expected quite such a response. "What's got into you?"

His mouth drew down at the corners. "Those guys aren't after you for your intellect."

She screwed up her nose. "How nice of you to point that out."

"You know what I'm saying."

Yes, she did. Unfortunately she knew it was true. And that would have been fine if she'd been the least bit interested in the other men. As it was, she still felt a little guilty using them, though no doubt they were big enough to look out for themselves.

She tilted her head and knew she had to say this. "If I didn't know better I'd think you were jealous."

"And if I am?" he challenged without warning.

She felt giddy but she couldn't let herself get her hopes up. "I'd have to ask why. Is it because you know I'm leaving soon and you only want what you suddenly can't have?"

"What the—"

"Or is it because you might actually want *me?*"

For a moment he looked like he would move in close. "You ask me that after the kiss we shared?"

Her breath came quickly. "I—"

And then something changed in his expression and his jaw thrust forward. "This isn't the time to discuss it. You need your rest. You should go lie on the couch."

Her throat blocked with disappointment, but then understanding dawned and she realized he was pulling back for *her* sake. If it hadn't been for her accident, she was sure he would be making love to her right now.

Frustration weaved through her, despite appreciating that he was doing the right thing. "I think I'll go read in bed. It's getting late." He went to come with her and she put her hand up. "No, I can manage by myself. Good night, Blake. And thanks."

He nodded. "Make sure you sleep in the spare bedroom. I still want you close to me."

She could feel heat sweeping up her face. Did he have to say it like that? "Okay."

He seemed mesmerized by her reddening cheeks. "I'll be checking on you a couple of times in the night." His voice had a gravelly edge to it now. "So I apologize in advance for disturbing you."

She looked away; the thought of him coming into her room during the night was enough to disturb her *now*.

Then she went up to bed with stars in her eyes. And they weren't from the hit on the head either. Unfortunately she knew he wasn't about to take advantage of her while she was injured, and certainly not during the night when she was sure he'd remain a perfect gentleman. But he'd better watch out when she was back on her feet.

Six

Blake looked at the bedside clock and grunted to himself. It was almost seven o'clock and still dark outside, but he needed to get up and check on Samantha before he did anything else this morning. Today he planned on working from Pine Lodge so he could keep an eye on her, but he needed to go to the Manor and get some things out of the way first.

He'd spent a restless night, getting up every couple of hours to check on a sleeping Samantha in the bedroom next door. Of course it was easy for her to sleep so peacefully. She didn't have to stand over an attractive member of the opposite sex who wore satin pajamas and looked deliciously alluring in bed. And she didn't have to reach out to touch that person's shoulder to shake them awake, nor rigidly ignore the urge to slide into bed next to her warm body and pleasure her senseless.

He would have done it, too—if he hadn't had to

wake her and ask questions to make sure she wasn't suffering any sort of confusion. Even now the thought of her having any sort of aftereffects from the head injury still managed to clench his gut tight. He'd hated seeing her hurt. If he hadn't been so focused on getting her away from that Ralph, then none of this would have happened.

Not even the kiss.

No, that kiss *would* have happened—if not there, then somewhere else. There was something going on between them now. It had started happening the night she'd handed him her resignation and it hadn't let up.

And it wasn't one-sided either. She'd dissolved in his arms so quickly yesterday he'd thought the marrow had melted in her bones. No woman had ever reacted quite like that for him before. It certainly made a man feel good.

Remembering the feel of her lips beneath his, he was tempted to just lie there and think about her, but he knew he'd never get out of bed if he did. And then Samantha would be bringing *him* breakfast in bed. The thought was more than pleasurable.

Giving a low groan, he tossed back the covers and shoved off the mattress in his pajama bottoms, then headed for the bathroom to take a shower. But as he opened the door and went to reach for the light switch, the light flicked on anyway and Samantha came through the connecting door.

She jumped back with a gasp. "Blake!"

A lick of fire sizzled through his veins as his eyes slid down over her slim contours, registering that what he thought had been green satin pajamas was an emerald midthigh nightshirt. It looked so sexy on her, suiting her complexion and rich brown hair.

He lifted his eyes back up to her face. "How's the head?" he asked huskily.

She seemed to become flustered. "Er…it doesn't feel too bad." Awkwardly she spun to face the mirrored wall, going up on her toes to stare at her reflection. "I came to see if it was okay." She lifted her long tousled strands to check the injury. "Yes, it looks fine," she chattered. "There's a bit of a bump and no sign of bleeding."

He appreciated that she was okay, but did she know that stretching up over the sink like she was, the side split of her nightshirt was showing him more of her long silken legs than he'd ever seen before? All the way up her thigh to the line of her panties.

Suddenly she seemed to freeze in position as she stretched up at the mirror like that, and he realized right then she was looking at *him* in the mirror, with a hungry look that drifted down over his bare chest and the pajama bottoms he'd worn last night for her benefit. He tensed with arousal and she must have noticed. Their eyes locked together in the glass.

And then she slowly pushed back from the sink and turned to face him with her body, her chin tilting provocatively, her eyes inviting him to take her. Caught off-guard by such an unfamiliar look from her, he swallowed hard. His assistant was certainly showing him a new side of herself lately.

"Samantha," he said thickly, galvanized into taking a step toward her. "Do you know what you're—"

"Yes, Blake, I do."

He reached her and she tumbled against him, her hands flattening against his chest, her mouth seeking his, her lips parting beneath his without any pressure at all.

Their kiss was hot and urgent and demanding, their bodies pressing closer and closer together, reveling in each other. Then a soft moan of hers breathed into him, and in a haze of desire, he deepened the kiss until he finally had to break away to suck in air.

But only for a moment, until he began planting quick, soft kisses down that creamy throat, before coming back up again to her lips, needing to be inside her mouth once more, needing to breathe her in once more.

He pulled her harder against him, running his hands hungrily over the satin material and feminine curves. She quivered all over from head to toe, wildly gripping his shoulders like she needed to hold on to him.

Mouth to mouth, he backed her to the full-length sink and lifted her up onto a folded fluffy towel. Her thighs fell open and he heard a button pop from the front of her nightshirt. He gave a groan of approval and wedged himself between her legs....

And the coldness of the marble touched his erection through his pajamas.

The shock of it made him still. Heaven knew he could do with cooling down...slowing down...but Samantha sat in front of him with her head tilted back and her eyes closed. Her cheeks were overheated, her breathing unsteady, and despite that come-to-me look she'd given him a short while ago, she appeared to be about to lose control. God knows he'd felt the instantaneous spiral of desire himself, but this was more and he really had to wonder just how inexperienced she actually was. He swallowed hard. Could she even be a *virgin?*

He wasn't sure how he felt about that, but he did

know he couldn't continue this right now. His previous lovers knew the score but this woman may not. And if he was playing with more than her body…if her emotions were more than involved…he could cause her a lot of heartache. He didn't want to do that to Samantha.

Yet this wasn't the moment to talk about it, with her looking all sexy and ready for the taking. There was too much hunger in the air in here. It would only confuse things. He liked her too much to do this to her.

Unwrapping her arms from around his neck, he lifted her down off the bench, hating that he had to walk away from her. "I'm sorry, Samantha."

Bewilderment spread over her face. "What's the—"

"I just can't do it," he rasped. "Not like this." As hard as it was to leave her side, he turned and went back to his room.

He badly wanted to turn right back around, sweep her up in his arms and carry her to his bed. He shuddered as he closed the door between them.

They would talk later and perhaps it would turn out that he'd have to keep the door closed permanently between them. Maybe she would be his road not taken. But he had to think what was best for Samantha. She deserved better than becoming his temporary mistress.

Samantha didn't know how she made it back to her own room. Humiliation scorched through her. She'd done exactly what she'd wanted to do and given Blake a come-on. She hadn't deliberately gone into the bathroom to entice him in there, but the opportunity had presented itself and she'd thought it had worked. Then he'd just upped and walked away and, despite his obvious arousal, he said he couldn't do it.

Couldn't make love with her.

She knew it had nothing to do with her having a minor head injury this time. He might say it was, but she knew this was about him not wanting her enough. His body had automatically responded to a female in his arms, but his mind had been elsewhere. As he'd said the evening before, any woman with the right equipment could attract a man. Unfortunately the attraction he felt for her hadn't been enough. Not for him.

It was Carl all over again.

She plopped down on her bed as her legs gave way. Had she unwittingly done something wrong back there? Something to annoy him physically? Clearly he hadn't been invested in the moment like she'd been. It had been wonderful in his arms but she hadn't realized he'd been feeling different. She thought he'd felt the same way. It was obvious now that he could turn himself on and off at a whim—just like he had after their kiss on the mountain.

Unlike her.

Her emotions whirled like a spinning top let loose on the floor. Oh, God, what was she going to do? How was she going to face him? Worse, would he insist on letting her out of her contract now? She had the feeling he would tell her to leave sooner rather than later.

At the thought, her emotions stopped spinning. They stopped dead. Her chin lifted. Right. Okay. If she was being given the heave-ho, then she would certainly leave without protest. It's what she needed to do anyway, she told herself. She regretted she would leave with this between them, but things had gone too far. It was a good lesson in being careful what she wished for. Now she simply wished this nightmare would go away.

Samantha took a shower and carefully washed her hair, but wasn't sure if she was dismayed or relieved after she came out of the bathroom and heard Blake's car leaving. Going over to peek out her bedroom window, she saw him driving toward the Manor in the early morning light. Evidently she was okay to be left alone now, she thought with a stab of hurt.

Then her heart dropped to her feet. Perhaps he was going to tell his family that she was leaving sooner? Would he tell them why? That she'd made a play for him and put him in an awkward position? Her cheeks heated at the thought and she wanted to curl up in a ball and not see any of them again.

Yet pride wouldn't allow her to do that. She'd held her head high when Carl had rejected her and she would do it again now. She would go up to the Manor and finish her tasks, and she would arrange her replacement. If she smiled at the others and acted carefree, then no one would know how bad she felt.

No one except Blake.

Half an hour later she sat at her desk at the Manor, relieved not to have seen anyone she knew on the way here. She didn't want to answer questions about her accident, or anything else for that matter.

Thankfully the door to Blake's office was shut, though the red light on the telephone told her he was making a call. Quickly she got herself organized, then found the number she was after and reached for the phone, hoping someone at the employment agency would be at their desk early like her. She knew that as soon as the red button on his phone lit up with her extension, Blake would learn she was here, but it couldn't be helped.

She got the answering machine. Having dealt with this employment agency before for other office matters, she decided to leave a message. At least that would get the ball rolling. "Yes, this is Samantha Thompson calling on behalf of Blake Jarrod Enterprises. Could Mary Wentworth call me back as soon as possible…" The red light on Blake's phone went off. Her heart started to race as a second later his door was flung open. "It's about a position that's become available." He strode to her desk. "It's—"

He pressed the button to disconnect the call, his eyes slamming into her. "What are you doing?" he demanded in a low tone.

She angled her chin as she looked up at him. "I'm trying to work."

"I thought you'd have enough sense to rest up today."

"I don't need to rest up. I did plenty of that yesterday." Calmly, she placed the telephone back on its handset. "I'm perfectly fine now."

His eyes narrowed. "And why the hell are you calling someone about your job?"

"You need a new assistant."

"I'm happy with my old one."

She arched one eyebrow. "Really? It didn't seem that way to me this morning," she said, staying cool when all she wanted to do was fall in a heap and cry her eyes out.

He swore.

"Don't worry, Blake. I'll be leaving Aspen soon, so

you don't have to worry that I'll attack you. I know you're not that into me."

He blinked, then, "What the hell!" He swore again. "We need to talk."

"It's a bit late for talking, don't you think?" She went to pick up the phone again. He grabbed her hand, not hurting her but not letting her make the call either. "Stop manhandling me, Blake."

He tried to stare her down. "No."

"Blake, this isn't getting us anywhere."

"Listen, Samantha. You're—"

Erica walked into the office and stopped dead, blinking in surprise as her gaze went from one to the other, then down at their hands gripped together. "Er… Blake, your car is here to take you to the airport."

He casually let go of Samantha's hand. "Thanks, Erica."

Samantha felt the blood drain from her face. "You're leaving?"

Like Carl?

He looked at her oddly. "Something cropped up overnight at one of the hotels and I need to go to Vegas and sort it out. I'll tell you about it later."

As fast as it had tightened, the tension unscrewed inside her. So he *was* coming back. It had been crazy of her to even think he wouldn't. Blake wouldn't give up all this because of *her*.

She went to get to her feet. "I'll come with you." Once she was in Vegas, she would start bringing her life there to a close.

"No, you stay here. You shouldn't be flying with a head injury," he said firmly, surprising her. She'd have thought he'd be eager to get her out of Aspen now.

He cast his half sister a look. "Erica, can you keep an eye on Samantha and make sure she doesn't stay here too long today? I don't want her overdoing things."

Erica looked startled then pleased. "Of course." It was obvious she valued being asked by her brother to help out, but Samantha was still surprised that Blake wanted *her* to stay in Aspen.

He nodded. "Thanks. I'll just grab my stuff." As he spoke he headed back into his office before coming out with his briefcase and coat. He looked at Samantha. "I'll be back tonight. I'll explain everything then." He started toward the door then hesitated. "You *will* be here when I return, won't you, Samantha?"

It hadn't occurred to her to leave behind his back, though she couldn't discount that it might have. Then she remembered how she'd thought he might have issues with feeling abandoned over his mother's death. Did he think *she* was about to abandon him, too? Tenderness touched a part of her that wasn't reeling by the latest events. "I promise."

He looked satisfied then he gave Erica a jerky nod as he passed by. He left behind a meaningful silence.

After a couple of seconds, Erica came toward the desk. "Are you okay?"

"My head's fine now, thanks."

She tutted. "You know I mean more than that."

Samantha grimaced. "Yes, I suppose I do." Then as she looked at the other woman, she wondered if Blake would eventually discuss her with his family. Would he even tell them she had made a play for him? Her breath caught. She'd never known him to talk about his affairs before to anyone. Huh! Affair? There *was* no affair. That was the problem.

"He's concerned for you, honey."

"He's concerned for the job."

"You're wrong." Erica paused. "Give him a chance to explain whatever it is he needs to explain."

The telephone rang then, and Erica said she had to go check on something but would be back later. Samantha answered it and heard Mary Wentworth's voice, and knew she needed to slow everything down a little. So she apologized to the other woman that she couldn't talk right now and would call her back tomorrow. By then, she should well and truly know the score between her and Blake. Either way, she still had to leave. It was just a matter of when.

After she hung up, the workday began with the phone ringing, then the mail arrived. Samantha worked through it all, but a part of her mind was on Blake's reaction earlier. He'd said he was perfectly happy with his old assistant.

Her.

And that made her wonder if he might still want her to work out her contract. Her heart raced at the thought, then came to a shuddering halt when she remembered this morning in the bathroom. She probably couldn't stay at Jarrod Ridge past tomorrow, but at least on his return tonight she might learn what had turned him off her. It may not be something she wanted to hear, but she needed to know or she would always wonder.

Erica returned an hour later, but Samantha still felt physically fine and convinced her not to worry. She'd decided to work until lunchtime, then she got a ride back to the lodge, where she made herself a light lunch. Afterward she felt tired, so she stretched out on the couch and took a nap.

The front doorbell woke her sometime later. It was a florist with a vase filled with the most gorgeous yellow tulips she'd ever seen. Something flipped over inside her heart. Her family wasn't into sending flowers, and only one person here knew she loved yellow tulips.

There was a card with them. "Dinner tonight. Pine Lodge. All arranged. See you at seven."

Her throat swelled with emotion as she carried the vase over to a side table and set it down. They looked so stunning that she was about to race upstairs to get her camera, but then wondered if that was a good idea. Did she really want to take away more memories of Blake?

The telephone rang then.

It was Joel. Oh, Lord. She'd forgotten her date with him tonight. The tulips caught her eye and she knew she'd rather spend her last hours here in Aspen with Blake than go to the movies with Joel.

She opened her mouth to speak but before she could say anything, he apologized and told her that his cousin was in town overnight and this was his only chance to catch up with her. Did she mind? No. Could they go to the movies tomorrow night instead? She said she would let him know. She had no idea whether she would still be here tomorrow night. Then he mentioned that he was in town right now and would get the nurse to check on her later today, but she thanked him and said it wasn't necessary.

More than relieved, Samantha looked at the tulips as she hung up the telephone, Joel already relegated to the back of her mind. Blake might just want to discuss her job tonight, but right now she didn't care. She needed to know where it had all gone wrong this morning. More importantly, she wanted to know if there was even a slim chance it was something that could be fixed.

Seven

Samantha hadn't been sure what she should wear for tonight. While the flowers and the dinner were very thoughtful of Blake, and while he'd said he would give her an explanation as to why he walked away from her this morning in the bathroom and that sounded promising, none of that meant he *wanted* her.

In the end she decided to keep it fairly low-key, just like she would if she were dining with him for business reasons. She wore a thin brown sweater over cream slacks and a pair of low-heeled pumps, adding a gold chain at her neck to make it a little more stylish.

Just after six-thirty one of the hotel staff arrived as sunset spiked through the lodge. He placed a cooked casserole in the oven to keep warm, dessert in the refrigerator, then lit the log fire before beautifully setting the table in the small dining alcove. Had Blake requested the two candles on the table? She was about to ask the young waiter when Blake came in the front door.

"Blake!" she exclaimed, her pulse picking up at the sight of him. Realizing she might be giving herself away, she pulled herself back and toned it down. "You're early," she said more sedately. "I didn't expect you quite so soon."

"We had a tailwind." He nodded at the waiter. "It looks good, Andy. Thanks."

Samantha wasn't surprised that he knew the man's name. Blake was good with people—as long as you did the right thing by him.

"No problem, Mr. Jarrod." Andy's smile encompassed them both. "I'll come and collect everything tomorrow." He nodded good-night, then went through to the kitchen.

Blake stood there for a minute looking at Samantha, his eyes flicking down over her outfit then away. "I could do with a shower," he muttered, and made for the stairs.

She felt nervous all of a sudden. She twisted away herself. "I'll just make sure the food's okay." She left the room and went into the kitchen, glad that Andy was still gathering a couple of things together before he left. It brought the world back into focus and took it away from her and Blake. She needed the balance.

Andy left and she busied herself unnecessarily checking on the casserole, then poured herself a glass of water and stood there sipping it to calm her nerves. She could only stay in there so long, and soon she wandered back into the lounge area and drew the drapes against the encroaching night, before switching on the lamps.

It was too quiet, so she put on a CD to fill the silence

and sat down on the couch to wait. The wood scent from the burning logs in the fireplace wafted throughout the room, and after a few minutes, she could feel the soft music begin to ease the tension inside her. And then it hit her and she realized how romantic the whole place looked. She groaned slightly. It hadn't been intentional but would Blake believe that? It all looked so intimate.

Panicking that he might think she was trying to seduce him, she was about to about to jump up and turn off the music when she saw Blake coming down the stairs. He wasn't looking at her and she ate up the sight of him. He was so handsome in light gray pants and a navy crewneck sweater, but it was his magnetic aura of masculinity that caught her breath.

He reached the bottom step and all at once he glanced up and his gaze quickly summed up the ambiance in the room. She could feel warmth steal under her skin. This guy never missed a trick.

"You must be tired," she said, hoping to ignore what he might think was obvious.

"A little. It's been a long day."

And then their eyes met—memories of this morning between them.

She moistened her mouth. "Blake, I—"

He shook his head. "Not yet, Samantha. Let's eat first. I'm starving and I need to relax a little."

"Of course." She swung toward the kitchen. "I'll serve the dinner."

"I'll pour the wine."

She hurried away, expelling a shaky breath once she reached the privacy of the kitchen. Blake wouldn't discuss the matter until he was ready, so she would just have to have a little patience. Perhaps it would be best if she had some food in her stomach first.

When she came back carrying the plates of chicken casserole, he was sitting at the table, having poured the wine. He stood up as she approached and took the plates from her. He'd always been a gentleman where she was concerned, holding out her chair or opening doors for her. She knew it was something he did on autopilot.

"You lit the candles," she said for something to say. "They look really nice."

He put the plates down on the table. "Andy knows his job."

She wasn't sure if that meant Blake had asked for them or if Andy had merely improvised. Did it matter, she asked herself as he held her chair out just as she'd expected.

As she sat down, she glimpsed the tulips on the side table. That was probably why he'd looked at her strangely before going upstairs to change. He must think her so ungrateful.

"Oh, Blake, I should have said something earlier. Thank you so much for the tulips. They're absolutely gorgeous."

"You like them, then?" He looked pleased as he sat down opposite her.

"I love them."

He considered her. "You getting hit on the head was very good for me."

She blinked. "It was?"

"I learned two things about you. What your favorite flower is, and your favorite color."

"Want to know my favorite perfume, too?" she joked, touched by his words.

Only he didn't laugh. "It's Paris by Yves Saint Laurent," he said with an unexpected thickness to his voice that made her nerves tingle.

"You know?"

"You bought some the first time we went to Paris together, remember?" He made it sound like they'd been together in Paris for something other than business.

Surprised he remembered that time two years ago when she'd first gone to work for him, she dropped her gaze and fanned her napkin over her lap, though she rather felt like fanning her face instead. "This looks delicious."

There was a slight pause. "Yes."

She could feel his eyes on her as she picked up her fork and finally looked at him again. "So, what was the problem in Vegas that you needed to go there in such a hurry?"

A moment ticked by then he picked up his fork. "There was a problem with one of the chefs. He was being a bit too temperamental, and the kitchen staff was threatening to walk out. It was beginning to escalate into a big commotion with the unions. It started to get ugly."

"And it's sorted out now?"

"Of course."

She had to smile. "Naturally. You wouldn't have come back otherwise, right?"

Suddenly there was an air of watchfulness about him. "What happened to your date with Joel tonight?"

She'd wondered if he'd mention it. And then something else occurred to her. Could he have arranged to get Joel out of the way tonight? The thought made her pulse race. "His cousin's in Aspen for the night and he wanted to spend time with her." She tilted her head. "You didn't have anything to do with that, did you?"

His brow rose. "Me? Am I that good?"

"Yes!" she exclaimed on a half chuckle.

A flash of humor crossed his face. "Believe me, I'm not *that* clever."

It did sound silly now. Blake could make things happen, but this time he'd have to find Joel's cousin and get that person to come to Aspen. Why would he bother? He knew he merely had to send her flowers and arrange dinner and she'd capitulate like every woman before her.

"Anyway, how are you feeling?" he asked.

"Terrific."

He searched her face, then inclined his head as if satisfied. "At least you only worked half the day."

Her eyes widened. "How do you know that?"

"I checked with Erica. She said you'd left at lunch-time."

She smiled wryly. "Did she also tell you she checked on me nearly every hour after that?"

"She promised me she would."

Why was she *not* surprised? "That was a bit over the top, wasn't it?"

"I don't think so."

She tried not to look more into it than there was. He probably wanted her all better so he could get rid of her faster. Then she knew that wasn't fair of her and she pulled her thoughts back into line. "You always were concerned for your staff, Blake. Thank you."

He looked at her strangely, as if he couldn't under-stand why she was putting herself in with the rest of his staff. But if that were the case, didn't that mean he was thinking she was something more to him than she actually was?

God, she had to stop thinking so much!

She picked up her wineglass. "You know, Blake. Erica isn't as bad as you imagine her to be. I suspect she'd still have kept an eye on me even without you asking her." She took a sip of her drink but watched him carefully over the rim of her glass.

His brows furrowed. "I guess so." As much as he appeared to concede the point, he didn't look totally convinced about Erica's intentions.

Samantha understood why. "You think she's only doing something nice for a reason, don't you?"

"Maybe."

"Has it occurred to you that the reason is *you?*" She let him consider that, then added, "Maybe she wants to get to know her brother, and she knows the only way she can do that is to show him she is willing to help him out?"

"Maybe." He paused. "But she cares for you, too."

She felt a rush of affection for Erica. "And that goes to show she's a nice person and worthy of your friendship… if not your love."

His lips twisted. "The hit on the head seems to have muddled your brain. You think you're a psychoanalyst now, do you?"

"Where you're concerned I have to be," she said without thinking, but knew it was her mention of the word *love* that had got his back up. Love and Blake Jarrod did *not* go hand-in-hand.

And neither did Samantha Thompson.

Not with love.

Certainly not with Blake Jarrod.

A curious look passed over his face. "Why would you want to psychoanalyze me anyway?"

This time she thought before speaking. No use giving away more of herself than she needed to. It was best she keep up a wall. He would appreciate her more for that.

She managed a thin smile. "A person likes to figure out how their boss's mind works. It helps with the job."

He leaned back in his chair. "Yes, you were always good at that."

Then…just as she thought she had it all under control, all at once everything rose in her throat. She couldn't take any more of this subterfuge and talking around things that mattered. "Blake, don't you think it's time we talked about last night? You took such good care of me, and then this morning…"

He stilled. "Yes?"

She swallowed hard. She had to ask the next question and she had to be prepared to accept the answer. "I'd like to know what I did wrong."

His face blanched as he sat forward. "Nothing, Samantha. You did nothing wrong."

"Then what—"

He drew a breath. "Samantha, are you a virgin?"

She felt her cheeks heat up. "No."

He looked surprised. "I thought you might be."

"Well, I'm not," she said, hunching her shoulders, wondering where this was going to lead.

His expression softened a little. "But you're not very experienced, are you?"

Okay, so it led to further embarrassment.

She could feel her cheeks redden further. "You must know I…er…haven't been with a lot of men."

"How many?"

Her eyes widened. "None of your business."

"You made it my business this morning."

She hesitated, then, "One lover when I was a teenager."

His brow rose. "And none since?" He must have read her thoughts. "You can tell me. I'm not going to tell anyone else."

So, okay, she would accept that. "Well, there was a man back home…."

He didn't blink an eye but she knew she had his attention. "And?"

"We didn't become lovers, but I was in love with him."

"What happened?"

Her lips twisted with self-derision. "He wasn't in love with me."

Blake nodded. "That explains why you haven't had any relationships since I've known you," he said, almost to himself. Then his eyes sharpened. "Are you still in love with him?"

"No. Carl left to go overseas and ended up marrying someone else. I realized I'd been in love with the *idea* of love and that's all it was." She sighed. "But it was a good lesson in learning that you can never be sure of another person's feelings." Realizing that she was suddenly giving too much away, she tried to be casual. "So, you see, I can only lay claim to one lover and that was a long time ago."

"I could tell."

Her composure lurched like a drunken sailor. "I'm sorry. I thought my enthusiasm might make up for any lack of experience."

"Don't apologize. Your enthusiasm was great. Damn great," he said brusquely. "I had a hard time walking away from you."

Her heart faltered. "You did? I thought you didn't want me."

He expelled a harsh breath. "Did my body *feel* like I didn't want you?"

She remembered the tense cords of his body burning her flesh through her nightshirt. "No," she croaked, then had to clear her throat before speaking again. "But what do I know anyway? I thought a man could easily turn it off and on." Carl certainly had been able to put a stop to anything beyond a few kisses.

"I'm not made of stone like that other guy," Blake scoffed, reading her mind, but his voice had gentled. "And all this goes to prove to me that I did the right thing this morning. I'm the experienced one here and that means I have a responsibility to you. I'm glad now I didn't take something from you that you might regret giving later on."

"You mean my virginity?" Her heart rose in her chest at the respect he'd afforded her.

"Yes."

"But I'm *not* a virgin," she pointed out.

"I know that now."

He'd rejected her all for nothing? It was admirable, but… "You should have asked me at the time."

He pursed his mouth. "It's not only that," he said, sending her stomach plummeting.

"I see."

"No, I don't think you do." He clenched his jaw. "You were so damn generous, Samantha. You were giving me everything and I was worried that you…er…might look more into this than you should. I just wasn't sure you could handle any emotional involvement."

She appreciated where he was coming from with this, but her heart still managed to drop at his words. What *was* it about her that every man felt they had to warn her off?

"Don't worry," she assured him. "I'm not planning on repeating history and losing my heart to anyone in the future."

His eyes searched hers. "Are you sure?"

"Positive." Suddenly she felt all-knowing. "Maybe it's *you* who can't handle it, Blake."

He looked startled, then scowled. "I admit it. I can't. And to be blunt, I don't want to even try." He paused. "But this isn't about me. I'm thinking of *you*, Samantha. Not me."

Her heart tilted. She appreciated his honesty but she could look after herself. And to be equally as honest, how could she give him up without a fight now that she knew he wanted her?

"Blake, thank you for that but you're doing me an injustice. I'm a grown woman. I know sex doesn't always mean commitment. I have needs and I know my own mind. I know what I want, and while I'm here…" She looked him straight in the eye. "What I want is *you*."

"Hell."

She flinched. "I'm sorry if that makes things more difficult."

"Don't be. It's your directness, that's all. It blows me away."

She felt a rush of warmth. "I do want you, Blake. Very much."

"Your head—"

"Is on the mend." She paused, preempting him. "And yes, I'm sure."

His eyes flared sensuously. "Then do me a favor."

She moistened her mouth. "What?"

"Go upstairs and put your nightshirt on for me," he said, his voice turning heavy with huskiness.

She blinked in surprise. "My nightshirt?"

"You looked so sexy in it this morning. I've been thinking about it all day. It's been driving me crazy."

Sudden awareness danced in her veins. "Does this mean we're going to—"

"Have sex? Yes." A tiny pulse beat in his cheekbone. "But only if you're sure you can handle a purely sexual relationship," he said, giving her one last out.

Excitement washed over her. He still wanted her.

She nodded. "I can handle it, Blake."

"Then go change."

She got to her feet. It was now or never. And right now *never* definitely wasn't an option.

Samantha couldn't deny she was nervous as she came out of her room in her nightshirt and descended the staircase in a pair of high-heeled gold sandals she'd put on at the last moment. The bottom button was missing from her nightshirt, but the material covered her and what did it matter now anyway?

Blake had turned the lamps off and stood by the log fire, watching her in the flickering light with the same look he'd had on his face last Saturday night when she'd dressed for her date with Joel. She'd been trying to capture Blake's attention that night to make him jealous. Tonight she'd definitely caught more than his attention.

Tonight they both knew they would be a part of each other. The power of that thought stunned her.

"Come over here, Samantha," he said huskily when she reached the bottom step. The air throbbed between them and she quivered, moving forward without a falter as she made her away across the carpet to him.

His blue eyes moved slowly down over her, and something flared in them. "You're still missing the button," he said, as if to himself.

She blinked in surprise as she reached him. "You knew it was missing?"

"Oh, yes. It came off this morning in the bathroom… when I lifted you up on the sink."

She could feel herself go hot all over. "Oh. I hadn't realized."

"I know you didn't," he said, with a pointed look. He pulled her up against him. "God, you're so damn sexy, Samantha Thompson," he murmured, gathering her close. "My very sexy lady." His body was hard and she trembled. "Now, does that feel like I can turn myself off so easily?" he said thickly, his breath stirring over her face.

The solid warmth of him pressed against her stomach. "No." The word emerged on a whisper.

"There's no going back this time," he said, reassuring that this time he would not walk away.

The deepest longing stirred within her. "Kiss me, Blake."

He did.

Once…twice…long and slow…

And then he eased back and looked deep into her eyes.

She looked back at him.

Blue on blue.

"I want you in front of the fire," he murmured, sending her pulse jumping all over the place. "Here. Lie down on the cushions." She saw he had placed two big cushions near their feet. "Be careful of your head," he said, helping to lower her to the thick rug, so sweet and caring. She wanted to say it was too late, that she was about to lose her head anyway, only the words wouldn't come.

Soon she was lying there in her nightshirt and her gold sandals and he was standing over her in the firelight, his gaze scanning the full length of her, before stopping at the junction to her thighs. "You left your panties on," he mused throatily, telling her the front of her nightshirt must have fallen open at the hem.

She moistened her mouth. "I wanted to take them off, but…"

"I'll be happy to do the honors…" he said, and her heartbeat quickened, "but in a minute."

All at once she wanted him so much. "Take off your clothes first, Blake. Don't make me wait."

His eyes darkened and he dragged his sweater up over his head, along with his T-shirt, tossing them aside. He kicked off his shoes and his hands went to his belt.…

He hesitated.

"Your trousers, too." She was desperate to see him fully as a man for the first time, the thought making her lightheaded.

Another second, then his hands dropped away from the buckle. "Not yet." He dropped to his knees beside her, and let his gaze slide along the full length of her, like he was committing her to memory.

But his bare chest beckoned her and she reached

out to touch him, her fingers tingling as she came into contact with the dark whorls of hair over hard muscle. He groaned and slammed his hand over hers, stopping it from moving.

"Not yet," he repeated, putting her hand back down beside her.

And then with slow deliberation he began to undo her top button. She gasped as he undid another and slid her nightshirt off her shoulder a little. "I've wanted to do this since this morning," he murmured, lowering his head and trailing a kiss from the curve of her shoulder to her throat, then down to the valley between her breasts.

He inhaled deeply, then lifted his face and undid another button, exposing her breasts. Soon he was leaning over her, using his mouth to possess the tip of one nipple before moving to the other, gliding his tongue back and forth over them, imprinting them with his taste.

"Oh, my God," she muttered, shuddering at such an exquisite touch. "I…"

"Steady, my lovely." He shifted back a little. Another button undone allowed him to drift kisses along the exposed skin to her belly button. She shuddered again when he stroked his palm over her stomach, before the rest of the buttons were unfastened and the material finally parted, falling away to her sides and revealing her near-nakedness to him.

"Beautiful," he murmured, dipping his fingers under the waistband then peeling the panties down her body. By the time he'd finished, he'd moved to kneel between her thighs. She moaned faintly, suspecting a blush was rolling all the way down to her feet.

"So beautiful." He slowly reached out and slipped a

finger through the triangle of curls, making her gasp. "You like that?"

She moaned again. "Oh, yes."

For long, heart-stopping moments he toyed with her dampening skin, sending tremors through her. And then he slid his hands under her, cupping the cheeks of her bottom and tilting her lower body up to him, the satin material of her nightshirt falling away fully as his head lowered to the dark V at her thighs.

But before he touched, he stopped and looked up again, his eyes catching hers, holding still. He didn't speak or move a muscle, but there was a primitive look in his eyes that swept her breath away.

Slowly he lowered his head again and sought her out, his mouth beginning a slow worship of her femininity. She gasped as his tongue slid between her folds, teasing and tantalizing her, stroking her in erotic exploration, taking her to the brink, then bringing her back…once… twice…then finally he took her right over the edge, any remnants of her control disintegrating as she pulsed with the purest of pleasures.

Long moments later, she was still trying to recover when he rose to his feet and stripped off his trousers. She watched mesmerized as he put on a condom, thrilled that she had the power to make this man so hot and hard for her.

He was soon kneeling back down between her legs, and kissing his way right up the center of her until he found her mouth. He gave her one long kiss, then suddenly he was part of her.

In her.

She held him deep inside, finally one with Blake

Jarrod. She'd been waiting so long. It was the most wonderful feeling in the world.

He kissed her deeper as he began to thrust, long strokes time after time. Soon she began to tremble around him, toppling over the edge again, the flickering of the flames in the fireplace nothing compared to their own fire burning within.

Samantha lay amongst the cushions in front of the fire and watched Blake stride toward the downstairs bathroom. He'd covered her with the throw from the couch, and she enjoyed lying there watching his bare back and buttocks that were all firm muscle and arrestingly male.

She smiled to herself in the gentle glow from the fireplace. She couldn't believe it. She'd made love with Blake. She felt marvelous. He'd been so generous and loving and…

All at once, she found herself blinking back sudden tears. Their lovemaking had been so much more than sex. She hadn't admitted it to herself until now lest she back out, but when he'd said earlier they were having sex, something had gnawed at her as she'd gone up the stairs. It had sounded like they would merely be having sex for sex's sake. And while that was somewhat true, that wasn't what she was *only* about.

She'd known the same was true for Blake. He'd already proven that by not taking advantage this morning when he'd thought she was a virgin. She'd "made love" with Blake, despite love not being involved. There was respect between them and that was more important to her.

Right then she heard him coming back and she

quickly blinked away any suggestion of tears. He wouldn't want to know. Otherwise he'd think she *hadn't* been able to handle it, when it was merely because she hadn't expected to be quite so touched by all this.

He gave a sexy smile as he dropped down and leaned over to kiss her. "How do you feel?" he murmured, pulling back and looking into her eyes.

She was fully aware of his nakedness next to her. She could easily reach out and touch him. "Wonderful."

He looked pleased as he lifted the throw and slid under it to lie on his back, pulling her against his chest and kissing the top of her head but being careful of her injury. "Is that better?"

She was glad he couldn't look into her eyes. "Much."

He chuckled, his breath stirring her hair. "Who knew, eh?"

"What?"

"That we'd be so good together."

She'd never doubted it. "We work well together in business, so why not in bed?"

"True."

After that, they lay in quiet. The fire crackled and the clock on the wall ticked the seconds by. Samantha began to feel sleepy. There was no place she'd rather be in the world right now, she thought, as her eyelids drifted shut and she listened to the tick tock…tick tock…tick…*she loved him*…tock.

Startled, she jumped. Dear God, *she loved him*.

"What's wrong?"

Her brain stumbled. Panic whorled inside her. The ability to speak deserted her for a moment…and then somehow she pulled herself together. "What? Oh, nothing. I think I fell asleep too fast."

"Don't worry. There's no chance of that happening again just yet." He put his hand under her chin, lowering his head and lifting her mouth up to his. She quickly closed her eyes, hiding them from him, hiding her deepest secret. She'd betrayed him by falling in love with him. And she'd betrayed herself. She hadn't wanted to love him. She had never intended for that to happen.

Then he kissed her and the slow, delicious process of making love to her started again. She prayed to God for the strength not to reveal her love for this man who was leaving his mark on her like no one had ever done before. She couldn't afford to give her feelings away, or their relationship would be over before it had really begun. Wanting Blake had been hard enough.

Loving him was going to be intolerable.

Eight

Blake made love to her many times during the night, both downstairs and in his bed. Samantha had never known such bliss, but by the time the next morning rolled around and she'd gone back to her own room to get dressed for work, she had a thousand worries inside her head. She loved Blake and that presented so many problems. She'd virtually promised him she wouldn't fall for him. Now it seemed like she'd gone back on her word.

Worse, somewhere along the line she hadn't exactly "fallen" for him. No, she'd skipped that bit and had progressed straight to loving him. They'd worked together so closely these past two years, she already knew Blake was the type of man she admired and respected. And falling "in" love implied she could fall "out" of love with him—like she'd done with Carl. With

Blake, she knew there would be no retracting her love for him.

If only she could.

Oh, God, loving Blake had taken her further with her emotions than she'd ever dared venture. And now she had to survive until she could leave for good. She had to remain tough. She would constantly have to keep something of herself back. Last night during their lovemaking, she'd only managed to keep a lid on it through sheer terror—only by telling herself he would run in the other direction if he knew how deep her feelings went. Talk about emotional involvement on her part!

And now more than ever she had to leave at the end of her month's contract. She couldn't stay permanently. Blake had been honest enough to admit he couldn't handle emotional involvement and she believed him. If he discovered she loved him, he'd be horrified. He'd probably have her on the next plane out of Aspen before she could blink. Even if he didn't, she couldn't risk giving him such a strong emotive power over her. A power he might use in and out of the bedroom to get her to stay.

For all the wrong reasons.

Yet would Blake manipulate her in such a way? He was, after all, the man she loved. An honorable man. Would he really do any of those things? Her heart remembered his generous lovemaking and said no. Her head remembered the hard businessman and said maybe.

Making love to a woman certainly changed things, Blake decided as he watched Samantha eat breakfast in the hotel restaurant. He'd sat opposite her like this many times in the last two years but it had always been about work. Now all he could think about was being inside her again.

She'd been so generously tight last night when he'd finally buried himself in her softness. It had almost sent him straight into orgasm. Only the need to give her more pleasure had held him back. Never before had that happened to him. He'd always made sure his partner had been fulfilled before taking his own pleasure, but this time her pleasure had been totally his. It had been the ultimate experience for him. How could that other man—that Carl—not have wanted her in his bed? Idiot!

"Tell me something, Blake," she said, cutting into his thoughts as he buttered a slice of toast.

"Anything." Well, not quite anything. He wasn't up for a meaningful discussion this morning. He merely wanted to sit here and soak up this beautiful woman in front of him.

She tilted her brunette head to one side. "Did you tell Andy to add the candles last night at dinner?"

He was relieved at the simple question. "Sorry, no. I wasn't planning on seduction. At least, not until I was sure you could handle becoming my lover." He smiled. "I'll light you some candles tonight, though."

A feathery blush ran across her cheeks but she looked pleased. "I've just realized something. You're a romantic, Blake Jarrod."

"Sometimes." He liked to romance a woman as much as the next guy. "But don't get the wrong idea that I'm a softie."

She nodded. "Got it. Hard in business. Good in bed."

He gave a low laugh. "I like that assessment." He also liked to think he was both things in and out of bed, but he wouldn't embarrass her further. Not here.

But tonight…

"I keep forgetting to mention this," she said, "but I haven't thanked you for taking such good care of me the other night."

"Oh, I think you did thank me," he said pointedly. "And you can thank me again later."

"Blake!" she hissed, but he could see she was enjoying this sexual interplay.

"What?" he drawled. "I'm just saying—"

A figure appeared at their table. "There you are, Sam," Joel said, giving them both a smile but causing Blake's mouth to clamp shut. "I'm glad I caught you. How are you this morning? How's the head?"

"Fine, Joel. No aftereffects at all," she assured the doctor.

"You're taking things easy, I hope?"

Her eyes made a quick dart across the table then back up at the other man. "Yes." Her cheeks had grown a little warm and that in itself appeased Blake.

"Good. Then how about we take in that movie tonight?"

She looked at Blake again. "Oh, Joel, I'm sorry, I can't."

"Tomorrow night, then?"

Blake held his tongue. He wanted to lay claim to Samantha and tell the other man to shove off, but he'd first give her the opportunity to do it.

"Um, Joel. Perhaps not." She shifted in her seat. "I'm returning to Vegas in less than two weeks' time and then I'm going home to Pasadena for good once I wrap things up there. So, you see, there's a lot to be done here right now. I need to work full-on with Blake until then."

Blake was dumbfounded.

"You're leaving?" the other man said, sounding shocked, echoing Blake's thoughts. "I can't believe that."

Another echo of his thoughts.

She looked slightly uncomfortable. "Yes, I know. I'm sorry I didn't tell you, but it was something that hadn't been finalized until now."

Joel gave a small nod. "I understand. Maybe we can get together in Pasadena sometime in the future? We'll at least have to get together for coffee before you leave."

She slipped him a smile. "That would be lovely."

Blake was vaguely aware of the other man walking away from the table, but he only had eyes for one person. "Samantha," he growled. "What the hell is going on?"

Her look seemed cagey. "I didn't want him knowing the truth. Our affair is our business and no one else's."

Anger stirred inside him. "I'm not talking about our affair, and you know it. Dammit, don't tell me you don't know what I'm talking about."

She lifted her chin. "You're talking about me still leaving," she clarified. "I'm sorry, Blake. Did you think that I would change my mind?"

"Yes, I damn well did." He'd expected her to stay now, not because he'd enticed her into staying but because she *wanted* to. And hell, she didn't seem to understand that he'd made a big concession in not seducing her in the bathroom yesterday morning. Now it felt like she'd slapped him in the face. He'd given. She'd taken. And now she was giving nothing back.

"But why, Blake? Our lovemaking hasn't changed

anything. We both decided it would only be physical and nothing more. No commitment, remember?"

Her words appeared to be reasonable, but for all that she had a peculiar look in her eyes he couldn't decipher. "That's still got nothing to do with you leaving."

"Doesn't it? I was leaving before we made love and I'm still leaving, so what's changed?"

Damn her. She was right. Even so, he couldn't explain it. He just knew something *had* changed and he didn't want to decode it. He just wanted her to stay and enjoy what they had for a while. They could at least get a couple of months together. Why leave while the going was good?

She shot him an unexpected candid look. "Blake, you asked me if I could handle a sexual relationship, and I said I could. It sounds to me like *you* aren't handling it."

His mouth tightened. "I'm handling it."

She shook her head. "No, I don't—"

"Blake," a male voice called out, and Blake instantly knew who it was. He stiffened. Damn the world! His twin brother was the last person he wanted to see. Guy had always understood him—sometimes more than he understood himself. Right now wasn't a good time to put that to the test.

He shot to his feet, turned and headed for the private elevator. "It'll have to wait until later, Guy," he muttered, striding past his brother.

Guy's steps faltered as he approached the table. Then as he came closer, he looked at Samantha with mild amusement. "Was it something I said?" he quipped in that easygoing way of his.

Samantha couldn't smile if her life depended on it. "He's got a lot on his mind."

Guy sobered. "Yeah, I know." He sent her a penetrating look that reminded her of Blake. "I hear you're leaving."

She nodded, still surprised word had gotten around the family so fast, and even more surprised that they were genuinely sorry to see her go. It wasn't like she was a friend of the family…or marrying into it.

"I'm glad I saw you," Guy said, drawing her back to the moment. "Avery and I would like to have you around for dinner before you go."

Somehow she managed a faint smile. "That would be very nice."

"Blake, too, of course." Silence, then, "He'll miss you when you leave."

"Maybe." *Maybe not.* "I'll find him an excellent replacement."

"It won't be the same."

Her throat constricted. "He'll get over it." She stood up. "You'll have to excuse me, Guy. I need to start work. There's a lot to do."

Guy stepped back and let her pass, but he was frowning and she could feel his eyes on her all the way out the eatery. Thankfully she had a few moments of privacy as the elevator took her to the top floor.

If only Blake wanted her to stay because he loved her, then things would be perfect. But for him this was only about two things—the job and sex. It wasn't about love. She sighed. She'd have to be crazy to think he would make a commitment. And she hadn't wanted a commitment before anyway, so why the heck was she even considering it now?

She must have rocks in her head.

Or have been hit *on* the head with a rock. It must have caused more damage than she'd thought. Why else would she be unwise enough to love a man who wouldn't let himself love in return? That bruise must have addled more than her brain. It had addled her heart.

Thankfully Blake's door was shut when she entered her office so she sat at her desk. Come to think of it, she felt a little better knowing she had hoisted Blake with his own petard. That was rather clever of her. He'd sprouted all that talk about not getting emotionally involved, but clearly his emotions *were* involved, albeit not enough and not the ones that mattered most to her.

They didn't entail love.

God was merciful just then, when not only did the phone start to ring but one of the staff who had a meeting with Blake walked into her office. Samantha got busy, putting on her professional persona as she placed the caller on hold, buzzing Blake on the intercom to tell him his first appointment was here. At his request, she ushered the staff member into his office, all the while keeping her face neutral whenever she looked at her boss. He seemed equally as disinterested in her, though she knew otherwise. What he was and what he seemed were two different things. She could recognize that in another person. After all, wasn't she an expert at the same thing?

Midmorning while Blake was busy at a staff meeting in the Great Room, Samantha picked up the telephone with a heavy heart and did what she had to do. She called Mary Wentworth back and spoke to her about a replacement. The other woman was surprised to hear she was leaving, but was more than happy to help. Mary promised she would e-mail some résumés of suitable applicants within a few hours.

Blake returned after the meeting, formally asked if there were any messages, then strode straight into his office. Samantha's heart sank at how cold he was, but there was nothing she could do about it. She still had to leave.

At lunchtime she had some sandwiches sent up from the kitchen, and Blake made it apparent that he preferred to eat at his desk by himself, with his door closed between them. Usually they ate together while discussing work. Or if they ate at their own desks, the door remained open.

Not this time.

And that was fine with her, she decided, growing more and more upset. She needed a filter to stop the waves of anger coming out of his office anyway. To clear her head, she went for a walk in the fresh air. Blake didn't ask where she'd been when she returned and she didn't offer. It was plain to see he was no longer concerned about her.

By late afternoon, Samantha had had enough of his attitude. He'd chastised her after she'd put through a call he hadn't wanted to take. He'd found fault with a letter she'd typed up for his signature. And he'd told her to go recheck some figures on a report that she knew were correct.

When she brought the report back, she deliberately placed another folder on top of it.

His head shot up. "What's this?"

"Résumés. They all come highly recommended."

His lips flattened. "I didn't ask you to do this."

She angled her chin. "It's what you pay me to do."

"I pay you to do what you're told."

She gasped, then held herself rigid. "That's unfair of you. You don't mind me being proactive in other things with my job. It's why I'm such a good assistant and you know it."

"We're talking fairness now, are we? *You're* the one leaving *me*. How fair is that?"

"I'm not leaving *you,* Blake," she lied. "Anyway, don't take it personally, remember? That's what you said to me when you reminded me of my contract obligations."

He muttered a curse, but for Samantha the last straw had already broken the camel's back. "I can't continue under these conditions, Blake. If you won't treat me right, then I'll pack my things and leave tonight. And I don't care if you take me to court for breach of contract either." She hesitated, but only for a second. "I believe I could make a good case for justifying my leaving anyway, considering the personal turn our relationship has taken."

There was a lengthy silence.

His eyes challenged hers. "Would you go that far?"

She gave a jerky nod. "If pushed I would. Don't doubt that."

He held her gaze with narrowed eyes.

And then suddenly something happened and a suspicion of admiration began to glint in them. "Way to go!" he said softly, startling her. "You're a tough little madam. I always knew you could hold your own in your job, but I never thought to see the day when you used it against *me*."

A little of the tension went out of her. "So things will return to normal?" she asked cautiously.

"No."

Her heart dropped.

"Things can never be normal between us again. Not since last night." He drew a long breath, as if taking a moment before making a decision. "I don't want to see you go, but I don't want to keep you here against your will either. If you want to go then I have to accept it."

It wasn't what she wanted at all.

It was what she *had* to do.

"Thank you, Blake."

"But at least stay until your contract runs out." He waited a moment. "I'm not asking for the job and I'm not asking for the sex. I'm asking for *me*."

She caught her breath. This was the best she could hope for, the best it could get, and she wasn't about to argue with that. She would take her happiness where she could.

A whisper of joy filled her. "Okay, yes. I'll stay until my contract runs out, Blake," she said, and watched him let out a shuddering breath that touched her greatly. He really *did* want her to stay so that he could be with her.

Clearly satisfied now they were back on an even keel, he leaned back in his chair with a look she had no trouble translating. "Go over there and lock the door."

A tiny shiver of anticipation went down her spine. "Blake, I can't… I don't…"

"You can." His eyes turned deeper blue. "I seriously need to make love to you, Samantha."

Her heart tilted. Oh, she wanted that, too. She darted a look at the door. "The others—"

"Will think we don't want to be disturbed." He gave a crooked smile. "And they'd be right." He waited a moment. "You can always race into my washroom if anyone comes."

Wanting this…wanting him…she went and locked the heavy wood door, but ducked her head out into her office first to make sure no one was there. "I can't believe I'm doing this," she muttered, turning the lock.

"Don't think about it." He looked amused and she decided that if he wanted her, then he was going to have her. And she would wipe that amusement right off his face.

Fingers going to the buttons of her long-sleeved blouse, she began to undo each one as she approached him across the plush carpet.

One eyebrow lifted. "Are you teasing me, Miss Thompson?"

"Actually I think I am."

He smiled, and she smiled, then his smile started to slip as she completely undid the blouse, leaving it hanging open over her black bra. She marveled at where this seductress in her was coming from, but didn't let it deter her. She wasn't about to waste a minute of it.

She reached the side of the desk. "More?"

"Oh, yeah."

"You're the boss."

Her hands were shaking a little as she slid the zipper of her slacks down, pushing them and her panties all the way to the floor, then stepped out of them. She heard a rasping sound escape Blake's throat and there was a blaze in his eyes that seemed to emit from his whole body.

Gratified by his reaction…satisfied by his amusement now turned to desire…she climbed onto his lap, knees

on either side of his thighs, her blouse covering her
bra—and then only just.

After that, passion overtook all rational thoughts and
the air hummed with soft, sensual sounds.

Nine

They dined together back at Pine Lodge, then made love again that night, and when Samantha woke the next morning she lay there and wallowed in a sense of occasion. Her memories of them together like this were all she could take away with her. Her heart, she would leave with Blake.

He woke up then and made slow love to her again. Afterward she put on a bright face and they went about their business as usual, neither of them showing any outward sign to the others that they were lovers. They hadn't discussed it, but Samantha was glad about it. Already his family seemed to have taken a special interest in them, and she didn't want anyone guessing she loved him.

Late morning, Samantha left her office and went down to the hotel kitchen to get some fresh milk for their coffee. She could have phoned down for it but she needed to stretch her legs.

In the hallway, she ran into Erica. They chatted a few moments but Samantha could see the other woman was preoccupied. "Erica, is something wrong?"

Erica wrinkled her nose. "Yes, unfortunately. I've been arranging a surprise party for tonight for this man who lives in town. It's for his wife's fortieth birthday and she thinks she's coming here for dinner." She clicked her tongue. "I've been working on this for weeks."

"So what's the problem?"

"We've got a DJ for later in the evening, but the husband particularly asked for someone to play piano music in the background during the meal, and now the piano player has come down sick." Her smooth forehead creased as she began thinking out loud. "The DJ could probably play some soft music as an alternative, but I really don't want to disappoint the husband. He said his wife loves the piano and he wants to give her the best party. I was hoping there might be someone in town I could find, but it's probably too late."

All the while she was talking, Samantha's heart began thumping with a mixture of excitement and panic. "You may not believe this," she said, not believing she was actually saying this, "but I can help."

Erica's eyes brightened. "You can? Do you know someone who plays the piano?"

"Yes." *Did she really want to say this?* "Me."

Erica stopped and blinked. "*You* play the piano?" She grimaced. "Sorry, that came out wrong. I just mean—"

Samantha smiled a little. "I know what you meant."

Regardless, Erica still looked doubtful. "You *really* play the piano?"

Samantha nodded. "Yes, *really.*"

"You're sure?"

Samantha chuckled as her anxiety faded. "Lead the way to the piano and I'll show you. Just don't expect perfection. I have to tell you I'm a bit rusty."

Erica began to grin. "As long as it's not 'Chopsticks,' then I'll be happy. Follow me."

A few minutes later, Samantha did a warm-up then started playing a quick medley of popular tunes. Her fingers felt a bit stiff because she hadn't played since last Christmas at home in Pasadena, but she was soon enjoying herself—and enjoying the look on Erica's face.

"That's wonderful!" Erica murmured, once the music ended.

Samantha smiled with relief that she hadn't lost her touch nor made a fool of herself. "Thanks, but it's nothing special."

Erica shook her head. "No, you're very good."

"Not really."

"Yes, *really,*" Erica teased. "Good Lord, I didn't know we had Liberace living here at the resort."

Samantha laughed. "Just be grateful my mother made me take piano lessons growing up."

"Oh, I am. Play some more, Samantha." All at once Erica's eyes widened and she chuckled. "Oh, my God, I don't believe I'm about to say this but 'play it again, Sam.'"

Samantha laughed. She knew she needed the practice so she was happy to oblige and felt more confident with each touch of the keys.

Afterward, they talked for five minutes then Samantha continued on her way to get the milk. Blake had a business lunch in town and had already left by the time she returned to the office, so she didn't get to tell him about it all until late afternoon.

He fell back in his chair. "*You* play the piano?"

A wry smile tugged at her mouth. "Why is that so far-fetched?"

"I don't know." Then he shook his head as if he wasn't hearing right. "Let me get this straight. *You're* going to play the piano at a party here at the resort tonight?"

She shrugged. "It's just background music during dinner." But she wasn't quite so calm inside, and talking about it now was making her kind of nervous.

He tilted his head at her. "Why didn't you tell me you could play the piano?"

"It wasn't a job requirement," she joked, more to calm her growing anxiety than anything.

His mouth quirked. "No, I guess it wasn't."

Her humor over, she bit her lip. "Actually, do you mind if I leave a little early? I need to get myself ready and I'd like some time to myself."

He gave a wayward smile. "You creative types are all alike."

"Blake—"

"Feel free to leave early," he agreed. Then his eyes slowly settled on her mouth. "But before you go…" Hunger jumped the distance between them. "I do think there is one requirement of your job that needs revisiting."

She knew what he was getting at. Her heart raced with a growing excitement. "Blake, we can't make love in here every afternoon."

"Who said we can't?"

"But I have to go now," she said, knowing she was weakening.

"In a minute," he murmured, sending her an intimate look across the desk. "Come and give me a kiss goodbye first."

She wagged a finger at him. "That's all, Blake. One kiss and no more."

"Trust me."

She moved toward him. "Okay…"

Half an hour later she left the office a very satisfied woman, amused at how easily she had fallen for his trickery. Of course, she couldn't fully blame her boss. She'd *wanted* to fall for it.

"Lady, you're far too dangerous to let loose on our male guests," Blake said, watching Samantha step into high heels. She wore a beaded jacket over black evening pants that flattered her slim figure, and she'd curled the brunette strands of her hair into a bubbly halo around her gorgeous face.

"You think I look okay?"

"More than okay. You'll knock 'em dead." He stepped closer and went to pull her toward him but she put a hand against his chest, stopping him.

"Wait! You'll mess up my lipstick."

Blake was amused. "I'd like to mess up more than your lipstick, beautiful."

Her blue eyes smiled back at him. "You already did that this afternoon. 'Trust me,' remember?"

He gave a low chuckle. "I remember." Even now he felt the stirrings of desire, so he stepped away from temptation. "Come on. I'll drive you up to the Manor."

"I can call the valet."

"That's okay. I want to look over those documents Gavin gave me about the new bungalow. It'll be a good chance to study them without the phones ringing." It was an excuse but she looked so good that he wanted to make sure she got home okay. If anyone hit on her they'd be sorry.

Ten minutes later they walked down the corridor toward the ballroom, but as they got closer she suddenly stopped. "Blake, please. Don't come in with me. You'll only make me more nervous."

"Okay. I'll be in the office until you're ready to go home."

"But—"

He leaned forward and dropped a kiss on her forehead. "I'll wait for you."

He looked up and saw Erica and Christian coming toward them. They were a distance away so he nodded at them then turned and walked in the other direction, taking the private elevator up to the office. He didn't care that they'd seen the kiss. He *did* care that they might think Samantha was his weak spot.

Christian had proven his integrity months ago, but the other man had his own weak point—Erica. It could make him blind to whatever his fiancée was up to, Blake thought, then winced. She may not be up to anything at all, he corrected, aware his hard attitude toward his half sister was diminishing with each passing day.

Yet he couldn't discount Erica was fooling him as well as Christian, though he was feeling less and less that was the case. He was usually a pretty good judge of character—when emotions weren't involved. Unfortunately finding out he had a half sister *had* brought out an emotional response in him. He hadn't liked that.

And he didn't like the emotional response he was feeling now as he sat down at his desk and saw the file with the résumés. It all came back that Samantha was actually going to leave. It had either been let her go in three weeks' time or lose her now. He hadn't been able to bear the thought of the latter.

And he wasn't up to reading those résumés right now either, he decided, putting them to the side. He would deal with it when he had to and not before.

He wasn't sure how long he'd been working when he heard piano music drift up from the bottom floor. He sat back in his chair and listened. Samantha was clearly talented as she went from one tune to another, even throwing in some classical music. He heard clapping at the end of that one, though whether it was for Samantha or in honor of the birthday guest, he wasn't sure. The music started up in another medley of popular tunes, so he figured it was for Samantha.

And rightly so.

Unable to stop himself, he knew he had to see her play in person and not merely listen from afar. He got up from his desk and went downstairs, hearing the clink of glasses and cutlery and the murmur of voices, but it was the music that drew him as he approached the ballroom.

Pushing open one of the large doors, he slipped inside and stood at the back, watching people half listening and half talking as Samantha played another piece of classical music. She didn't see him, but she appeared totally at ease at the piano, concentrating on the music, her hands flowing across the keys, looking very feminine and beautiful. Suddenly he was so proud of her that a lump rose in his throat.

"She's good," a female voice murmured, and he glanced sideways at an attractive woman in her late thirties who'd come to stand beside him.

He wasn't interested. "Yes," he said, looking back at Samantha.

"You're new here." She thrust a manicured hand in front of him. "I'm Clarice, by the way."

It would have been rude not to shake her hand, but he still wasn't interested. "Blake." He wished the woman would leave him alone so that he could concentrate on Samantha.

"Do you know the guest of honor?"

For a moment he thought she meant Samantha, then he realized she was talking about the birthday lady. "A casual acquaintance." He didn't feel the need to explain.

"I went to boarding school with Anne. We've been lifelong friends."

"That's great." The music ended on a high note and everyone started to clap and it gave him the chance to move away. "Excuse me," he said, taking a step.

Clarice put her hand on his arm, stopping him. "Would you care to have a drink later?"

He'd been approached like this many times but for some reason now he found it distasteful, though he hid it. He only wanted to see Samantha. "I'm sorry," he said, being as nice as possible so as not to offend. "Not tonight." He walked away.

And headed straight for Samantha getting up from the piano. She was laughing as some people rushed to talk to her, and as Blake weaved his way through the tables he could only think how much she lit up the room.

Then she saw him. "Blake," she murmured, her blue eyes lighting up *for him,* sending an extraordinary feeling soaring inside his chest.

He reached her and put his hand on her elbow. "I think the lady needs a drink," he told the group at large, making no apologies as he led her away.

"What are you doing here?" she said as he took her over to the bar.

"I could hear the music upstairs. It drew me to you." He paused. "I'm totally in awe of you," he murmured, pleased to see a hint of dusky rose color her cheeks.

"Thank you," she said in a breathy voice.

For a moment they held one another's gaze.

"Samantha," Erica said, rushing up to them and kissing Samantha on the cheek. "You were wonderful!" In her excitement she kissed Blake's cheek, too. "Isn't she wonderful, Blake?"

For a split second he froze at Erica's friendliness, but then he found himself relenting toward her even more. Anyone who liked Samantha so much deserved a little more consideration.

He gave his half sister his first ever warm smile. "Yes, she's pretty wonderful."

Erica seemed a little taken aback at his friendliness, but her self-possession soon returned as she spoke to Samantha. "The minute you started playing this afternoon, I knew you were good."

Samantha laughed as she looked from one to the other. "Do either of you have an ear for music?"

"We know a class act when we see it," Erica said, then winked at her half brother. "Don't you agree, Blake?"

Blake nodded, his gaze returning to Samantha and resting there. "I couldn't agree more," he said, as everything inside him went still.

Samantha was class all the way.

Just then, the real guest of honor and her husband came up to thank Samantha for playing so beautifully. Then Anne asked Samantha if she'd play her a special piece of classical music.

And as Blake watched Samantha start to play the piano again, he realized this woman could be destined for better things than being his assistant. He wasn't an expert at piano playing by any means, but he knew when something sounded good. It hit home then that he had no right to keep her here and hold her back from what could be her true vocation. He really did have to let her go. Somewhere at the back of his mind he'd still believed she wouldn't leave. Now he knew different.

"You're amazingly good at playing the piano," he said later, once they were inside Pine Lodge and alone together.

She sent him an amused glance as she took off her coat. "Don't start that again."

He frowned as he took off his own coat and hung it on the rack. "I don't understand why you didn't take your music further. I'm sure you could be a world-class pianist."

She lifted her shoulders in a shrug. "I'm an average pianist. I know my limitations."

He'd been raised to push himself to the limit. "Aren't you putting those limitations on yourself?"

She shook her head. "No, I don't think I am. There are lots of mildly talented people who don't take it all the way. It doesn't mean they're wasting their lives. They can use it in other ways. Some people teach. Some people play for themselves. Others play at parties," she said, her lips curving wryly.

"But—"

She put her hand against his chest. "I don't have the passion for it, Blake. Really, I don't. I like to play occasionally but that's all."

He finally understood what she was saying, but the world had better look out if she ever decided to further her talent.

He felt her palm still against his chest. "What *do* you have a passion for?" he said huskily, bringing it back to the two of them as much as he could. That's what he would focus on from now on. Them and only them.

She rubbed herself against him, seeming to delight in making him aware of her. "Right now? You."

By the time they reached the bedroom they were both naked. After they made love, he pulled her into his arms and let her sleep, but listening to her soft breathing, he admitted to himself that never before had he felt as comfortable after making love to a woman as he did right then. This woman felt right at home in his arms.

And he wasn't sure he should like the feeling.

Ten

One advantage of sleeping with the boss was that she didn't have to jump out of bed and hurry to get to work, Samantha thought lazily, after she woke late the next morning and lay in Blake's arms. He was still asleep.

Then he moved a little and she tilted her head back to look up at him. "You're awake?" she said unnecessarily.

He opened his eyes. "I have been for a while."

That surprised her. Usually the minute he woke up he made love to her.

"Is something wrong?"

"No," he said, but she felt his chest muscles tighten beneath her.

She saw that he had a closed look about him. Something must be on his mind, though she didn't know what. He'd been fine when they'd made love last night. Now he seemed...distant.

She could only think something had occurred to him during the night and upset him. For some reason a wall had been erected between them now. Then she remembered how Erica and Christian had seen him kiss her on the forehead before the party. It hadn't been a passionate kiss but it was clearly more than friendship. So perhaps Blake minded that his family knew about them now? As far as she could tell, it was the only thing that had changed overnight.

"Erica and Christian probably realize we're lovers now," she said, testing the waters.

"They'd be stupid if they didn't." It wasn't said nastily, but it still made her wonder.

She tilted her head back a little. "You don't mind?" He'd looked more at ease with Erica last night. He'd actually seemed to like his half sister.

"Why should I?"

"True." She swallowed. "I'm leaving soon so it doesn't matter anyway, does it?" she said, trying to get a reaction out of him. *Any* reaction. One that didn't lock her out.

There was nothing.

Feeling disheartened, she pushed herself out of bed and hurried to the shower, a tightness in her throat. Their remaining time together was so short. She didn't want to spend it like this.

No sooner had she stepped under the spray than he opened the sliding doors. "What's the matter?" he said, frowning at her.

She thanked goodness the water streaming over her head hid any tears that threatened. "Nothing."

His look said he didn't believe her as he stepped inside the cubicle and joined her. He didn't say a word, and he had a fixed look about him as he soaped them both up and then made love to her with an urgency that startled her. By the end of it she was none the wiser, but at least she knew he still wanted her.

Her heart twisted inside her then. As much as it was a compliment to her, was he still refusing to accept that she was leaving? If so, he was only making it harder for himself. They *both* had to accept it, she thought, her heart aching at the thought.

She managed a blank face as they went to the manor for breakfast. It was either that or cry, and she couldn't allow herself that luxury.

As they entered the lobby, a woman practically jumped out at them. "Blake Jarrod!" she exclaimed, in a you-are-a-naughty-boy tone. "You didn't tell me you owned this hotel." Her gaze slid to Samantha, "Or that your assistant was the piano player."

Blake put on a practiced smile but Samantha could tell he didn't like the woman. "It's Clarice, isn't it?" he said, making it clear he wasn't interested. "This is my assistant *and* piano player," he mocked, "Samantha."

Samantha inclined her head and the woman gave her a cool smile. "I'm Clarice Richardson. Mrs. Clarice Richardson, but I'm *divorced*." Her gaze slid to Blake, instantly dismissing Samantha. "I was wondering, Blake. How would you like to have that drink tonight?"

Blake shook his head. "Can't do, I'm afraid. I have a prior commitment tonight."

"Then how about a cup of coffee now?" the woman said, not giving up. "I have a free morning. In fact, I'm free for the whole day. I'm looking for someone to take me for a drive to Independence Pass."

"Sorry, but I have to get to work."

Clarice gave a tinkle of a laugh that grated on Samantha's nerves. "But you're the boss."

"Which is exactly why I'd better do some work," he said smoothly, then put his hand under Samantha's elbow. "If you'll excuse us."

"Oh. Of course," Clarice said, but Samantha saw her mouth purse with irritation as they walked away.

Then she realized Blake was walking her to the elevator instead of the eatery. "Aren't we having breakfast?"

"We'll get something sent up."

She gave a soft laugh. "Don't tell me you're scared of Mrs. Richardson?"

He shot her a wry look that said he wasn't scared of anyone. "No, but I don't want to deal with her."

"She's persistent, that's for sure." Samantha paused, thinking about something as they stepped inside the elevator and the doors shut. "So you're going out tonight?" She didn't want to sound demanding like Clarice, but as his lover she hoped *she* had a temporary claim on his time right now.

"No, I'm staying home. *You're* my prior commitment."

"I am?" Relief went through her.

He slipped his hand around her waist and pulled her hip against his. "And if I go for a drive to Independence Pass it will be with only one lady."

"Melissa?" she teased.

"You." He kissed her quickly on the mouth just as the doors started to open.

They met Erica as they stepped out of the elevator and into the corridor. She came hurrying forward with a big smile on her face. "Samantha, I want to thank you once again for the fabulous job you did last night."

Samantha returned the smile. "You're very welcome, Erica. I enjoyed it."

Erica considered her. "You know, I've already had a call from the president of the local music school. They heard about you and want to meet with you," she said enthusiastically, making Samantha's heart sink. "They have this huge summer festival where nearly a thousand students and faculty come together from far and wide. There's orchestral concerts and chamber music and—"

Samantha had to stop her there. "I'm sorry, Erica. It wouldn't be any use. I'm leaving soon." She felt Blake stiffen beside her.

Erica's eyes widened. "Oh, I thought—"

Blake muttered something about starting work and stalked off. For a moment Samantha wondered if he was still thinking about her not taking her piano playing seriously, but she soon dismissed it. This wasn't about her not playing the piano. It was about her leaving.

Erica looked at her and winced. "Sorry if I said something out of place."

Samantha tried to smile. "You didn't." She started to follow him. "But I'd better get to work."

Blake was closing his door behind him as she entered her office, and Samantha's heart sank. So. They were back to that again. Talk about a temperamental boss!

Shortly after, he buzzed her for coffee. When she took it into him he seemed okay if a little preoccupied, and she realized she was reading more into this than she should. He had the resort issues to concentrate on and was trying to get the feel for it, that's all. Besides, just because she was now his lover, it shouldn't upgrade her status from his assistant. On the contrary, here at work she'd be upset if it did.

Around eleven he opened his door and strode through her office, scowling. "I'll be with Trevor in his office." He left before she could make any acknowledgement.

Getting to her feet, she went to empty Blake's out tray. There were some letters he'd signed and…all at once she noticed he'd been reading through the files with the résumés. Her heart dropped. That file had sat on his desk untouched all day yesterday, but now he must be thinking ahead.

She should be pleased he wouldn't be left without an assistant, but she could only feel upset. And that was made worse as she went back to her desk and opened the agenda for tomorrow's meeting and saw one of the items was to discuss her replacement.

Oh, God.

So she didn't need Clarice to make a sudden appearance in her office about fifteen minutes later. "Mrs. Richardson, how did you get up here?" she asked, as the woman came toward her desk. A card key was needed for both the private elevator and the back stairs.

"I told one of the staff that I urgently needed to see the person in charge. And I do."

After seeing how Clarice had operated downstairs with Blake, the other woman would have refused to take no for an answer. More than likely she'd even given the staff member a monetary "donation."

Samantha frowned. She would deal with the security breach later. "This is a private area. You shouldn't be here at all. If you needed anything, you should ask at the front desk."

The woman sent her a haughty look. "I'd prefer to deal with Blake, Miss…"

"Thompson." Samantha recognized being put in her place. "Blake's not here at the moment," she said his name deliberately, "but I can pass on a message when he gets back. Now let me walk you to the elevator."

Clarice looked disappointed. Then, "I'll give you my room number." She picked up a sticky-note pad from the desk and wrote on it. "You'll make sure you tell him Clarice called, won't you?" she said, tearing off the slip of paper and handing it to Samantha.

"Of course."

Clarice went to turn away then spun back. "Tell him that I have a proposition for him," she said in a breathless voice.

"Fine." There was nothing to worry about with Blake, but it annoyed Samantha to have to deal with another woman who threw herself at him. There had been so many of them over the years. Clarice was very attractive, but so were the other women who had chased Blake.

Samantha stayed at her desk and waited for Blake to return for lunch. Knowing she was being contrary, she was still upset that he was looking at replacing her, and now she just wanted to spend more time with him. But he didn't return until after lunch, and she spent a quiet lunch break by herself.

"There's a plate of sandwiches on your desk," she said when he walked back through to his office.

"I ate lunch with Trevor."

It would have been nice to be told, she decided, then admitted to herself that as her boss, Blake didn't owe her his time.

She followed him into his office. "Here are your

messages. You'll see there's one from Mrs. Richardson."
When his face remained blank, she said, "Clarice."

He let out a heavy sigh. "What does she want?"

"For you to call her. She delivered it in person."

He scowled. "How did she get up here?"

Samantha told him. "I've passed on my concern to
the front desk. They're going to look into it."

He nodded. "Good."

"By the way, Clarice left her room number for you to
call her back. She says to tell you she has a proposition
for you."

"A proposition?" He grimaced. "I bet she does."

Samantha picked up the plate of sandwiches and put
them in the refrigerator near her desk, feeling better
that Clarice hadn't fooled him. Not that she expected he
wouldn't see through it all. He knew more about women
than she did herself.

It was fairly quiet for the next two hours as Blake
returned messages and she typed up some reports. Then,
he came out carrying his coat. "I have to go into town
for a meeting. It'll take a few hours."

She almost asked if she could go with him, then
stopped. Her place as his assistant was here.

Suddenly he came over and kissed her hard. "I'll see
you later at the lodge. We can go out for dinner if you
like."

She shook her head, pleased. "No, let's eat in. I'll get
something from the hotel kitchen on the way home."

His eyes flickered, and she suspected he'd noticed
her mention of the word *home*. "Okay." He left.

Not long after that, Samantha decided to go down
to the kitchen to see about tonight's dinner. She took
the plate of sandwiches down to the front desk, as one

of the staff might appreciate them for later, rather than throwing them in the trash.

She was walking through the lobby toward the front desk when out of the corner of her eye she happened to glance over at the bar. Her heart stuttered. Blake and Clarice were sitting in there having a drink. Both of them were focused on each other, though she noted Clarice was leaning toward him and doing the talking, more with her cleavage than not. Was this where the other woman offered her "proposition?"

So much for his appointment in town, Samantha thought, not sure what she was doing as she spun around and headed back to her office, giving herself time to adjust to what she'd seen. She had to put this into perspective.

Okay, so there was probably nothing to it, but she just didn't like that Blake was telling her one thing, then doing another. And wasn't he getting Clarice's hopes up even by sitting with the woman? Then again, he was a free man and once *she* left Aspen he would get lonely. The other woman was certainly beautiful.

Samantha threw the sandwiches in the trash, unable to face going back downstairs again. Instead, she phoned the kitchen and ordered two meals for dinner, though she wasn't sure she would feel hungry.

Blake seemed lost in thought when he returned to the lodge that evening, so Samantha didn't mention it straightaway. Besides, she didn't want to sound like a harping wife.

She managed to wait until they had almost finished dinner before saying offhand, "By the way, Blake. Next time you *don't* plan on having a drink with Mrs. Richardson, don't do it in the bar."

His eyes narrowed. "What does that mean?" he said coolly, thankfully not looking the least bit guilty.

"I saw you with her," she said, still keeping her voice casual.

He frowned. "So?"

She lifted one shoulder. "I just thought it odd that you weren't 'free' to spend time with her…and then you were."

He had an arrested expression, before a look of male satisfaction crossed his face. "You sound jealous."

She tried not to look flustered. If he thought she was jealous then he might realize she was more emotionally involved with him than she was letting on. "It's not in my nature to be jealous," she lied, quickly disabusing him of that.

His eyes sharpened. "So you don't mind if I go out with other women, then?"

"While I'm here in Aspen, I *do* mind," she said, seeing his jaw tense. "I think a person should show respect for their lover, don't you?"

There was a moment's pause before he gave a brief nod. "I totally agree, Samantha. Lovers should be true to each other."

"Thank you."

He broke eye contact and took a sip of his wine. "Anyway, you have nothing to worry about with Clarice. She waylaid me as I was leaving for my meeting in town and I felt I had to hear her out. Her proposition is a business one. She owns a chain of high-end boutiques and she wanted to know if she can put one here at Jarrod Ridge."

Samantha digested the information. Now she felt foolish for jumping to conclusions about Clarice.

Yet not.

"It's purely about business," Blake assured her. "I'm going to speak to the family about it at tomorrow morning's meeting."

Her heart constricted at the thought of what else was on tomorrow's agenda—the résumés for her replacement. She noted he didn't mention that right now.

Trying not to think about it, she concentrated on what the other woman's proposition would mean. "Clarice will be here in Aspen a lot, then." And *she* wouldn't be. Clarice would have a clear field with Blake.

He frowned. "I'm not sure. I'd say while it's being set up, she'll visit on and off from L.A." His eyes caught hers. "Why?"

She schooled her features. "No reason. I was merely thinking out loud." She planted on a smile. "And of course I won't be here anyway, so it doesn't concern me."

His eyes turned somewhat hostile. "That's right. What do you care anyway?"

"Exactly," she agreed, her heart breaking. She stood up. "I'll get dessert." She hurried out of the room, aware that he still didn't understand why she had to leave and thanking God he didn't. She took comfort knowing he had no idea she loved him.

Unfortunately the marvelous chocolate concoction in the refrigerator wouldn't lessen her inner pain. She doubted anything ever would.

"…And now that the Food and Wine Gala is completely out of the way for this year," Blake said the next morning, looking down the boardroom table at his siblings, "let's move on to the next thing on the agenda.

Gavin, can you give everyone an update on the bungalow project."

Blake already knew the details of the project, so he found his mind straying back to Samantha. Last night at dinner he'd actually been pleased that she might be jealous of Clarice. Never before had he wanted a woman to feel jealousy over him. Samantha had soon disabused him of that, but appeared to deliberately bring up the fact that she was leaving soon just to goad him. And he'd retaliated by lashing out with an I-don't-care attitude.

Only trouble was…he *did* care. And he couldn't shake that feeling. It kept hitting him in the face no matter where he turned. She didn't seem to realize how much he was going to miss her. If she did, would she still leave? He'd already made it clear he didn't want her to go. Hell, she should be here at his side right now taking notes. Instead, he deliberately told her not to bother attending the meeting today. Not when *she* was on the agenda.

"Blake, I've finished," he heard Gavin say.

He blinked and saw the others staring at him. He had to get back to business. "Right. The next item on the agenda is mainly for you, Trevor. One of the wealthy guests has approached me about opening a boutique here at the lodge." He explained further.

Trevor nodded as he listened. "Sounds good. We could see—"

There was a tap at the door.

Samantha came into the room, looking slightly apologetic. "I'm sorry for the interruption, but Trevor's assistant asked me to give him a message." She walked toward Trevor and passed him a piece of paper. "I ran into Diana downstairs," she said directly to him. "She was on her way up here, so I said I'd hand it to you and save her coming up." Then she gave a general smile and turned to leave the room.

Blake watched her walk away with a slight sway to her hips that emphasized the soft lines of her body, but as she closed the door behind her, he heard Trevor mildly curse.

"What's the matter, Trev?" Guy was the first to ask.

Trevor looked at the note and shook his head. "I don't know what's going on. It's some woman called Haylie Smith. She left a message the other day saying it's important she speak with me but that it's private and she won't discuss it with anyone else. I've never even heard of her."

"Maybe she's got a crush on you?" Gavin mocked.

Trevor shot his brother a look that wasn't amused. "I don't mind a novel approach but this is getting ridiculous."

"Perhaps you should call her back," Melissa suggested.

Trevor shook his head. "No, if it was that important she could leave a message as to why." He grimaced. "I'll have to let Diana know not to interrupt my meetings in future."

"Maybe you should get a tap on your phone," Christian said, ever the lawyer.

Erica looked at her fiancé. "Darling, the woman's only left two messages. Hardly enough reason to put a stalking charge on her."

"Hey, who said anything about a stalker?" Trevor choked.

"I think—" Melissa began.

"People, can we focus here," Blake cut across her. "We have other matters at hand."

A few seconds ticked by.

Then Trevor nodded. "Yes, of course." His forehead creased as he thought. "Now, where was I? Right. I think we can give this Mrs. Richardson a short-term lease and see how it goes. I'm sure she won't want a long-term lease anyway."

Blake agreed. "Good idea. Perhaps you'd like to check out her business practices and financial situation before we decide anything further."

"Sure."

Blake turned to Melissa. "How's the spa going, Melissa?"

Melissa launched into a brief report.

"And now we need to discuss plans for the upcoming ski season." Blake looked at his half sister. "Erica, I believe you were going to prepare a report on how the Christmas bookings and the hiring of staff are going."

Erica inclined her head, looking very efficient. "Yes, Blake, that's right. I've drawn up a presentation, so if you'll all just look at the screen…"

Blake glanced at the screen, immediately impressed by Erica's attention to detail, and he couldn't help but surreptitiously glance at Christian sitting down the table on his right. The other man was looking at Erica with pride and admiration. But Blake saw something in the other man's features that reminded him of how *he* felt whenever he looked at Samantha.

Samantha.

Something twisted inside him. In less than ten days she would return to Vegas to wrap up everything. Then in another two weeks she would be out of his life and gone for good. He swallowed hard. There was nothing good about her going, he decided, dropping his gaze to the paperwork in front of him in case the others saw his thoughts.

The next agenda item jumped out at him.

Samantha's replacement.

Dammit, he had to do this. It was time to bring to the table a list of suitable applications for her position. It was only fair he keep his family up-to-date. After all, the new applicant would be mainly working out of here now and he wanted everyone to—

Just then there was another tap at the door and Samantha stuck her head around it, then entered the room farther. "I'm sorry, Blake, but there's an urgent message here for you from Mrs. Richardson. She wants you to call her back as soon as you can. It's to do with her boutique."

Here was the woman who was leaving him. The woman who could so easily walk away from what they had. Resentment rose in his chest and up his throat. He was tying himself up in knots for her and she was standing there looking so damn poised and polite.

And so damn beautiful.

Something snapped inside him right then. "I'm sure whatever Mrs. Richardson has to say can wait. Please keep any other messages for us until we finish this meeting," he dismissed, hearing himself talk in that harsh tone like he was listening to someone else talk to her.

Samantha flinched, then went to leave but turned back and squared her shoulders, a rebuke in her eyes. "Of course, Mr. Jarrod," she said primly and left the room with quiet dignity.

The door closed behind her.

All eyes were turned on him.

"I don't think there was any need for that, Blake," Guy said quietly.

Blake felt bad. If she hadn't come in at that moment then he wouldn't have verbally attacked her. It had been a reaction to her leaving him, not a reaction to *her*.

He looked at them. They were staring back at him with reproachful eyes that reminded him of Samantha. His mouth tightened. "I know, I know. I'll apologize later." He put thoughts of that to the side. "Now. Speaking of Samantha, as you know she's leaving. I'm looking at other applicants and I think one of them will be eminently suitable to replace her."

Guy arched a brow. "Can anyone replace her?"

"Guy," Blake growled.

"Blake," Melissa began, "don't you think—"

"No, Melissa," he said firmly, without being rude, knowing what she was going to say. "All of you listen to me. This is private between Samantha and myself. It's none of your business. Now. Let's talk about finding me a new assistant so that we can end this meeting and get on with other things."

The tension in the air was palpable, but he ignored both it and the looks on their faces. He owed no one any explanation. Hell, what explanation could there be anyway?

Samantha wanted to leave.

Samantha *was* leaving.

And he hated himself for embarrassing her just now.

"I apologize, Samantha."

Samantha had heard him enter the office but she'd

ignored him. Now she lifted her head to find Blake standing in front of her desk. Anger and hurt rioted inside her. She had to keep busy.

She rose to her feet and went to put some papers in the filing cabinet. "I'm glad I'm leaving now."

"Don't be like that."

She spun around. "Like what, Blake? Standing up for myself?"

His eyes clouded over. "Look, I know I embarrassed you in front of the family. I shouldn't have done that. I'm sorry."

She lifted her chin. "I was only doing my job. I'm not a novice at this. The woman said it was urgent, and seeing that her proposal was on the agenda for the meeting, I assumed you'd want to know any important developments."

"I know. And you're right. You did the right thing." His expression turned sincere. "You may not believe this, but the reason I snapped was because of you. I was angry because I had to bring up mention of your replacement. I don't want a replacement. I want *you*."

Her heart skipped a beat and she began to soften. She didn't doubt him. She never doubted what he said. If he said something, he meant it. He wasn't manipulating her. He'd accepted that she was leaving and he had nothing to lose by being honest. Why fight with him when time was so precious between them?

She thawed. "Oh, Blake."

He came toward her and slipped his arms around her waist. "Forgive me for being a pig? The others know I feel bad. Their sympathy was all on your side, believe me."

"Let's forget it." But it was nice to know his family had stuck up for her, especially against their big brother.

He lifted his hand and stroked her cheek. "Are you sure you don't want to change your mind about leaving? It would be good between us."

She drew a painful breath. "No, I can't." He wanted short-term. She wanted forever. And he wasn't a forever type of guy.

His eyes shadowed with regret and he lowered his head and kissed her. She opened her mouth to him, knowing this was the only way she could let him inside herself.

The telephone rang just then and they both ignored it.

It stopped, then rang again.

She pulled back. "I should get that," she said, and Blake nodded with a grimace.

It was Clarice.

Samantha looked at Blake as she listened. Then, "Yes, I passed the message on, Mrs. Richardson."

Blake's mouth tightened and he held his hand out for the phone. "What's the problem, Clarice?" he said, after she handed it to him. There was a pause as he listened. "Look, I'm pretty busy right now." He winked at Samantha and her heart soared with love.

Another pause.

"It was discussed at a meeting this morning. My brother, Trevor, is going to work with you on this." He listened. "Yes. Fine." He hung up, shook his head at it, then kissed Samantha quickly. "I need to go see Trevor and fill him in before Clarice gets to him. Unfortunately I'm not sure he knows what he's coming up against with that woman."

Samantha considered him. "You really worry about your brothers and sisters, don't you?"

"Yes, I suppose I do."

She went up on her toes and kissed him briefly. He looked a little surprised as he turned and left the office. He was a good brother, she decided, her heart beating with love for him.

And a good man.

Eleven

Just before lunch, Melissa popped into the office as Blake was discussing a letter with Samantha. "I've booked you in for a spa treatment with me at four, Samantha. You need some major pampering."

Samantha blinked. "Oh, but—"

"No arguments. I don't give many massages these days but I've decided to give you one." Melissa smiled slyly at her big brother. "Anyway it's Blake's treat."

Blake lifted his brows. "What is it with my sisters bullying me?" Then he smiled at Samantha. "Keep the appointment."

"Okay, thanks." Samantha smiled at Melissa. "And thank you, too, Melissa."

"You're very welcome. See you at four." Melissa started to leave then stopped to consider her big brother. "It would do you good to have one, too, Blake." Her face lit with mischief. "You could share with Samantha. I'll even throw in a bottle of chilled champagne and some chocolate truffles. It's quite decadent."

"Not right now, thanks. I've got a lot to do."

"And that's exactly why you *should* have a massage."

"Soon."

"I'll keep you to that."

After she left, Samantha looked at Blake. "I wish you could come with me."

Heat lurked in the back of his eyes. "So do I, but I've got that meeting in town this afternoon."

His look warmed her through as she tilted her head. "You don't realize, do you?"

"What?"

"That you said *sisters* before."

Not *sister* and *half sister*.

Sisters.

Something flickered across his face, then he shrugged. "Yeah, well, don't make a big deal out of it." He went back into his office and Samantha went back to work, but she felt he'd made a big step in his relationship with his family and she was pleased for them all.

At four, Samantha walked over to the Tranquility Spa. Just stepping into a place that exemplified sophistication and sheer indulgence in a mountain setting relaxed her. It was gorgeous.

Melissa was waiting for her and led her to one of the treatment rooms that had serene music playing in the background. "I'll leave you to take off your clothes. Then slide under that sheet there and lie facedown on the bed. It's heated. I'll be back in a minute."

Samantha did as suggested and five minutes later, Melissa came back. "Good. Now I think a gentle massage should do the trick." There was the sound of her moving about. "Hmm, I'll have to be careful with your head. How is it, by the way?"

Samantha appreciated that Melissa remembered her injury. "Much better, thanks. It's healing well."

"I'm pleased. It could have been so much worse." Melissa started to rub oil on Samantha's back. "I hear Blake was quite upset about it."

"He blamed himself because he insisted I go with him for a drive."

"My brother's deep at times."

"I know." Samantha groaned as Melissa began long strokes to help soften the muscles.

"Am I hurting you?"

"No, not at all. It's exquisite."

Melissa laughed. "There's nothing like a massage." She continued working wonders, finding the right spots with unerring accuracy. Then, "Blake was pretty hard on you in the conference room today."

Samantha was glad she was lying on the bed with her face turned to the other side. "He apologized later."

"I knew he would. He's a man who knows when he's in the wrong."

"A rare boss," Samantha said, trying to make light of it.

"And a rare man."

"Right on both counts," Samantha just had to agree, then gave a little moan of pleasure as the massaging reached the base of her neck. She hadn't realized how badly she needed this.

Conversation ceased for a bit, before Melissa said, "I think Blake might be getting used to Erica."

Samantha wasn't surprised by the comment. "So you noticed that he said *sisters,* did you?"

"Oh, yeah."

"Erica's really nice."

"I love her already." Genuine warmth filled Melissa's voice. "It's like we're full sisters, not half sisters. We connected together right from the start."

"You've been really great at welcoming her into the family, Melissa. Erica must have appreciated that, especially when it came to the cool attitudes of her brothers."

"Those guys are so stubborn at times, and now look at them. They'll protect her to the death. I suspect even Blake would, too."

Back to Blake.

It always came back to Blake.

Time to change the subject. "So how is business doing at the spa?"

"Quiet right now, but next month it'll start picking up. And in December we'll be run off our feet. Of course, Shane worries about me and the baby, so I've promised him I'll put on extra staff."

"I can understand that."

There was a tiny pause. "This baby means so much to us," she said, with a little catch in her voice that tugged at Samantha's heartstrings.

"Pregnancy suits you. You're glowing."

Melissa cleared her throat. "Thanks. I can highly recommend it." All at once there was a slight change in the air. "What about you, Samantha? Do you plan on having children one day?"

Samantha swallowed the despair in her throat at the thought of having Blake's baby. She forced herself to sound natural. "Yes, I'd love to. But only when the time is right and with the right man."

There was no immediate reply. Then, "Forgive me for saying this, but isn't Blake the right man for you? Wouldn't you like to have his baby?"

Samantha's heart constricted as she was forced to face something she hadn't dared let herself think about now that she knew she loved Blake. This was dangerous territory for her. Loving him like she did and having his baby would be so absolutely wonderful, but knowing it was never going to happen was like a knife through her heart.

She swallowed hard again, then somehow said calmly, "You should know your brother by now, Melissa. Blake isn't into commitment, and having a baby would be a *huge* commitment."

Besides, Blake was already a father figure to his brothers and sisters, and he was already married to his job. There wasn't room for her, even if he actually *wanted* her to be a part of it all.

"Is that why you're leaving?"

She didn't hesitate. She couldn't afford to. "No. I'm leaving because it's the best thing for me."

There was a short silence, then, "I see."

Much to Samantha's relief, Melissa changed the subject and they talked about more desultory things on and off until the massage was over.

"Now," Melissa finally said, after she'd tidied up. "How do you feel?"

"Like I'm about to slither off the bed."

Melissa laughed. "That's what we aim for. Right, I'm going to leave you to get dressed. Take your time and don't rush. And make sure you drink lots of water for the next couple of hours. The massage releases toxins and if you don't flush them out you'll end up with a toxic headache."

"That sounds lethal," Samantha joked as she managed to push herself into a sitting position and wrapped the sheet around herself. "Thank you so much for this, Melissa," she said sincerely. "I didn't know how much I needed it. I really do feel wonderful."

Melissa smiled as she headed for the door. "Then I've done my job."

Samantha watched her leave, her smile fading as soon as the door closed, leaving her alone. Her body might feel better, but how did a person continue with a broken heart? Unfortunately no one could fix that.

"How was the massage?"

Samantha closed the front door behind her and saw Blake leaning against the kitchen doorjamb, as if he'd been waiting for her to come home. This was how it would be if she were to stay here with him. Yet how long would it last? Certainly not forever. Eventually things would become awkward between them and he would start to avoid her.

And then she'd know he would no longer want her.

"Wonderful," she said, giving him a smile that somehow felt empty.

"What's the matter?"

She looked at him and her heart felt sore. She couldn't seem to shake herself out of her despondency. "I think I need you to hold me, Blake."

"Why?"

"I just do, okay?"

He pushed himself away from the wall and came toward her, pulling her close. "Is that better?"

She slid her arms around him. "Yes." But a shiver went through her.

His brow wrinkled as he looked down at her. "What's going on with you?"

She drew a breath. "We won't have this for much longer."

He stiffened. "And?"

His reaction told her all she needed to know. "I feel… sad it's coming to an end."

"It's your choice to leave, Samantha."

She kept her face perfectly straight. "I know." He didn't understand and she couldn't say any different. "I want to go to bed, Blake. Let's make love until the sun comes up."

It could have sounded silly but he didn't smile and she was glad about that. It was as if he knew this meant a lot to her. And regardless of him avoiding any type of commitment, she hoped it would mean a lot to him, too.

In his bedroom she kept her eyes closed as she made love to him with everything in her heart. The thought of leaving him…of never having his child…of not sharing his life forever…was utmost in her mind. She'd never before felt such profound depth of emotion and she cried softly afterward. It would be so much worse once she left Blake for good.

Blake carefully eased out of bed the next morning just before sunrise, drew on his pajama pants and robe and left Samantha to sleep as he went downstairs to make himself some coffee. He felt restless, with a hard knot in his gut that he couldn't shake. Samantha had cried last night after they'd made love. She hadn't done that before. And it made him wonder. It was obvious she had strong feelings for him and he was certain now those feelings were the reason for her leaving. She hadn't said the words out loud, but he'd felt it every time she touched him and in her cry of release. Could she *love* him?

He couldn't love her back.

Hell, he should have seen this coming. *He* was the experienced one after all. Okay, so he'd invested more of himself in this relationship than he'd planned, but falling in love with Samantha, or any woman, wasn't on his agenda. It never had been and never would be. He'd never allow any person that much control over him.

Never.

So where did they go from there? Exactly nowhere. She'd leave and he'd let her go. End of story. There would be no happy ending for them. He couldn't give her that. He wished to heaven he could. He hated hurting her like this, especially knowing her last boyfriend had rejected her, too. She must feel so totally unwanted. Cast-off. Discarded and abandoned. God, how he hated to do this to her. It really pained him to do this. He shuddered, then reminded himself. He *had* warned her. And now that it came down to the crunch *she* had to be responsible for her own reactions.

Just then, the security light came on over the back decking and he saw a figure coming up the steps. The man was wrapped up to ward off the pre-sunrise chill, but he'd know that gait anywhere.

He opened the back door just as Gavin reached for the handle. "I see you smelled the coffee."

His brother smiled as he stepped inside the kitchen. "Sure did."

Blake went to get another mug down from the cupboard. "What are you doing out and about so early?"

Gavin began taking off his thick gloves. "I was going for a walk to clear my head and saw the light on."

Blake frowned a little as he poured coffee into the mugs. "Anything in particular bothering you?"

"Not really."

He handed one of the mugs to his brother. "Is the bungalow project worrying you?"

"Not at all." Gavin shrugged. "I guess it just feels strange being back home again. It hits me most at this time of the morning, and that means I usually need to get some fresh air."

Blake understood. "I know what you mean."

Gavin shot him a curious look. "I'm surprised. Don't you have a lovely lady warming your bed, helping keep those thoughts at bay?"

Blake kept his face blank. "Do I?"

Gavin shook his head. "You always were the same about never sharing your feelings with anyone."

Blake's lips twisted. "Yeah, like *you* do?"

"All I can say is that you must be losing your touch where Samantha is concerned."

"Why?" He knew he shouldn't bite, but Samantha was so much on his mind this morning.

"I thought for sure you wouldn't be dumb enough to let her go."

Blake immediately went on the defensive. "Why would I want her to stay?"

"You need to ask?" Gavin shook his head. "How about she's excellent at her job, she's a looker and a nice person to boot, and as much as I hate to say it, she's damn good for you, that's why. You'll never find an assistant who anticipates your needs the way she does."

Blake dropped his gaze to the mug of coffee in his hands. What Gavin said was true, except the bit about Samantha being good for him. He didn't need any woman to make him feel good.

And he didn't like his brother getting too close and figuring out something that didn't need figuring out. Certainly he didn't want his brother figuring out that Samantha was in love with *him,* and that he couldn't return her love. He had to protect her. He didn't want anyone talking about her even after she left here. He owed her that much.

"Yeah, she's more than competent at her job and she's beautiful, too, but so are many other women. As for being good for me…yeah, we've had some fun while it lasted but it's coming to an end now and I'm more than happy with that."

Gavin sent him a challenging look. "So you feel nothing more for her?"

"No," he lied, feeling like Judas.

"I'm sorry to hear that," Gavin said slowly.

Suddenly a figure stepped into the doorway. "Don't be, Gavin," Samantha said quietly, hurt in her lovely eyes but dignity in her face. "I'm not."

Blake's heart cramped. "Samantha, I—"

"No need to explain, Blake. I shouldn't have eavesdropped but I'm glad I did. I would never have guessed you felt so little for me," she said, a catch to her voice.

He took a step toward her. "Samantha—"

She put up her hand. "No, Blake. You've said more

than enough." She turned and hurried away so fast all he saw was her shadow.

Shit!

Gavin lifted a brow. "Seems to me she might mean more to you than you think."

Blake tried to focus. "No, you're wrong."

Gavin stared hard, then put his mug down on the bench. "I'll leave you two to sort things out."

Blake gave a jerky nod as his brother headed for the back door and left him to it. He stood there in the kitchen for a minute as regret washed over him before he took the steps to follow her. He'd do his best to mend this damage as much as possible, but if he were to be honest, things between him and Samantha really couldn't be fixed. It was probably best this had come to a head.

Samantha could barely see as she fled up the staircase for the sanctuary of her room. After waking up, she'd gone downstairs in her nightshirt looking for Blake, surprised to hear Gavin's voice and never dreaming they were discussing *her*.

Oh, God. She couldn't stay in Aspen any longer. Not now. This was it. She was leaving as soon as possible, come hell or high water.

She grabbed her suitcases out of the wardrobe and threw them on the bed. She'd always been neat and tidy and fast at packing, but who cared anyway, she decided, swallowing a sob. All she wanted was to throw everything in her bags and get to the airport. She was going home to Pasadena where she would lick her wounds. Beyond that she couldn't think.

"Samantha?" Blake's voice came gently from the doorway.

Refusing to let him see her cry, she blinked back her tears as she carried her sweaters over to one of the suitcases.

"Samantha, stop. We need to talk."

She looked at him but continued what she was doing. "No. I'm leaving. It's time for me to get out of your hair."

And out of your life.

He swore low. "I'm sorry."

She dumped her clothes into the case. "You're only sorry that I overheard you," she said tightly, then took a shuddering breath as humiliation and hurt swelled inside her. "You made it sound so…cheap. You made *me* sound cheap. As if I don't matter."

"You *do* matter," he said, looking pained, but she knew better.

"Just not to you, right?" she derided, despair wrapping around her heart and not letting go.

"I didn't mean to speak like that about you. I just didn't want Gavin to know what was going on between us."

She snorted. "Of course. How silly of me? We can't have the great Blake Jarrod show any feelings now, can we? Not to his family and not to me." It was never about his feelings anyway, and that was the hardest part to take. She'd dared hope he might at least have a high opinion of her. "Your words show me that you never even respected me as a person, Blake. And certainly not as your lover."

His face blanched. "Don't say that," he growled. "I respect you. There's no one I respect more."

"It didn't sound like that to me back there." All at once she took a shuddering breath and admitted that she couldn't blame him for everything. "But I'm doing you a disservice. You made me no promises, I'll allow you that. You tried to warn me not to get involved with you."

His gaze sharpened. "And did you?"

What did she have to lose now? "Of course I did. I…" She couldn't say she loved him. She just couldn't. That would be too humiliating. "…I thought we had something special."

"We do."

She shook her head. "We *did*. It's over." Suddenly she caught a subtle change in his face—a change that Carl hadn't shown when he'd rejected her. She stilled. Her breath stopped. Did Blake have feelings for her after all? "Unless…" *Dare she ask?* "Can you give me one good reason to stay?"

Silence fell.

She waited. She couldn't say the words but he must know what she was asking. If ever there was a time he might let down his guard…a time when he could allow her into his heart…it would surely be—

His face closed up. "No, I'm sorry. I can't give you a reason to stay."

As hard as it was to pull herself together, she recovered her breath. "That's what I thought."

"Sam—"

A hard laugh escaped then. "Too late to call me that, Blake. Far too late." She held her head up higher. "Now, please leave me to pack in peace. It was good while it lasted but it's over between us now."

He stiffened, withdrawing into himself. "I'm really sorry I hurt you."

She held his gaze. "So am I. And as horrible as this

sounds, I wish I *was* capable of hurting you back." It would at least show she had meant something to him.

Turning away, he stopped and said over his shoulder, "The family jet is at your disposal. It'll take you wherever you want to go."

The words stung her heart. "Thank you."

He strode down the hallway to his suite, going inside and quietly closing the door behind him, shutting her out of his life. For good.

Samantha made herself move. She walked to her door and closed it, then went and sat on the bed and picked up a pillow to muffle her sobs. She figured this time she was entitled to cry.

Twelve

Half an hour later, Blake had showered and dressed and now sat in his office at the Manor, his leather chair turned toward the picture window. An early fall snow that wasn't unusual at this time of year had begun covering the resort, and now a weak sun was shining on the surrounding mountains. Usually at this time he was back at Pine Lodge making love to Samantha. All he could think now was that she was leaving.

God, she'd been so hurt back there. It had pained him to realize how much. And yet he hadn't been able to say the words to get her to stay. He'd known what she wanted, of course. She wanted him to say he loved her, but those words were no longer in his vocabulary. The last time he'd used them had been all those years ago to his mother—just before she died. He'd never said them again to anyone. He'd accepted he never would.

His upbringing—his whole life since—had been about avoiding commitment.

And now Samantha had to accept that, too.

Just then he heard a noise behind him and his chest instantly tightened. She'd come to say her final goodbye.

"What happened with Samantha, Blake?"

Erica.

He twisted his chair around, forcing his brain to work as he looked at the unhappy face of his half sister. Clearly she'd spoken to Gavin not too long ago.

He picked up a pen. "She's packing to leave."

"So you're just going to let her go?"

He gave a shrug. "She wants to go. I can't stop her."

She came closer to the desk, frowning. "What's gone so wrong with you two?"

He shot her a hostile look. "It's none of your business, Erica."

"You're my brother. I'm making it my business."

"Half brother," he corrected.

"I'm so sick of this," she snapped, drawing her petite frame up taller than she was, glaring down at him, standing her ground. "We have the same blood in our veins and that makes me a Jarrod, Blake. You're my brother, like it or lump it."

He stared up at her, a growing admiration rising inside him as he looked at this woman who was related to him, no matter how much he didn't like it. The angle of her chin. The light of battle in her eyes. That stubbornness in her mouth. Oh, yeah. Erica *was* a Jarrod, through and through.

"Blake, for God's sake, when are you going to drop your guard and let people in?"

He tensed. "I don't know what you mean."

"I mean, you won't let a half sister into your life because you think I might let you down like your mother did when she died. And you won't let Samantha into your heart because of the same thing. You're frightened you'll get hurt."

"That's ridiculous," he snapped. Sure, he wasn't willing to get involved with anyone and lay himself open to hurt, but that was only because he couldn't be bothered with the ramifications of it all. He was too busy to introduce any complications in his life.

"Then tell me why you're letting a beautiful woman like Samantha walk away from you?"

"She wants to go."

"No, *you* want her to go and she knows it."

His jaw clenched. "This has got nothing to do with you, Erica."

"Look at yourself, Blake. You're deliberately making it hard for Samantha to stay. You're pushing her away and abandoning her before she can abandon *you*."

He swore. "Just stay out of this."

"Think about it. Your mother died when you were six, so it stands to reason that you would be affected by her death. And what about your father? Donald Jarrod shut up shop with his emotions when his wife died, and the only way he could cope was by focusing on his offspring. He pushed all of you to be the best you could be, and none more than you as eldest."

"Erica…" he warned.

"I suspect he wanted his kids to be fully reliant on themselves. He didn't want any of you to get hurt. Not like *he* got hurt."

"That's enough."

"So you effectively lost not only your mother when you were little, but your father, as well. Is it any wonder you don't want to let anyone get close to you?"

He opened his mouth again....

And then somehow, without warning, her words began to hit him right where it mattered. But still he had to say, "What I want is not to listen to this drivel."

Her eyes said he wasn't fooling her. "People have their breaking point, Blake. Your mother's death was your—I mean, *our* father's breaking point. A person can do silly things in their grief. Everyone reacts differently. Our father turned to my mother, looking for solace. Who's to say you wouldn't do the same thing?"

"I would never want another woman after Samantha," he growled. "Never."

"Do you hear yourself?"

He stiffened and blinked. "What?"

She stood there watching him in silent scrutiny for a moment. "If Samantha died how would *you* feel?"

"Don't say that," he rasped, the thought slicing down through the middle of him.

"You love her, Blake."

His head reeled back. "No."

"Yes. Don't let yourself realize it too late. You may never get a second chance."

He swallowed as something deep inside him lifted up like a shade on a window and he finally admitted what was right there in front of him.

He *did* love Samantha.

And right then, he finally understood the depth of his father's loss. He still didn't understand how Donald Jarrod could have shunned the children who were a legacy of his beloved wife, nor how his father had turned to another woman, but the idea of Samantha dying squeezed his heart so tight he could barely breathe.

He surged to his feet. "I have to go to her."

"Thank God!"

He glanced at his watch. "She may not have left the lodge."

"She's already taken the valet car. I saw her leaving." Erica made a gesture toward the door. "Go. I'll make sure they stop the plane. And hey, take it easy getting to her, okay? We've got our first snow, and she'll want you in one piece."

"I will." He was almost at the door by the time she finished speaking. All at once he stopped, conscious that he had to take a moment more for something else. He returned to Erica to kiss her on the cheek. "Thanks, sis."

She beamed at him. "You're welcome. Just remember you'll have a few brothers and sisters who'll expect your firstborn to be named after them."

He grinned. "That's a lot of names."

"Well, maybe you can have a lot of kids."

He chuckled as warmth filled him at the thought of Samantha carrying his child. But first things first...he wanted only one person right now.

Samantha.

As he raced down to the lobby, he remembered how after their lovemaking the other night he'd felt so at home in her arms. Now he knew it was more than that.

In Samantha's arms he *had* come home.

"Is it going to be much longer, Jayne?" Samantha asked, after she'd boarded the Jarrod private jet and nothing seemed to be happening. They hadn't even taxied out onto the runway yet.

"I'm sorry about this, Ms. Thompson," the stewardess apologized. "It's the weather. There's a storm ahead. We have to sit tight until it passes."

Samantha swiveled her leather chair around on its base a little to glance out the cabin window to the snow-dusted airport. A few weeks ago, before she'd decided to resign, she'd been eagerly looking forward to the first of the snow falling over Jarrod Ridge. Now she had to return to the warm California weather and try not to imagine how magical it would have been here in Blake's arms.

Somehow she faked a small smile back at the other woman. "Okay, thanks, Jayne."

The stewardess smiled, then went to the back of the plane, leaving her alone to stare out the window. She'd done her best to repair her face after her crying session back at the lodge, but the longer she sat here the more likely she might burst into tears.

And if she did that she would be humiliated in front of Jayne. She wanted no one knowing how painful this was for her. Blake knew she'd been hurt, but he really had no idea at the depths of her despair. How could he? He didn't love her. He was going to move on. He'd probably already written her off as a bad debt, she thought with a touch of hysteria.

Oh, God. This was it. She was actually leaving Aspen…leaving Blake for good. Fresh tears were verging in her eyes when there was a sudden flurry of movement near the doorway. She quickly took a shuddering breath and glanced ahead to check what was happening.

Blake!

He stood there looking at her…so dear to her heart. And then he moved toward her through the wide cabin, and her thoughts kicked in. Was he here merely to make sure she left? She dared not think otherwise.

He stopped in front of her seat and looked down at her. "You didn't say goodbye, Samantha."

She moistened her mouth. "I didn't think you wanted me to."

"I didn't," he said, and her heart twisted tight at his honesty. "The fact is…I didn't want you to say goodbye at all. I still don't want you to leave. I want you to stay with me." He pulled her to her feet, looking at her with an emotion in his eyes that almost blinded her. "I love you, Samantha."

She knew in a heartbeat he was telling the truth. "Say that again," she whispered.

"I love you."

She threw her arms around his neck. "Oh, my God! I love you, too, Blake. So very, very much."

He kissed her then and she clung to him, loving him with every ounce of her being, feeling the pounding of his heart in time with hers. Forevermore.

Finally he pulled back, but kept his arms around her. "I love you, Samantha. I love you more than life itself."

She sighed blissfully. "I feel the same."

He gave her a soft kiss. "After we made love last night, I suspected you loved me."

At the time she'd hoped she'd masked her feelings well. "I gave myself away when I cried, didn't I?"

"Yes, I'm afraid you did, darling."

She went all sappy inside at the endearment, so she

could forgive him anything. "Yet you were still going to let me go."

"You can thank Erica that I didn't. She made me see sense about a couple of things."

"Thank you, sweet Erica," she mused out loud.

He smiled, then it faded on his handsome face, making him more serious. "I hope you can forgive me for what I said to Gavin. You were right. I didn't want anyone knowing my feelings for you. I was even hiding them from myself," he added with self-derision. "And I hope you can believe this, but I was trying to protect you. I didn't want them realizing you had feelings for me either." He lifted his shoulders. "Loving someone is a private thing."

She thanked him with her eyes. "I agree, though they probably suspected anyway. And yes, I do forgive you, darling," she said, loving the sound of that on her own lips and seeing his eyes darken. "If you hadn't said what you did to Gavin, then all this may not have been resolved."

He chuckled. "Erica would have made us resolve it, don't you worry about that. My sister is a very determined woman."

Her heart swelled. So he'd let Erica into his heart, too. How wonderful. Now he could be the man he was meant to be with his family.

And with her.

All at once there was so much to talk about. She'd have to tell him about when she'd actually realized she loved him, and she'd have to come clean about trying to make him jealous. He was bound to get a laugh out of that.

"Samantha," he cut across her thoughts. "I insist you

don't give up your music. I want you to contact that person Erica mentioned at the music school as soon as you can."

"Oh, Blake, I'm not giving up anything," she said softly, and ran her fingers along his chin, loving the feel of its masculine texture. "I've got all I ever wanted right here."

His brows drew together. "But—"

She smiled at the worried look in his eyes. "Okay, I'll contact them. Perhaps sometime in the future I'll be able to help out in some minor way, but please believe that playing the piano isn't important in my life. I enjoy it. I might even take some more lessons, or give lessons for that matter, but living here with you, and being part of your family, will be more than enough for me."

He gave her a searching look, then his shoulders relaxed. "While we're being honest…"

Her heart caught. "Yes?"

"I know you feel I'm letting you down in some way, but…"

She swallowed hard. "But?" What wasn't he telling her? Was he actually in love with someone else? Was she his second choice? Perhaps he—

"Forgive me, Samantha, but I don't think I'll ever be able to call you Sam."

It took a moment to sink in. She laughed and lightly punched his chest. "You think that's funny, don't you?"

He put his hands on either side of her face and looked at her lovingly. "You're Samantha to me. *My* Samantha. Do you mind?"

She blinked back silly tears of happiness. "Of course not." Not anymore. "It makes me feel very special."

"You *are* special, my darling." He placed his lips on hers, then, "Let's go to Vegas right now and get married."

She blinked. "Married?" As crazy as it seemed, she hadn't thought that far ahead. She'd been too busy taking in that he loved her. "You really want to marry me, Blake?"

He stroked her cheek. "Yes. I want your kisses for the rest of my life."

She drew his mouth down to hers and kissed him softly. "Here's one to start with."

When the kiss finished, he said, "Speaking of giving, you haven't *given* me my answer. Will you marry me?"

"Is there any doubt?"

"Not really."

"You're a conceited man, Blake Jarrod," she teased.

"And that's a good thing in this situation, right?"

She sent him a rueful glance, then something came to her. "But don't you want to get married in Aspen with your family present?"

"No. I'm an impatient man. I want to marry you now. Today." He scowled. "Unless *you* want a big wedding?" He didn't wait for her to answer. "I suppose I shouldn't cheat you of a wedding with your family."

She shook her head. "No, I don't need my family there. I love them dearly but they'll understand. All they want is for me to be happy."

"I can guarantee that."

"Then a wedding for two will be just perfect, my love," she murmured, a flood of emotion making her voice husky.

Blake lowered his head to place his lips against

hers. Outside the plane more snowflakes fell in a hush, blanketing everything in a fairy-tale setting. And that was appropriate. Their love was, after all, a fairy tale come true.

* * * * *

WEDDING HIS
TAKEOVER TARGET

BY
EMILIE ROSE

Bestselling Desire™ author and RITA® Award finalist **Emilie Rose** lives in her native North Carolina with her four sons and two adopted mutts. Writing is her third (and hopefully her last) career. She's managed a medical office and run a home day-care, neither of which offers half as much satisfaction as plotting happy endings. Her hobbies include gardening and cooking (especially cheesecake). She's a rabid country music fan because she can find an entire book in almost any song. She is currently working her way through her own "bucket list," which includes learning to ride a Harley. Visit her website at www.emilierose.com or e-mail EmilieRoseC@aol. com. Letters can be mailed to PO Box 20145, Raleigh, NC 27619, USA.

From the Last Will and Testament of Don Jarrod

…And to my son Gavin I leave my stable of horses. I have such fond memories of you spending hours in the big barn, taking care of all the animals. How many meals did you miss, insisting you had to feed the horses first? It gave me such pride to see you grow into your own, riding "your" horses across the field. How carefree you were… Did you know it broke my heart when you left and didn't look back? I hope being responsible for the horses once more will help you find your way home.

One

"You said urgent. Here we are," Gavin Jarrod said as he preceded his oldest brother Blake into Christian Hanford's office Monday morning. Not a great way to start the week.

The attorney handling their late father's estate indicated the chairs in front of his desk and waited until Gavin and Blake sat. "I appreciate your coming in. Unfortunately, the news is not good."

Gavin shot a *what now?* look at his brother. "Not surprising since none of the news since our father's death five months ago has been good, beginning with him requiring each of us to put our lives and careers on hold and spend a year at Jarrod Ridge or we all forfeit our inheritance."

"This regards your project and the permits needed to build the new bungalow you've designed on the resort property."

Gavin tried not to let his frustration and resentment show. Leave it to their father to try to control their lives from his grave with posthumous demands.

"What's the holdup? It's November first. We need to get the foundations dug and poured before the ground freezes solid."

"You can't get the permits because the land isn't part of your father's estate."

"What?" Gavin and his brother exclaimed simultaneously.

Blake leaned forward in his chair. "The site is in the middle of Jarrod property. How can the family not own it?"

Christian pulled an aerial map of Jarrod Ridge from the file in front of him and slid it across his desk. He indicated an X on a five-acre tract outlined in red.

"This is where you wanted to build. When we researched the deed we discovered your grandfather transferred ownership of this plot to Henry Caldwell fifty years ago."

Gavin searched his brain for Caldwells and came up empty. He'd spent the first eighteen years of his life in Aspen, but he had no reason to know any of the locals anymore. He'd escaped the town and his domineering father when he'd left for college a decade ago—he only returned when he absolutely couldn't avoid it. To say he and his father hadn't gotten along would be a gross understatement. "Who in the hell is Caldwell?"

"He owns the Snowberry Inn, a bed-and-breakfast here in Aspen that's been around as long as Jarrod Ridge."

"Why would our grandfather sell him a defunct mine?" The old mine had been Gavin's favorite hideout as a kid. He and his brothers had spent countless hours wandering through the tunnels, and in high school Gavin had taken girls there to make out.

"The real question is why would anyone want to buy it?" Blake countered. "There's not enough silver on the site to make extraction cost-effective."

"That's the interesting part. In my digging, I discovered

your grandfather didn't sell the acreage. He wagered it in a poker game. And lost it."

Surprise pushed the air from Gavin's lungs. "We'll buy it back."

Christian eyed him across the map. "Good luck with that. There are numerous letters in our files indicating that your father tried and failed to repurchase the land more than a dozen times over the years. Caldwell refused to sell."

Blake sat back in his chair looking more relaxed than he should given the revelation that had just blown their plans to hell and back. "The plans are already drawn for a high-security bungalow for the resort's A-list guests. The construction crews have been contracted and the materials ordered because we had no reason to expect a glitch like this. We'll have to choose another site."

"No," Gavin insisted. "If I'm condemned to waste another seven months here I'm not giving up on the only place on the estate that holds good memories for me. I'll convince Caldwell to sell."

One corner of Blake's mouth lifted. "You just want to do what Dad couldn't."

A smile tugged Gavin's lips. His brother knew him and his competitive streak too well. Gavin never had been good at passing up a challenge. "I wouldn't mind besting the old man. He'll probably roll over in his grave when I succeed."

"*If* you succeed," his brother cautioned.

"I will." Having older twin brothers who'd often teamed up against him had given Gavin a persistent streak that some called stubborn, but that same trait had taken him to the top of his field.

Blake pulled his wallet from his pocket and flashed a Ben Franklin, then laid it on the desk. Gavin caught a gleam of gold on his brother's finger. *What in the hell was that?* It couldn't be what he thought it was. But first things first. The mine. He'd deal with the new jewelry after they left Christian's.

"A hundred bucks says you won't," Blake challenged. "Dad might have been an uptight pain in the ass, but he was a shrewd businessman. If there was a way to get that land back, he would have found it."

Gavin shook his head and withdrew a matching bill. "You're on. If there's one thing engineering has taught me, it's that there's a solution to every problem. It's a matter of whether you're willing to pay the price. All I have to do is find Caldwell's price and that land will be ours."

"Hey," Gavin called out before Blake could climb into his car outside Christian's office. "What in the hell is that thing on your finger?"

Blake smiled, looking as satisfied as if he'd just finished a five-course gourmet dinner. "Samantha and I got married in Vegas."

Shock popped Gavin in the gut. "I thought you were there for work on your hotel."

"Not this time. We were there for our wedding and honeymoon. We're going to tell the family tonight."

"Are you out of your mind?"

Blake looked him dead in the eye. "Yes. With happiness."

"Samantha's been around for years and you never noticed her in that way before. In fact, you always said never mix business with pleasure unless you want pleasure to bite you in the ass."

Blake's skin reddened. "What can I say? I was a little slow on the uptake."

"You did this because you didn't want to lose her as your assistant, right?"

"Our romance started that way, but it's more than that now. I love her."

Gavin laughed. And then he realized Blake wasn't joking. His brother's expression was serious and more than a little sappy. "You're kidding, right?"

"No. Love is the only reason to take that step."

Not in Gavin's world. In his world love was something to avoid, like standing in front of moving trains or jumping off a bridge. "You're saying you love Samantha—the 'til death do you part kind of thing?"

"Yes, I am."

Blake looked happy instead of miserable. How had that happened? It didn't matter how, the euphoria wouldn't last long. His brother was as much of a workaholic as Gavin. Women hated that. And when they'd had enough solitude they packed up and left. "Is she pregnant?"

"Not that I know of, but I wouldn't mind if she were."

"Did you get a prenup?"

"I'm not worried about a prenup."

"Blake, I've never known you to be blind or stupid."

"And I'm not now. In fact, I'm seeing clearly for the first time. Samantha is the only woman I want and I trust her implicitly."

Poor deluded sucker.

"You'd risk it even knowing how crazy losing Mom made Dad?"

"I'd be just as crazy, maybe more so, if I were too much of a coward to try to make this work."

"I can't talk you into an annulment?"

"No." Blake wore his stubborn, don't-mess-with-me face. "And I'd suggest you back off. Remember, you like Samantha."

"As your assistant, yes, she's damned good at her job,

probably the best assistant you've ever had. But marriage?"
He faked a shudder.

"Yes, marriage. You should try it."

No way. He and Trevor were the only ones who'd eluded
pairing up in the past few months. Good thing he knew he
wasn't susceptible. Otherwise he'd be worried. "I guess all
I can do is wish you luck and tell you I'll be here when you
need me."

"To pick up the pieces? I won't be needing those services."

"You hope."

"I know. Samantha is the one for me. The only one."

Gavin opened his mouth to continue the argument then
swallowed the words. Blake was infatuated and probably
brain-dead from getting laid well and often. Gavin wasn't
going to be able to change his mind. The best he could do
is hope like hell that when the marriage ended, Samantha
wouldn't take a chunk of Jarrod Ridge with her.

The Snowberry Inn looked as homey as Jarrod Ridge
was opulent, Gavin decided as he ran an assessing eye over
the large Victorian after circling the block to appraise his
opponent's property. Located in the heart of downtown, the
B and B had a homey charm reminiscent of Aspen's silver
mining boom in the 1880s, whereas his family's resort catered
to affluent guests who demanded modern amenities and world-
class service.

He pushed open the door of one of The Ridge's fleet of
luxurious black Cadillac SUVs, and the irregular beat of an
unskilled carpenter's hammer striking wood greeted him as he
slid from behind the wheel. Glancing up and down the street,
he surveyed the area, his breath fogging the chilly autumn air.
The location couldn't be faulted. Guests could easily stroll to
the shopping district's art galleries and designer boutiques

or to the upscale restaurants overlooking the Roaring Fork River.

A prime piece of valuable real estate and a relatively large parcel if the barns beyond the main structure were included.

He followed the winding walk through bare Aspen trees and leafy snowberry shrubs with their white fruits glistening in the afternoon sunlight. It seemed like a lifetime ago that he and his brothers had used clusters of the small berries as ammunition for their homemade slingshots whenever they'd stolen a few moments away from their father's eagle eye.

Though the B and B appeared structurally sound, the clapboards could use a fresh coat of forest-green paint. The butter-yellow railing wobbled slightly in his grip as he climbed the brick steps leading to the front porch. His offer would give Caldwell an influx of cash that would more than cover the cosmetic work.

Rather than ring the bell by the front door Gavin followed the banging sound around the wide covered porch spanning the front and side of the building, hoping to find Caldwell or someone who could direct him to the man. He found a red-coated, hammer-wielding female, kneeling with her back to him. A matching red toboggan capped long, dark curls winding down her back. Definitely not Henry Caldwell.

"Ow. Oh. Dammit," a feminine voice cried out. The hammer clattered on the floorboards.

"You okay?"

The handywoman shot to her feet and spun around, clutching her left thumb in her right hand. Wide, bright blue eyes found his.

"Who are you?" Pain tightened her voice.

"Gavin Jarrod. Need some help?"

"Are you looking for a room?" She ignored his question.

"No. I'm here to see Henry Caldwell."

He automatically catalogued her assets. Early- to mid-twenties. Smooth, clear skin. Above average height and probably slender beneath the parka if her long, jeans-clad legs were any indication. In short, beautiful and worth getting to know better.

Then he appraised the problem, a half hammered-in nail, toenailing the railing to the column. Not an easy angle for an amateur. "Let me get that for you."

He bent and scooped up the hammer—one too heavy for her—and slammed in the nail with one swing. "There you go."

"Thanks," she offered grudgingly. Still holding her injured hand close to her body, she accepted the tool he offered with her other.

"Let me look at that." He grabbed her wrist and inspected her reddened thumb. The unpainted nail plate remained intact with no blood pooling beneath it.

The warmth of her soft skin heated his and did something wacky to his pulse rate. *Single?* Her ring finger was bare. He dragged his thumb over her palm.

With a quick hiss of her breath, she jerked away.

Too bad. He hadn't reacted that instantly to a woman's touch in a long time. "You've probably just bruised it. Work gloves would have offered a little protection."

Her eyes narrowed, drawing his attention to a thick fringe of black lashes that looked real. In fact, if she wore any makeup, it was the kind a straight guy couldn't see. "I couldn't hold the nail with gloves on. Is Henry expecting you? He didn't mention an appointment."

"I didn't make one." He'd wanted to catch the man off guard and perhaps get him to agree to sell on impulse.

"Are you selling something?"

"No. I didn't catch your name."

"I didn't throw it." She gathered the box of galvanized nails, her discarded gloves and the hammer. "Follow me."

She headed toward a back entrance and led him into a warm kitchen. The combined scents of pot roast and freshly baked bread made his mouth water and his stomach growl as he followed her down the center hall to the front parlor. "Wait here. May I tell him what this is about?"

"An old poker bet."

Her dark eyebrows dipped. "He owes you money?"

"No." And that was all she'd get out of him. No matter how attractive she might be he wasn't sharing personal business with her—unless it was over dinner.

Her curious gaze slid over him, making him overheat under his ski jacket. "You don't look like one of his poker buddies."

"I'm not."

"Then you are…?"

"Here on personal business."

She stood straighter, her chin snapping up. "I'll see if Po—Henry's available."

Gavin hadn't dated since arriving in town, and watching her peel the knit cap off those thick, gleaming curls and then unzip her coat reminded his libido of the long dry spell. He visually tracked her until she turned a corner out of sight.

He'd definitely have to take this one to dinner. And then maybe to bed. His heart pumped faster in approval of the plan.

Unzipping his coat, he surveyed the room. Antiques. But not the kind a man would be afraid to sit on. Lace, velvet and flowery fabrics predominated. But not enough of the girly stuff to threaten his manhood. The inn wasn't bad. But it definitely wasn't competition for The Ridge.

"Are you related to the Jarrods of Jarrod Ridge?" she asked from behind him.

He hadn't heard her return. She'd shed her outerwear, revealing a purple turtleneck sweater clinging to a long, lean torso with curves in all the right places. Nice. And definitely worth pursuing. "Yes."

Her lips mashed together as if his reply displeased her—drawing attention to the fact that she'd added some gloss to her wide, red mouth. An encouraging sign. If she wasn't interested she wouldn't have bothered.

"My grandfather will be with you in a moment."

His plans sputtered and stalled like a faulty airplane engine. "Your grandfather?"

"Yes."

The revelation killed any chance he had of taking her on a date or to bed. With his relationship track record, he couldn't risk souring the sale with another romance wreck. Business came first—especially family business. But perhaps after the deed had been transferred…

He couldn't imagine going a year without sex, but he'd ended his last relationship two months before his father's death, and thus far none of the women he'd met at the lodge had tempted him like this one did.

"You're not from here, are you?" he asked. Not that many people were Aspenites these days between the celebrity invasion and the ski season's tourist ebb and flow.

"No." She folded her arms across her chest, looking protective, defiant and delicious. *Down, boy.*

"I've worked all around the globe, but I can't place your accent."

"Good."

Man, she had it in for him for some reason. "Have I done something to offend you, Ms. Caldwell?"

"Taylor."

He hiked a brow.

"My last name is Taylor."

He noted she'd ignored his question. Again. Apparently, Ms. Taylor, like him, operated on a need-to-know basis. His gaze flicked briefly back to her bare ring finger. "Married?"

She glanced away, but not so quickly that he didn't catch a glimpse of pain, and then she checked her watch. "Not anymore. Can I get you something? Coffee? Tea? We usually have high tea at four."

That would give her an excuse to leave the room, and he wasn't ready to let her go yet—not until he'd made sense of her cool demeanor. "No thanks. Are you visiting your grandfather?"

"I manage the B and B for him."

"Been doing that long?"

"A while."

He almost laughed at her quick, succinct response. He'd never met a woman who made him sift so hard for information, like a miner panning for precious metals. He was used to ones who chattered nonstop. He'd have to employ a different strategy if he wanted to get details out of her.

"I am a local—or I used to be. But I'm only back for...*a while*." He mimicked her words.

"Yes, I heard."

"Did you?"

"Don't get excited. I wasn't fishing for information about you Jarrods. In a city with a population of roughly six thousand residents, most of those not full-time, the gossip mill works overtime. Your father's death and the stipulations of his will are a hot topic. My condolences on his passing."

He digested the *you Jarrods* part of her reply. "Thanks, but if the grapevine is working efficiently, then you know there was no love lost between my father and me. I'll only be here another seven months and then I'm gone."

"Your loss. Aspen is beautiful."

He let his gaze wander to her booted feet and then back

to her eyes. "Exquisitely beautiful. But not as warm as I'd like."

She stiffened, obviously receiving the message that he wasn't discussing the city's climate. A fresh rush of color flooded her cheeks and her lips parted.

"Yeah, well, you're old enough to know you can't always get what you want."

A clearing throat preempted further discussion. An older gentleman, tall, thin, but bearing military-erect posture and a shock of snow-white hair stood in the entry. Blue eyes the same shade as his granddaughter's met Gavin's. "Jarrod, huh?"

"I'm Gavin Jarrod. I'd like to talk to you about—"

Caldwell held up a blue-veined hand. "Sabrina, be an angel and get me some coffee to wash away the cobwebs my nap always leaves behind."

Not a good start. Gavin fought the urge to check out the brunette's backside as she left. "I apologize if I woke you, sir."

Caldwell waved his apology aside. "Fell asleep watching the news channel. Damned depressing babble. All gloom and doom even if it is delivered by hot blondes in short skirts and high heels. Time to get up anyway. Can't sleep what's left of my life away. What can I do for you, Gavin Jarrod?"

"I'd like to buy back the property my grandfather lost to you."

"Should have known one of you would pick up where your father left off. Badgering me seems to be the Jarrod way. At least you had the gumption to pester me face-to-face instead through a damned lawyer. Can't respect a man who won't handle his own dirty work."

Gavin digested the animosity. He'd have to work around it. "As you've no doubt discovered, the mine is worthless."

"Depends on what you consider the valuable part. Ain't necessarily the minerals."

Cryptic old coot. "The acreage is in the middle of Jarrod Ridge."

"And me owning it is like a burr in your butt, ain't it, boy? Drove your daddy nuts, too." Mischief fanned crinkles from the old, but sharp eyes.

"My oldest brother and I would like to build a bungalow on the property."

"Don't you folks have enough going on up there already? Lodges all over the damned place plus Jarrod Manor."

"This would be a different caliber accommodation for guests needing more privacy and additional security than the hotel or existing lodges could provide."

Henry snorted. "Married Hollywood types sneaking off with somebody they oughtn't to be with."

Another strike. "We were thinking more along the lines of heads of state."

"Don't care if you're putting up the president. The land's not for sale."

Gavin struggled to keep his frustration in check. "What purpose does keeping it serve you, Mr. Caldwell? There's no road access which means you can't build on it. You can't even get to it without obtaining written permission to cross Jarrod property."

"Y'think so? Son, I've been visiting that mine for fifty years—often enough to know you're one of the young'uns who used to camp down in the shaft."

Interesting. Until his most recent return Gavin had never seen signs of anyone visiting other than him and his brothers. The entrance was pretty well hidden. "Yessir. All three of my brothers and I did, but I probably spent more time there than the rest of them combined."

"Cleaned up after yourself, too."

"Our father forbade us to go there. We didn't want to leave any tracks."

"He forbade you because he didn't own it."

"A fact he didn't share with us, and one we'd like to rectify. I'm prepared to offer you—"

"Don't matter how much you offer. I'm still not selling. Which one are you? The architect, the engineer, the marketing man or the restaurateur?"

Caldwell knew quite a bit about the Jarrods, but considering the family had been a fixture in Aspen for generations, the interest in their lives wasn't surprising. "I'm a construction engineer. My brother Blake is a developer who commissioned the design for the bungalow we'd like to build. Our offer is more than generous."

"Don't care about your money."

"Your inn could use a little work."

Caldwell snorted. "I'll get to it."

"Opening day for the ski slopes is only a few weeks away."

"That's not news."

Gavin didn't like bringing personal issues into a business problem because it gave his opponent leverage, but he had no choice. "Mr. Caldwell, as you've noted, that mine has sentimental value to me. I spent a lot of my youth there. The site holds some good memories."

Those intensely blue eyes held his. "For someone who never comes home, you're sure tied to the place. Could be the mountain's dug her claws into you. Some folks claim once she gets hold of you, she never lets go."

The old man's folktales didn't change the fact that Gavin intended to get the hell out of Dodge as soon as he'd fulfilled his part of the will. "Our plans will preserve the mine and its historical value. The bungalow will blend into the setting."

"I'm still not interested in selling."

"What can I do to change your mind? Would you like to see the blueprints?"

"I don't care about any blueprints."

Gavin clenched his teeth so hard he was lucky he didn't crack a molar. He had to find a way to get through to the man, and at the moment his mind was blank. He pulled the written offer from his pocket and offered it to Caldwell. "Take a look at our price."

When the man made no move to take the envelope, Gavin laid the package on the coffee table. "Think it over. Thank you for your time."

He strode toward the entry.

"What'd you think of my Sabrina?" Caldwell called after him.

Gavin stopped and pivoted. "Excuse me?"

"Liked her, didn't you?"

What was the old man up to? "Your granddaughter is quite attractive."

Caldwell nodded. "She's easy on the eyes, that's for sure. Like her grandma, my Colleen. Shut that door."

Unsure of where the conversation was headed, Gavin complied. The envelope remained unopened on the table where he'd left it.

"How badly do you want that land?"

That sounded like a loaded question. "I want to see the Jarrod property intact."

Caldwell scratched his chin. "A deed will earn you the deed."

What in the hell did that mean? The man seemed lucid, but Gavin wondered if he'd misjudged him. Gavin slowly crossed the rug. "I'm not following."

"Marry Sabrina and I'll sell you the land."

Shock knocked Gavin like a wrecking ball to the chest.

Was everybody marriage-crazy today? First Blake, now this. "*Marry* her?"

"It could work."

Gavin shook his head. Caldwell had to be senile. But Gavin couldn't afford to offend him. "I just met Sabrina, sir, and you weren't in here long enough to notice she's not exactly impressed with me."

Caldwell smiled, smirked, really. "She's interested."

Gavin's pulse spiked. "She told you that?"

"Nope. I just know."

This conversation seemed surreal. What could be so wrong with the woman that her grandfather had to bribe someone to marry her? "Mr. Caldwell, you don't know me well enough to wish me on your granddaughter."

"My Colleen was one of those mail-order brides. Didn't set eyes on her until the week of our wedding. But we had chemistry from the minute we met at the train station. Same as you and Sabrina."

Gavin didn't bother to deny the attraction. "I'm glad that worked for you, but frankly, I'm not interested in marriage. My career keeps me on the road. I move from site to site, usually only staying in one place for six months to a year. No woman wants to live like that."

He'd learned that the hard way.

"The mountains still call you home. Court Sabrina. Marry her. And I'll sell you that parcel for whatever you've written on that paper."

"You haven't even looked at the offer."

"I told you. Money ain't the issue, son."

Hell. Ask anything else of him and he'd be all over the deal. *But marriage?* "I'm sorry, Mr. Caldwell. I'm not your man."

"Sabrina's all I have left. And you might have noticed, I'm not a spring chicken. I'm seventy-five, and my health ain't what it used to be. But that's between my doctor and me and now you. Sabrina doesn't need to know. Once I'm gone there won't be anyone around to look after her since my head-in-the-clouds son and his wife can't be bothered. I want to see to Sabrina before I'm gone."

The genuine concern in the tired blue eyes yanked at something in Gavin's chest. *Sap. He's playing you like a fiddle.*

"I'm not the man for the job," he repeated.

"I think you are. The fact that you turned me down despite the fact that Sabrina could inherit everything I have only reinforces my opinion. I ain't talked to you more than ten minutes, Gavin Jarrod, but I can already tell you're twice the man your daddy was. He used the land, stripping away whatever got in his way, without thought for anything more than the profit he could make. You, with the way you took care of one good-for-nothing hole in the ground, proved you're smarter. You respect the land and nature."

True. "That's a broad assumption, Mr. Caldwell."

"But a valid one. You'll treat my girl with the same respect."

Gavin backed toward the door. "The answer's still no."

"If you're thinking you can wait 'til I drop dead and buy the property from Sabrina, think again. If I die before she marries I've willed that plot to the National Parks Service."

Damn. The park system would condemn land to get road access to the mine. Jarrod Ridge would end up losing even more property and have to deal with tourists wandering off the path. Their secluded retreat atmosphere would be shattered.

"If you agree I have one more stipulation. I don't want our girl knowing anything about our little agreement. Ya hear? You'll court her like a woman deserves to be courted. She won't marry ya without loving ya. That much I know."

In Gavin's opinion, making a woman fall for him under

false pretenses was about as low as a man could get. How could he respect himself if he pulled that kind of crap? Refusal hovered on his tongue.

"Son, if you want that five acres, this is the only way you're gonna get it. That's my deal. Take it or leave it."

Man, this was insane.

A tap on the door preceded Sabrina returning with a laden tray. Gavin's pulse thudded harder and faster.

Marry her?

There are worse things than being married to a beautiful woman.

This had to be flat-out the craziest scheme he'd ever heard in his life. So why was he still standing here?

If marriage was the only way to get the land back, to succeed where his father had failed and to keep his family from losing even more acreage, what choice did he have? For the good of his family and Jarrod Ridge, he had to accept the deal.

But the marriage would be temporary. Once he returned to his regular job nature would take its course and, aided by his long absences, the relationship would die a natural death—as had all his previous liaisons.

Hell of a way to start a relationship—planning its demise.

But he was attracted to Sabrina and the idea of sharing her bed appealed tremendously.

He'd need an ironclad prenup.

"Can I get you anything else?" Sabrina asked, her suspicious gaze drilling his. The familiar clench of desire fisted in his gut and pounded through his veins.

"This'll do, love," Caldwell answered.

She left the room, her protectiveness of her grandfather clear in her reluctant steps.

Gavin took a deep breath, willing sanity to return and offer him a better option. It didn't. "I'll do it."

Two

Her grandfather had closed the door.

Sabrina couldn't remember any other time in her life when Pops had shut her out of a conversation. She blamed their unexpected visitor—one who couldn't be bothered to make an appointment—for the exclusion.

Gavin Jarrod epitomized everything Sabrina disliked about the soon-to-be-arriving ski season guests. Rich guys like him, with their perfectly tousled hair, flawless faces and gym-buffed bodies swaggered into town like they owned the place. They threw around their money and entitled attitudes, expecting the world to revolve around their wants and acting like the local businesses should kiss their expensively-shod feet and be grateful for whatever crumbs the rich guests threw their way.

Well, not her. She'd had enough of that holier-than-thou behavior throughout school from the wealthy snobs who'd attended the elite private college where her parents had taught.

Those snotty students had made sure Sabrina knew she was not one of them. As if being a professor's daughter made her somehow genetically inferior to someone born to money.

She swished the cleaning cloth over the countertop and tried to ignore the anger and worry making her stomach churn. She knew her grandfather's health wasn't as good as it had been when she'd arrived three years ago. He slept more, ate less and had trouble keeping up with the inn's routine maintenance—a job he used to tackle with enthusiasm. But he wouldn't let her hire anyone to help him. He always claimed he'd get to the tasks, but the to-do list kept growing and the clock ticked down on the upcoming Thanksgiving holiday when the ski slopes would officially open and the guests would arrive— whether the inn was ready or not. Unless a miracle happened, this year the inn wasn't going to be ready.

Was Gavin Jarrod here to try and buy the inn? She couldn't imagine her grandfather handing over the reins, but that day was coming, she realized with a heavy cloak of sadness. She'd hoped—*prayed,* really—he'd let her take over, but a few months ago while cleaning his office she'd come across a pamphlet on his desk on donating property to the historic trust. When she'd asked him about it he'd told her not to worry, he had everything under control. But how could she not lose sleep? If he donated or sold the inn she'd have to find a new home and job.

In the meantime, the only thing she could do was try to help more. She glanced at her sore thumb. Carpentry wasn't her strong suit, but she'd get better with practice.

The sitting room door opened, and footsteps—too sure and firm to be her grandfather's—approached.

"Thanks for the coffee and snack."

Who was Gavin Jarrod and what business did he have with Pops? Reluctant to face the brown, gold-flecked eyes that seemed to see straight through her, she turned slowly. "You're welcome."

"Your coconut cake is probably the best I've ever tasted."

Pleasure sent another blast of heat through her already warm body. She struggled to suppress the reaction. No doubt his charm and flattery combined with his money and looks made it easy for him to coast through life. "It's my grandmother's recipe."

"Henry said you don't have any guests tonight."

Why would Pops volunteer that? "No. Early November is like the lull before the storm."

"It's been the same back at The Ridge ever since the Food & Wine Gala ended. I'm exploring the area restaurants before the tourists hit town. Show me your favorite tonight."

She fought a grimace. He wasn't the first of his kind to assume she could be had as easily as booking a room. "I don't have a favorite, and I've already prepared dinner for myself and my grandfather."

His eyes narrowed. "Henry can serve himself. Let someone cook for you for a change."

Eating someone else's cooking was tempting, but not with Gavin Jarrod or his ilk. She'd been led on by too many rich boys and then dumped when she wouldn't get naked for them or get her parents to give them better grades.

"No. But, thank you." She tacked on the last hastily because she could almost feel the ghost of her grandmother rapping her knuckles for being ungracious and impolite.

His steady gaze continued to drill her. She felt like a butterfly fighting to get free of a collector's pin. "Henry is worried that you don't get out often enough."

Embarrassment bubbled inside her. *Thanks, Pops.* "That's because I don't date."

"Ever?"

"No."

His square jaw dipped. "Are you gay?"

Typical. "Do you assume every woman who turns you down is gay?"

A slow smile curved Gavin's full lips. "Only the ones who ignore the obvious chemistry between us."

So he'd caught that, had he? She hadn't experienced that rush of response since before her husband had died and it had caught her off guard. She had no interest in pursuing it. "There is no chemistry."

The fire in Gavin's eyes told her she shouldn't have challenged him. Two long strides brought him within touching distance. Within *smelling* distance. An outdoorsy, woodsy and clean scent mixed with a hint of something spicy and exotic clung to him.

She stared into his handsome face, alarm prickling the hairs on her nape and arms. He wasn't particularly tall— six feet, maybe a little more—but he seemed bigger in an intimidating, turf-conquering way despite the snowboarder-disheveled hair that should have made him appear easygoing and approachable.

"No chemistry?" He lifted a hand.

Sabrina backed out of reach. "Don't."

"Don't prove you're lying?"

"Calling a woman a liar is a unique way to win points. Does that approach usually work for you, Mr. Jarrod?"

The corners of his eyes crinkled. "You seem like the type who'd appreciate honesty."

"Good deduction. Let's start with what business do you have with my grandfather?"

"I'd be happy to tell you." Gavin's smile broadened, revealing an orthodontist's dream of straight white teeth. "Over dinner."

Sabrina ground her molars in aggravation. How could she

protect her grandfather and the inn without information? "Nice try. The answer's still no."

"Not even if I tell you your grandfather has something I want?"

Warning sirens blared in her head. "What?"

"Join me and I'll tell you."

She really hated being backed into a corner, but she wasn't going to let Gavin have the upper hand.

"Make it lunch." It wouldn't be a date. It would merely be a fact-finding mission.

Those gold-flecked eyes probed hers. "I'll pick you up tomorrow at eleven. Dress warmly. Wear walking shoes."

Without waiting for an answer he brushed past her and exited via the back door.

Dress warmly? Wear walking shoes? What had she gotten herself into? At the sound of the lock catching, the tension deflated from her muscles like air escaping from a balloon.

The creak of a floorboard brought her around. Pops made his way down the center hall, his steps lacking the vigor that had once radiated from him. She tucked her concern away for later and parked her hands on her hips. "What was that about?"

"Jarrod's just being neighborly."

The fact that he didn't look at her when he spoke sent tingles of worry down her spine. "Baloney. What does he want?"

"Can't a body converse with a neighbor?"

"He told me you had something he wanted."

He shrugged. "The Jarrods own half the damn valley. What more could they want?"

When Pops wore that stubborn expression trying to get him to talk was a waste of time, but she didn't believe the just-being-friendly story for one second.

"Pops, why did you tell him I don't go out?"

"You don't."

She shook her head. "You know I'm not interested in—"

"You should be. Your husband died. You didn't."

She flinched at the quick stab of pain. "I'm not ready."

She'd never be ready. She'd given up everything for love, and when Russell had died she'd had nothing left—nothing except Pops and the Snowberry Inn. And now she could lose those.

His shoulders drooped. "When I'm gone—"

"Stop. You know I hate it when you talk that way."

"Hating it doesn't change the facts, girl. You can't run this place by yourself. It's too much. You need someone to help you. Someone who doesn't punch a time clock or resent the long hours."

"I don't have to be married to be a good businesswoman. I can take care of the inn the way you and Grandma taught me."

He shook his head. "You're missing the point, Sabrina. Life is meant to be shared and enjoyed, not endured. If you try to run this place on your own you won't have time for a life. Russell would be the last one to want you to sit on the bench for the remainder of your days."

Sabrina swallowed to ease the grief tightening her throat at the mention of her husband. "I haven't noticed you dating since Grandma passed."

"That's because I already had forty-six years with the best woman God ever created. No one else can measure up. I don't want to lead a lady on only to disappoint her, 'cuz I ain't settling for second-best, and I ain't getting hitched again. I'm too old to change my ways to suit another. You're only twenty-five. Too young to quit living. Tarnation, I have more of a social life than you do."

"I could always join your weekly poker club." Her tongue-in-cheek comment deepened the concern shadowing his eyes.

"Don't sass me, Sabrina. You once talked about traveling the world and filling your home with a passel of young'uns. You still have time for both. But not if you keep hiding here."

The cold ashes of dead dreams stirred inside her. "I'm not hiding. I'm working. And I don't need children to have a full life. As far as seeing the world, I have everything I want right here, Pops. The world's travelers come to us."

"The world might come to Aspen, but hearing about somebody else's adventures secondhand and watching from the sidelines ain't the same as playing in the game."

"I certainly don't have a future with some rich guy who's only counting days until he can leave town."

"He ain't your father. Jarrod might have left town, but he came back the minute his daddy died. Don't try to tell me you're not interested in him. I saw you putting on lip gloss in the hall."

Guilt burned Sabrina's cheeks. "I was working outside trying to fix the loose railings when he interrupted me. My lips were dry."

"Yep, I'm sure that explains why you couldn't take your eyes off each other when you were in the same room."

She didn't bother to deny it. "You don't know him. How can you or I trust him? I've heard you refer to the Jarrods as land-hungry thugs too many times to count."

"That was their daddy. Donald Jarrod turned into a heartless, selfish bastard after his wife died. He gobbled up everything around him, and he rode his kids so hard it's no wonder they all skedaddled as soon as they could. But I know more about the Jarrod boys than you think. I watched 'em grow up. The whole town did. And while those boys might have gotten up to some high jinks like reg'lar kids, they were hard workers and always respectful."

Hard workers? She couldn't imagine anyone with the Jarrods' wealth doing anything that required them to break a sweat except maybe watching the stock market play with their investment portfolios. Jarrod Ridge catered to the wealthiest clients who wanted pampering and spoiling. Their guest list read like a global who's who of famous names, and a day at the resort's spa cost more than she made in a month's salary. She knew that much from the grapevine and the local paper.

But that didn't tell her why Gavin had come here and secluded himself in a room with her grandfather. Was Pops going to donate the inn to the historic preservation society or was he thinking of selling to the Jarrods? "He's not here to buy the inn, is he?"

"He's not interested in the inn."

"Then what?"

"Nothing you need to worry about." But again, his gaze drifted away from hers.

She had to find out what was going on. The only way she'd get her answers was to get as wily as Pops. She wouldn't tell him she'd already been coerced into lunch.

"I'll go out with Gavin if you'll agree to let me hire a handyman to get this place in shape. We're booked solid beginning the Monday before Thanksgiving all the way through mid-March."

His pride obviously ruffled, Pops puffed up his narrow shoulders. "I can handle the chores."

"I'm sure you can. There's not that much to do. But this way you can focus on the important items and let someone else sweat the small stuff."

His eyes narrowed and his thumb jabbed his chest. "You got yourself a deal but only if I get to pick the handyman. And you'll give Jarrod a fair shot. Y'hear?"

"I'll go out with him once. It's up to him to make me want more." And she could safely guarantee that would never happen. She was through with love and all the heartaches that went with it. And she specifically wanted nothing to do with Gavin Jarrod.

The knock on the front door filled Sabrina with dread. She'd rather slam her thumb with the hammer again than go on this outing.

Determined to get this over with, she shrugged on her coat and zipped it to her chin, then marched across the foyer and opened the door. Gavin, wearing a black ski jacket that accentuated his broad shoulders, filled the entry. Her insides did an inexplicable gelatin jiggle thing, and the frosty air sweeping inside did nothing to cool her suddenly warm cheeks.

Okay, so he was attractive. But nothing was going to happen between them no matter what Pops hoped.

Gavin's dark gaze skimmed Sabrina from her barely behaving curls to her scuffed boots. "Bring gloves and a toboggan."

She glanced past him and spotted a Jeep with monstrously large tires in the inn's parking lot. No luxurious Cadillac today. "Where are we going?"

"On a picnic."

Was the man stupid or just into torturing her? "It's forty degrees outside."

"I won't let you get hypothermia."

"And how exactly do you plan to keep me warm? If this is some rich-boy ruse to get physically close you're going to be disappointed."

"It's not. Trust me. I know what I'm doing."

Trust him? Not on her life. She snagged her gloves and hat from the hallstand. "Let's go."

The gold flecks in his eyes glittered with amusement. "Said with the enthusiasm of a woman on her way to have cavities filled at the dentist's office without Novocain."

"Does your ego require me to pretend I'm eager to go out with you? You know I only agreed because you're withholding information."

His grin broadened—like a shark's—at her sarcasm. "You won't regret spending the day with me."

"That remains to be seen. And it's not the day. Just lunch. Two hours, at the most. I have chores to do this afternoon."

His confidence—or was it arrogance?—came through loud and clear in the cocky way he indicated the four-wheel drive vehicle with a sweeping arm and a slight bow. Sabrina traversed the walk, conscious of him looming behind her. He reached past her to open the door. Avoiding contact, she climbed inside the Jeep.

She caught a glimpse of her grandfather's face at one of the inn's windows. Why did he look so serious? He was getting his way. She hoped he appreciated her sacrificing an afternoon of repairs for this. But he'd agreed to hire help, and that would make suffering through the next couple of hours worth it. Resigned to her fate, she buckled her seat belt.

Gavin slid into his seat and started the engine. He turned the car toward Jarrod Ridge. Sabrina sat back and took in the scenery of Aspen's grid of streets. Art galleries, designer clothing and jewelry boutiques and famous chefs' restaurants lined the sidewalks, alternating old-world charm with more modern architecture. For such a small city, Aspen's downtown and the surrounding ski areas brought in a lot of tourists and generated a lot of jobs and revenue. She was lucky to be a part of it. And she didn't want to lose it, but there was no way she could afford to live here without the inn.

All too soon Gavin turned through the resort's arched entrance. She'd never had a reason to come down this road, and her curiosity got the better of her, but before she could catch more than a glimpse of the reportedly ultra-luxurious lodges, Gavin veered off the driveway and onto a dirt track.

"Where does this go?"

"My favorite spot." He shot a short, stabbing, breath-stealing glance her way. She shut down her response. Charming or not, she wasn't interested in him or a bored, rich guy's flirtation.

The track grew rougher and steeper. She gripped the seat and stared out the window rather than at Gavin. The Jeep bounced along until he took a sharp turn around a boulder and stopped on the edge of a small clearing. "We're here."

She swept her eyes across the snow-dappled scene. No picnic tables. Nothing, in fact, except nature. Dirt. Rocks. Trees. "This is it? We're in the middle of nowhere. How far are we from the lodge?"

"Not far as the crow flies, but I wouldn't recommend trying to hike it unless you're a seasoned climber. The terrain is pretty rough."

She wasn't an outdoorsman. She shoved open the car door and cold air gusted inside making her shiver. "Maybe we should eat in the car."

"Coward." He delivered the insult as a challenge, then climbed from the vehicle and walked to the back to retrieve a bulging backpack which he shrugged on. After tugging on her hat and gloves she followed.

When she reached his side he tossed a thick blue blanket at her. "Think you can carry that?"

"Sure." She'd probably need to wrap up in it.

After locking the Jeep he headed down an almost indecipherable trail scratched through the low-growing junipers. Sabrina trudged after him, inhaling the crisp, clean air. This is what Gavin smelled like, she realized. Evergreens and earth and sunlight. An odd combination for a city guy.

"Watch your step," he cautioned over his shoulder as the ascent steepened. "Do you need a hand?"

"I can manage." She hadn't been hiking in ages—not since the summer before she'd run away to get married. Back then her grandfather had had the energy to take her exploring in the mountains around Aspen, sometimes on horseback, but usually on foot. When the inn hadn't been busy her grandmother had joined them. Those carefree days had been some of the happiest in Sabrina's life.

Brushing off the sadness and worry, she studied the green firs, pines and bare aspen trees around her rather than the taut leg and butt muscles flexing in front of her. Gavin probably paid a trainer an obscene amount of money to keep him in shape.

For the next ten minutes she concentrated on her footing and her breathing. Just when she thought her lungs would burst from the unaccustomed exercise he stopped. "This is it."

She scanned the clearing at the base of a rock face, noting the carefully laid fire pit stacked with split logs and surrounded by stones. He'd obviously been up here earlier to prepare for this outing. "There's nothing here."

"That's where you're wrong." He shrugged off his knapsack, removed his gloves and then lit the fire. The dry wood caught quickly. "How much do you know about Aspen's history?"

Sabrina moved closer to the crackling flames even though the climb had warmed her. She shed her gloves to enjoy the heat on her palms. "I know Aspen began as a silver mining town called Ute City in 1879, but I'm sorry to say that's the extent of my knowledge even though I spent most of my summers here while my parents went away on research trips. I only learned enough of the city's history to point the inn's guests in the right direction."

"What kind of research do your folks do?"

She considered dodging the question, but what did it

matter if he knew? "They're university professors back in Pennsylvania specializing in animal science. They're always jetting off somewhere around the globe to study behavior patterns of some critter or another."

"You didn't go with them?"

"They claimed it was safer for me to stay with my grandparents." Personally, she didn't think her parents wanted to be distracted by looking after her when they had much more interesting things like polar bears or penguins in their sights.

He spread out the blanket on an area that had been raked clean of snow then proceeded to lay out an assortment of covered containers, a pair of thermoses, and finally a loaf of crusty bread wrapped in a cloth napkin.

Her instinct was to offer to help, but he'd forced this outing on her, so she let him do the work. Shoving her hands in her pockets, she wandered a few yards from the fire, trying to see what lay beyond the next turn in the path. Even though Gavin appeared occupied with the preparations, she could feel his attention focused on her like an alpha wolf's would be aware of his pack—or his next meal.

He glanced up, finding her instantly and proving her point. "We'll explore after we eat. Lunch is ready. Have a seat."

Skeptical of how she'd enjoy a meal when she was so cold, she returned and eased down onto the blanket, trying to stay close to the fire and in reach of the food but not too close to her unwanted companion.

Gavin Jarrod unsettled her. Being near him made her feel as if she were perched at the top of the highest double black diamond ski trail and teetering on the verge of plunging downhill at breakneck speed. She wasn't an expert skier by any means, and Gavin, like the most advanced slopes, was far out of her league.

"The mining heyday didn't last long, did it?" she asked to change the subject to something less agitating.

His gaze hit hers like a falling tree, knocking the wind from her. "Most of the mines closed down after the Panic of 1893 and by the 1930s Aspen had less than a thousand inhabitants after maxing out at close to fifteen thousand. The region didn't recover until the mid-1940s when it became a designated ski area. Jarrod Ridge weathered it all."

The pride in his voice spurred her own. "So did Snowberry Inn. My ancestors have been here just as long as yours."

"So they have." He indicated the thermoses, giving her an excuse to break the connection his eyes seemed to have forged with hers. "You have your choice of hot coffee, hot chocolate or bottled water. We're having chili for lunch. There's freshly shredded cheddar in that tub, sour cream in this one and raw vegetables and dip in there."

"This is a pretty decent spread," she admitted grudgingly.

"For a guy?" He unscrewed the cap on one of the containers and steam mushroomed into the air. The aroma of the spicy chili filled her nose and her mouth watered.

She shrugged. "For a *rich* guy."

He hiked a brow. "What did you expect?"

She shrugged. "An unimaginative, candlelit meal in some fancy place that doesn't put prices on the menu, has obsequious waiters and a wine list the size of a telephone book."

He studied her, and she couldn't tell from his neutral expression if she'd annoyed him. "If I did that you might think I was trying to impress you."

Was that deadpan humor or was he serious? "You're not?"

He poured the thick chili into a bowl and passed it to her along with a spoon and a mug. "If I were, you'd know it. Eat before it gets cold."

She frowned as she tried to make sense of the conversation and took a bite of the chili. The rich beefy flavor exploded on her tongue. "Mmm. This is good."

"It's one of my older brother's recipes. Before Guy got too big for his britches he used to be a good cook. Now he owns a restaurant and lets others man the stove."

"My compliments to the chef."

He lifted his mug in a toast. "Glad you like it."

"You cooked?" Surely he had a staff at his beck and call at the resort.

"Even rich guys have been known to stir a pot now and then."

Chastened, she broke off a piece of bread, dipped it into her bowl and then ate while she tried to figure out what Gavin wanted from her. There were certainly far more attractive available women in town. Why her? Boredom? Slumming? The inn?

"What brought you back to Aspen?" His question chiseled into her thoughts.

Sabrina chose her words carefully. The full truth tended to elicit either pity or an anti-war tirade, and she wasn't in the mood for either, so she edited. "My grandmother died and Pops needed my help with the inn."

"Planning to stay?"

"Yes."

"What did you do before moving here?"

"Work and school." *Wife.* But enough about her. She shifted on the blanket. "What about you?"

"Work. Travel."

She guessed she deserved the brief response. "Travel to where?"

He shrugged. "Anywhere the job or the mood took me."

That sounded like heaven. She and Russell had intended

to work their way around the country when he'd gotten out of the service, but his death on his last mission had derailed their plans.

The remainder of the meal passed with nothing but the sound of some small animal foraging for food in the background interrupted by an occasional jet overhead. After he'd packed away the dishes he extracted graham crackers, chocolate bars and marshmallows from his backpack along with a couple of skewers.

The ingredients looked familiar. "You're making s'mores?"

"It's a tradition. My brothers and I used to make them whenever we camped here."

An image of him as a gangly kid chipped away at her dislike. "I haven't had s'mores in a long time."

She focused on his hands as he skewered the marshmallows then roasted them over the fire. His weren't the pampered hands of a pencil-pushing millionaire. Small scars marred the tanned flesh and his palms had calluses. The imperfections didn't fit with the Cadillac-driving, Tag Heuer watch-wearing, swaggering image she had of him from yesterday. "What do you do when you're not killing time in Aspen, Gavin?"

"I'm a construction engineer."

She'd been wrong. He wasn't a man of leisure, and an engineer had to be smart despite the evidence to the contrary of his bringing her here to freeze her fanny off. But now that she considered it, she wasn't all that cold with the warmth of the fire in front of her and the outcropping of rocks behind her to block the wind.

But his occupation told her nothing about why he'd be interested in her grandfather or the Snowberry Inn. "Working on what?"

"Bridges, dams, mines, buildings. I go wherever the project sounds the most interesting."

"You love your job." The enthusiasm in his tone gave it away.

"I never wanted to do anything else."

"Then I can see why being grounded here for a year must be hard." He had the world waiting for him.

"I'll survive it." He sandwiched a gooey semi-melted marshmallow and a piece of chocolate between two crackers and offered it to her.

She took it, bit into the crisp crackers and chewed, savoring the rush of memories the sweet treat brought back. She and her grandmother had made s'mores often. "Okay, I have to admit, I was skeptical about your picnic, but this was a good idea. It's beautiful up here."

"It's better at night when you can see the stars." He took a bite of his dessert.

"It's a little late in the season for that with the night temperatures in the single digits." She licked a sticky bit from her lip. "You still haven't told me what my grandfather has that you want."

"This." His gesture encompassed the area around them.

A tiny dot of chocolate clung to the corner of his mouth. She had a weird urge to reach out and wipe it away with a fingertip. Or her tongue. Shocked by the errant thought, she averted her gaze and rescanned the setting rather than focus on that strangely tempting spot. "And what is 'this' exactly?"

"Five acres surrounded by Jarrod territory and a defunct silver mine started by one of my ancestors before Aspen was founded."

When she looked back, the tempting daub of chocolate was gone, thank goodness. "Pops owns this land? But you said something about a poker bet."

"Henry won the plot and the mineral rights from my grandfather fifty years ago. I want both back."

"That's all? Just this land? If he sells it to you, you'll leave him alone?"

He picked up a stick and poked the fire, avoiding her gaze—exactly the way her grandfather had. "Yes."

She didn't believe him. Cradling the now-empty mug of coffee in her hands she searched his tense face. "And what do you want from me? Do you expect me to convince Pops to sell it to you?"

"We've already agreed on the terms."

Something didn't add up. "If Pops has already promised to give you what you want, then why am I here, Gavin?"

Silent seconds stretched between them. "Because I want you, Sabrina Taylor. And you want me, too."

Her stomach swooped and burned in a way that had nothing to do with the spicy chili or the gooey, yummy dessert. Denial galloped in, making her heart pound like stampeding horses. "You're mistaken."

His teeth flashed in a brief, but predatory smile. "One of these days you'll learn I rarely refuse a challenge. Looks like I'm going to have to prove you wrong."

He hooked a hand behind her nape and pulled her forward, covering her mouth with his.

Three

Gavin took advantage of Sabrina's surprise-parted lips to sweep his tongue across the slick surface of hers. Her squeak of protest filled his mouth, but before he could force himself to let her go, her shocked stiffness eased and the hands she'd planted on his chest flexed into his coat, anchoring him. His heart pounded approval.

He hadn't expected a deal with the devil to taste this good, but the combination of sweet dessert, spicy chili and hot woman hit him like a prizefighter's right hook, making his head spin.

God help him, he wanted Sabrina in a way he shouldn't want a woman being forced down his throat as part of a business deal, but they had something between them, and while the chemistry might be temporary, it was damned impressive and worth exploring.

She returned his kiss, tentatively at first, with soft flutters of her lips against his, then with increasing pressure and hunger. Her hand slid upward until her short nails teased the underside of his jaw. Her fingertips were cool against his overheated skin, but her kisses burned hot. He snaked an arm around her waist and tugged her forward onto her knees. She leaned against him, her weight supported on his chest, her hands braced on his shoulders, digging into his muscles.

Cursing the insulating layers between them as their tongues tangled and their breaths mingled, he deepened the kiss, tunneling his fingers into her curls, surprised to find the coils soft instead of wiry. He couldn't get enough. Air or her. His body steamed inside his coat. Skin against skin would be good right about now. He reached for the zipper tab under her chin.

She gasped, pushed his hand away and jerked back, falling onto her butt. Eyes wide with horror, her breath panting as rapidly as his made clouds in the air between them. She scooted away on the blanket and pressed her fingertips to her mouth. "What was that?"

"Proof," was all he could force out. Her taste lingered on his damp lips, making him ache to tug her down on the blanket and cover her body with his.

Her dazed expression morphed into disbelief. "Proof of what?"

His blood slowly drifted north, reviving brain cells her kiss had decimated. "That you want me. And trust me, Sabrina, the feeling is mutual."

Shaking her head, she shot to her feet. "No. You're wrong. I'm not interested in getting involved with you. Or anyone. Take me home, Gavin."

He could argue that her actions contradicted her words, that even now the flush on her cheeks and the rapid rise and fall of her breasts gave away her arousal. But he didn't want to scare her off. Instead, he rose slowly, being careful not to jar the lingering ridge behind his zipper. "Not yet."

"Then I'll walk."

He couldn't let her go. Not with the bargain he'd made. If he did she'd never agree to see him again let alone marry him. And at the moment, marriage wasn't looking like the death sentence it once had.

He caught her elbow. "I don't recommend walking out. It's a long way and it's cold. I brought you up here to show you the mine. Take a look, then I'll drive you back."

She scanned the area as if searching for the mine portal. Or the path to freedom.

Cupping her shoulders, he steered her to the left and pointed. She stiffened in his hold. "The entrance is behind that line of firs. I planted them when I was a teenager to conceal my hideaway."

She shrugged off his hands. "I've seen old mines before. The area is littered with them. I don't need to see another one."

"Even though your grandparents spent time spelunking in this one?"

She bit her lip, curiosity invading her blue eyes, then stomped her feet and shoved her hands into her pockets. "Did Pops tell you that? I mean, I know you said he owned it, but how do you know he or my grandmother were ever here?"

"After I discovered Henry owned the mine I realized the initials I'd found carved into one of the beams were his, and when he told me your grandmother's name was Colleen I guessed the set beside his might be hers."

"Maybe he carved both."

"Come and see. Judge for yourself."

"I could just call him and ask." She pulled out her cell phone.

"You get poor, if any, reception up here."

She checked the phone, frowned, then shoved it back into

her pocket. Her eyes clouded with suspicion. "Is this your version of showing me your etchings?"

Her accusation surprised a bark of laughter out of him. Sabrina was a tough case, and she really didn't like him. He had his work cut out for him to win her over. "I confess I used that trick when I was a dumb kid, but I don't need a cold, dark tunnel and a repertoire of ghost stories to get women these days."

She folded her arms. "And yet here we are. I had given you points for originality with your hearty picnic, but now you tell me this is your old tried-and-true seduction routine?"

Guilty. "This is my favorite place. I wanted to share it with you. Put on your gloves and let me show you a bit of history—your history. *Our* history."

Shifting on her feet, she looked back down the trail, blew out a frosty breath, then snatched up her gloves. "Make it quick."

If she was half as curious as he hoped she'd be, "quick" wouldn't be an option. He still had a lot to learn about his wife-to-be, and the only way to figure out if the old man had hoodwinked him into agreeing to marry a nut-job was to spend time with Sabrina. "Follow me."

He stepped into the adit running horizontally into the side of the mountain and lit the kerosene lantern he kept inside the portal. "Once in a while we get a few bats, but they shouldn't bother you."

She flashed a startled glance at him. "That better not be a cheap trick to get your hands on me again."

Give her points for intelligence. He hid a grin by ducking under a crossbeam. "Guess you'll have to figure that out yourself. Stick close and watch your head. It's a small mine, but I don't want you to get lost."

"Gee, thanks. Should I drop bread crumbs?"

"Not unless you want wildlife to come looking for you."

She gasped and hung back.

"I'll take care of you, Sabrina. Come on."

He was used to the deep shadows cast by the lantern, but she wasn't. Every now and then she jumped and hustled closer to him.

She paused at the first ventilation shaft, looked up into the dark hole and then down and stomped her foot. "I didn't expect a wooden floor."

"A solid surface makes rolling the ore cart out easier. The boards have held up well because it's dry and cool in here. If you've toured larger mines then you know most have tracks, but this was a one-man operation for the most part, although my great-great-grandfather must have had help setting the supports."

She eyed the square-set timbers warily. "How safe are the supports?"

He heard the apprehension in her voice and stopped, making her jerk to a halt just short of colliding with him. The small circle of light forced an intimacy between them. She stared up at him with dilated pupils and parted lips, and the need to kiss her again seized him. With the taste of her still fresh on his mind and mouth, it was difficult to remember to take it slow rather than act on his desires and risk scaring her.

He suppressed the hunger. "I spent countless hours in here as a kid and more as an experienced engineer. The mine is as safe as any mine can be. There are always risks when you're underground."

"There you go trying to scare me again."

"Relax. Short of an earthquake—which is unlikely—you're safe. I've been in here several times since returning home and checked to make sure there aren't any unwelcome visitors hibernating." He hadn't intended that to be a cheap shot, but she startled and shuffled closer.

She scowled. "Cut it out. But I'm warning you, Gavin

Jarrod, if there are any bears or fanged creatures, I'm pushing you into them and running for it while they feast on you."

"Thanks for the heads-up." Her feisty attitude would definitely make their relationship interesting. He led her toward the mine's newest section. "Some mines have steep drops or winzes that go straight down. Our ancestors kept the tunnels relatively level, but there are plenty of drifts to explore."

"Drifts?"

"Dead-end tunnels. The one where your grandfather left his mark is ahead on your right." He lifted the lantern, illuminating a broad beam as they approached the turn. "The depth and shape of the second set of initials is different from the first. It doesn't look like the same person carved the letters."

She stepped closer, brushing against him in the narrow space. He caught a trace of her flowery scent over the earthy smell of the tunnel and his pulse quickened. She peeled off a glove and lifted her hand to trace the letters of the second trio. "CDC. Colleen Douglas Caldwell. You're right. These are my grandmother's initials. She always used to put a little heart like this one after her name."

He had a crazy urge to coil a curl around his finger, but focused instead on why he'd brought her here. "The carvings and this section weren't here when I left for college, and I don't remember seeing them when I came home on school breaks. Your grandparents must have dug this sometime in the last six years."

"My grandmother died five years ago."

The pain in her voice sounded fresh. "You were close?"

Her fingers lingered, then her arm slowly lowered, as if she hated breaking the connection. "She was more of a mother to me during those summer months than mine was for the rest of the year—not that my mother was or is a bad parent. She's just totally absorbed with her Arctic mammals."

"I'm sorry for your loss." He reached into his pocket and dug out his pocketknife then flicked open the blade. Sabrina stumbled back, fear flashing in her eyes. He'd never had a woman be afraid of him before, and he didn't like it.

He offered her the butt of the knife. "Keep the family tradition alive and carve your initials into the beam."

The wariness faded from her face, replaced by a vulnerability that jump-started his pulse and made him want to take her in his arms, but if he did that he was going to kiss her again—and reinforce her suspicions that he was using old tricks on her.

"Thank you. I'd like that." She took the knife from him.

She tucked her tongue into the corner of her mouth as she worked. The gesture was damned adorable. And sexy. Then in the lantern light he caught the glistening of tears brimming in her eyes and rolling down her cheeks, and it hit him low and hard that Sabrina could be hurt by the marriage scheme.

But what choice did he have except to carry on? His family was counting on him.

She had to get rid of Gavin Jarrod, Sabrina decided as he shadowed her to the inn's front door as the sun set. But more immediately, she had to avoid kissing him again.

Guilt and fear intertwined inside her. For a moment up on the mountain she'd weakened and let herself be swept away by the strength of Gavin's arms as he held her and the passion in his kiss as his lips plied hers. She'd taken pleasure in the leashed power of his muscle-packed form against her, the smell of him, the taste of him—all that manly stuff her life had been lacking lately—and her body had awakened with a rush of desire.

In that moment, she'd forgotten Russell.

She'd forgotten how much loving him had cost her, how much losing him had hurt and the vow she'd made while standing at his graveside to never open herself up to that kind of pain again.

Determined to keep her distance from Gavin, she stopped at the door, pivoted and offered her hand. "Thank you for lunch and for showing me the mine."

Eyes narrowed, he studied her extended arm, then searched her face. "You're welcome."

His long, warm fingers closed around hers, but instead of shaking her hand and releasing her, he anchored her in place and bent his head. Her heart sputtered in panic. She ducked at the last second to dodge his kiss, and his lips settled on her temple. She tried to pull away, but he kept her tethered with his strong grip, then he feathered a string of soft branding caresses along her cheekbone. A shudder of awareness shimmied over her. She struggled to clear her head with gulps of chilly autumn air.

"Stop, Gavin," she croaked and pushed against him with her free hand. How could she tell a man that he'd made her feel and she preferred being numb?

Without loosening his grip Gavin slowly straightened. "I'd like to take you out again—maybe to one of those restaurants you described—the ones with no prices on the menu and a long wine list."

She blinked up at him. Was he teasing or serious? His direct gaze held no humor. It held something much more frightening—hunger. Alarm prickled through her followed by a chaser of heat that started at her core and radiated outward, making her skin hypersensitive.

"I really—today was—I'm sorry. No, thank you." She couldn't string sentences together when he looked at her like he wanted to devour her mouth…and then the rest of her.

"I don't give up that easily, Sabrina. We have something worth exploring."

Even though she'd failed in her mission to discover what Gavin really wanted from her grandfather she couldn't risk another outing. Pops was a safer target. She'd work on prying the details out of him. "We don't share anything more than a history of ancestors settling in the same town about the same time."

One corner of his mouth lifted in a sexy half smile. "You love issuing challenges, don't you?"

She wriggled her hand free and hugged her arms around her middle. "That wasn't a challenge. I'm sure you're a nice guy, but I just don't have time for a social life right now. There's too much to do before the season starts. Go play with one of your lodge bunnies."

"I'm not interested in lodge guests. I'm interested in you."

Her stomach flip-flopped at the intensity of his gaze and his low, gravelly tone. She shook her head. "Good-bye, Gavin."

She fumbled behind her for the doorknob, but the door swung open before she could locate the brass orb.

"Don't keep the man out in the cold, Sabrina. Invite him in," her grandfather said.

Denial screamed through her. "Pops, Gavin has to g—"

"Thanks, Henry, I appreciate it." Gavin overrode her objection and moved forward, forcing Sabrina to scramble out of his path. *Now what?*

The three of them stood in the foyer with an odd, expectant tension she didn't understand stretching between them. Sabrina could feel Gavin's and her grandfather's gazes on her. She didn't know what they were looking for and she couldn't come up with an acceptable excuse to escape.

Gavin shifted his attention to Pops. "I'm trying to convince Sabrina to join me for dinner."

Her grandfather nodded. "Good idea. I have a hankering for leftover pot roast, so there's no need for her to cook tonight."

"Pops," Sabrina squeaked in protest. "I've explained to Gavin that I have too much to do getting ready for our guests."

"Not if I hire that handyman you insisted on to help with your to-do list." Pops looked at Gavin. "Know anybody who's skilled with power tools and has a few hours to spare each day over the next three weeks?"

"As a matter of fact, I do. Me."

"No," Sabrina all but shouted on a wave of panic. "We're going to hire someone local. Someone who needs the work." She shot her grandfather a warning look—to which he seemed oblivious.

Gavin shrugged, splaying his big hands, palms up. "I need the work. Not financially, but because I'm going stir-crazy up at The Ridge with nothing to do. We already have a full staff. They don't need me. I'll donate whatever salary you intended to pay to the charity of your choice."

"Well, ain't that nice." Pops sounded far too smug for Sabrina's liking.

"I'd rather hire a local, Pops."

Gavin smiled. "I am a local, Aspen born and bred."

She gritted her teeth. "You know what I mean. There are unemployed people in town who actually need the income."

Pops clapped Gavin on the shoulder. "Glad to have your help. And if you two aren't going out tonight you can stay for dinner. By the time I finish going over Sabrina's list with you, she should have something ready. She's a pretty good cook. My Colleen taught her."

Sabrina wanted to scream. The only thing she wanted to cook up for Gavin Jarrod was food poisoning. "I'm sure Gavin has better things to do."

"My evening's free," the pig-headed rat replied with an innocent expression she didn't buy for one second. "Henry, show me that list, and we'll see what tools and supplies we'll need. I can be at the builder's supply store tomorrow morning as soon as they unlock their doors."

"Sounds like a good plan," her grandfather said before turning and heading for his study with a spring in his step Sabrina hadn't seen in a while.

Having Gavin underfoot for three weeks sounded like a disaster to her, and the glint in his eyes as he smiled at her made it clear he knew he was irritating the daylights out of her—and was loving every second of it. He followed her grandfather. If she'd had her grandmother's cast-iron skillet in hand, Sabrina would have hurled it at his head.

For her grandfather's sake and to get the work done that the inn desperately needed, she would endure Gavin's company. But that was it. There would be no more dates.

And there definitely wouldn't be any more kisses.

"I took Sabrina to the mine," Gavin told Henry as the old man rifled through the slips of paper piled on his desk.

Henry's chin popped up. He examined Gavin over the top of his gold-rimmed bifocals. "Why in tarnation would you do that?"

"She wouldn't go out with me until I bribed her. Is she always that stubborn?"

"If she's strong-willed it's because life's made her that way. Ain't necessarily a bad thing. Reminds me of my Colleen. In my day we called it 'grit,' and we wanted our women to have it. The ones who lacked it didn't last long."

The declaration raised red flags. Gavin had kept Sabrina at the mine for an extra hour, showing her through the tunnels, explaining the mining process and subtly grilling her, but getting information out of her was damn near impossible.

"What made Sabrina tough?"

"You'll have to figure that out yourself. I'm not making it easy for you. Hiring you to help with the inn's as far as I'll go. If you want her you'll have to work to woo her, and I won't lie and tell you it'll be easy. But we agreed to keep the whys and wherefores of this deal between us. You breaking your word already, Jarrod?"

"No, sir. I intend to be as honest with Sabrina as possible and still keep to our agreement. I told her you'd agreed to sell me the land, but not the conditions of the sale."

Caldwell drilled him with a hard stare. "Guess that's fair enough. Once you sign the marriage license, I'll sign the deed."

Henry extracted a piece of paper and passed it to Gavin. Neat, loopy, girly script covered the page. Sabrina's. Gavin scanned down the list. Nothing major. "This won't take three weeks."

"Then you'd better work slow on the chores and fast on Sabrina."

What choice did he have with the winter freeze approaching and the old man's obstinacy? Gavin knew if he didn't seal this deal soon, he'd have to wait until next spring to break ground. Postponing meant staying longer in Aspen, and that wasn't going to happen. For his siblings' sakes he'd stay his year, but not a day more.

The old man chuckled. "Gotta admit, this is gonna be fun to watch."

Four

It was hard to remember a day Sabrina had dreaded as much as she did this one. She shuffled toward the kitchen Wednesday morning, intent on preparing breakfast, leaving it on the buffet and getting out of the way before Gavin arrived.

Last night she'd taken the coward's way out by claiming the necessity of paying bills. She'd put dinner on the table for the men and then retired to her office to pick at her meal at her desk. Avoiding Gavin wouldn't be as easy today.

At the sound of male voices, she stopped abruptly in the back hall. She identified Pops's then Gavin's and her stomach sank. He was already here. She checked her watch. Six-thirty. Pulse accelerating, she backed out. A floorboard squeaked beneath her foot, betraying her presence. She cringed.

"Coffee's ready, girlie. C'mon in," her grandfather called.

Ugh. Trapped. She debated ignoring the summons, but she'd be darned if she'd let Gavin Jarrod think her a coward.

Squaring her shoulders, she fluffed her damp hair, took a deep breath and marched forward.

The men sat at the table, her grandfather with his paper, Gavin with a mug cradled between his big hands. He looked good in a white turtleneck that showed off his tan. His light brown hair looked like a snowboarder's after a lightning-fast run down the mountain. The mussed strands seemed somehow sexy.

No. Not sexy. Messy.

His gaze drifted from her eyes to her mouth and her stomach did a swan dive. Knowing how he kissed and how he tasted changed everything.

No, it didn't. She still wasn't interested.

She gulped. "Good morning."

He nodded. "Morning."

She forced her attention to her grandfather. "You're up earlier than usual for a day when we have no guests."

He shrugged. "No point in lying abed when there's so much to do. You'll want to go over the repairs with Gavin before the two of you head to the builder's supply center."

Aghast, she stared at Pops. "I thought you were going with him."

"Storm must be brewing. M'bones are aching this morning. I'll take it easy today."

She worried more than a little that his aches and pains had worsened in the past year, making it impossible to ignore his physical slowdown. Was he also losing his mental acuity?

All the more reason for her to make sure Gavin Jarrod wasn't trying to pull a fast one on her grandfather and cheat him out of the mine and/or the inn. Hadn't Pops groused on more than one occasion about Gavin's dad, Donald, being a greedy, land-hungry bastard? Were all the Jarrods a bunch of swindlers?

She could feel Gavin studying her and headed for the

coffeepot to avoid letting him see he'd unsettled her. She wanted to escape this excursion, but if she did then Pops would go. A no-win situation. She didn't want to go, but she didn't want Pops and his checkbook alone with Gavin either.

She focused intently on the dark brew streaming into her favorite mug and tried to pretend she couldn't feel Gavin's gaze boring into her back like twin laser beams. The way he always watched her—as if she were a puzzle he couldn't quite figure out—made her nape prickle. She turned toward the sink, reaching for the faucet.

"You won't need to water down your coffee," Pops said. "Gavin made it instead of me."

The territorial invasion made her hackles rise. The man had been messing with her coffeepot.

The perfect excuse to avoid Gavin came to her as she stirred sugar into the liquid. "Your joints are a pretty accurate weather gauge, Pops. Maybe we should postpone repairs until after the front passes."

"No, ma'am," Pops snapped. "You're the one all fired up to get through this list. Best to start now and have spare time at the end than to be pushed to work 'round the clock before our guests arrive."

True, but that didn't make it any easier to work with her new handyman.

"I can go with you," Pops offered grudgingly, "if you're afraid the job's too big for you."

Her spine snapped with indignation. She was practically running the inn single-handedly now. "Do you really believe I can't handle the shopping?"

"I don't know, girlie. The maintenance on this place is a daunting job."

She didn't like the sound of that. "It's a job I love and do willingly. I lack a few skills, but I'm learning every day."

Gavin rose and crossed the kitchen, invading her space and

making her move out of the way. He casually refilled his mug as if he weren't a guest. Pushy bastard. "I borrowed a pickup truck from The Ridge, but it's a single cab. The bench seat will hold the three of us, but it'll be a tight squeeze."

And she'd be sandwiched between the man she loved the most in the world and the one she wanted to avoid at all costs. One who'd stirred up all kinds of dormant feelings she'd prefer to leave sleeping. No more passion for her. No passion meant no pain. She liked it that way.

She tipped her head back to glare at Gavin. "I can do the shopping. In fact, I don't need your help."

"Your van isn't going to carry twelve-foot timber, and I can't loan you the truck because of liability issues."

She clenched her teeth in frustration. Did he have to be logical? "I'll have the order delivered."

"You'd lose several days' work time waiting for the materials."

He had an answer for everything, she fumed silently, and it didn't help that he was right. "Fine. I'll ride with you. Pops can stay here."

Instead of returning to the table, Gavin leaned a hip on the counter right beside her. She scalded her tongue on her first, hasty sip of coffee.

"Did you know our grandfathers were friends?" Gavin asked.

"Best friends," Pops added. "'Til your grandpappy stiffed me with a bum mine. He claimed he'd found silver chunks the size of a goat's head in there, but that was bull."

"I've never found anything that large," Gavin confirmed, "but I still do a little digging and look for a vein each time I come home."

The comment instantly carried her back to the seclusion and intimacy she'd discovered in the mine—not a mental journey she wanted to revisit. She pivoted away. "What would you like for breakfast today, Pops?"

"Y'might want to ask our guest that since you're gonna put him to work."

She bit the inside of her lip. Gavin wasn't a guest. He was a temporary employee and a pain in her backside. "Gavin?"

"Henry's been bragging about your blueberry pancakes. Might as well see if he's all talk."

"And bacon," Pops added without a trace of guilt. "Crisp."

She glanced from man to man. They'd been discussing her? Why? Surely her grandfather wasn't matchmaking? He knew better. And he knew what kind of man she preferred—one like Russell. Generous, smart, loyal and fearless, as an army medic her husband had been willing to put his life on the line and even die for any member of his unit—a point he'd proven by throwing himself on a grenade to save his team.

Egotistical jerks who swaggered around being excessively bossy and sneaky did nothing for her.

She narrowed her eyes on Gavin. He gave her a half smile. "If you don't have the ingredients, I could always take you to breakfast at Jarrod Ridge."

No way. She'd walk barefoot over broken glass to get what she required before she'd have breakfast with him on his turf. It was bad enough he'd forced his presence on her for the shopping trip and chores, but if she wanted to keep her life flowing in the comfortable groove she'd carved for herself since moving to Aspen, avoiding additional one-on-one time with Gavin was a necessity.

"I have everything I need. If you'll excuse me…?" She made a shooing motion with her hand and waited for him to return to his seat at the table before she pivoted back to the pantry.

She'd made the recipe a hundred times, and she assembled

the ingredients by rote. But this time felt different. Her hands were clumsy, her movements awkward as she furiously whisked the egg whites. She realized her frenzied actions were probably giving away more than she intended and deliberately slowed her strokes. She folded the froth to the flour mixture, egg yolks and milk, then ladled the thick liquid onto the hot griddle. The sizzle of butter and batter didn't drown out the sounds of the men's voices as they discussed politics, cars and sports. No matter how hard she tried to block them out, she couldn't escape Gavin's deep, velvety tone.

Escaping gained appeal by the second, and it seemed to take forever to fry the final piece of bacon and pile the last golden disk on the platter. She carried the plates to the table and turned to leave.

"Whoa, girlie. Sit down and eat."

"I need to wash the dishes." She'd done most of the work while cooking, but still—

"I'll do them while you're at the store. You're not hiding in the office like you did last night. These chores were your idea. You need to contribute to the planning."

Her cheeks burned at being called out in front of Gavin, but again, Pops spoke the truth. Refusing to join them would be both ungracious and cowardly. She retrieved her coffee, a carafe of orange juice and three glasses, stalling, she admitted, before returning to the table.

She had no appetite. How could she when awareness of Gavin made her jittery? Russell had never made her uncomfortable. He'd been dynamic and exciting, but he'd never made her feel crowded, breathless or restless.

She forced down a pancake without tasting a bite. She'd almost finished when Pops pulled his checkbook from his back pocket. She smiled at his old-fashioned gesture. Almost everyone she knew used debit or credit cards these days. No one wrote paper checks anymore—except Pops.

"Pops, I can charge our purchase to the inn's card."

"Don't trust that electronic junk. Too many accounts get hacked." He made the check out to the store and signed it, leaving the amount spaces blank, then tore it out of the book. She put down her fork to take it, but he passed the check to Gavin.

Tension snarled in Sabrina's stomach, turning her fluffy pancake into a lead brick. How could Pops be so trusting to a virtual stranger? He'd literally handed Gavin a blank check.

It was up to her to make sure Pops's trust was not abused. She wasn't letting Gavin Jarrod out of her sight until this job was done and he crawled back under the rock from which he'd come.

Sabrina surreptitiously checked her watch, willing time to pass quickly.

"Relax and drink your coffee. The cashier said our order would be ready in an hour," Gavin said from across the table.

She pleated her paper napkin. "I've never known them to take so long to pull an order."

"They only have one guy licensed to drive a forklift working today. Are you sure you don't want something to eat? You barely touched your breakfast."

"I'm fine." With her nerves already stretched to the breaking point, the last thing she needed was more caffeine. As for eating…no way. Her stomach churned like the cement mixer rattling the diner's windows as it thundered down the street.

Gavin's calmness only agitated her more. But then *he* was getting his way. "Dragging me to a restaurant has been your goal all along. Congratulations. You've succeeded."

"And the enthralled expression on your face will make every woman on the sidewalk want my phone number."

His dry sarcasm made her lips twitch. She wasn't going to like him. No way. Not after the past hour.

In a store as large as the one they'd just left, how could there have been such a shortage of space that she and her unwanted shopping partner had repeatedly made contact? But they had. Their hands had bumped over banisters and their hips by the hedge trimmers. Every time she'd turned around he'd been in her personal space, crowding her and not giving an inch.

Her pulse hadn't been in the normal range since she'd climbed into his cramped truck cab, and she'd gasped so many times while shopping that anyone who didn't know her would think she had a chronic lung condition.

How could she get rid of him and still protect Pops? She traced the lip of her mug, then glanced at Gavin. His attention seemed riveted to the movement of her finger, and then abruptly shifted to her face. The impact of his dark gaze swept her into an out-of-control, lighter-than-air feeling that made no sense considering she was sitting in a diner in the middle of downtown Aspen. But she felt as if her parasail had suddenly been caught by a strong gust and she'd been lifted off her snowboard, off solid ground and carried up the mountain.

She snatched her hands from the table and gripped the booth's bench waiting for her breathlessness to ease. She scrambled to find a rational thought. "Did you have to order top-of-the-line everything?"

"The more expensive products have better warranties. If you have problems the replacements are free."

That much was true. But still…the total of the supply bill had been about twenty percent higher than she'd anticipated. Luckily, she'd balanced the checkbook last night and knew the account had enough to cover the amount. The inn wasn't hurting financially yet despite some zero occupancy days, but it was the principle of Gavin being so free with someone else's money that bothered her.

She sipped her unwanted coffee, grudgingly admitting the brew he'd made this morning was better than the trendy diner's—maybe even better than hers, and she prided herself on making great coffee for the inn's guests.

So the man made decent coffee. Big deal. That wasn't a reason to keep him around.

"What do you want from my grandfather?"

"I told you. The mine and the acreage surrounding it." He sounded sincere, but the way his eyes turned guarded and he tensed ever so slightly contradicted his words.

With almost fifty years between him and Pops, the men's sudden friendship seemed unnatural and calculated. Gavin had to be up to something. That blank check he'd managed to get from Pops spoke volumes. There had to be more. She just didn't know what yet, and the only way to figure out his agenda was to get to know him better. Not a project she relished.

What made Gavin Jarrod tick? "Where do you live when you're not here?"

"I divide most of my time between Vegas and Atlanta."

"Why two such different places?"

"Because Vegas is where my brother's hotel is located and Atlanta is close enough to the Appalachian Mountains for hiking and river rafting and has a major airport hub."

"You're an outdoorsman?" The breadth of his shoulders implied as much.

"Yes."

"A hunter?"

"I shoot nature with a camera these days, although I have nothing against putting food on the table through hunting."

Good answer. She'd have to find something else to dislike about him—other than that he was rich, he'd forced his company on her and she didn't trust him. As if that weren't enough.

"What makes you think you're qualified to be our handyman? Aren't construction engineers pencil pushers?"

"I'm a hands-on manager. I work with my team, and I worked part-time construction jobs during college."

He worked construction? That might explain the faded scars on the backs of his hands. So much for proving him unqualified for the job. "Didn't your father pay your bills?"

"He paid tuition, and for that I had to come back and work at The Ridge every summer. But during the academic year I earned my own wages rather than answer to him on how I spent my money."

So maybe Gavin hadn't lacked responsibilities the way so many of her parents' wealthy students had. "Why engineering?"

"I like figuring out how things work and finding ways around obstacles that others consider impossible. What about you?"

She startled. "What about me?"

"Did you always want to manage the inn?"

She bit her tongue on the automatic no. In high school all she'd cared about was getting as far away from her parents and their stilted, judgmental university community as she could. She'd had no grand goals beyond escaping. Initially, she'd been drawn to Russell because he'd been everything academics were not—big, brawny, into action more than higher learning. He also wanted out of their small college town, and he'd had a plan to achieve his getaway.

She'd fallen head over heels in love with him and ended up pregnant. Her parents' ultimatum—terminate the pregnancy or get out of their house—had left her with no choice. She and Russell had eloped on her eighteenth birthday—just days after her high school graduation. She'd planned to be a good military wife and raise Russell's babies. But that hadn't happened.

She pressed a hand to the empty ache in her belly, then blinked to chase away the past. "Does it matter? I'm where I'm needed right now, and I'll never let my grandfather down. Nor will I let anyone take advantage of him."

"What would you do if your grandfather sold the business?"

Alarm raced over her. She'd come to love making a warm, welcoming home away from home for their visitors, the way her grandmother had always done for her. She couldn't imagine doing anything else now, nor did she have the qualifications for anything else. "He wouldn't do that. He knows I love Snowberry Inn."

Pops knew the inn was her refuge, the one place she'd always felt wanted and loved regardless of her choices. But she'd seen that blasted pamphlet and she had her doubts. However, she wasn't giving Gavin Jarrod that information.

His brown eyes searched her face. "What if you marry someone who lives elsewhere?"

"I won't."

"You sound certain."

"I am." She'd done that before, and during her four-year marriage she hadn't seen Snowberry Inn or her grandparents. Russell had been stationed in North Carolina, too far from Aspen to drive the distance in their old car, and she'd been too proud to tell her grandparents she couldn't afford the airfare for a visit. During that time her grandmother had died, and Sabrina hadn't been able to say good-bye. She'd had to borrow money from Russell's friends to come to the funeral because her own parents wouldn't loan it to her.

Time to change the subject. "Why did you leave Aspen?"

His face hardened. "My father was determined to turn us into clones of himself."

"And that was a bad thing?"

"Yes. He was excessively controlling. But I escaped. We all did. Until now." Anger flattened his lips into a thin line.

Demanding parents and a desire to escape were two things they had in common. Her perfectionist parents had never forgiven her for failing to meet their standards. They'd considered her an embarrassment and she hadn't spoken to them in years.

But this wasn't about her. "What about your mother?"

He focused on the mug cradled in his big hands. "She died from cancer when I was four. I barely remember her."

Her mother may not have been the milk-and-cookies type, but she'd always been there at least physically…until Sabrina had needed her the most. "I'm sorry."

"It happens. If we finish the repairs on time you'll have a few days to relax before your guests arrive. What will you do with the time?"

Relax? What was that? She'd been so busy doing her job and picking up Pops's slack that she couldn't remember the last day off she'd had. She shrugged. "I don't know. I used to ride horses on the trails, but—"

She bit off the thought. She didn't want to imply the inn wasn't financially secure to a shark like Gavin. Besides, her hobbies were none of his business.

"I didn't see any horses."

Busted. "Pops sold them after my grandmother died because they were too much work for him to manage alone and they reminded him of her."

"We have horses at The Ridge."

They had everything at the resort. "Goody for you."

"That was an invitation, not a boast. If you want to ride I'll take you."

Tempting—except for the part about having to endure his company. The man irritated her like a blister forming on her heel halfway through a long hike. She just knew he wasn't going to get better as time passed. "Thanks, but no."

She had to get out of there and away from him even if all she did was freeze her fanny off with an hour of window shopping. The waitress provided an opportunity when she strolled by with the coffeepot. Sabrina caught her attention with a wave. "Excuse me, could I get the check, please?"

"Sure." The woman peeled off the ticket and laid it on the table.

Sabrina reached for the bill, but Gavin moved a split-second faster. Her hand landed on the back of his. The contact uncorked something in the pit of her stomach, releasing a flood of fizzy heat that gushed through her like froth from an ineptly opened bottle of champagne.

She snatched back her hand, severing the connection, but her palm continued tingling, and her body bubbled with excitement she never expected or wanted to experience again. "Hey, I was going to pay that."

He shook his head. "I'll get the coffee. It's the least I can do considering you're going to be feeding me three meals a day for the next three weeks."

Horrified, she stared into his dark eyes in dismay. "Says who?"

"Henry. He actually offered me room and board, but I already have a place to stay."

Thank God for small favors. "I'm sure the food will be more to your liking at Jarrod Ridge."

"I've been eating gourmet food for months. It's time for a change. I'm looking forward to your good home cooking."

At that moment she didn't like her grandfather very much. What had he gotten her into?

Five

Caldwell's old bones had been right, Gavin concluded as a cold gust of wind cut through his turtleneck, chilling the sweat he'd worked up while unloading the building supplies from the truck bed.

He monitored Sabrina's progress as she carefully picked her way down the brick sidewalk through the snow that had begun feathering down five minutes ago. The stubborn woman had insisted on helping him empty the truck despite the worsening weather. And while he admired her grit, as Henry called it, Gavin didn't want her doing any heavy lifting or slipping and cutting herself on the pane of glass she carried toward the porch. If that made him a male chauvinist too bad.

After he stacked the last two gallons of paint inside the storage closet he grabbed his coat from the railing where he'd tossed it then let himself into the warmth of the cozy, good-smelling kitchen. The kitchen at Jarrod Manor had never had this welcoming atmosphere.

The glass pane lay on the table, still in its brown paper wrapper, but there was no sign of Sabrina. He caught the tap of her boots down the hall as he hung his coat on a peg by the back door, shed his gloves and mentally shuffled the chore list. Having weather change a timeline on a job was nothing unusual for him, but usually there were tens of thousands of dollars in penalties at stake. This time the delay was a reward rather than a punishment because it worked in his favor.

Sabrina returned. "Pops is napping."

Her discarded knit cap had ruffled her curls, giving her a sultry, just-out-of-bed look that contrasted with her reserved expression. She'd shed her outerwear giving him another chance to appreciate her lean curves in a body-skimming sweater, this one a pale blue that accentuated her eyes. Her gaze met his and he experienced a now-familiar punch to the solar plexus.

"Go home, Gavin. We can't work in the snow."

She wasn't getting rid of him that easily. If the only thing they had going for them was chemistry, then he intended to exploit it shamelessly to get what he wanted. "We can't paint when it's snowing. I'll start with replacing the window."

Her breath hitched. Wrapping her arms around her middle, she briefly glanced away. "That can wait."

"It's the quickest job on the list, and with the temperature dropping it makes sense to fix the broken glass rather than lose heat. Show me which room."

She pinched her bottom lip between her teeth and shifted on her feet. "Pops can do it. Or you can tell me how and I will. It's something I need to know anyway."

"It's easier to show you. Sabrina, I'm here to work. I can either get on with it, or I can spend the afternoon sitting in the kitchen watching you cook and waiting for the weather to clear enough for me to tackle another job."

Wide-eyed horror morphed into resignation in her features. "This way."

He'd never encountered anyone so determined not to like him, and he had to admit the novel experience wasn't an enjoyable one. He picked up the glass, points and glazing compound and shadowed her down the hall instead of upstairs as he'd expected. He took the opportunity to enjoy the angry sway of her hips. She had a nice butt—slender, but with just enough meat on it for a man to grip.

She paused, puffed out a breath and then pushed open a door and motioned him to go ahead. He stepped through the doorway. A subtle, but unmistakably familiar scent filled his nose and stopped him in his tracks. Sabrina's cinnamon, vanilla and flowers scent. This wasn't a guest room.

"This is your room," he stated.

"Yes."

His attention shot to the bed—a bed they would share in the near future because, damn it, he would not fail. He couldn't wait to see her hair spread across those pristine white pillows and feel her naked body against his beneath the old-fashioned quilt. He might even shove one of those prissy lace pillows under her shapely behind to improve the angle when he drove into her. The pressure in his groin increased and his pulse pounded in his temple.

He exhaled and examined the rest of the space, searching for clues about his mysterious bride-to-be. The furnishings were traditional and uncluttered, but feminine nonetheless with white painted furniture and a mostly white décor dotted with pastel shades. The only thing that didn't fit the pale color scheme was the U.S. flag in its triangular glass and dark cherry wooden case sitting on a desk in the corner.

He wouldn't have pegged her as the patriotic type.

A picture frame rested on each bedside table. Henry and a woman, presumably Colleen, smiled in the photo Gavin could see from his position by the door. The angle of the other concealed the subject. Intent on seeing who else Sabrina kept by her bed when she slept, he stepped deeper into the room.

Sabrina moved between him and his goal. "The broken window is in my bathroom. That way."

Rather than reveal his curiosity, he headed in the direction she indicated. She followed him. Her bathroom seemed to shrink in size with the pair of them in it. They stood within touching distance, and he was tempted to reach out and stroke the smooth, flushed skin of her cheek. But she seemed on edge. There was a time to make a push for the finish line and a time to maintain the current pace. This was the latter.

Rather than moving in for kiss number two prematurely and risking spooking her, he scanned the work space. A white claw-foot tub with brass feet sat in one end of the room. His mind instantly filled with images of Sabrina naked and wet with her damp dark curls streaming over the rounded tub edge as she waited for him there. His heart pumped faster.

Hoping to derail the train of heat steaming south, he averted his gaze to the vanity which, like her bedroom, lacked the clutter of makeup, perfumes, toiletries and junk the women he'd known in the past deemed necessary for life.

She pointed to the window. "I'm not sure what broke the glass. A bird, maybe. I didn't find one outside."

A diagonal line, patched with wide clear tape, split the pane. But her rushed speech interested him more than the cracked glass. Why was she so uneasy around him if not for the sexual chemistry? She might deny it, but she felt it.

"Should be a simple repair. I'll talk you through it."

She backed a quick step. "No. Go ahead. I'll leave you to it."

He caught her hand and she gasped. "I thought you wanted to learn how?"

Her gaze flicked to his, then away. A line formed between

her brows. She tugged at her hand and he let her smooth fingers slide through his. The rose of her cheeks darkened. "I—I need to start lunch."

"This will only take a few minutes. We can remove the sash and work inside rather than tackle the job from outside. It will take a couple of extra steps, but you can handle them."

"I'll learn another time, and I'll close the door to keep the cold air from sweeping into more than this room." She left hurriedly, the door snapping close behind her.

More curious now than ever, Gavin let her go. There was no doubt his touch affected her as strongly as hers did him, but she was resisting. The question was why?

He quickly finished the simple job, then gathered the broken glass and tools and returned to her bedroom, determined to see whose face she looked at when she laid in bed.

The photo frame was gone. Sabrina must have moved it.

What did she have to hide? It was imperative that he uncover her secrets and get on with his plan.

Sabrina tried to be as quiet as possible while washing the lunch dishes, but no matter how hard she strained, the men's voices didn't carry clearly enough from the living room for her to make out their words.

Eavesdropping! How low was she going to have to go to get rid of Gavin Jarrod?

She shouldn't leave Pops alone with him, but until she made sense of her jumbled thoughts, she had no choice, and washing up was her first break away from Gavin's intense scrutiny since he'd returned from fixing her window.

Having him in her bedroom had felt like an invasion—but in an agitating way, not a repulsive one. Her skin had flushed and her pulse and respiratory rates had increased.

Only because you haven't had any man other than Pops in your bedroom since Russell.

Right. She'd been uncomfortable, not anything else. She definitely had not been turned on.

When Gavin's gaze had looked toward the flag, then moved on to Russell's picture, shock quickly followed by panic had seized and chilled her. She used to end each day looking at the flag and remembering her husband had been willing to die for a cause he'd passionately believed in. Every night before she'd closed her eyes she'd told the image of Russell's beloved face good-night.

When had she stopped? She couldn't remember.

Guilt poured over her. Shaken and weak, she'd hidden the photograph because she couldn't bear Gavin asking about Russell. And he would, the nosy bastard. She hated that she'd been so rattled she hadn't even been able to stay and learn basic window repair. How could she take care of the inn if she didn't tough it out?

And then Gavin had watched her throughout lunch with that wolf-like predator's awareness of his. Her nerves had stretched to almost the breaking point as she'd waited for him to voice the questions in his eyes and rip the scabs off barely healed wounds. But he hadn't. Instead he and Pops had discussed the dam Gavin had built in Namibia. If she'd been less tense she would have been fascinated by the stories Gavin told of his adventures. He'd worked in places she'd only dreamed of seeing and done things she couldn't even begin to fathom. It must be amazing to look up at a massive dam or bridge and know you'd had a part in its creation.

Pops shuffled into the kitchen, followed by Gavin. The men headed for the coatrack.

She quickly dried her hands. "Where are you going?"

"Henry wants me to take him to the mine," Gavin answered.

No. "But it's snowing."

"It stopped an hour ago and we checked weather radar. The

next band of snow won't move through for a couple of hours." Gavin helped Pops with his coat.

She scrambled for excuses. "The ground will be slick."

"I'll drive him as close to the mine entrance as possible," Gavin replied in a deep, patient tone that made her want to scream. "With the forecast we have we won't be able to make the trip later in the week."

If she couldn't make the lug head see reason, she'd work on Pops. She turned to her grandfather. "What about your aches?"

"They've eased a might since my nap. The exercise will do me good. Might even loosen me up."

She couldn't let them go alone. Gavin had already gotten a promise to sell land and a blank check. No telling what else he would wheedle out of Pops. "I'll go with you."

"We're taking the pickup," Gavin warned.

She smothered a grimace. That would put her in the sandwiched-between-two-men position she'd fought so hard to avoid this morning. "Fine."

Gavin held out her coat, leaving her no choice but to turn her back and let him assist her. She shoved her arms into the sleeves and before she could step away he scooped his hands under her hair to pull it free of her collar. His fingertips grazed her nape. A shiver of awareness trickled down her spine.

Startled, she jumped out of reach. She was not attracted to him. Absolutely not. She wouldn't let herself be. She had too many good reasons to dislike and distrust him.

"Pops, wouldn't you prefer your beaver hat?"

"B'lieve I would." He shuffled toward his bedroom.

Sabrina waited until he was out of earshot, then scowled at Gavin. "The climb will be too much for him."

"He can handle it if I take it slow and stop to show him points of interest along the trail." He kept his voice at the same low volume as hers.

"Gavin—"

"He needs to do this and you need to let him." His firm I'm-the-boss tone warned her not to argue. But that wasn't going to stop her from trying to protect Pops.

"He doesn't have to do it today. He can wait until it's warmer."

"Today is the anniversary of the day he and your grandmother carved their initials into the beam. He claims it's the last time they were happy together before her pancreatic cancer was diagnosed. He wanted to go alone, but I insisted on tagging along."

Sabrina's heart clenched and her anger deflated. Could Gavin be a complete ass if he were this considerate of Pops?

"I didn't know about the anniversary. He's never said anything before. In fact, they never told us about the diagnosis until close to the end. I guess I should thank you for insisting on going."

He snagged her knit cap from the peg and tugged it over her head. The intimate gesture startled her and made her chest tight, but she couldn't move away since he still gripped her cap.

"Sabrina, I like your grandfather. You have nothing to fear from me as far as he's concerned."

Gavin looked and sounded sincere—and she wanted to believe him—but there was too much at stake to risk being wrong. "You'd better not be lying."

"I don't lie." He slowly trailed his knuckles down her neck and then his palms over her shoulders, her arms. His fingertips raked along the back of hers, making her jump at the jolt. *Static electricity. That's all it is.* He ended the contact seconds before Pops entered the kitchen.

With her pulse banging wildly in her ears, she trailed the men to the truck and reluctantly climbed into the middle of the bench seat. Gavin slid in beside her. His big body pressed hers from knee to shoulder and not even several layers of clothing could block the heat radiating from him. Her skin tingled. Her heart skipped. Awareness pooled in the pit of her stomach, heavy and hot. She wanted out of this vehicle, and yet she couldn't avoid this excursion and still protect Pop.

Time seemed to crawl as they crossed the valley and ascended the ridge with each bump in the road making her burn from the friction of Gavin's hard male body chafing against hers. Relief surged through her when Gavin finally parked the truck. She jumped out of the cramped cab as soon as Pops was out of her way and took a deep, sobering breath. But a nagging part of her noticed and missed the warmth Gavin had provided.

Gavin took a different path than the one he'd hiked with her last time. They hadn't gone a hundred yards before she noticed her grandfather's raspy, rapid breathing. Before she could say anything Gavin stopped. "This is the best view of the valley. If I ever decided to return to Aspen for good, I'd build a house here."

Pops leaned against a rock. "You could be right. I can see the inn and Colleen's favorite spot by the river."

The sadness in Pops's voice tugged at Sabrina's heart. She hooked her hands through Pops's elbow, offering support. She ached over losing Russell, but she'd only had him for a fraction of the time her grandparents had been together. How would it feel to lose someone who'd shared almost a lifetime with you? She didn't want to know because she didn't think she could survive it. Would she always ache for Russell the way her grandfather did for her grandmother?

The old anger stirred. She only half-listened as the men made small talk about the city's history as if they'd known each other for years. She'd wanted the rest of her life with Russell and she'd been robbed of it. He'd sacrificed his life so others could return to their wives. He'd chosen his men over her.

When Pops caught his breath, Gavin continued up the path only to stop again at the first sign of Pops struggling and point out some odd rock formation. She was both impressed and appalled at the smooth way Gavin manipulated her grandfather. This consideration was the last thing she'd expected of him, and if he hadn't warned her what he'd planned she never would have guessed each pause in their trek was deliberate and not incidental. But that he did so without giving a clue to his motive worried her. How else could he fool her—and Pops?

When they finally reached the clearing her grandfather tramped ahead of them toward the mine entrance.

She held back with Gavin. "That wasn't the way you brought me the other day."

"You could handle a more strenuous ascent."

The rat bastard. "You had me huffing and puffing and sweating just for fun?"

"The tougher trail is more picturesque, but I doubt Henry could handle it."

He was right on both counts. Her anger died quickly. She turned to follow her grandfather. Gavin's big hand curled around hers holding her back and making her wish she'd taken time to put on her gloves.

"Give him a few minutes alone."

He had to stop touching her. Each time he did, something inside her fanned an ember she didn't want rekindled. She tried to pull free, but he held fast and stuffed his hand, along with hers, in his coat pocket. His body emitted heat like a roaring fire. "You left your gloves in the truck. Your hands are cold."

So she had. "I can get them."

"No need. We won't be here that long." His fingers laced through hers, pressing her knuckles against his abdomen and narrowing her focus to his flesh against hers, his calluses against her palm, his height looming over her. "Who hurt you, Sabrina? Who made you so wary?"

Her breath caught. "No one. No one hurt me. I'm fine."

"Yes, you are fine, quite beautiful, in fact." The words should have sounded like a cheesy pick up line, but the sincerity in his eyes held her transfixed. He lifted his free hand and stroked her cheek. Despite the cold, she felt flushed and too hot in her down coat. His proximity messed with her head, making her slightly dizzy. Tension stretched between them.

Back away.

But then his gaze dropped to her mouth and it was as if her feet had grown roots anchoring them in the hard ground. Her stomach fluttered. He bent and she gasped in surprise, then his lips settled over hers with a brush, a nudge, a sip. The heat of his tongue swept her bottom lip and a shower of sparks rained over her. He cradled her head in his palm, holding her captive as he ravaged her mouth with hot, hungry kisses.

She needed to push him away, but he tasted so good, like the mint chocolate chip cookies she'd served for dessert and like…Gavin. She didn't mean to kiss him back. But somehow, her tongue twined with his. Somehow she moved closer until his hard chest supported her. He released the hand he held captive in his pocket to wrap an arm around her waist and pull her even closer.

Excitement coursed through her, making her feel alive and womanly and desirable—a trio she hadn't experienced in far too long. A combination that had brought her nothing but pain. A sobering chill rushed over her.

She jerked free, backing up one step, two. Her heavy breaths fogged the air between them. "I don't want you to do that again."

"When was your divorce final?"

The question blindsided her. "I'm not divorced."

His eyes narrowed. He lifted her hand. "But you're not still married. You don't wear a ring."

She yanked her hand free and debated telling him to mind his own business. But maybe a dose of the truth would scare him away. "My husband was an army medic. A hero who died saving his team in combat."

Gavin's jaw shifted. "That was his funeral flag on your desk and his picture on the nightstand."

"Yes."

"How long ago?"

"Three years."

"And you're not over him."

"I'll never be over him, Gavin. You never forget a love like that."

"You can't move forward when you're living in the past, Sabrina."

"Maybe I don't want to move forward." Because forgetting the past meant opening her heart to that crushing pain again.

He was competing against a damned saint, Gavin realized. No wonder Caldwell had to bribe someone to woo his granddaughter. The old geezer had deliberately set an unattainable goal. Had Henry known all along that Gavin didn't stand a chance of winning?

The hell you don't.

Gavin wanted Sabrina more than ever—not just for the mine or because he liked her protective lioness attitude toward Henry, but because the passion she ignited inside him promised to be stronger than any he'd experienced before. Convincing her to test that passion would be a challenge, but he liked nothing better than tackling obstacles. He'd built his professional reputation on making a success out of projects others deemed impossible.

Peeling off his gloves, he stomped the light dusting of snow off his boots and knocked on the kitchen door Thursday morning. Caldwell opened the door and glanced past him. "Bringing out the big guns, ain't you?"

"Yessir."

"C'mon in and pour yourself a cup of coffee. Sabrina will be in momentarily."

"Thanks, but I have a thermos of coffee in the carriage along with breakfast. I hope you don't mind if I kidnap her for an hour or two."

Henry raised his mug and smirked. "Good luck with that."

"You could have warned me about her husband."

"And have you quit before you started? Now that would spoil the fun, wouldn't it?" The old man's eyes twinkled with mischief.

"Glad I can entertain you."

Sabrina's soft tread carried down the hall. Gavin saw her before she spotted him. The softness of her face before her expression turned guarded had his heart slamming hard against his rib cage. Sabrina Taylor was definitely worth the battle.

She glanced from him to her grandfather and back, her wariness palpable. "Good morning."

"Gavin here has a surprise for you."

"What?" Suspicion laced the word and narrowed her eyes.

"A carriage ride," Gavin told her.

Her lips parted. Interest flickered across her face before she shut it down. "It's snowing."

"It's barely coming down. I have blankets, coffee and breakfast waiting in the rig."

She brushed past him, heading for the window. The gentle bump of their shoulders aroused him like a damned schoolboy getting his first peep at a girl's panties. If he ever— *When* he got her into bed, they were going to generate enough heat to melt the snowcaps surrounding the valley.

She looked over her shoulder at him. Excitement pinked her cheeks and sparkled in her baby blues. "I shouldn't. Pops—"

"Go on, girlie. I'll fine for a few hours. We both know how much you miss the horses."

Biting her lip, she hesitated. Outside the horses shifted and the tinkle of sleigh bells carried inside. He could feel her excitement, sense her indecision, and decided to give her a nudge. "If you want to see the sun rise over the mountains we need to leave now."

"Go, Sabrina, before the road gets slick. He's got wheels on the thing, not runners. Time's a-wastin'."

Gavin observed her changing expressions, and it was a toss-up whether he'd win or lose this round. He'd never met a woman more difficult to decipher.

She huffed out a breath. "Just a quick ride."

Victory pumped through his veins. One step closer to his goal.

Six

She needed to end this Christmas card moment *now,* Sabrina decided as the carriage turned the corner and the inn came into view. But telling herself to snap out of the romantic fantasy Gavin had created with his horse-drawn tour of the city at sunrise and doing it were two different things. She adored horses and buggy rides—thanks to her grandmother.

Warm and toasty despite the frosty temperatures, she snuggled deeper into the fur blankets. Gavin had plied her with hot coffee, fresh beignets and stories about growing up in Aspen, and sometime during the past hour the steady clip-clop of the horses' hooves and the quiet tinkling of the bells on their harnesses had combined with the light drifting snow and the crisp start of a new day to blur the line between reality and fantasy.

"You have good hands," she offered grudgingly.

He shot her a look filled with sexual intent and the fire in his dark eyes nearly roasted her.

She gulped. "I meant you're good at this carriage-driving thing. Your grip is steady but firm on the reins. My grandmother always said good hands were the mark of a good horseman."

"My father made us work a variety of jobs. I drove the carriages when I had the chance."

"What other jobs did you have?"

"We did whatever needed doing. Dad wanted us to learn the resort business from the bottom up."

Once again, Gavin blew her preconceptions out of the water. Could he truly be that different from the spoiled men who'd attended the college where her parents taught? "You were good with Pops yesterday. How did you know how to handle the situation? Every time I try to talk to him about Grandma he gets ornery."

"I've learned from experience with friends and co-workers who've lost loved ones to listen if they want to talk and give them space and privacy to grieve when they need it. Men don't like to share their tears."

When he said insightful things like that it was difficult to believe he was scheming to steal the inn from Pops. In fact, at the moment she actually liked Gavin. And that wasn't good. Her guard was down, and she needed to keep a clear head around him. Being with him threatened the inner peace she'd fought so hard to find. But as long as they stayed out in the open nothing could happen.

He guided the horses into the inn's driveway and then steered the carriage toward the barn. She straightened, letting the fur blanket slip. "Where are you going?"

"Henry's letting me keep the horses in your barn while I'm working here. This pair is good for riding as well as pulling the carriage. You miss riding. So do I. We'll ride together."

No. No. No. "I don't have time to ride."

"You have to make time for the things that matter. Besides,

Henry likes watching you. He says you and your grandmother rode together."

Making it a request from Pops made it impossible to refuse. "She's the one who taught me to ride. Her horses were her babies."

He climbed from the carriage and opened the barn's double doors then returned. The coach rocked as he resettled himself in the seat, his body nudging hers and bumping her heart rate right off the charts, then he clucked to the mares, driving them inside.

The barn smelled different. Instead of dust and disuse, Sabrina smelled fresh hay, shavings and oats. She scanned the stalls as she descended. Two of the four had been prepared. "When did you do this?"

Gavin made closing the heavy sliding doors look easy when she knew it was anything but. She grunted and groaned and had to put her entire body weight into it when she opened them. "Henry and I cleaned up after we returned from the mine."

She'd wondered where the men had gone. "Usually Pops naps in the afternoon."

"He naps because he has no sense of purpose. He needs to feel useful," he said as he began unhitching the harness from the horses.

Without the pale sunlight the shadowy interior created an intimacy she didn't want—not while she battled this push-pull thing between them. "But the inn's chore list—"

"Is beyond his capabilities at the moment. He's not ready to admit it yet." One corner of his mouth lifted in a half smile that made her stomach flutter.

"Mucking stalls is too much for him."

"I had him clean the tack room while I did the heavy work."

His consideration surprised her yet again. How could he

be a swindler? She automatically helped him remove the tack from the horses. Her fingers fumbled with the once familiar task of slipping pliable leather through buckles. Gavin, she noted, did not fumble. After they finished and the gear had been hung on the wall, he handed her a brush. She caught herself watching him, specifically his hands, and unconsciously matching his rhythm as she stroked the bristles over the mare's glossy hide.

Would his hands be as gentle on a woman?

She pushed the disturbing thought aside. Gavin was as good with the horses as he was with her grandfather. But was it an act? A means to an end? Or was he the real deal? Evidence said he was no stranger to hard work, but her years of experience with men of his ilk said otherwise.

She needed to focus on something besides his positive attributes. "So your twin brothers, Blake and Guy, are a year older than you, and Trevor is a year younger?"

"Yes." He bent over to clean his horse's hooves and her attention zeroed in on his backside. Tight, firm, with enough muscle development to keep it from being flat.

Gavin straightened. She pried her gaze away and kept it focused on the dust motes dancing in the murky light while he tended her horse's hooves. Then he led the bay mare he'd been grooming into the first stall. She led the sorrel into the second and latched the door. The slurp of the horses at the water buckets broke the silence.

Sabrina cleared her throat. "Are you and your brothers close?"

He shrugged. "Close enough."

"Then there's Melissa and…Erica Prentice? But she's not a Jarrod, right?"

"We share the same father, but he never acknowledged Erica when he was alive."

The bitterness in his voice caught her attention. "Don't you like her?"

"Erica's nice enough."

"But?"

He pitched the brushes into a caddy. "My father had an affair immediately after my mother died."

"You think he forgot her, and you're angry that he moved on."

"I don't care."

But he did. It showed in every stiff line of his body as he carried the caddy and blankets to the tack room.

She followed him inside. The smell of Lexol brought back memories of spending hours in here cleaning and oiling saddles and bridles. A small window filled the room with diffused light.

"Gavin, maybe he simply needed someone to prove he hadn't died with her."

He dropped the blankets on the sofa. "Is that what you need? Someone to prove you didn't die with your husband?"

The unexpected attack and resultant stab of pain made her flinch. "This isn't about me."

He closed the distance between them in two long strides. His dark gaze burned into hers. "I think it is. It's about you being afraid to let go of the past."

She shook her head as denial raced through her, quickly chased by a thrill of something exciting and energizing. She tried to squash the latter, but failed. Her heart raced and her palms tingled. "No. You're wrong."

"Not this time. Come out of hiding, Sabrina." He cupped her shoulders, and before she could convince her feet to carry her out of trouble's way, he bent and settled his mouth over hers.

His lips were warm, firm, sure. *Persuasive.* A response she couldn't prevent streamed through her like a waterfall pouring over the mountains and crashing into her stomach, but instead of filling her veins with icy mountain water, a warm thermal spring bubbled in her veins.

Her brain and body worked against each other. One demanded she push him away. The other stubbornly held on tight. If her internal battle wasn't enough, Gavin's passionate embrace evoked so many long-suppressed memories. She'd forgotten the experience of having a man's strong arms hold her tight, forgotten the heat of a muscle-packed body pressed against hers, and she'd forgotten how deliciously feminine the combination made her feel. But mostly she'd forgotten how it felt to crave more.

More deep kisses. More firm, but gentle hands buffing her body. More of this heady, dizzy, free-falling sensation that made her cling even tighter to him for fear of losing her balance.

This wasn't supposed to happen. Not with him. Apparently she didn't have to trust the man to desire him. He was attractive and she hadn't had sex in a long time, so her reaction to him was probably just deprived hormones at work. But he and Pops were wrong. She wasn't hiding. She wasn't afraid.

She wanted Gavin Jarrod, she admitted as their tongues dueled. And what was wrong with that? What was wrong with wanting to experience hot, sweaty mind-numbing passion one more time? It didn't have to mean anything. In fact, she wouldn't let it mean anything. She'd already had a man who'd loved as ardently as he'd lived, and like her grandfather, she'd never settle for second-best.

Gavin's hands skimmed her waist, her breasts, and her heart banged wildly. He lowered her coat's zipper tooth by tooth. The rasp shattered the silence of the small room, then welcome cool air soothed her overheated skin. He parted her coat and spanned her rib cage, palms burning hot through her sweater as he stroked his thumbs back and forth beneath her breasts with breath-stealing effectiveness. The urge to press herself into his palms surged through her. It had been so long she almost didn't recognize the bite of lust gnawing her middle.

And then his hands slipped under the hem of her sweater and his skin found hers. She jumped. The chilly air contrasting with the heat of his touch set her core on fire. Breaking the kiss, she threw her head back and gasped for breath, for sanity, for control. Her head spun. Her knees wobbled. His lips scorched a path from her cheek to her temple then down the side of her neck. Desire thundered over her like a storm coming over the mountains, rumbling with a strength she couldn't remember experiencing before. But she must have. With Russell.

Was she making a mistake? Playing with fire? Taking on more than she could handle?

The heady rush caused by Gavin's warm breath on her skin combined with the slick heat of his tongue teasing the sensitive spot behind her ear and his teeth grazing the cord of her neck provided her answer. She *had* to taste the passion, *had* to sample the need of a hungry man. She'd missed that feeling so much. Too much. She'd allow Gavin into her life long enough to take the edge off. But that was it. Nothing more. No promises. No long-term. Just this. Today.

She shoved Gavin's coat off his shoulders. He whipped hers down her arms. Breathing heavily, he cupped her face, traced her jaw as if he were trying to slow down. Then he pressed his lips together, and with a rueful grimace shook his head and yanked her close.

The impact of his ravenous kiss robbed her breath, her balance, her reason. He kissed her as if he couldn't get enough of her and a similar sensation swelled inside her. She clung to him. The hard length of his erection burned against her hips. Cool air swept her midsection, then he eased his upper torso

away only far enough to whisk her sweater over her head.
She had a moment to feel uncomfortable and exposed in her
plain white bra before he ripped off his own shirt, and then
her doubts vanished and her appreciation focused on him.

His chest was all male—wide shoulders, brawny pectorals,
dark swirls of hair, tiny, puckered nipples, and hot, so, so hot
to the touch. She dragged her fingertips down his sternum.
Satisfaction rose in her when she left a crop of goose bumps
in her wake. She pressed her cheek to his chest and inhaled
deeply, filling her lungs with his masculine scent, then she
licked his golden skin and tasted a slight tang of salt.

His breath hissed and his grip tightened on her waist as
she licked across the tiny hard tip. A groan rumbled from his
chest. "I like your mouth, your hands on me, Sabrina."

Hot palms buffed her back, her waist and then he covered
her breasts. He captured her gasp with his mouth, swallowed
the *Mmm* of pleasure she couldn't contain. She wanted, *needed*
skin on skin. Her bra was in the way. She reached for the
hooks in the middle of her back, but he beat her to them and
dispensed with the garment. He cradled her aching breasts in
his palms. His thumbs teased the tips, sending bolts of need
straight to her center. *Intense. Too intense.*

She eased back to map the supple skin covering the ropy
muscles of his shoulders, his thick biceps, his hard pectorals.
She flicked her short nails over his beaded flesh then raked
downward over his six-pack abs to his waistband.

He shuddered an inhalation, then swept her into his arms
and carried her to the sofa where he laid her on top of the fur
blankets before following her. His weight pinned her down
and being trapped beneath him felt good. So good. She lightly
raked his back and then his mouth found her breast. Hot. Wet.
Slick. Pleasure bathed her as his tongue laved her, and she
moaned. He sucked, nipped, rasped her with his chin stubble,
and all she could do was struggle to control her growing

urgency. Her legs shifted restlessly, trying to soothe the knot of nerves between them.

She ached to tear off the remainder of their clothing and fill the emptiness expanding in her belly. Her fingers tangled in his hair, holding him close. He worked his way down her midline until he reached the button of her jeans. He released it. The fabric gave way and the zipper parted letting in a kiss of cool air. He skimmed her pants and panties down her legs, leaving a trail of open-mouthed kisses in the fabric's wake. Then her pants, boots and socks were gone.

She lay naked before him and she should have had second thoughts, but she didn't, not with the way he devoured her with his eyes. She attributed the depth of her hunger to the length of time it had been since she'd allowed herself even a teensy sexual urge. Why else would this feel so right, so necessary? She reached for the fly of his jeans.

He covered her hands, pressing them to the ridge beneath his denim, groaned and then shook his head. "Not this time. I can't handle it."

She took comfort in knowing she wasn't alone in her over-the-top response. He brushed her hands aside and quickly stripped. His body was long and lean, but corded with thick muscles. She wanted to stare, to map his contours with her fingertips, but she also wanted him on her, surrounding her, inside her. She lifted a hand to him, beckoning him. He rejoined her, pressing her into the soft blankets with his weight.

While his mouth consumed hers she palmed the muscles of his back, his buttocks, his strong thighs. He kissed and laved his way to her breasts, sucking, licking, nipping until she squirmed beneath him, impatient for more. Then he blazed a trail down her middle. Her muscles clenched in anticipation, and then he was there—his hot breath a prelude to the scalding sweep of his tongue. He found exactly the right spot instantly.

How did he do that? Pleasure quivered through her, making her whimper, causing her to bow off the sofa and toward the mouth working magic on her body.

Tension built, adding more and more pressure until she cracked like a dam and an orgasm erupted though her in wave after wave of breathtaking release. It wasn't enough. She'd waited so long for this. She needed more. Digging her fingers into his arms, she tugged him upward. He resisted, forcing one more breath-robbing climax on her before he rose above her, spread her legs and positioned himself. He paused.

Confused and gasping for air, she looked into his lust-darkened eyes. His passion was too intense. She lowered her lids. "Please, Gavin. Now."

"Open your eyes," he rumbled almost inaudibly.

Reluctantly, she did as he ordered. Once their gazes locked he eased into her, inch by inch, filling her, stretching her.

"You're so wet."

Having a lover talk was a new experience, and surprisingly it increased her arousal. He felt good. So good. And then he withdrew. She pulled him back again and again, chasing another climax with each thrust and withdrawal, feeling the heaviness build low in her belly and waiting, waiting for the explosion. When it hit, it hit hard, racking her body with spasms. "That's it, baby. Squeeze me."

She bit his shoulder to muffle her cry, and then before the aftershocks faded he groaned as he found his own release.

Gavin rested atop her, the majority of his weight braced on his forearms as she struggled to catch her breath and to still the quaking of her legs. His long, hot thighs burned against hers and his chest pressed hers with each rapid breath.

Reality slowly nudged fantasy aside. How had she and he come together so naturally when she and Russell had worked long and hard to achieve such satisfaction? Guilt settled heavily on her at the traitorous thought.

It's only because you and Russell were inexperienced kids when you first made love. You and Gavin are experienced adults.

As she mentally withdrew from him she became aware of the soft furs tickling her back, the unheated air cooling her skin, the hot, damp man still buried deep inside her and the stickiness joining them.

Stickiness?

They hadn't used a condom. Shock raced over her, quickly chased by panic. What had she done? She hadn't simply answered a biological call as planned.

She'd made a mistake of potentially disastrous proportions—one that could have lifelong repercussions. She'd risked a pregnancy—something she'd sworn she'd never, ever do again.

Satiation and satisfaction blended in Gavin's blood like a top-shelf cocktail. His heart pumped faster and yet his limbs felt weighted. His brain raced, searching for the next step in his plan to seduce Sabrina Taylor into marriage. But for some crazy-ass reason he was having trouble thinking about anything except the warm, soft woman beneath him, the hot, wet grip of her body and the smell of sex hanging in the air.

He ought to feel ashamed for enjoying the act as much as he had considering he was using her as a means to an end. But he didn't because she'd enjoyed it as much as he had.

She stiffened beneath him, jarring him out of Shangri-la.

"That shouldn't have happened."

Not what a guy wanted to hear when he was still buried deep inside a woman. "With chemistry like ours it was inevitable."

She squirmed as if trying to get free, and the slick slide of her body on his signaled his erection for an encore. "No. It wasn't. I don't do...*this* with men I barely know."

"Good to know." Marriage and more of *this* appealed more with each of her wiggles.

"Gavin, we didn't use a condom."

The statement rocked him, instantly dousing the smoldering embers of desire. He never neglected to practice safe sex. "My company requires physicals on a regular basis. I'm clean. You?"

Face flushing, she pushed against his chest, her fingers digging into his pectorals until he eased off her and sat beside her on the sofa. "Of course."

"Good." Without the warmth of her body pressed against his, the chill of the unheated tack room—and the woman beside him—penetrated his consciousness.

She sprang to her feet, frantically scooping up clothing and clutching the wad of fabric to her spectacular chest. Her breasts might not be large, but they were perfectly formed. A handful. A mouthful. The pink tips lured him ba—

"You're ignoring the big picture. I'm not on the pill."

Arousal once more derailed, he processed the bad news. Their union was supposed to be temporary. A baby was a long-term commitment—definitely not in the works for a rolling stone like him who didn't know how to be a good father. "The odds of you conceiving from one encounter are slim. We'll take precautions next time."

"There won't be a next time, and any chance is too big of a chance." She tugged on her bra, concealing the breasts he hadn't had enough of yet, then her shirt. Without the delicious distraction, he had to focus on her eyes—eyes filled with regret.

"We'll deal with that situation if it arises."

She bent to look for her panties and he shamelessly enjoyed the view of her long legs and tight, round butt. He couldn't help reaching out and skimming his hand down her flank and savoring the satiny smoothness of her pale skin.

She jumped out of reach and spun around, shielding the dark triangle of curls between her legs with her jeans. "Stop that. And there is no 'we.' We have no future. You're leaving Aspen. I'm not."

Why did her words hit him like a punch in the gut? They were true. But admitting the truth could cost him everything.

She stabbed her legs into her jeans—sans panties, zipped and buttoned them. "And if any situation requires a decision it will be my decision. Not yours. I don't want anything from you."

It would be partly his decision if he married her. "Don't expect me to walk away from a connection like ours without a fight."

Panic widened her eyes even more. "There is no connection. It was just sex."

"Great sex."

She bowed her head and took a deep breath, then lifted her chin. Her eyes were hard, determined. "Look, Gavin, this was a mistake that won't be repeated."

Yes it would. Often, if he had his way. But not in an unheated barn. As much as he liked the way her nipples tightened from the cold and pushed against her shirt, he wanted her naked and spread across his Egyptian cotton sheets, warm and willing.

He rose and stepped closer to her, enjoying her quiet gasp of surprise. "Not repeating what we just shared would be the mistake."

Her pupils dilated, her lips parted and her cheeks flushed. He could see the hunger in her eyes and waited for her to admit he was right, but instead she shook her head and backed away. "No. Pretending this never happened would be the wisest course of action. That's what I intend to do. What we both should do."

He couldn't allow that to happen. He caught her face in

his palm. Her body stilled and her expression turned wary. "There's no way you can forget how good we are together. I guarantee it."

She jerked her head out of his grasp and set her jaw at a stubborn angle. "Watch me."

Seven

She might have been a little overconfident in her ability to ignore Gavin, Sabrina admitted Friday afternoon.

In the eight hours since they'd made lov—had sex, she hadn't been able to get him out of her head. Thoughts of him lurked around corners of her mind, leaping out to startle her at inopportune moments. It didn't help that he was rarely out of sight, and even when he was she could hear the low baritone of his voice as he talked to Pops.

Worse, she still smelled of him—of *them*—because she couldn't sneak off to wash his scent away without making Pops question why she'd taken a second shower in the same day. And the seam of her jeans rubbed sensitive places—places that should be covered by panties, but weren't since she hadn't found hers and hadn't wanted to linger in the barn to search.

How could she have become intimate with someone she'd only known four days? Shame burned her cheeks. That wasn't like her. Russell had been her only lover, and it had taken three months and falling head over heels in love with him for him to talk her out of her clothes. Luckily, she'd figured out the guys before him had only wanted one thing from her—copies of her parents' course exams—before she'd done more than heavy kissing and a little uncomfortable groping.

Footsteps approached—her grandfather's soft shuffle followed by Gavin's purposeful tread. Her spine snapped straight and her pulse went wacky. She wanted to run, but she wouldn't give Gavin Jarrod the satisfaction of knowing she was uncomfortable around him.

Pops preceded Gavin into the kitchen. "I'm off, girlie."

Alarm raced through her. "Off where? What about dinner?"

"I'm eating with my poker buddies."

"But this isn't your usual night, and I was about to grill steaks." She couldn't care less about the steaks. She didn't want to be left alone with Gavin.

"Save mine for tomorrow. Horace is making his famous venison stew."

"Why don't you take Gavin with you? He might enjoy meeting your poker pals."

"I'm not about to bring a card shark to the table. He'd steal the pot, and the boys would never forgive me. Good night. Don't wait up." Pops grabbed his coat and hat and let himself out the back door, leaving Sabrina staring after him in dismay.

Now what?

Get rid of Gavin, that's what.

She delayed facing him until she absolutely couldn't anymore, then turned. He leaned against the doorjamb, ankles and arms crossed, watching her. The wolf-like watchfulness and hunger in his eyes as his dark gaze rolled over her thickened her tongue and made the spot between her legs tingle.

She gulped. "You're a card shark?"

He lifted one muscled shoulder. "When we're stuck on a job and the weather's not cooperating we sometimes kill the time with cards. I do okay."

She shifted on her feet, searching for a way to rid herself of his company. "You have an evening off. Go home."

"Not without my date."

Her stomach swooped. Good. She was glad he had a date. She wanted him to bother some other woman and leave her alone. But that burn in her belly felt a lot like anger. How dare he romance her and then hours later turn to another woman while her scent still clung to his skin. But what had she expected? Hadn't those spoiled college boys tried the same tricks? They'd flirted with her, plied her with beer neither she nor they had been legally old enough to drink, then they'd gone back to their girlfriends when she hadn't given them what they wanted.

"I hope you have a nice time," she forced through clenched, smiling teeth.

He moved closer, making her retreat until the counter bumped her spine. The look of intent on his face caused her legs to quiver. "We will. Grab whatever you need. Let's go."

She blinked in confusion, then when his meaning sank in panic prickled her skin. "We? Go where?"

He parked a hand on the counter on either side of her, effectively boxing her in. "We're having dinner at my place."

"Your place," she parroted back and then could have kicked herself for sounding like an idiot.

"The lodge I'm using at Jarrod Ridge."

No way. She folded her arms, intent on avoiding that trap

and forcing a few inches between them. "I am not going to your place."

"Would you rather your grandfather come back unexpectedly and catch us in bed?"

Her chest hurt. She realized it was because she'd forgotten to breathe. She inhaled shakily, hoping the oxygen would clear up her light-headedness and slow the rush of blood through her veins. It didn't. "That's not going to happen."

He checked his watch, giving her just enough space to dodge out of reach. "The lobster, buttered asparagus, maple-glazed carrots and German chocolate cake will be delivered in an hour."

Her favorites. Her mouth watered like one of Pavlov's dogs'. "Pops has been talking."

"You're his favorite subject."

She cringed. "I'm sorry you have to endure his ramblings."

"I'm hanging on every word because pleasing you, pleases me."

Oh, boy. The man personified testosterone in a turtleneck, and when he spoke in that low sexy growl she wanted to lap up everything he said like a dog in heat. Good thing she wasn't that gullible.

"Come for dinner, Sabrina. If you can resist the pull between us I'll bring you home—untouched—afterward. But if you can't..." He dragged a knuckle down the side of her neck, making her shiver. "I'll spend the rest of the night exploring every inch of you. First with my hands. Then with my mouth."

Her knees melted. She clutched the counter for support. Shattered by the image he painted with his words, she shook her head, trying to clear it. "I'd rather have a quiet night. Alone."

A smile of pure devilment curved his lips, and her heart

flipped like a pancake on a hot griddle. "No, you wouldn't. I can't erase the taste of you or the feel of your skin from my mind. This morning was only an appetizer. I want more, and I'd bet my truck you're fighting the same battle. You've watched me all day with the same hunger in your eyes that's chewing up my insides."

Could her skin possibly get any hotter? Her heart beat any faster? Had she ever been more tempted to throw caution to the winds and seize what he offered? No, no and no.

And then her panic subsided as quickly as it had risen and a sense of calm settled over her. Well, a sort of calm if you discounted the tremor racking her limbs and making a cold sweat bead on her upper lip.

Why couldn't she accept his proposition? Why shouldn't she enjoy a brief, temporary affair with Gavin? He was the perfect candidate to help her work the logjam of hormones from her system. He was rich, entitled, and even arrogant—qualities she would never find attractive. He'd be leaving Aspen as soon as he fulfilled the terms of his father's will. It wasn't as if she'd fall for someone who was counting the days until he could break free. Not when she understood how all-consuming that yearning to escape could be. It overrode everything, including reason.

An affair. Seven months of sex.

Excitement rippled through her, then waned. Her last affair—with Russell—had cost her so much. Her home. Her family. Her friends. And then when she'd lost her baby and hit rock-bottom she'd had no one to turn to because Russell had been deployed overseas. But that had been years ago. She wasn't a naïve eighteen-year-old anymore. And her family, other than Pops, already acted as if she'd died.

What did she have to lose? Certainly not her heart. Not to a man like Gavin "His Family Owned Half the Valley" Jarrod.

It didn't matter that he was handsome and hellaciously good at finding her pleasure points. She couldn't—*wouldn't*—love him. Not in this lifetime.

You have no idea how to have a no-strings affair.

But she could learn. She could learn anything if it meant finding a way to hold onto the inn and easing the discomfort Gavin had created.

But her grandfather could never find out. He wouldn't approve.

"I'll get my coat."

The flash of victory in his eyes gave her pause, but she pushed it aside. She would not let this be a mistake.

Sabrina wiped her damp palms on her jeans and swallowed the lump of nerves rising to block her throat. "Black Spruce Lodge," she read on the tastefully carved wooden sign outside the building. "Are all Jarrod Ridge's lodges named after trees?"

"Yes," Gavin said as he pulled the key card from his pocket.

From the outside the structure looked extremely rustic— like a miner's cabin with its rough cedar siding and steep shingled roof—unless you paid attention to the details. Every element of the building's design and landscaping had been intricately planned and cared for in a way that only those with a surplus of money could achieve. The windows gleamed like diamonds in the setting sun, and not even a trace of the snow that had fallen on and off during the day remained on the walk or front steps.

Gavin opened the door. "Come in."

Said the spider to the fly. Her legs trembled as she climbed the steps.

The only way to conquer your fears is to face them.

Russell's voice echoed in her head, startling her. She didn't want to think about him now, didn't want to remember his overlapped-tooth smile, his bravery or anything else about him when she had another man's seed still deep in her womb and she was about to embark on something as sordid as a cheap, temporary, meaningless affair.

The urge to turn and run barreled into her chest like a runaway horse, but she gathered her flagging courage and crossed the threshold. Strangely, excitement intermingled with shame.

Gavin flicked a switch and a chandelier made from antlers and candelabra bulbs cast a cozy light over the large open space with its steep vaulted ceiling. "I'll take your coat."

Before she could protest he stood behind her, waiting to help her remove the garment. She reluctantly shrugged it off and hugged herself, not because she was cold, but because she was totally out of her element. How did one go about a tempestuous affair anyway?

After hanging their coats in the closet he crossed the room to light the logs stacked and waiting in the massive stone fireplace, giving her an opportunity to scan her surroundings. The lodge looked more like someone's home than a temporary accommodation. Hardwood floors gleamed in every direction. One side of the rectangular room housed the kitchen and dining area, and on the other a pair of black leather sofas jutted perpendicular to the hearth. The walls on either side of the fireplace were made of glass, offering a breathtaking view of the mountains fading to a dusky pink as the sun set.

Black dominated the decor. Charcoal sketches graced the walls. She strolled closer to a rendition of an ice-covered lake and noted the artist's signature—one she recognized from her trips to the many art galleries in downtown Aspen. An original. Translation: very expensive and not even remotely within her budget.

She turned a slow circle. The black marble vases flanking

the mantel and the onyx-framed mirror hanging between them screamed money in an understated, elegant way. Ditto the knickknacks sparingly dotted along the flat surfaces. She'd seen enough of this type of art through exclusive shops' windows to know the value.

She lifted an exquisitely carved wooden bear. Nope, it wasn't nailed down, and yes, the artist's initials had been burned into the bottom. No mass-produced decor here. She set the bear back on the polished surface. What hotel could afford to risk a guest tucking even one of these objects into his bag?

The fire popped, startling her and drawing her gaze back to the man watching her in silence. Gavin's sensual expression made her shiver. Rubbing the goose bumps popping up on her arms, she glanced away and spotted a staircase. "What's in the loft?"

"An office."

"Are you working while you're here?"

"I'm doing some consulting and preliminary work for future jobs. It's not enough to keep me busy, but it staves off insanity."

Another surprise. She'd expected him to enjoy his year of leisure. Oh, sure, he'd claimed he needed the handyman job because he was bored without work, but she hadn't really believed him.

He crossed to a black slate-topped wet bar, pulled a bottle of white wine from the refrigerator, opened it and poured two glasses and brought one to her. "To our mutual pleasure."

She gasped and nearly choked on her own saliva. Having him verbalize the purpose of this visit sent a jolt of adrenaline though her. He'd said he'd brought her here for dinner, but she knew better. One look at his eyes told her getting naked was on the agenda.

The chime of his rim tapping hers sounded light compared

to her dark and dangerous thoughts. She tried to focus on something besides making lo—having sex on the white fur rug in front of the fire. But she couldn't seem to shove that idea from her head now that it had burrowed into her brain.

Tonight was all about sex. Nothing more. Nothing less. Just physical pleasure with a man she didn't particularly like but one who knew how to ring her bell.

She gulped her wine and tried to work up the courage to jump him and get it over with. Not happening. She licked her lips. "You said during the carriage ride that most of your siblings were staying in lodges or hotel rooms. How can the resort afford for so many of your family members to take up guest quarters?"

The twitch of his mouth told her he'd noted her change of subject. "Our budget can handle it, but I'll move to the main house when the tourists arrive and we reach maximum occupancy. For now, I'm enjoying roughing it here."

"Roughing it?" She snorted, touched a pewter horse statue and rolled her eyes. Three of her and Russell's old military base apartments could fit into this great room alone, and there would be even more space in what she suspected were massive bedrooms through the archway on her right. One of which she'd probably see tonight. Her abdominal muscles contracted. She took another hearty swallow of wine. "You call living in the lap of luxury *roughing it?*"

"It is compared to living in the hotel where the concierge hovers, the maid comes by two or three times a day and you can have your own personal chef and wine steward serve a meal in your suite whenever you desire it. At Jarrod Manor every want is anticipated and provided for before I even make the request. Even my underwear gets ironed."

Don't think about his underwear.

That anyone could see having their needs taken care of as a nuisance astounded her. "I can't imagine living that way."

"Our guests demand it. Jarrod Ridge is known for pampering its clientele."

"Moving away and leaving all this…*assistance* behind must have been difficult for you."

"Not at all. It's impossible to figure out who you are and what you want out of life when someone else is forcing you down his path, telling you who he expects you to be and making all your decisions for you."

Again, she heard the bitterness and she understood it. She didn't like having this in common with him. "Your father."

He inclined his head.

"My parents did the same. They pressured me to follow in their footsteps and get multiple degrees. They couldn't understand that college just wasn't for me even though I scored high on all the entrance exams."

"Why wasn't college for you?"

She sipped her wine, trying to figure out why she'd just volunteered something she'd not shared with anyone before. Must be the liquor loosening her tongue. She wasn't much of a drinker. "I don't like taking classes. There's too much reading and talking about stuff and not enough doing it."

"You're a hands-on learner. Nothing wrong with that."

Something in her softened. She'd never had anybody understand her like that before. And how could he? He barely knew her. Even though her grandparents had emotionally supported her, they had assumed she was delaying college, not skipping it altogether. She'd eventually caved and taken several business classes to keep herself occupied during Russell's deployments, but she'd hated being confined to a classroom. However, she was grateful for those classes now. They helped her manage the inn's budget.

Gavin moved closer—close enough to touch. But she didn't reach out. She wasn't ready to take that step—the one that would end up with the two of them bare-skinned and against each other. But her belly clenched in anticipation of having him deep inside her.

"Let's soak in the hot tub while we wait for dinner," he said in that low rumbling jets-coming-over-the-mountain voice of his.

Her skin flushed hot and her gaze shot to the glass doors leading to a deck. "I didn't bring a swimsuit."

"You don't need one. The tub is completely private."

"But…what about the staff serving dinner?"

"They've been instructed to leave it in the kitchen."

"I—I—" Planning to be bold and actually doing it were apparently two different things. And then she noted something out of place in Gavin's perfect world. "There's still snow on the deck. I'm surprised the grounds crew didn't sweep it away like they did on the front walk."

"I asked the staff to leave it. There's nothing like sitting in a bubbling hot tub, surrounded by snow and staring up at a clear blue star-filled sky through the steam rising from the water."

The man had a way with words.

"The stars aren't out yet," she replied hastily.

"True."

"And more snow is predicted. Won't it be too cloudy to see them?"

"So it will. You're quite practical, aren't you?"

She'd had to be. She'd run away from home on a romantic fantasy of love and collided with cold, harsh reality. While Russell had been off doing his job and supporting his country, she'd been home alone, trying to learn how to manage on a meager budget and hold onto what was left of their life together after she'd miscarried. Luckily, she'd had the guidance and support of a few experienced and big-hearted military wives to point her in the right direction.

"I'm sorry. I don't mean to be a wet blanket."

Gavin set his glass on the table. "Sabrina, you have nothing to fear from me."

Like she believed that. The moisture between her legs already proved she had plenty to fear. He had decimated her scruples this morning. And where were those scruples now? She was very tempted to take him up on his offer. To see those broad shoulders glistening wet in the moonlight. To feel those big calloused hands rasping over her skin, on her breasts, between her legs. She'd barely been able to think of anything else all day.

She exhaled shakily, turned her back on him and took another sip of wine. *C'mon. You can do this.* "All right. Let's get in the hot tub."

She started shaking even before she finished the sentence. Golden liquid sloshed around the bowl of her glass.

Gavin moved up behind her. She felt the heat radiating from him even though he didn't touch her. One long arm reached around her and removed the glass from her hand. "Why don't we take a walk before dinner and save the hot tub for later?"

Suspicious, she spun to face him. "Why?"

"You said you'd never toured Jarrod Ridge. We'll burn off a little excess energy and then relax afterward."

That sounded suspiciously like him being considerate, and she hadn't expected that from him. But she'd take the reprieve. Maybe by the time they returned she'd have found her courage to plunge into the affair. "I'd like to see the grounds."

He retrieved their coats and then pulled a couple of his thick scarves from the closet. He draped a white one over her head, covering her ears, and then he wound it around her neck. His scent clung to the soft cashmere caressing her cheeks.

He wrapped the black one around his neck, but left his head bare. Within moments they were back outside, their breath fogging the air. Snow had begun falling while they were inside. Big, fat flakes floated down, piling up on the grassy surfaces. With the temperature dropping it wouldn't be long before it stuck to the sidewalks despite the diligent landscaping crew's efforts to remove it.

She hadn't brought gloves. Bad habit. She tended to forget. Before she could shove her hands into her pockets Gavin caught one and folded his long fingers around her palm. She jumped and tried to pull free.

"Easy. I just want to hold your hand."

Holding hands. Something so basic and innocent. Something she'd once taken for granted and hadn't bothered to do often enough with her husband. And now she was palm-to-palm with a virtual stranger, and the simple contact rocked her entire body. Gavin's heat seeped into her, traveling up her arm and down her torso to pool in an area that had been dormant for a long time.

He led her along the sidewalks winding through the resort. Snowflakes sparkled in his brown hair like gold dust. Lights glimmered through the trees from the windows of the occupied lodges they passed, then streetlamps flickered on as the sun slipped behind the mountains in the distance.

"Why me, Gavin? You could have your pick of women." She blurted the question that had been haunting her.

He briefly squeezed her hand, sending a pulse of energy through her. "Why not you? You're beautiful, intelligent and your touch ignites me."

His quick, decisive answer blew her away. She stumbled. He caught her elbow, keeping her upright. His eyes searched hers then his expression changed from concerned to challenging. "Are you up for a little fun?"

Adrenaline pulsed through her veins. "Maybe. What did you have in mind?"

"Come with me." He walked a little farther down the sidewalk then ducked between a pair of tall cedars, tugging her along in the near-darkness to a better lit area. He broke into a jog. She hustled to keep up as he zigged and zagged through the trees. A few hundred yards later, he slowed to a halt in a well-lit clearing behind a shed that looked as if it might house landscaping equipment. Her quickened breaths fogged the air. He wasn't breathing any faster, she noted. He released her, then knelt to open a door hidden in the foundation and pulled out a flat-bottomed wooden snow sled with a curled end.

He straightened with a huge, devilish, big-kid grin on his face that was so contagious she couldn't help smiling back. "It's still here. I wasn't sure it would be after so many years." He knocked on it in several places with his fist, the sound echoing off the buildings around them in the near-silence of the evening. "The wood is still solid."

Flakes drifted down around them, heavier now than before. "You're taking me sledding?"

He swept the dust off the surface. "Sure. Why not?"

It was a far cry from flipping her on her back and having his way with her, but as he said…*why not?* "I've never been sledding."

His eyes narrowed. "It snows in Pennsylvania."

"My parents weren't the sledding type. And snow wasn't common in the eastern part of North Carolina where Russell was stationed."

"Russell? Your husband?"

Speaking his name in front of Gavin seemed…strange, but it had just slipped out. And it felt…okay. "Yes."

"And you never sledded with your grandparents?"

"I was usually only here in the summers except for quick trips some Christmases with my parents. My father didn't get along with Pop—his father—and he couldn't wait to get out of here, so we didn't stay long."

"Then it's time to make up for what you've missed." He

tucked the sled under one arm, draped the other across her shoulders and guided her through the darkness away from the lights of the resort and across the snow-covered slope. Their torsos and thighs bumped and nudged with each step, overloading her senses so much she barely noticed the cold.

"Watch your step. The ground is slick."

"Where are we going?"

"Up the mountain a bit. This same path leads to the mine." At the top of a slope he turned. "Climb on. Put your feet against the front."

Nervous, she shifted in her boots. "How do you steer this thing?"

"By shifting your weight or dragging a hand. But let me worry about that."

She reluctantly eased onto the flat surface. Gavin settled behind her with his strong legs flanking hers, his hips snug against her bottom, and his chest flush with her back, warming her in the rapidly dropping temperature. His arms encircled her and her breath hitched. He held the rope in his fists. "Ready?"

"Ummm." Excitement and anxiety shimmied over her. "I guess so."

His cheek pressed hers. He nudged her scarf aside until his lips brushed her ear. "You're going to have to trust me, Sabrina. I won't let anything bad happen to you."

Trust seemed a lot to ask from someone he barely knew, but it was too late to back out now. "Let's go."

Eight

Sabrina had never looked more attractive than she did now, flat on her back with her cold-reddened nose and cheeks, excitement sparkling in her eyes and a huge smile on her face.

For about two seconds Gavin considered making love to her out here in the open in the powdery snow. But while instant gratification might be exciting and physically satisfying, it wouldn't be comfortable for either of them. First, it was too damned cold, and second, security was bound to spot them out here in the milky moonlight.

So he offered her a hand and tugged her to her feet instead of giving in to his body's demands. Her fingers felt like ice in his and white clumps of snow caked the ends of her long hair as she turned to admire the snow angel she'd made in the deepening snow. Her third. But she'd been having such a good time he'd hated to interrupt.

"Your hands are frozen and your clothes are wet. Let's get you back to the lodge to warm up."

"Do we have to?"

Her enthusiasm acted as one hell of a payoff for his patience. "There's no need to risk frostbite."

"That was fun." She grinned up at him. "Thank you."

"For?"

"Teaching me to play in the snow."

Her sincerity tightened his chest. As much as he'd hated his childhood, hers must have been worse. At least he and his brothers had had those stolen moments when they'd escaped their father. "You're welcome. I'm glad I could share a few firsts with you."

And he meant it. Her enthusiasm and excitement these past two hours had been contagious. From her squeals as they raced down the slope to her learning to make snowballs and snow angels, he'd found more enjoyment watching her have fun than he'd had in a long time. Meeting Sabrina almost made his year of exile worth it.

And then because he couldn't resist, he bent to taste her smile. She met him halfway, going on tiptoe, leaning into his chest and wrapping her arms around his neck. Her lips and nose were cold, but her kiss was hot—hot enough to make his head steam and his groin heavy.

Their tongues sparred, their breaths blended. How could he possibly want a woman this badly when he'd already had sex once today? The hunger gripped him so tightly he reconsidered risking an embarrassing encounter with The Ridge's security staff. His brothers would never let him live that down. But once he got Sabrina back to the lodge he could linger over her soft skin, her long legs, her—

Scratch that. He'd linger the second time. The first time was going to be fast. And hot. And hard. He pried his mouth from hers to suck air into his lungs. Chest bellowing, he grabbed her hand, snatched up the sled and towed her toward a warm bed.

"In a hurry?" she panted a few minutes later.

He slowed his steps. "I want you naked."

She gasped and tripped. He caught her and kissed the O of her mouth, adding fuel to the fire in his gut. Her earlier reservations apparently forgotten, she clutched his jacket and held him close. But not close enough. The layers of down and assorted shirts and sweaters and wet denim blocked him from what he wanted.

He broke the kiss. "Let's go."

He avoided the paths that would take him past his siblings' accommodations because he didn't want to be waylaid. Sabrina hurried alongside him. His plan to get her to relax by taking a walk had succeeded beyond his wildest dreams. Now she seemed as eager to get back to the lodge as he was. And he was the one wound up. Embarrassingly so.

He said a silent thanks when his temporary home came into view. After propping the sled against the porch wall he wasted no time swiping the key card and shoving open the door. Warm air, carrying the scent of dinner, rushed through the portal to greet them. His stomach grumbled, but he had a more urgent appetite to satisfy before he could eat. He craved the taste of Sabrina. Her mouth. Her breasts. The sweetness hidden within her dark curls.

"It feels good in here," she said as she reached for her coat's zipper.

"Over here." Grasping her shoulders, he steered her to the fireplace. He pitched another log onto the flames then turned to face her. "We'll leave our clothes by the fire to dry out."

A moment of doubt flickered over her face, but he wasn't going to lose ground now. He reached for her scarf, unwound it from her head, then dispensed with her coat. He draped each over a chair which he angled toward the flames, then shed his own gear. Her shirt, like his, was dry because of the outerwear but her jeans were wet from the melted snow.

"Sit." He pointed to the raised hearth.

With a hiked eyebrow, Sabrina sank onto the stones. He removed her boots and socks, then massaged warmth back into her cold feet. "I kept you out too long. You're cold."

Her smile nearly blinded him. "No. Not too long. Tonight was perfect. I wouldn't have wanted to miss a minute of it." Then as his thumbs dug into her instep, she purred, "That feels good."

He'd make her feel even better before the night was through. "Stand."

"You like giving orders." But she rose.

"Hazard of the job. Comes with being the one in charge." He unbuttoned and unzipped her jeans, then peeled the soggy fabric over her hips. It bunched around her thighs. She wasn't wearing panties—the reminder punched him hard in the solar plexus. She wasn't wearing them because he'd spotted them on the tack room floor earlier and stuffed them into his coat pocket. "You're missing something."

He retrieved the plain white cotton bikinis from his coat and dropped them on the floor.

"You had them in your pocket all day?"

Her scandalized tone made him chuckle. "Yes." And the knowledge had driven him wild. He hadn't forgotten until the sight of her playing in the snow had overridden the idea.

He eased the wet, clingy jeans down her legs. "Sit."

"Are you always this bossy?"

"Only when there's something I want very badly. And I want you so badly my jaw aches from gritting my teeth against the need to be inside you."

Her lashes fluttered and her pupils widened. "Are you always so...verbal?"

"Yes. Does it bother you?"

"No. I—I think I like it." She sat. He stripped the garment from her and tossed it onto the hearth where it could dry without catching fire, then he chafed her cold, reddened thighs with his hands.

But as her skin warmed beneath his palms, he discovered touching her legs wasn't nearly enough. The hem of her shirt played peekaboo with the dark triangle between her thighs, mesmerizing him, tantalizing him, beckoning him. He whisked her shirt over her head, then released and removed her bra and tossed both aside.

He considered planting his face in her lap and bringing her to a climax, but he wanted more. "I want to caress you, to taste you—your skin, your breasts. But I specifically crave this spot." He dragged a fingertip beneath each soft curve, making her gasp. "You smell so damned good there."

He rose, his legs unusually unsteady as he took in her almost naked form in front of the fire. His erection pulsed behind his zipper, demanding release.

She arched her back to the heat, thrusting her puckered nipples in his direction with mouthwatering effectiveness. The fact that she was probably trying to dry her wet hair and seemed unconscious of the eroticism of the move made it all the more irresistible. He stripped off his boots and clothing, pulled her to her feet and yanked her close.

She gasped and stiffened. "You're cold."

"No, baby, I'm burning up. For you. Feel what you do to me." He pressed his erection into her belly and her soft skin teased him.

He lost control of the kiss even before his lips met hers. He wanted to absorb her, better yet, to burrow under her skin. Instead, he wound his arms around her as tightly as he could and devoured her mouth with hungry bites and greedy swipes of his tongue—all of which she returned.

How had she done this to him? He usually had more control.

He tried to tame the need, tried to slow his caresses. But

she felt too good in his arms and the fire in his belly burned as hot as molten steel. He couldn't get enough of her. He cupped and massaged her breasts, tweaking her nipples until she whimpered into his mouth. He thrust his leg between hers, and gripping her hips, encouraged her to ride him. She eased back and forth, hesitantly at first and then found her rhythm.

"You are so wet," he groaned against her cheek, then gasped for air. The knowledge sent a sharp stab of hunger straight to his penis. Her moisture eased the glide of her flesh over his thigh. She trembled ever so slightly, but enough to let him know she was as turned on and close to the edge as he. "Are you ready for me?"

"Yes," she whispered breathlessly.

He couldn't wait any longer. He eased his fingers between them and found her slickness. The scent of her arousal rose up to greet him, and his heart slammed against his chest.

He stroked her center, circling her tender flesh again and again until her back bowed over his arm, granting him access to the sweet taste of her nipple. He rolled the tight bud with his tongue, grazed it with his teeth, then sucked it deep into his mouth. He sampled the other, licking, biting, sucking. "Do you like me touching you, Sabrina?"

"Yes. Yes. I do." Her cries of release echoed off the high ceiling. Then, near the breaking point, he bent his knees, determined to take her on the rug in front of the fire and pulling her down with him.

"Wait." She remained standing as he kissed his way down her tummy. "Do you have a condom?"

Her question yanked him back to reality. "In the bedroom."

The bedroom seemed a mile away. But they couldn't take any more unnecessary risks. He swept her into his arms and carried her to his room. Despite her height, she weighed practically nothing in his arms.

The maid had already been in and turned on the bedside lamp, folded down the covers and left chocolate truffles on the pillows. He laid Sabrina on the sheets and pushed the confections away. The only thing he wanted to feast on was her.

On second thought…

He snatched up one chocolate and unwrapped it, watching curiosity fill her eyes. He licked her nipple, dampening it, then pressed the chocolate to the tight tip.

She gasped and flinched. "It's cold."

"It won't be for long." He circled her puckered flesh, leaving a melting chocolate trail on first one hard, dusky pink areola, then the other. Desire flushed her face and chest. Her eyelids fell to half-mast, and she bit her bottom lip which was already swollen, red and damp from his passionate kisses. Beautiful.

She shifted restlessly beneath him, her breaths stuttering in, then out again. "That feels…g-good."

He lapped up the chocolate, being sure to do a thorough job before he reapplied the confection once, twice, a third time until the only thing left was the smudge on his fingertips. When every trace of the chocolate was gone from her breasts, he offered her his hand. "Lick me."

Without hesitation, she grasped his wrist and sucked a chocolate-covered finger deep into her mouth. The sight of his flesh disappearing between her lips combined with the swirl of her tongue over his skin pushed him perilously close to the edge.

"You're driving me crazy, baby. I like your mouth on me." He shook with hunger, and could barely wait until she cleaned the last of the chocolate from him before he kissed her, their mouths mingling the tastes of candy and desire.

Gasping, she pushed him away. "Condom."

He groaned, then yanked open the nightstand drawer and grabbed protection. Where was his head? He didn't make stupid mistakes like forgetting precautions. Certainly not twice.

After he'd taken care of business, she extended her arms, beckoning him. He stroked her thighs apart and savored the sight of her glistening sex, then moved into position. Her lids drifted shut, her head turned away.

"Open your eyes. Look at me."

Her lashes fluttered upward and their gazes locked. Gritting his teeth against the urge to drive deep and hard, he eased in, one arm-quaking inch at a time. His pulse hammered in his ears. Need burned his gut, licking like the flames of a wildfire at the base of his spine and snaking out in hot streaks. Watching pleasure expand her pupils and part her lips magnified every sensation. "Tell me what you want."

Sabrina grasped his hips. "Please, now. Hurry. I'm so close."

The dam of his control broke. He thrust deep, hard and fast, riding the crest of desire. He tortured himself with restraint, teetering on the edge as he stroked her to climax with his thumb. Her inner contractions put another crack in his control but he fought off his release. He wasn't ready for this to end. Not yet.

She arched off the bed, banding her arms around his neck, and then her breath fanned his ear a split second before her tongue outlined the rim, then her teeth closed on his lobe. The love bite sent him reeling and he lost it. Wave after wave of hot, molten pleasure erupted through him until spent, he collapsed to his elbows above her with her cries echoing in his ears.

Her body spasmed around his with aftershocks, and the gentle clutching and releasing was almost too exquisite to bear. He eventually found the strength to separate from her and ease onto his back beside her. Shaken by the intensity of the experience, he stared at the ceiling.

Why her? Why did this woman who'd been forced upon him have the power to rock his world and decimate his control like no other?

He'd be damned if he knew. But he would find out.

Because if he didn't, losing her could destroy him the way losing his mother had destroyed his father.

She had to get out of here, Sabrina decided once her lassitude eased and her brain resumed functioning.

She turned her head to study Gavin through the steam rising from the hot tub and visually traced the strong line of his jaw and throat and his broad, wet shoulders—the same line her hands and mouth already had taken three times today. She tried to work up a little shame for her day of debauchery… and failed.

With his arms and head resting on the rim of the hot tub and his breathing deep and even, he appeared totally relaxed. Was he asleep? He hadn't moved since he'd dragged her out onto the deck to sink into the steaming water after their impromptu fireside dinner followed by round two of lov—sex. Her body quivered at the memory of his devilishly talented tongue making her climax again and again on the rug by the fire.

She blew out a silent, shaky breath and prayed she wasn't courting disaster. She couldn't afford to care for him. No matter how much fun she'd had with him tonight. Or how good the sex—all three times—had been. He'd done something to her, cast some spell over her to keep her from thinking straight. If she wasn't careful she'd forget this temporary relationship was all about physical fulfillment.

An urgent need to run surged through her. She started to rise. "I have to go."

Without cracking an eyelid, Gavin snagged her wrist and pulled her back down into the water. It was as if he had some sixth sense or mental GPS or something that told him where she was without looking. "Stay with me tonight."

Her heart slammed against her chest like a racing horse against the gate, then it pounded like thundering hooves. "I can't. Pops will be waiting for me."

Without releasing her Gavin turned his head and their gazes met. "Henry will understand."

She'd be lying to herself if she didn't acknowledge she was tempted. Tempted to give in to the passionate demand in Gavin's dark eyes, tempted to lie in his arms, tempted to hold and be held throughout the dark night. And that was exactly why she had to go. She broke free of his grip, the lubricant of the water enabling her escape, and bolted to her feet.

The biting cold temperature slammed against her hot, wet skin like an iceberg. "There's nothing to understand. We were both answering a biological need and we had sex. That's it."

He rose and stood beside her, water streaming over his corded muscles, flat belly, groin and thighs. Involuntarily, her eyes tracked the cascade. He caught an escaped curl and tucked it back into the knot she'd made at her nape, then lifted her chin with a knuckle. "It's more than that. You know it. I enjoy your company, Sabrina. I had more fun tonight than I have had in a long time."

The hint of surprise in his eyes and voice undermined her resistance. Was he as shaken by this sudden attraction as she was? She struggled to rally her defenses because she needed room and privacy to think and reevaluate her plan. "I enjoyed tonight as well, Gavin. But I nee—I want to go home. If you can't take me, then please call me a cab."

She couldn't—wouldn't—call Pops. She knew he'd come

get her instantly, but even if he didn't have trouble driving after dark, she didn't want him to know about tonight—today—any of it. As much as he'd been nagging about her lack of a social life lately, he was incredibly old-fashioned. He wouldn't approve of an affair with no future.

Telling him about the affair would be a great way to drive a wedge between him and Gavin.

She debated the option, but decided she couldn't handle Pops being as disappointed in her as her parents had been when they'd found out about Russell. Especially since, like that first time with Russell, she'd forgotten to use birth control. Surely she wouldn't be as unlucky as to have the same consequence. Worry churned in her stomach. She fisted her hands rather than give in to the aching need to cover her belly. And what if she was wrong about Gavin? What if he was being honest and wanted nothing more than the mine? But her doubts niggled.

"I want to go home."

Without moving, Gavin's body seemed to coil with tension. "I'll drive you."

She suddenly felt uncomfortable and exposed being outside and naked, and she wanted to duck back into the water to cover up. Instead, she forced herself to climb from the tub, knowing Gavin had an unobstructed view of her butt—which she'd never been fond of. Dripping, she stood on the wooden deck, hugging herself and getting colder by the second. The snow chilled her feet. Now what? She couldn't track water all over the floors. The heck with the polished wood. Better a wet floor than hypothermia. "We should have brought out towels."

"No need." Gavin climbed from the water, mesmerizing her with his ropy arm muscles, defined chest and wet, long legs. He opened a cabinet built into the wall of the lodge and withdrew a large bath sheet which he unfolded and draped around her shoulders.

She gasped in surprise. "It's warm."

"The cabinet is heated." He gripped the ends of the fabric, trapping her arms by her sides. His attention dropped to her mouth, and before she could move, he dipped his head and kissed her. Her senses overloaded with the cold air, the warmth of the towel and touch of his mouth.

The easy brush of his lips across hers might be considered innocent compared to their earlier, more carnal exchanges, but nonetheless it slammed her with the full force of desire, weakening her knees and making her want him all over again. *How did he do that?*

She dug up the strength to push away. Grabbing the towel and hugging it close, she put a yard between them.

Your hormones are making up for lost time. It's nothing special. He's nothing special.

Gavin extracted a second towel and dried himself as casually as if he were in the privacy of his bathroom instead of outside on his back porch in freezing temperatures. Not that anyone was likely to see them with the way every Jarrod Ridge lodge was secluded, and with the hot tub tucked into a little nook, but still…

She caught herself admiring the ripple and flex of his muscles beneath his taut skin and the tightening of his nipples due to the cold. The temptation to drag her tongue across the tiny brown bumps drove her to bolt through the French door and race for her clothes.

The sound of the door closing and the quiet, confident pad of footsteps told her Gavin had followed. When she risked peeking at him and noted he'd wound a towel around his hips she exhaled in relief. He threw another log on the fire. The pop and hiss drew her like a flame does a moth. But getting closer to the fire meant getting closer to him and standing in the exact spot where he'd pleasured her so many times earlier.

Turning her back to him, she hastily dragged on her bra and shirt, and then reached for her jeans. The denim had dried in front of the fire, and if it was stiff and rough against her skin, then the discomfort was no more than what she deserved.

Consider it penance for using the man to scratch your sexual itch.

She yanked on her socks and boots, then prowled the room rather than watch Gavin dress, but she couldn't block out the *swish* of his jeans sliding over his hair-dusted legs, the *rrrp* of his zipper or the thump of him stomping his feet into his boots. Her brain filled in the gaps with graphic images collected over the past three hours, and her body hummed like a beehive.

She couldn't recall ever being this aware of anyone before— not even Russell, and she'd thought she'd memorized her husband's every gesture. Being so attuned to a near-stranger concerned her.

She had to get out of here. *Now.* She hastily donned her coat, then turned and found Gavin immediately behind her. She staggered back at his close proximity.

"You planning to love me and leave me, snow angel?" he asked with a teasing half smile that didn't carry to his searching eyes, and it was his eyes she focused on rather than the way his "snow angel" rumbled through her like an avalanche. Why was he so solemn?

"Pops will wonder where I am."

"He knows you're with me and that I won't let anything happen to you."

"It's late." And her will to escape was weakening. "Ready to go?"

Bracing a hand on her waist, he reached past her for his coat, pressing the length of his body against hers. Her hormones clamored to attention despite the workout they'd already been given. She was more physically sated tonight than she'd ever been in her life. How could she still want him? She gulped.

He shrugged on the garment, staying in her personal space as if laying claim to it. "Let's go."

Then he moved out of scent range and opened the front door, giving her an opportunity to fill her tight lungs with fresh, cold, sobering air. She stepped outside into a world of white and stopped to admire the scene. Inches of fresh snow blanketed the ground and low shrubs.

She glanced up at him. "The weather forecast wasn't calling for this much snow, was it?"

"No. And it's still coming down heavily. It would be safer for you to stay until morning when the roads have been plowed."

Alarm raced over her. She wasn't ready to play house or sleep with him all night. He'd already shaken her defenses. "I can't. I have to make sure Pops takes his medicines."

"Then I'll get you home." Gavin led her to the Jeep he'd driven that first day and helped her into the passenger seat. He took her hand, uncurled her fingers and pressed the keys into her palm. "Start the engine. Warm up the car."

After closing her door he scraped the windows, then joined her in the cab. The Jeep slipped a bit as he backed out of the parking space, making her pulse skip. Maybe staying would be safer. No. Too big of a risk.

Gavin drove slowly through the resort's winding roads. The short drive into downtown seemed to take forever. He reached across the seat and briefly covered her cool hands with the heat of his. "I'll get you there in one piece. Relax. I've driven in worse."

She winced when she realized he'd caught her fisting her fingers so tightly that her nails had dug into her palms. "Sorry. I just haven't mastered driving on slick roads yet."

The inn finally came into view. She heaved a sigh of relief.

Gavin pulled as close to the back door as he could get and killed the engine.

"Who plows your parking lot?"

"Pops has always done it with the tractor we have in the barn."

"I'll come by and do it in the morning."

"You don't have to do that, Gavin."

"The ground's going to freeze tonight. Henry doesn't need to risk slipping and breaking a hip."

When he put it that way, how could she refuse? And yes, his consideration touched her. "Thanks."

"Not a problem." He shoved open his door.

She stiffened. "You should get home before the roads worsen."

"I'm walking you to the door," he said, his voice firm and insistent.

Determined to keep the good-bye short and sweet, she slid from the cab. Gavin caught up with her, grabbed her arm and offered support as she made her way through the powdery snow. She wanted to cast off his help, but the back door opened before she could. Pops stood in the threshold.

"Should have known my bones weren't wrong about the storm front."

"They never are, Pops." She turned to Gavin, trying to figure out how exactly you said good-night to a lover when you didn't want anyone to know about the intimacy. "Thanks for the ride, and the sledding and dinner."

He searched her face. "You're welcome."

"Get out of the way, girlie, and let the man inside," Pops said from behind her. "You're not sending Gavin back out in this weather. It's late and we have a houseful of beds. He can stay here and go home in the morning after the roads are plowed."

No. Panic rose inside her. "But, Pops—"

"B'sides, I'll need his help cranking the old tractor and putting the plow blade on it in the morning."

Her stomach plunged to her cold feet and a trapped sensation banded her chest. Spending a night under the same roof as Gavin Jarrod was the last thing she wanted to do.

But the choice had been taken from her.

Nine

She should be exhausted, but instead Sabrina fidgeted in bed, staring gritty-eyed at the ceiling and worrying her bottom lip with her teeth. She could still taste Gavin on her lips, smell him on her skin and feel the residue of their coupling between her legs. Maybe a shower would wash away her tension so she could sleep. But no. Since her bathroom backed up to Pops's, he would hear the water running through the pipes in the walls of the old house.

That left her stuck with traces of Gavin all over her and the same old unanswered question playing over and over in her head. Had she made a mistake in getting involved with Gavin?

A noise jerked her from her rumination. Holding her breath, she listened until she heard the click-click again, then bolted upright, climbed from the bed and eased open her door. Was someone in the house? The muffled sounds came from the laundry room just down the hall. No trespasser would break in there and close the door.

Panic subsiding, she exhaled in relief. No doubt Pops was sneaking one of his contraband cigars with the back door open to try and alleviate the odor. It wouldn't be the first time she'd caught him defying his doctor's orders in the middle of the night when he thought he wouldn't get caught. And with the storm still blowing, his aching bones were probably keeping him awake.

Without turning on the lights she shuffled down the hall letting the sliver glowing beneath the door act as her beacon. She sniffed, but she didn't smell a pungent tobacco aroma. Ready to scold Pops and rehash the old argument *again,* she shoved open the laundry room door. The sight of Gavin, with his back to her and a pair of her grandfather's sweatpants riding low on his hips sent her staggering backward.

He pivoted, all bare-chested, barefooted and delicious.

A thin line of pale, untanned skin showing just above his waistband drew her eyes. She forced her gaze upward. "What are you doing?"

"Washing my clothes. We worked up a sweat on the slope tonight."

And again in his lodge. Twice. She pushed the heat-inducing memories aside. "You know how to use the machines?"

He tilted his head and gave her a patient look. "Of course. I know how to wash my own clothes."

He washed his own clothes, she silently parroted. Somehow that fact made him seem more human and less rich, obnoxious and entitled. And she had to admit, albeit reluctantly, she found his confidence in being able to handle anything that came his way extremely attractive.

Yet another thought to squash. *Focus on the fact that he's invading your turf. Again.* "I usually do our guests' laundry if they ask."

"Henry gave me free run of the place and told me to make myself at home. Do you have anything you want to throw in here?"

"No." Rejection sprung automatically to her lips. How could something as commonplace as sharing an appliance's washtub seem so...personal, so intimate? But the idea of their clothing intertwining in the water the way their bodies had earlier made her pulse skip and her skin flush.

And then there was her grandfather's new open-door policy. What was up with that? Normally he wasn't as trusting as he'd been with Gavin. Why the sudden change? What did she not know? There had to be something.

Gavin closed the lid and leaned a hip against the machine as water splashed into the basin. "Did I wake you?"

"No."

Fighting the temptation to ogle his body, she focused instead on his face, and because of that she didn't miss his gaze roving over her, starting with her hair which was probably a frizzy mess from her tossing and turning, then he studied her face, her chest, her torso and her legs. The return trip dragged on equally as long, stirring up a storm of awareness inside her. For a few precious seconds she regretted wearing her old, boring flannel nightgown.

What do you care about his opinion of your wardrobe? You don't.

A rueful smile twisted his mouth. "Considering the day we've had, we should both be sleeping soundly tonight. But here we are. Awake well past midnight."

Because of the orgasms, he meant. She couldn't even remember how many she'd had. Russell had always allowed her one, sometimes two, then he'd gotten down to business. Not that their sex life hadn't been good, but it had never been...stupendous.

Uncomfortable with the traitorous thought, she shifted on

her feet. "If you're tired you can go to bed, and I'll switch your stuff to the dryer when it's done so you'll have clean clothes in the morning."

"I can handle it. I make a mean hot chocolate. It'll help us unwind." He leaned forward, snagged her wrist and tugged her toward the kitchen.

She tugged back, but trying to pull free proved useless. His grip remained tight. Hijacked in her own home. How had that happened? "What if I don't want hot chocolate?"

"You will once you taste mine. Like me, it's irresistible."

His cockiness combined with the playful attitude he'd displayed while sledding tonight startled a laugh from her. The man had an ego the size of the Rocky Mountains. "You think so?"

He stopped abruptly and snatched her forward. Their bodies collided with a soft, heart-skipping thump. "I know so."

Her breasts, overly sensitive from the attention he'd already showered on them today, nonetheless welcomed the pressure of his chest against them. His lips settled on hers, sipping and sampling softly at first, then with increasing pressure and urgency. Her pulse rate tripled and her body seemed to come alive in his arms, wanting more of the magic she knew he could deliver. Before she could work up a protest or convince her hands to rise and shove him away, he grasped her upper arms and set her back. "Wait and see. Where do you keep your cocoa and spices?"

Dizzy from the abrupt change, she blinked to clear her head, then pointed toward the pantry and sank bonelessly onto the nearest barstool. She wasn't used to letting someone wait on her. And she wasn't sure she liked it. But she'd give it a try. It wasn't as if she'd get used to it and get lazy since the relationship was short-term.

Gavin found a pot, then gathered and combined the ingredients. After he'd stirred the mixture into the milk and turned on the burner he leaned against the counter watching her with those predator's eyes. Was he trying to read her mind or looking for a vulnerable spot to attack? Her nipples tightened and her breathing quickened. Sexual tension sizzled in the air between them. She didn't know how to handle it.

"Come here, Sabrina."

Her breath caught at the hungry look in his eyes. "Why?"

"Because you want to."

She did, and that scared her. For that reason alone she should refuse, but she slid from the barstool and circled the work island on trembling legs because… Well, she didn't know why exactly. She just did.

He cupped her jaw. "I haven't had as much fun as I did today in a long time. We're good together. In bed. And out."

When he spoke in that low, knee-melting rumble and looked at her as if he wanted to eat her up she had trouble remembering her name, let alone why they were so wrong for each other. "It's just sex."

He caressed her cheek, and the urge to lean into his palm, into his body, surprised her. "Tell yourself that if it makes you feel better."

"You don't agree?"

"No. I don't." He paused and sniffed. "Hold that thought and prepare to be impressed." He turned back to the stove, stirred the mixture.

Confused by her disappointment, she hugged her arms around her chest. She should go back to her room. If she stayed there was no telling what would happen.

"Do you have marshmallows?" he asked.

She retrieved the bag. He dropped a few of the white puffs into each mug then poured the steaming liquid over them. The scents of chocolate and cinnamon filled the air.

He lifted his cup for a toast. "To us and the good times we have yet to share."

The statement implied more of a future than they had.

"To good times," she corrected and clanked her mug against his. She really should hate him. He was encroaching on her territory, possibly threatening the roof over her head and her grandfather's security. But distrusting Gavin grew more difficult by the second. And then she sipped his hot cocoa, and disliking him became easier. First his coffee was better than hers, now this.

"Your cocoa is better than my grandmother's recipe," she offered grudgingly.

"Told you I'm good." But his suggestive tone and the hot look in his eyes implied he wasn't talking about the beverage.

Rather than deal with the sexual innuendo that tangled her thoughts and her tummy, she gulped another mouthful, savoring the sweetness of the marshmallows and the richness of the chocolate. "I can't see you slaving over a hot stove perfecting a recipe."

"You're right. My brother is top chef in the kitchen. But make it campfire rations and I'm king. I made hot cocoa whenever my brothers and I camped out at the mine."

King. Yes, she'd just bet he liked that. She enjoyed the peeks into his past more than she should since they were completely irrelevant to whether or not he was trying to swindle her grandfather. "I want your recipe."

"You'll have to earn it."

"How?"

His lips curved slowly upward, stealing her breath and sending a rush of warmth to her lower regions. "Drink up and I'll show you."

Every fine hair on her body rose to attention. Gavin Jarrod excelled at whatever game he was playing. He was so far out of her league, how could she even begin to compete? And if she wasn't careful, she was going to fall under his spell.

Who are you kidding? You already have.

Her heart went splat like a thrown snowball and settled like a cold, heavy blob in her stomach. She was falling for Gavin Jarrod despite her aversion to rich men and emotional involvements, and her fear that he had ulterior motives for befriending Pops.

She'd let him get too close. And she didn't know how to push him away. Or even if she wanted to anymore.

A creeping awareness of pins and needles prickling Gavin's left arm woke him slowly. He flexed his fingers, trying to work the circulation back into his limb. That's when he noticed the warm, soft, sweet-smelling weight on his biceps and remembered where he was and why.

Sabrina. He'd slept with her last night. In her bed. Under Henry's roof. Not smart considering the deed had not been signed over. But he was close—damned close—to closing the deal.

He'd intended to sleep alone just to prove a point—the point being that he controlled the hunger he felt for his soon-to-be temporary wife rather than the hunger controlling him. But the marshmallow foam on Sabrina's upper lip had been his downfall. One cocoa-flavored kiss and he'd lost control and his common sense, apparently. Even then, he'd intended to leave after the sex, but when he'd tried, Sabrina had whispered, "Stay," and he'd caved like a damned fool.

To make matters worse, dawn outlined the curtains, and his clothes were still in the washer. Henry would be expecting him to help with the tractor soon.

Gavin grimaced. He had to get up. But he didn't want to move. The narrow queen bed should have felt cramped since he was used to stretching out in a king. Instead he liked it because it forced Sabrina to lie against him, his body spooning her warmth, her hair tickling his chin and chest. He felt better rested than he had in months—as if he'd had his first good night's sleep since returning to Aspen.

What in the hell had she done to him?

He had to get out of here before he started believing their relationship could be anything other than temporary. Any marriage to him would be doomed to failure—his past relationships and those of his co-workers had proven that fact repeatedly. He didn't do failure. And he sure as hell didn't want to end up like his father—a cold heartless bastard who had driven his children away and had to die to get them to come home.

He eased out of bed, being careful not to wake Sabrina. She sighed in her sleep and rolled onto her back, one pink-tipped breast peeking above the sheet. Hunger speared him and he nearly reached out to stroke the soft swell. He searched her face from the dark fan of lashes on her cheeks to her red lips, and smooth, flushed skin. Beautiful. The urge to say to hell with Henry and climb back between the sheets hit hard, but he stifled it and reached for the borrowed sweatpants. Business came first, and his family was counting on him.

He made his way to the door and escaped as silently as possible. The smell of strong coffee was his first indication of pending disaster.

He ignored it and made his way down the hall to the laundry room. He opened the washer. Empty. It was still too early for Henry to be up, but he hadn't felt Sabrina leave the bed during the night to switch the clothes to the dryer. He was a light sleeper, but maybe he'd been so drained he'd missed it. Doubtful. He opened the dryer. His clothes were inside and still warm. The warmth was a bad omen.

He had a feeling he'd been busted by Henry. Gavin dressed quickly by the machine, and dreading what lay ahead, made his way toward the kitchen. Henry sat at the table, cup of coffee in his hand, a newspaper in front of him and a scowl on his face so fierce it would blister paint. Anger shot from his eyes like lasers and stiffened his frail body.

Aw, hell. A sinking feeling entered Gavin's stomach. He squared his shoulders, prepared to fight the battle since he couldn't avoid it.

"You've abused my hospitality and my trust."

Yep. Busted. "You asked me to romance Sabrina. I'm doing it. My way."

"You'd better not hurt that girl."

"I have no intention of hurting Sabrina."

"If you do, you'll never get what you want out of that land. I'll tie it up in so many legal knots you won't be able to untangle it."

"You said you'd sign over the deed to me."

Henry's mouth flattened into a straight line. "An' *I* won't go back on my word. I may not have the money you Jarrods have, but I've been in this city a long time. I have connections. You'll find it impossible to get your permits or even your trash picked up if you cross me."

Great. Just what he needed. He'd made a potential enemy out of his only ally.

The men had been outside for over an hour. The sound of the back door closing had jarred Sabrina from her deepest sleep in years. Her face warmed as she recalled the cause of her near-comatose state. Gavin. Sledding. Multiple orgasms.

But she'd yet to hear the growl of the old tractor's engine. Knowing the pair of them, they'd probably started talking and weren't getting any work done. They must be frozen by now.

Juggling the thermos and a couple of mugs, Sabrina stepped onto the back porch. The snow had stopped and the sun was making a weak effort to peep through the clouds, but the bite of cold still lingered in the air. A narrow path to the barn had been shoveled clear. Gavin must have done it. Her grandfather had given up shoveling more than a year ago. Like other chores, it had become her job. This year she needed to look into hiring a high school boy to do it.

She made her way to the barn, entered and pulled the side door closed behind her. Other than the horses crunching on oats in the stall, she heard nothing—no conversation, not even the radio her grandfather usually listened to while he tinkered in his small workshop. The two of them working in silence struck her as odd.

A small kerosene heater had warmed the interior to above freezing, but she sensed a chill in the air that had nothing to do with the weather. What could it be?

Your imagination, probably. Or maybe their frustration over not getting the machine running.

Her grandfather sat stiffly on the tractor's seat. He glanced at her, then he stared straight ahead at Gavin bent over the front of the plow blade with a wrench in his hand. Gavin had stripped off his coat and his shoulder muscles flexed beneath his turtleneck as he yanked on something. Desire trickled through her like melting snow sliding down the mountainside.

She cleared her throat, breaking the silence. "I brought coffee."

Both men looked at her, but neither made a move in her direction. Gavin and Pops had never been short of conversation and yet they weren't talking.

"Is something wrong with the tractor?" she asked.

Gavin straightened. "One of the nuts is rusted. I'm having trouble breaking it loose from the bolt to attach the plow. If soaking it in motor oil won't free it I'll have to cut the bolt and wait until the store opens to get a replacement."

She searched his face, seeking the man who'd held her and made love to her so tenderly last night. Instead she found no welcome in his expression. Confused and slightly hurt, she turned to her grandfather. "You've been out here a long time. Why don't you take a break and warm up?"

Pops swung down from the seat and made his way to her, stopping between her and Gavin. His eyes seemed to probe hers. "How're you this mornin'?"

A smile she couldn't hold back curved her lips, but then the odd undertone in his voice registered. What did it mean? Did he know Gavin had been in her room? *No. He couldn't.* They'd been quiet, and her last memory of Gavin had been of him kissing her good-night and telling her he was going upstairs to his room. She'd mumbled, "Okay," through lips almost numb from his ravenous kisses, and then, oblivion. She didn't remember him actually leaving.

"I'm fine. How are your bones this morning?"

"Good enough." The succinct answer wasn't like him.

Gavin joined them, but kept out of her personal space— unusual for him. He silently met and held her gaze. She wished she could read him well enough to know what he was thinking. But she hadn't even known him a week. Way too soon to be getting as serious or as intimate as they had. They'd skipped a lot of get-to-know-you steps in the dating game.

Too late to worry about that now. As Pops would say, that horse had already fled the barn.

"Pour me a cup, girlie."

Blinking at the reminder of why she'd come out here, she filled the mugs. "I can call someone to clear the driveway if you don't think you can get our tractor working."

Gavin accepted a mug. "If I can't get this bolt loose I'll have the Jarrod Ridge crew take care of it."

"Don't want your damn charity," Pops grumbled.

"It's not charity. It's a neighbor helping a neighbor," Gavin countered tightly.

"Neighborly, huh. Is that what you call it?"

Alarm slithered over Sabrina and a sinking feeling settled in the pit of her stomach. She looked from one man to the other. The tension and antagonism between them was palpable. That could only mean one thing.

Pops knew Gavin had been in her room last night. Her lungs emptied.

Would Pops condemn her? Would he call her a slut the way her father had? Would he shake his head in disgust and stare at her with disappointment-filled eyes? Would he order her to get out because he couldn't stand the sight of her?

She gulped. Her parents had been more concerned with the embarrassment her unplanned pregnancy would cause them and the potential backlash on their careers than they had on the effect of the situation on her life.

Bracing herself, she searched her grandfather's face and waited. For condemnation, for understanding or…or anything. Instead, like Gavin, he offered no clues to his thoughts or feelings.

The one thing she'd wanted just days ago—to break up the camaraderie between Gavin and Pops—had fallen into her lap. Right after she'd decided she didn't want it anymore. Not when she might be falling for Gavin.

And that enmity could very well spread to her.

Now what was she going to do?

How could she make it right?

She didn't have a clue.

Ten

"Sorry it took me so long to get here. I was in the middle of something," Gavin told Blake as he joined his brother in the Jarrod Ridge offices. Coming here still made him uncomfortable even without their father behind that desk dispensing orders and disapproval.

He'd received Blake's text message requesting a meeting hours ago, but he'd refused to leave the Snowberry Inn until he'd plowed the parking lot. Doing so would have meant Henry plowing it and possibly breaking a hip, and/or killing himself with that old tractor before the deed was settled. Besides, Gavin realized, he liked the old geezer and didn't want him to get hurt.

And then old habits had kicked in. He'd returned to the lodge to shower off the tractor grease and change clothes before putting in an appearance. Being dirty in the public rooms of Jarrod Ridge had always brought down their father's wrath. On second thought, he should have come here filthy, just to make dear old Dad roll over in his grave.

Blake gestured to a chair. "What's the status on the land?"

"I have the situation under control," he replied with a confidence he wasn't sure he believed. But damn it, he would not fail.

Blake grinned. "I remember saying that last month about me and Samantha."

"Yeah, and your assistant turned the tables on you. That won't happen with me. I'm close to getting the property back from Henry Caldwell."

"How close? Should I let the construction crew move on to another project?"

Frustration made his molars slam together. "If we do, then we'll lose them for months."

"That's right. We'll have to wait until they finish their next job. But they're about to wrap the current project and can't afford to stand idle."

Damn. He had to pick up the pace. Move the marriage forward. He weighed the idea, and surprisingly, it didn't repulse him as much as it once had. He also needed to get back on Henry's good side and marrying Sabrina would do it. The sooner, the better all around. "How'd you go about your wedding?"

"Excuse me?"

He eyed his brother. "Arranging a marriage, Vegas-style."

Blake's eyebrows lowered. "Why?"

"I've been seeing Sabrina, Henry's granddaughter, and I'm thinking of proposing."

"You?"

"Sure. Why not? She's beautiful. I enjoy her company, and the sex is good." Damned good. Phenomenal even. But his brother didn't need to know that.

Blake started shaking his head even before Gavin finished speaking. "That's not a reason to get married."

"No. It's three reasons. Three good ones."

Blake gave him a pitying look that chafed. "You might want to hold out for love."

"Who says I don't love her?"

"You haven't said you do, which means you don't."

Because he didn't lie. "I'm not the kind of guy who shares personal stuff like that. But I care about her. A lot."

And strangely, that wasn't a lie.

"Then take it slow and see what develops."

"I don't want to wait."

Blake frowned. "I'm not liking the smell of your urgency. This isn't tied to getting the land, is it?"

Gavin considered prevaricating, but Blake was too smart to be fooled. "Henry will be…encouraged to sign the deed sooner if I'm part of the family."

"Don't do it, Gavin. Don't tie yourself to someone you don't love. It's not fair to you and it's disrespectful to her."

"Says the man who seduced his assistant to keep her from quitting. I know what I'm doing."

"Those sound like famous last words—words you'll regret, I might add."

He brushed off his brother's concern. He didn't have a choice. "Like I said, I have the situation under control. Don't let the crew go. We'll be ready to break ground as soon as they finish their current job."

He rose, ending the meeting before his brother could ask more probing questions, and made his way to the door. The idea of whisking Sabrina off to Vegas was growing on him. No fanfare. No money down the drain. No witnesses. But he wasn't doing that until he had a prenup. For that he needed Christian, the family attorney and soon-to-be brother-in-law.

But first, he needed a ring and a pitch she couldn't refuse. Until he proposed and Sabrina accepted, the rest was a moot point.

"You win," Sabrina said after the waiter discreetly backed away from the table, leaving her and Gavin to their after-dinner coffee. In normal circumstances, a highfalutin place like the riverside restaurant wasn't her style. But with Gavin seated across from her at the candlelit table the evening seemed magical.

"How do I win? Aside from the great company," Gavin asked in that deep, rumbling voice of his that sent a shiver down her spine.

Her cheeks warmed. She didn't know where to begin. From the moment he'd shown up at the inn's front door wearing an immaculately fitted black suit and carrying a dozen red roses every single minute had seemed like a fairytale.

"You got me to a restaurant with a wine list the size of a telephone book and no prices on the menu and made me love it. The food was amazing. And this…" She flicked a hand to indicate the linen-draped table set in an intimate alcove overlooking the Roaring Fork River and the landscaping beyond the window decorated with twinkling white lights. "I don't know how you managed to get reservations on short notice when most people wait a month to get in, but this is so…perfect. The flowers, the wine, that decadent tiramisu… everything."

He smiled a little, but he seemed tense. "I'm glad you enjoyed it. I want nothing but the best for you. For us. From here on out."

Her heart hiccupped at the serious look in his eyes. She swallowed. "What do you mean?"

Gavin reached across the table and captured her hand. Her pulse did its usual skip on contact. She loved the strength and gentleness of his hands and the warmth of his skin on hers. He caressed the heart of her palm with his thumb, stirring up a fizzy sensation low in her abdomen.

"Sabrina, I want to go to sleep with you in my arms like we did last night and wake up with in you in mine every morning."

A thrill shot through her. At the same time, fear tickled her nape. But she'd promised herself seven months and she'd take it. A finite period of pleasure would be safe. But part of her—an itty bitty part—had begun to want more. She struggled to catch her breath. "I'd like that, too."

His fingers tightened. "I don't want to have to sneak around to be with you, and I don't want to upset Henry. I respect him too much for that. Him catching me coming out of your room this morning made us all uncomfortable."

Understatement of the year. Pops hadn't said a word, but the tension had hung over them like a dark cloud all day. "I thought you were going back to your room as soon as I fell asleep."

"You asked me to stay, and I didn't have the strength to refuse." Before she could correct him Gavin shifted, reaching into his suit coat pocket with his free hand and withdrawing a small black velvet box.

That couldn't be what she thought it was.

"Marry me, Sabrina, then we can share as many nights like this as we want." He flipped open the lid, revealing a pale blue stone set on a woven gold band.

She gasped. This couldn't be happening. Not to her. She wasn't ready.

"The stone reminded me of your eyes. Bright, clear and beautiful. And when the light catches it right, there's an inner fire that ignites. From the moment I saw it, I knew it belonged on your finger and that I wanted to be the one to place it there."

No one had ever said anything as romantic to her in her life. Her head reeled and her pulse pounded in her ears. She lifted a shaky hand to her chest. "It's—Gavin, the ring is beautiful, but we haven't even known each other a week."

His gaze remained steadfast. "Long enough to know we're as perfectly matched as two people will ever be."

Wanting to say yes was wrong on so many levels, but the tiny word danced on the tip of her tongue. And that was *crazy*. It was too soon to make such a momentous decision. Hadn't she sworn never to fall in love again because she didn't think she could survive the hurt of losing someone special? And wasn't Gavin still a rich guy?

But he is so much more than that, an insistent voice in her head argued. He's fun and sexy and smart. He made her feel alive and special. She'd been wrong about him on so many levels. He didn't act as if he were entitled to anything he wanted, and he didn't treat her as if she was less worthy because she was less wealthy.

Stop it. Just say no. Or ask for more time.

But what if she did and she lost him forever? Was she willing to risk that? No. And what if this moment was the one that she'd remember for the rest of her life? She fought to clear her head and use logic. "We barely know each other."

"Ask me anything."

"I don't even know you well enough to know what to ask. What about your job and your insistence on leaving Aspen?"

"I'll make Aspen my home base. That way you can be here for Henry."

"Where would we live?"

"For now, I have to live on Jarrod property."

"I can't leave Pops alone at night."

"I'll arrange for someone to stay with him."

He made it sound so easy. "Why are you in such a rush?"

"I don't want to miss another day with you."

If a heart could actually melt, hers would be a soggy puddle beneath her feet right now. So much for her resistance to his charm.

"I'll charter a plane and first thing in the morning we'll fly to Vegas."

Shock knocked her back in her chair. "Vegas?"

"In another week you'll be too busy for a vacation. We'll find a little chapel and get married and be back before Henry misses us."

A cold rock settled in her stomach, squashing all her warm, fuzzy feelings. "You want to elope? Tomorrow?"

"Why wait?"

"We're moving too fast."

"Do you love me?"

The abrupt and unexpected question stunned her speechless. She'd been trying very, very hard not to let her mind wander down that dangerous, slippery path. Her stomach churned, and her thoughts swirled wildly. Did she love him? The weight of the answer settled on her like a cold blanket of heavy snow. "I—I am falling in love with you."

He closed his eyes, squeezed her hand and inhaled long and slow. His emotional reaction to her confession touched her deeply. Then he met her gaze again with determination-filled eyes. "Marry me so we can be together."

He hadn't said he loved her back. But from what she'd learned of his childhood, of his mother's death when he was four and his father's overbearing nature, she suspected words of love wouldn't come easily to Gavin. She'd have to work on that.

"Gavin, even if I accepted your proposal, I wouldn't elope. I did that the first time." The hand in her lap clenched and released. Should she tell him? Yes. If their relationship had a future, then it had to be based on total honesty.

"There's something you need to know. The reason I was in such a hurry to get married the first time is because…because I was pregnant. I—I was still in high school when I found out. My parents gave me the ultimatum of getting rid of my baby or getting out of their house. In their circle, unmarried daughters didn't have unplanned babies." She searched his face, trying to read his reaction, but failed to see so much as a flicker of emotion.

"I told Russell, and when he came home from boot camp we eloped. I haven't been home since. I went with him when he reported to Fort Bragg. I was angry at my parents for not being there for me when I needed them, and I didn't tell them until after the ceremony, but I'll always regret not inviting my grandparents. Pops and Grandma were hurt by my selfishness, and I won't do that to Pops again, not after all he's done for me."

Gavin's eyes filled with compassion. "What happened to your child?"

Loss welled in her chest. "I miscarried shortly after Russell was deployed. The doctors don't know why. It just…happened. They said it shouldn't happen again, but we didn't try. We wanted to wait until Russell got out of the military. And then he—then he was gone."

He gave her hand another squeeze. "You had to go through that alone?"

"Losing my baby, yes. But Pops was there for me after Russell."

"I'm sorry. What about now? Do you want your parents at the ceremony?"

They wouldn't care enough to take the time away from their precious university. "They're probably too busy to fly out."

"Then it will be just Henry and us."

"What about your family?"

"That's up to you. As far as I'm concerned, as long as you're there I don't need anyone else."

Yet another of Cupid's arrows scored a direct hit to her heart. Pops would be happy to know he was right when he'd told her that when the right one came along love would hit hard and fast. She hadn't believed him. After all the pain she'd been through she'd believed herself immune to love. Apparently not. Her feelings for Gavin were far different from the slow-building affection she'd had with Russell.

"Could we wait a little while?"

"Would you be comfortable staying at my place every night until the wedding?"

She sighed. "No."

"Do you really want to sleep alone?"

He did have a point. "I'd rather be with you."

He removed the ring from the box and extended his hand, palm up. Tremors started deep in her belly. Why was she being such a coward when she could have more than she'd ever dreamed of—a passionate marriage to a man she loved and a chance to take care of Pops.

"Say you'll marry me, Sabrina," he encouraged without one hint of impatience. "On Monday we'll get our marriage license, and I'll set something up as soon as I can at the resort and we can be together. Possibly even as soon as Monday evening."

Her lungs emptied. Her head spun. Her conscience said *Slow down* but her heart said *Yes, yes, yes.* She offered Gavin a trembling hand and met his dark gaze. "Yes, I'll marry you, Gavin Jarrod. I want to be your wife and spend the rest of my life waking in your arms."

He took her hand and slid the cool ring onto her finger, then kissed her knuckles. "Thank you."

Teary-eyed, Sabrina stared at the ring—a symbol of the

kind of happiness she'd never intended to allow herself again. "The stone is beautiful. What is it? A sapphire?"

"A blue diamond."

Her heart went *ka-bump*. "Aren't those incredibly rare?"

"Not as rare as you."

The words added yet another fairy-tale twinkle to the evening. But a teensy part of her brain asked if a man who bought priceless blue diamonds would ever be happy with a plain-old-quartz kind of girl.

"Let's go back to the inn and share our news and a bottle of champagne with Henry."

Sabrina couldn't think of a better way to celebrate except maybe in Gavin's bed. But making love with her fiancé would have to wait.

The guilt knife twisted in Gavin's gut every time Sabrina beamed a smile in his direction. She loved him.

And he didn't deserve it.

But he couldn't allow his feelings to show. Not with Henry watching him like a hungry hawk. Sabrina had already been through so much, her parents' betrayal, losing her baby and then her husband. He had no right to pile more misery on her. But backing out of the deal now would hurt her more than sticking it out and letting her love slowly fade over time—as it undoubtedly would.

The inn's phone rang. "I'll get it," Sabrina said and hustled down the hall.

Henry waited until she was out of the room to set down his champagne flute. "You're determined to do this?"

"I make her happy."

Henry's snowy white head bobbed. "That you do. If not, I'd be calling off the whole deal despite my concern about her being alone after I'm gone. But I'll be watching."

"As you should be."

"Don't think that ring—no matter how much you paid for it—gives you carte blanche to anticipate your vows under my roof again."

"I understand. We'll have a private ceremony at Jarrod Ridge as soon as I can arrange it. I'm shooting for Monday."

"Why not here?"

"Because if the marriage doesn't work out, I don't want Sabrina to have any bad memories attached to the Snowberry Inn."

Henry grunted. Gavin didn't know if the noise indicated approval or disapproval.

Sabrina returned. The confused, or maybe dazed was the right word, expression on her face, made him want to hug her—not a normal reaction for him. He wasn't the hugging type.

"That was Samantha Jarrod. She said she's your sister-in-law. I've been invited to a bridal shower for your sister Erica on the nineteenth."

Blake must have said something to his new wife. Gavin's family was already bringing Sabrina into the fold. Too late to back out now—even if he could find another way to get his hands on that land.

Her wedding day.

Sabrina paced inside the atrium at Jarrod Manor Monday afternoon, struggling to settle her rattled nerves and slow her breathing before she hyperventilated.

She needed to remind herself why she was rushing into marriage. But between shopping for a wedding dress and several walk-in guests at the inn, she'd only seen Gavin once over the weekend before this morning's rushed trip to the Pitkin County clerk's office for their marriage license.

So much for it being bad luck for the groom to see the bride before the ceremony on her wedding day.

Was she doing the right thing?

Her conscience had been screaming that question since Gavin had presented her with the prenuptial agreement Saturday evening. Signing the document had seemed like planning the end of her marriage before it began. But Gavin had explained she needed to protect her interest in the inn, and he needed to protect his siblings' interests in Jarrod Ridge. Logically, everything he said made sense, but that didn't mean it didn't bother her.

To focus on something besides the emotional cauldron boiling in her belly she examined the location Gavin had chosen for their ceremony. She had to give him points for choosing a scenic setting.

The solarium with its vaulted ceiling had already been decorated for Christmas even though Thanksgiving was still weeks away. A massive Christmas tree decorated with red and white poinsettias and twinkling white lights dominated one end of the room, lending a festive air to what should be a simple exchange of vows officiated by one of her grandfather's poker buddies—a retired judge. At the opposite end of the solarium a poinsettia and greenery-draped stone fireplace dominated the wall. And in the center of it all, a beautiful brass fountain shaped like the jagged mountains beyond the windows gurgled. Under other circumstances, she imagined that gurgle would be quite soothing.

Chilled, she made her way toward the crackling flames and held out her hands toward the heat. Light from the overhead chandelier caught the Colorado-blue-sky diamond of her engagement ring, revealing the inner fire Gavin had mentioned. She'd fallen in love with the ring the moment she'd seen it, but when she'd learned the blue of the stone happened to be Gavin's favorite color she'd loved it even more. Finding a dress in the same hue felt as if destiny had stepped in to confirm her decision to marry a man she barely knew.

But that didn't lessen her nervousness.

She swept a hand down the long satin skirt and shifted her shoulders in the sheer lace and beaded bolero jacket overlaying the strapless satin sweetheart top. The dress was a little lower cut than she was accustomed to wearing, showing the top curves of her breasts. She turned to let the flames warm the skin left bare by the deep V-back of the dress.

She hadn't had a wedding dress when she'd married Russell. They hadn't had the money for one.

Stop. Don't think about Russell today.

The door opened, providing a much needed distraction, and Gavin strode in looking powerful and charismatic in his black suit, white shirt and blue-and-black-striped tie. He had a red rosebud in his lapel and one hand behind his back. Her heart quickened.

"Are you ready?"

If she said no would he wait? "I think so."

He swept out his arm, revealing a gardenia and red rose bouquet. "For you. Henry said these were your two favorite flowers."

His thoughtful gesture reminded her of one of the reasons why she'd said yes. Gavin was generous and considerate. He might not have said he loved her yet, but he did show it. "Thank you, Gavin. The flowers are beautiful."

"So are you." He traced a fingertip over her neckline beneath the sheer bodice, making her shiver as desire swept a few doubts under the expensive rug beneath her feet. "Your dress is sexy."

"I'm glad you like it." Blushing, she accepted the bouquet and lifted it to her face, drawing a deep breath of the heady fragrance. "Mmm. Smells good."

"Where's Henry?"

"Judge Roberts has cataracts and can't drive. Pops is picking him up."

"I could have sent a car rather than have you waiting here alone."

"It's okay. I've been…gathering my thoughts." More like gathering her nerve.

Gavin lifted her chin with his knuckle. "Sabrina, if you're having doubts, now's the time to say so."

The fact that he was giving her an out went a long way toward soothing her fears. "I want to marry you, Gavin."

"Good. Because I can't wait to hold you in my arms tonight. It's been a long weekend without you."

The last of her misgivings melted. "I can't wait either."

He took the bouquet from her, set it on a nearby table and pulled her into his arms. He lowered his head and she met him halfway, needing to feel his hunger. The kiss didn't disappoint her. From the moment his mouth opened over hers, she felt the restraint in his firm possession, in the deep sweeps of his tongue and the way his hands tightened on her upper arms.

He tasted of mints and coffee and Gavin. He shifted his stance, then his palms coasted downward to her waist. His hips pressed against hers, generating heat, hunger and enough eagerness on her part that she should be ashamed of her out-of-control desire. But she wasn't. As much as she'd enjoyed her numbness before meeting Gavin, she now relished the way he made her feel alive with nothing more than a glance or a touch.

The doors opened, startling them apart. Pops and Judge Roberts ambled in. Judge Roberts rubbed his hands and grinned. "Looks like we need to get this knot tied good and tight as quickly as possible."

"Amen," Gavin muttered beside her, making her smile. At least the passion wasn't one-sided.

And for better or worse, Sabrina decided she couldn't agree more. She wanted to get the wedding over with so she could stop questioning whether she was doing the right thing.

* * *

The gold band weighed heavily on Gavin's finger as he washed his last bite of wedding cake down with champagne at the end of the brief wedding reception he'd arranged for Sabrina. He owed her that much since she'd had none of the fanfare at her first wedding. His family would probably insist on something larger later since he'd kept them away from the ceremony, but for now he wasn't looking forward to playing the besotted bridegroom in front of the people who knew him—and his aversion to marriage—best.

He signaled the photographer he'd hired to give them a moment and smoothed a loose curl from Sabrina's soft cheek. She looked up at him from beneath her lashes with happiness shining in her eyes, and he felt the impact of that glance like a caress. It took him a second to recall what he'd been about to say.

He cleared his throat to ease the sudden thickness. "We need to get Henry and Judge Roberts on the road before dark. I'll walk them to the car."

She smiled and lifted her hand to lick a smudge of cake icing from her finger. He intercepted her and carried her finger to his mouth. The tastes of Sabrina and white chocolate buttercream icing mingled on his tongue. Her pink lips parted on a gasp and her pupils dilated, igniting a corresponding hunger in his belly. The woman had bewitched him, but not even a passion this strong could endure the absences his job would require.

But until that day, he would focus on the here and now. In a matter of hours he would have her in his bed, naked, wet, and begging him to taste her other sweet spots. He ground his teeth but he couldn't contain the groan rumbling up his chest. "Give me five minutes."

She licked her lips, unconsciously inviting him in for a

quick kiss that ended up lingering until he almost forgot he had business waiting. A flash from the camera jarred him away.

"Take your time. I need to run to the ladies' room anyway." Her voice sounded breathless and a flush tinted her cheeks.

And he didn't want to leave her. But the signed deed was the reason for this farce, and he wouldn't end the day without having it in his possession. Once he had it he'd call Blake and give him the go-ahead to contact the construction team.

Releasing her hand and backing away was more difficult than it should have been. He did it anyway and joined the men by the door. "Gentlemen, shall I see you out?"

Once the door closed behind them, Henry nodded to Gavin then turned to Roberts. "Elwood, can you give us a minute?"

Roberts nodded, slapped Gavin on the back and shook his hand. "Congratulations, son. You are indeed one lucky bastard."

More bastard than you know. "Yessir, I am."

After the judge walked away Gavin gestured to a small sitting area around the corner. He and Henry made their way to the secluded spot. "You have the signed deed?"

"I do." Henry offered the folded document. "A deed for a deed, as promised."

Satisfaction rolled through Gavin as his fingers closed over the paper. He finally had what he wanted—and he'd achieved something not even his father had been able to manage— getting the land back.

"What is that?" Sabrina's question jerked Gavin's attention away from his prize. She stood in the hallway. Holding Gavin's gaze, she quickly closed the distance and plucked the paper from his hand before he could think of a way out of this mess.

She unfolded it, scanned it and then looked up at him with confusion puckering her brow. "This is the deed to the mine."

"Yes."

"Tell me you were just doing business today and that this—" she rattled the page "—isn't connected to our wedding."

"It's nothing for you to worry about, girlie," Henry said and tried to take the deed from her. She snatched it out of reach and focused on Gavin.

"You said Pops agreed to sell the land to you."

He debated his options. Honesty was his only course. "I said we agreed on the terms."

She frowned. "If you bought the property where's the check?" She held up a hand before Gavin could reply. "Think very hard before you lie to me."

Henry shot Gavin a warning look, but Gavin ignored it. The pain in her eyes cut him to the bone, crushing his triumph over achieving his goal.

He had to fix this. Or he'd lose her.

Eleven

Sabrina searched her grandfather's face and then Gavin's. Both looked back at her with matching thin-lipped, guilty-as-sin expressions and her stomach sank.

"A deed for a deed," she repeated the words she'd overheard through numb lips, trying to make sense of them. Unfortunately, the only option wasn't a palatable one. Why would the two men she loved the most deceive her?

She focused on Gavin. "Did you marry me to get the mine?"

He shared a long look with her grandfather and each silent second ticking past deepened her misgivings and tightened a vise around her chest.

"Did you, Gavin?" she repeated.

"Jarrod—" her grandfather growled in what sounded like a warning.

"Sabrina needs to know the truth." Gavin's solemn dark eyes met hers. "That was the original plan."

An arrow pierced her heart, but this one hadn't come from Cupid's bow. This one had come from an assassin. Her marriage was a sham. "The original plan? Explain that, please."

Gavin paused and swallowed. "As soon as I met you on that porch I wanted you. And then we touched, and I knew I'd stop at nothing to have you. I've never reacted to a woman that intensely or that fast in my life. That was before I met Henry and he laid his suggestion on the table."

"His suggestion? And what was that exactly?"

Again, he hesitated for a moment as if choosing his words very carefully. "That I take the time to get to know you. Sabrina, with or without the land we would have ended up together one way or another."

"So all this…" Heartsick, she swept a hand to indicate her dress, the hotel, him. Her throat closed up. Her eyes burned. "You faked it."

He gripped her upper arm and led her a short distance away from her grandfather, then dipped his head to speak close to her face. "Do you believe I could fake the desire I feel for you? The hunger that eats me up inside until I can barely think? Name one thing that's happened between us that feels phony."

He'd lowered his voice to that sexy rumble that made her tremble. She didn't want to believe him, but for a man who was usually hard to read she couldn't deny the sincerity in Gavin's eyes. Her emotions churned wildly. How could his comments simultaneously hurt her and send her heart flying?

Did he love her or had he just used her?

She jerked her arm free and moved a few steps away from Gavin to try to regain control. That left her staring at her grandfather. "So this was your idea."

Pops's eyes and his hangdog expression begged for forgiveness. "Sabrina—"

Gavin's hands settled on her shoulders. "Henry saw the chemistry between us and prodded me to follow through because he loves you, and he doesn't want you to be alone if anything ever happened to him."

And then she realized there was a much larger issue here. For Pops to be this desperate he had to be hiding more than his matchmaking. "The pressure you've been putting on me to find someone over the past few months…it's because you're not well. Isn't it?"

Pops shrugged. "I've been better."

"Don't keep secrets," she warned. "Not about something this important."

"I'm feeling my age, girlie, that's all. Colleen would want me to see you settled, before—"

Before he joined her, she finished silently when he didn't. "I don't need a babysitter, Pops. You and Grandma taught me well. I can take care of myself and the inn."

"I'm not talking about a keeper. It's like I've told you. Life is meant to be shared. I want you to experience what your grandmother and I had, Sabrina. You need to know what it feels like to know that one person in this world will always support you and be there for you until God calls 'em home. You didn't have that with Russell. He was off doing his job—" She opened her mouth to protest but he held up a hand to cut her off. "I'm not denying his was a valiant mission, but he left you behind to fend for yourself. You never had the chance to be two halves of a whole before you were his widow and alone again."

She couldn't argue with facts.

"I saw you primping in the hall the day Gavin first visited. That's the first time I've seen you flushed and excited in years. Then Gavin here couldn't take his eyes off you, and I knew I had to act before yer blasted stubbornness kept you from finding the match standing right in front of you."

"But, Pops—"

"But nothing. Gavin is the first man you've shown interest in since you moved in. I wasn't letting him get away."

Her cheeks burned. "You could have given us a chance to work things out ourselves."

"Wasn't wasting time I can't guarantee I have. None of us knows how many days we have left, and happiness won't wait. You have to seize it while you can."

By marrying her off, he'd lessened his worries, she realized.

She turned back to Gavin, and her pulse did a little skip as it did every time she saw him. She loved him, and from what he'd said and from what he'd shown her in the short time they'd known each other, he did care about her. As he'd said, no one could fake that passion or that tenderness. Maybe he didn't love her yet. Maybe he did. But did she want to throw it all away because of the rocky start to their relationship?

No.

She licked her dry lips and took a breath for courage. "Are you sure you want to be married to me?"

Gavin held her gaze. "I wouldn't undo anything that has happened from the moment I met you, and I will do my best to make sure you never regret becoming my wife."

Then she would do her best to make her marriage work for her sake, but mostly for Pops's sake. "Let's get Pops home. I believe we have a honeymoon waiting."

"You know I can't leave."

"You won't have to leave Aspen for me to make you feel like you're flying."

The sensual promise in his eyes and voice made her tremble. For better or worse, Gavin was her future.

Pregnant.

Sabrina stared at the test stick.

The word in the tiny window explained so much: the slight nausea she'd experienced the past three days, the extra sensitivity in her breasts, and the way certain smells suddenly repelled her when they hadn't before.

She'd been blaming the changes on adjusting to married life. As much as she'd loved sharing Gavin's lodge with him for the past eleven days and nights and spending their mornings and evenings together, juggling her roles as wife, innkeeper and Pops's caretaker was a tough balancing act. Gavin had arranged for Meg, the inn's housekeeper, to stay with Pops at night, but Sabrina still worried about her grandfather.

She stared at the bathroom mirror and pressed her hand to her stomach. A baby. Excitement and fear battled for supremacy inside her. Part of her yearned to have Gavin's child. Another part worried that it was too soon to add a baby into the mix.

How would Gavin react to the news? Would he take it stoically and decide to make the best of the situation the way Russell had, or would he be upset? It was hard to know. They'd been so busy between finishing the chores at the inn and the beginning of construction on the new lodge on the property near the mine that they were still learning about each other, and they could barely have a conversation without ending up naked. A baby would change that.

It was early. Her period was only a few days late. So much could go wrong in the first trimester, as she'd learned the hard way. Maybe she should wait to tell him.

The doorbell rang, startling her. She glanced at her watch. "Oh, darn."

Her ride was here. She'd met Avery Lancaster last week when at the coffee the Jarrod women had organized to welcome Sabrina into the family, and Sabrina had clicked with Guy's fiancée instantly. When Avery had offered to give Sabrina a ride to Erica's bridal shower in downtown Aspen,

Sabrina had been touched by the way the Jarrod women had included her and she'd accepted. She hadn't known then that she'd need the quiet drive to get her thoughts together.

Sabrina huffed out a breath and hastily gathered the test strip and packaging and stuffed them back into the bag. She wasn't ready to face the world with her new knowledge. But what choice did she have? She crammed the pregnancy test into the garbage can, slashed on a swipe of lipstick and bolted for the front door, grabbing the shower gift from the hall table on the way. She'd have to worry about Gavin and her pregnancy later. And then she'd decide when and how to share her news.

She yanked open the door to Avery's smiling face. "Hi. Sorry I didn't hear you drive up."

"No problem." Avery's eyes narrowed. "Are you okay? You're very pale."

"I probably forgot to put on blush. Oops. I'll daub a little lipstick on my cheeks in the car. What did you buy for Erica?" she asked, trying to change the subject.

"Guy and I are going to provide a week's worth of gourmet dinners and matching wines for when Erica and Christian get back from their honeymoon."

"Good idea. I hope Guy is cooking the meals himself." She followed Avery to the car and climbed in.

As she buckled her seat belt she realized she didn't even know where she and Gavin would be living when their baby arrived sometime in—she did the math in her head—late July. Gavin's required year at Jarrod Ridge would be ending.

Would he be willing to move into the B and B? If not, maybe they could buy a place in downtown Aspen. Or would he be on the road for his job? She couldn't leave Pops or the Snowberry Inn to follow Gavin around the globe. Would this be like her marriage to Russell where she'd basically been alone most of the time? Would she be raising her child primarily as a solo parent? Would this pregnancy go full term?

There were so many unanswered questions. She now wished she'd pressed Gavin for details. But the sex—which was still amazing—kept getting in the way. In fact, she had wondered if Gavin didn't use sex to avoid serious conversations sometimes.

"Are you sure you're okay? You're very quiet today," Avery asked.

Sabrina grimaced. "Sorry. I was wondering where Gavin's next job would be once he finished his year in Aspen."

Avery glanced her way. "I heard him tell Guy he was working on some preliminary studies for a bridge in New Zealand."

Surprise stole her breath. Not even the same continent. "I didn't know he'd already accepted a job."

"He might not have. You'd better ask him before you get excited about living in such a cool place."

Only she wouldn't be living there, but Sabrina kept that to herself. Luckily, they'd arrived at the bistro and getting inside ended the conversation.

The other women had already arrived. Bride-to-be Erica glowed with happiness. Sabrina delivered her gift, kissed Erica's cheek and then scanned the others gathered in the private dining room. She recognized Melissa, Gavin's sister, and Samantha, who had married Gavin's oldest brother Blake just days before Gavin and Sabrina had met. The rest of the dozen or so women were new faces. She pasted on a smile and tried to work up the appropriate amount of enthusiasm.

A waitress passed with an order of buffalo wings. The sour smell reached Sabrina. Her stomach roiled. Surprised, she mashed her lips together. Normally, she loved the tangy hot wings, but apparently not now. Her mouth filled with saliva and a cold sweat beaded her brow and upper lip.

Avery touched her arm. "Let me introduce you to everyone."

Sabrina held up a finger. "Excuse me."

She spotted a sign marked restroom and darted toward it. She slammed through the door and into the cool tiled room. Before she reached the stall the nausea faded. Bracing her arm against the wall, she took several deep breaths. Wow. She'd never been sick like that with her first pregnancy. She turned on the sink, dampened a paper towel and blotted her face, noting that the amethyst cashmere sweater dress she'd chosen for today accentuated her pallor and the circles beneath her eyes. *Lovely. Not.*

The door opened behind her and Avery entered. "I hate to keep asking, but are you sure you're okay, because you don't look like you feel well."

"I—" Sabrina didn't know what to say. She hadn't told Gavin her news, and it didn't seem right to share it with anyone else until she had. "Don't worry. I'm not contagious."

"Ohmigod. You're pregnant," Avery exclaimed wide-eyed.

Sabrina didn't want to lie, and yet how else could she explain her odd behavior. "I'm pretty sure I am. But please don't tell anyone. Gavin doesn't know yet. I did the test right before you arrived."

"That would explain the shell-shocked look on your face when you opened the door. It's none of my business, but are you happy about this?"

Warmth seeped though Sabrina chasing away her chill. She laid a hand over her tummy. "Yes. I'd love to have Gavin's baby. But I'm not sure how he's going to take the news. It's so soon and we didn't plan this. We haven't even discussed having children."

Yet another conversation they should have had before rushing into marriage. Luckily, Avery didn't point that out.

Sabrina brushed a stray curl from her face. "I'm thinking about waiting a bit before I tell him…you know, feeling him out about the situation and figuring out how best to approach him."

"Sabrina, if you're already pregnant it's too late to test the waters on his thoughts about children. Besides, if what happened out there happens again you won't be able to hide your news anyway."

"No. I guess not. But…"

"Let me tell you something I've figured out. Gavin—like all the Jarrod men—is tough on the outside because he had to be with his father, but all the guys also have warm hearts. It shows in the way they care about each other and kept in touch even when they were scattered about the globe and in the way they dropped everything and rushed here for each other when Donald's will required it. Trust me on this. I should know since I'm engaged to Gavin's big brother." Avery gave a sympathetic smile.

"I guess you're right. I'll tell Gavin tonight."

And she prayed he'd be as happy as she was.

"Hey." Blake's shout jerked Gavin back to the present.

"What?" Gavin scanned the area and spotted a backhoe heading toward him. He moved out of the way without a second to spare.

Blake approached. "Didn't you see the tractor coming?"

Gavin shook his head. "My mind was elsewhere."

"On the Auckland job?"

"No. I—" He cut off the words rather than admit he'd been thinking about Sabrina, how flushed and satisfied she'd looked this morning when he'd climbed from their bed.

Blake grinned. "Thinking about your pretty new wife? Welcome to the club, man. Go home and get you some. I have it covered here."

"I don't need to leave. I'm fine."

"Cut yourself some slack. You didn't even take a honeymoon. Spend a little time with your woman."

Tempted more than he should be, Gavin checked his watch. It was almost quitting time anyway. He'd go because if he stayed his distraction was going to get someone hurt—probably him. Heavy equipment on-site meant everyone's head had to be one hundred percent in the game one hundred percent of the time. Today, his wasn't.

But he wasn't leaving because he needed to see Sabrina.

Who are you kidding?

Disgusted by what he considered a weakness, he waved good-bye to Blake and stomped across the mud and slush-covered ground toward the pickup. What had Sabrina done to him? How had she managed to shatter his concentration when his ability to focus anywhere and under any conditions had previously been one of his best assets?

He shoved the key into the ignition and glanced at the folder labeled *New Zealand* on the passenger seat. Blake had asked about the project. Before meeting Sabrina, Gavin had considered the bridge the most exciting opportunity of his career. But the sad fact was he hadn't been able to work up any enthusiasm for the job since he'd met Sabrina. He carried the file around intending to delve into it, but he'd only opened it a couple of times when Sabrina had been tied up at the inn, and then he'd been listening so intently for her key in the lodge's front door he'd had trouble concentrating on the geology reports.

"It's just the sex," he muttered under his breath. "Damned good sex."

Yeah, right, his conscience jibed. *And that mine is just a hole in the ground.*

The dashboard clock read four o'clock. At this time of day Sabrina would still be at the inn. He tromped on the gas, earning a warning glare from the Jarrod Ridge security man working the gate blocking access to the construction site. Within minutes he reached the inn's lot, pulled in and parked beside two other cars—probably tourists getting a head start on sightseeing before the crowds swept into town next week.

Using his key, he let himself in the back door. The smell of cinnamon hung in the air telling him she'd recently made a batch of her famous oatmeal cookies. "Sabrina?"

"In the office," she called back.

He made his way down the short hall. She sat behind the old wooden desk with her hair twisted up, baring her neck and that spot near her nape that she liked for him to nibble. Seeing her hit him with a pulse-accelerating punch of desire to the gut. "Where's Henry?"

"Out with the judge."

"And your guests?"

"Visiting art galleries."

He pushed the door closed and turned the lock. Her eyes widened. "It's early. Why aren't you at the construction site?"

"Blake has everything under control." He circled the desk, grabbed her hand and pulled her to her feet. He studied her from her face to her breasts outlined to mouthwatering perfection by the purple sweater and then down. He liked the surprise. "You're wearing a skirt."

"I attended Erica's bridal shower today."

He skimmed a hand over her hip and then beneath the hem and back up her thigh. She wasn't wearing pantyhose. But she was wearing panties. Too bad, but not for long.

She gasped as he tugged the cotton down her thighs. "Gavin, we need to talk."

Why did women always want to talk when they

communicated so much better on a more basic level? The panties fell to her ankles. "In a minute. First, I need this."

He hooked a hand around her nape, pulled her forward and kissed her, covering her soft lips, stroking them with his tongue and lapping up her unique flavor. "Mmm. You've been eating chocolate mints again."

Ever since the night he'd painted her nipples with chocolate she'd had a craving for the things.

"Just one." Her breath caught when he cupped her breast and found her tight nipple, then a moan slipped free. Her breasts were so sensitive a man couldn't help playing with them. But he wouldn't taste them today—not with the threat of Henry or the guests interrupting him.

He lifted her skirt, finding her curls already wet and her slick little nub swollen and waiting for his attention.

"Gavin, please." Her breathless voice egged him on.

"I will, baby. I will please you. I know exactly what you like." He caressed her until she trembled in his arms, then turned her, planting her hands on the desk's surface. He buried his face in her neck and her perfume filled his nose as he opened his mouth over the warm, satiny flesh beneath her ear. She bowed her back, pushing her bottom into his groin. Hunger surged through him, making his erection pulse in her warm crevice.

He quickened his finger, listening to the telltale sign of her panting breaths. When he thought she was close to the edge he ripped open his pants and shoved the fabric out of the way. Then when her muscle tension told him she was on the verge, he rolled on a condom and eased into her, filling her and sending her over the edge.

She felt so damned good. Slick. Hot. Wet. He gritted his teeth to keep from losing control right then as her muscles contracted around him with the rhythm of her orgasm. Once she settled, he stroked her again, this time using his penis as well as his hand to push her toward the next peak. He teased her as well as himself, alternating fast and slow strokes. Her body drew tight and he backed off once, then repeated the process a second time, making her wait for release. When he couldn't stand the pressure building in his gut any longer he caressed her past the point of no return and quit fighting.

Climax exploded through him in hot brain-numbing bursts leaving his legs weak and shaking in the aftermath. He had to brace his arms on either side of hers to remain upright. His chest burned as he struggled to fill his lungs.

How could it be that good every time? How long would it take before his craving for her waned?

Sabrina squirmed free long before his legs regained stability. She hastily righted her clothing, and ducked to scoop up her panties. "That was—"

"Fantastic." He dropped the condom in the trash can beneath her desk and refastened his pants.

"I was going to say unexpected." When she met his gaze again, the pink drained from her cheeks. Worry clouded her eyes. "Gavin, I have something to tell you."

Her tight tone indicated whatever it was couldn't be good. "Is Henry okay?"

"Yes, he's fine." She chewed her bottom lip and shifted on her feet. Her fingers tightened and relaxed on the panties in her hand. "I'm pregnant."

Shock winded him. The blood drained from his head and tension instantly knotted his previously relaxed muscles. "How?"

She searched his face as if trying to gauge his reaction. "I'm guessing I conceived that first time in the tack room. That's the only time we haven't used protection."

He didn't want to be a father.

He especially didn't want to be an overbearing, fault-finding parent like his had been. Gavin could almost smell the smoke of his plan for a short marriage going up in flames. He'd expected Sabrina to tire of his long, work-related absences and demand a divorce. And then they'd never see each other again. That blueprint had been part of the Auckland job's appeal. Distance of that magnitude meant fewer visits, less face time.

But now he and Sabrina would be permanently tied by a child. A child he would fail unless he found a better role model than Donald Jarrod.

Twelve

Gavin's bleak expression dropped a lead weight in Sabrina's stomach, erasing any lingering afterglow.

"Children were never part of the plan."

She blinked at his bluntness. "We didn't discuss them one way or the other. Are you telling me you don't ever want children? Or you don't want them with me?"

"My job involves too much travel for me to be a good father. I'd be an absentee one at best."

Her heart sank upon hearing him confirm her fears. "So you are going back on the road when your year in Aspen ends?"

"Yes."

"What about me? What about us? You know I can't leave Pops, and the inn has been in my family forever. I can't just abandon it or turn it over to strangers to manage."

"I never intended for you to leave the inn. I'm going back to the lodge."

"Wait. Don't you want to talk about this?"

"There's nothing to discuss. You're pregnant with my child. I'll make sure you have the assistance you need when I'm away on the job, and I'll provide for the kid."

Pain pierced her chest. She winced. "So you did marry me to get the deed. Then what? What was your plan after you had what you wanted, Gavin?"

He stared at her through eyes devoid of emotion—eyes that had only moments ago burned with passion. For her. She knew then that Gavin would never care for her the way she did him, and the reason he'd never said he'd loved her wasn't because he didn't know how to verbalize the words, but because he didn't feel them.

Getting buried by an avalanche would have been less painful, less chilling than the realization that sex and land were all that mattered to him. For her the relationship was about so much more than just physical satisfaction.

She wrapped her arms around her middle. "If you married me to get the land then you have it. Mission accomplished. You don't need me anymore. And I don't need you. I'll give you an uncontested divorce if you'll sign over your rights to my child."

"Our child."

Numbly, Sabrina shook her head. "I grew up feeling unwanted and in the way and like a burden to my parents. As long as I'm breathing, my child will never experience that. If you don't want him or her, if you don't want *us* in your life, then you and I have nothing more to say. I'll send someone for my things. Now please get out."

Gavin let himself into the Black Spruce Lodge a few minutes before noon. The heavy snow falling had shut down construction. Just as well. With everyone on the site yapping about tomorrow's Thanksgiving plans they weren't getting much work done anyway, and he'd been eager to escape the chatter for the solitude of his home-away-from-home.

He hadn't told anyone that he and Sabrina had split, but when he showed up at the family dinner without her they'd figure it out.

The silence of the house echoed around him and the sterile smell of hotel disinfectant lingered in the air. In the short time Sabrina had lived here she'd made her mark—particularly in the small kitchen. Each night when he'd come home from the site the delicious scents of the recipes she'd been testing had greeted him at the door, and the refrigerator had been filled with tasty and sometimes decadent morsels for him to munch on.

But not this week. This week the place smelled like sanitizer. His refrigerator was empty and Sabrina's flowery shower gel wasn't on the shelf by the tub. And even though he'd asked the maid not to, she still left chocolates on his pillows—chocolates that reminded him of making love to Sabrina, of painting her nipples and then lick—

He wiped a hand down his face, trying to sever that thought, but it was too late. Heat built like steam in his groin—heat that would have no outlet. He hung up his coat and headed for the minibar and a shot of Dewar's. It burned all the way down his throat.

An odd restlessness rode his back. Why? He was used to hotels. Hell, he spent most of his life in generic, temporary accommodations. Free. Unencumbered. Uncluttered. And he liked it that way. So why did it feel as if something were missing now?

Deciding to forego lunch due to a lack of appetite, he opened his briefcase and extracted the Auckland file. He'd work until he got through the data. He considered lighting a fire, but that too brought back memories of making love to

Sabrina in front of the crackling flames. He'd even given her rug burn on that—

He drowned the thought with another gulp of Scotch and headed upstairs to the loft office—where the fireplace was out of sight. He settled on the leather sofa and tried to focus on the geological reports, but it was slow going. His lids grew heavier with each passing second when normally the technical pre-construction specs fascinated him. He loved the challenge of anticipating problems before they arose. But not today.

What do you expect when you're not sleeping at night?

That was only because he was worried about failing a kid as badly as Donald Jarrod had failed his children. Gavin and each of his siblings had baggage from their father's brand of tough love.

Twenty minutes later—yeah, he was watching the clock—a knock at the door gave him an excuse to abandon his fruitless attempt. He made his way downstairs and opened the front door. A clean-cut twenty-something guy in a suit stood on the stoop. "Gavin Jarrod?"

"Yes."

"This is for you, sir." The young man handed over a thick envelope, then turned and departed before Gavin could dig a tip out of his pocket.

Curious, Gavin scanned the return address. An attorney's office. "What in the hell?"

He hadn't spoken to Henry since the separation, but the old man might have followed through with his promise to muck things up with inspectors since Gavin had hurt his granddaughter. The construction crew had barely begun. Plenty of stuff could go sour at this point.

He opened the tri-folded sheets expecting to find some kind of injunction to halt work on the lodge.

Divorce Petition.

The words hit him like a one-ton I beam slamming into his chest. Sabrina had filed for divorce. He flipped through the pages, skimming the legalese, most of it predetermined by their prenup, and then he came upon a second document—a form asking him to relinquish his paternal rights to the child she carried.

Gavin staggered backward until the living room sofa hit the backs of his legs. His knees buckled. He collapsed onto the cushion.

If he signed this then he'd have no reason, no *right* to contact Sabrina ever again or to see their child, and no reason to ever return to Aspen.

Sign it. It's the best thing you can do for both of them. You'll make a lousy husband and a worse father.

He pulled a pen from his pocket. His hand shook, quaking over the page until his eyes blurred. He couldn't do it. He dropped the pen, shot to his feet and walked away from the papers lying on the table.

The idea of going another day—let alone a lifetime—without seeing Sabrina made it hard to breathe. His chest and throat burned as if a hot steel band constricted him. He glanced over his shoulder at the papers on the table. Signing them was the easy way out of all his problems. So why did the idea of walking away from her feel as if he were ripping out a part of himself? He'd never wanted a wife, and he'd sure as hell never wanted children.

Because you've fallen in love with the woman you married under false pretenses.

The realization stunned him. He didn't do love.

Until now.

In their short time together, Sabrina had gotten to him and breached barriers he didn't let people cross. She'd shown him how warm and welcoming a real home should be and reminded him how much he loved Aspen when his father wasn't acting as a domineering killjoy. She'd taught him that real love meant sometimes putting another's happiness ahead of your own.

For a moment when she'd been telling him about the baby there'd been a glow of hope and excitement in her eyes making them sparkle more than the diamond on her finger. And he'd killed it with his knee-jerk reaction and cruel words.

He wanted to see those emotions light up her face again. He couldn't live a lifetime wondering if she and the child they'd created together were happy and flourishing. And leaving Aspen to avoid her the way he had his father seemed repugnant.

The most important lesson he'd learned from Sabrina was that bad parents didn't necessarily make an emotionally crippled child. Look at her. Despite her parents' lack of interest he'd never met a warmer or more generous woman. She relished making even strangers feel welcome in her home.

And she hadn't let losing her husband or her first baby stop her from trying love again. She believed her late husband was the courageous one, but that man had nothing on Sabrina. Any child would be lucky to have her for a mother. Gavin fisted and released his hands by his side. He wanted a chance to raise that child with her even though he didn't have the skills to handle the job.

Maybe with Sabrina's help he could learn how to be a father.

You could end up failing Sabrina, your child and yourself.

But that was a risk he had to take. If it wasn't too late.

But first he had to talk to his siblings. What he was considering wouldn't affect just him. He had to find a way to prove to Sabrina that she was worth more to him than a hole in the ground.

* * *

"Kinda overdid the cooking, didn't you?" Pops said.

Sabrina glanced up to see him looking over the top of his glasses at the kitchen work island laden with pies, cakes, cookies and an assortment of other dishes she'd prepared for tomorrow's Thanksgiving meal.

She shrugged and continued kneading the dough for Friday's sourdough coffee cake. "I had a lot of new recipes I wanted to try, plus all of Grandma's favorites."

"Did cookin' fix what ailed ya?"

Her fingers twitched in the malleable mix. "I'm sorry?"

"Colleen always baked when she was upset. I ate best when she had issues to think through."

Sabrina ducked her head. Was she so transparent? "I'm fine, Pops."

He snorted. "You gonna let him get away with it?"

She considered playing dumb and asking "Who?" but Pops wouldn't buy it. He'd been hovering since she'd moved back in, and his worrying about her wasn't good for him. His agitation would only worsen once she told him about the baby. She hadn't found the nerve to do that yet. "Let Gavin get away with what?"

"Running scared."

"He's not running scared. He married me for the land. He got it. He's history."

He shook his head. "If he was history you wouldn't have cooked enough to feed a church congregation."

Embarrassment burned her skin like a heat lamp. "The inn is at full occupancy. I want to have plenty to go around. You know our guests are ravenous when they return from the slopes."

He *tsked* and shook his head. "Never known you to back down from a challenge, girlie. Always admired your grit. Until now."

She flinched. "What would you have me do?"

"Nope. I'm not giving you the answer. You have to figure that out for yourself. But I'll tell ya this much. Hiding in the kitchen and baking into the wee hours every morning ain't gonna solve your problems or make you happy." He shuffled out of the room.

The spacious room suddenly felt crowded and hot. She needed a break. Sabrina quickly washed and dried her hands, then plucked at her cowl-neck sweater. If only she could turn back the clock to October, back to when she'd been normal and numb. No. She smoothed a hand over her tummy. She didn't want to go back. Going back meant undoing the miracle she and Gavin had created and forgetting those wonderful, magical, Christmas-card moments they had shared.

The only thing she'd change if given the chance was to slow everything down. Her relationship with Gavin had been too…everything. Too fast. Too intense. Too perfect. Too good to be true. And now…too painful.

What else could she do? She'd fought for her parents' attention and failed to get it. Then she'd begged Russell to come home and share her grief after she'd miscarried. And even though his superiors would have granted him leave, Russell had chosen to stay with his men and do his job over being with her. She wasn't going to set herself up for another rejection from Gavin.

If you don't have the guts to ask for something, then you don't deserve it. Sabrina heard her grandmother's voice as clearly as if Colleen Caldwell were standing in the kitchen kneading dough and dispensing advice the way she'd done every summer of Sabrina's life.

But was her grandmother's wisdom right?

Sabrina fussed with the tie strings of her apron. No. She wasn't going to beg for love. She wanted a man who chose to be with her, one who needed her as much as she did him. If Gavin wasn't that man then she didn't want him.

Yes, you do.

Sad, but true. She still loved him. Gavin had hurt her, but he'd also taught her how to play again, how to feel, and he'd shown her a side of Aspen she'd never experienced before—Aspen through the eyes of a native who truly loved this place, even though he let his father drive him away.

And that was the key, she realized. When you loved something or someone, you couldn't let them push you away. You had to push back and fight for what you wanted.

She couldn't walk away without at least making an attempt to see if what she'd shared with Gavin was more than just an act on his part. His touch, his lovemaking, his smiles had all seemed too genuine to have been nothing more than a pretense to seduce her into marriage.

And didn't her child deserve better than an emotionally and geographically distant father? Yes. And the only way this baby had a chance at having an involved father was if Sabrina found the courage to confront Gavin and demand he be a better parent to their child than his or hers had been to them. If he'd already signed the relinquishment papers her lawyer had sent him then she'd just have to change his mind.

And, as Pops had so wisely pointed out, she couldn't do that hiding in the kitchen.

"Meg?" she called.

The inn's housekeeper stuck her head around the corner of the laundry room door. "Yes?"

"Everything is under control here. Leave the dough to rise and I'll deal with it later. I'm going out."

"In this weather? Honey, you'll need sled dogs to travel now. The snow is really coming down. Visibility up on the mountains can't be good. Our guests will be returning from the slopes before dark, I'm thinking."

Surprised, Sabrina glanced out the kitchen window. Leaden skies dumped big, fat flakes. Her heart sank. "I guess I could put the chains on the tires."

"Can't whatever it is wait until tomorrow?"

"No. It can't wait another minute." She pulled on her coat, hat and gloves. "Dinner is in the oven. It'll be done at five if I'm not back."

"The girls and I can handle serving. Do what you've got to do. Just be careful out there."

Sabrina felt a twinge of guilt at leaving the inn's staff to cope, but that is why she'd hired extra help for the tourist season. She stepped out on the back porch and the cold hit her like a blow, but she gritted her teeth and headed for the barn to get the chains for the minivan's tires. She'd made it halfway to the building when the sounds of bells caught her attention.

Her heart skipped at the memory of the carriage ride with Gavin and what had happened afterward. They'd made love and made a baby. She'd never be able to hear sleigh bells again without remembering. But right now she had more important things to do than reminisce.

She ducked her head and trudged onward, but the bells kept coming closer. She stubbornly refused to look. "Probably tourists taking a sleigh ride."

She stepped into the cold barn, rummaged until she located the chains and headed back out the side door only to stop in her tracks. A sleigh she didn't recognize stood in the inn's driveway, but two familiar horses snorted frosty white clouds into the air from the harnesses. The man stepping down from the vehicle didn't glance her way, but she'd recognize that muscular frame and that confident bearing anywhere. Gavin. He marched toward the inn's back door.

"Gavin," she called out, her voice cracking.

He stopped and pivoted. Her heart swooped to her stomach

like a skier plunging down the mountainside. He closed the distance between them in long determined strides.

She wet her dry lips. "What are you doing here?"

He looked tired and tense as his dark eyes prowled slowly over her, resurrecting memories of his hands and mouth doing the same. He jerked his head toward the sleigh. "Get in."

Her breath hitched. "It's cold. Are you sure you wouldn't rather put the horses in the barn and go inside the inn?"

"If we go into that barn together, we're going to end up making love and not talking. And as much as I want you, it'll have to wait."

A quiver started deep inside her, then worked its way outward until her entire body trembled. "Oh. I—I—" The tire chains in her hands rattled. She swallowed and tried again. "I was coming to see you."

He took the chains from her, carried them back to the barn. She took the sixty seconds while he was out of sight to try and gather her shattered composure. Why was he here? The divorce papers? The relinquishment form? Both should have been delivered this morning.

He returned. "The sleigh is safer than slick tires. Let's go."

He gripped her elbow and pulled her forward, hitting her body with a bolus of adrenaline. How could his touch affect her so deeply? He'd married her for land. Or had he? Was Pops right? Was Gavin running scared? Heaven knew the way he made her feel terrified her.

"Are you sure the horses will be okay?"

"They're conditioned to the weather and they have the proper shoes." He helped her into the vehicle but this wasn't the one they'd used before. This one had runners instead of wheels. She settled on the seat and pulled the blankets over her legs. He climbed in beside her, his body only inches from hers, then released the brake and clucked to the horses. He guided them back to the road where, thankfully, the traffic was light due to the heavily falling snow.

"Where are we going?"

"Wait and see. Are you warm enough?"

"Yes." An electric blanket kept the chill away and the curved top kept the snow off their heads. But neither did anything for her doubts. She knotted her gloved hands and tried to find the words to broach her request. How did you order a man to be a good father? Giving him a chance to concentrate on maneuvering them through traffic was the perfect excuse to stay silent.

He turned the sleigh into the Jarrod Ridge driveway, then took the path toward the mine—the cause behind everything that had happened in the past twenty-four whirlwind days. Their meeting, dating, marriage, baby and separation.

"Look in the compartment," he said.

Sabrina leaned forward and opened the small box in the front dashboard of the carriage. She withdrew a sheaf of papers and unrolled them. She'd seen this document before. "It's the deed to the mine."

"Made out to you."

She scanned the words and saw her name, verifying what he said. "Why?"

He pulled the horses to a stop beneath a covered shelter that hadn't been here last time she'd visited the mine, then he set the brake and dropped the reins. She looked around, noting the stakes and the trenches in the nearby soil rapidly getting covered with snow. "I've halted construction on the lodge."

"Why?" she repeated.

"Because I married you under false pretenses, this land is rightfully yours." He paused and swallowed, his dark gaze unwavering. "But I'm hoping you'll share it with me. With our child."

Stunned, she stared at him. "What are you saying, Gavin?"

"I may have married you for the wrong reasons, but I fell in love with you for the right ones."

Her eyes, throat and lungs burned. She searched his eyes, seeing the truth, the emotion behind the words. He *loved* her. "Gavin—"

He held up a hand. "Hear me out. You stole my heart, Sabrina, with your smiles, your generosity and your courage. You reminded me why I love this place."

The pages crumpled in her hands. He took them from her and dropped them on the seat, then climbed down from the carriage and held out his hand. Too dumbfounded to do anything else, Sabrina placed hers in his and let him assist her from the carriage. Cold as it was, she resented the gloves separating their flesh. He led her toward the path and stopped a hundred feet away at the overlook where he'd allowed Pops to rest the day they'd hiked to the mine.

"I told Henry that if I ever returned to Aspen I'd build a house here overlooking the valley. That day I didn't have the courage to face the bitter memories I'd left here. Today, because of you, I do."

"Gavin, I don't want to be any man's anchor. You love your job."

"You're no one's anchor. You're the fulcrum on which everything else balances. The idea of not being able to come home to you every day, to hold you in my arms at night and to make love with you knocks me off center."

Her knees went weak. "You're not saying this just because of the baby, are you?"

He shook his head. "I never expected to find you. The baby is a bonus—first of several I hope to have with you. Let's build a home in this spot overlooking the inn and raise a family together."

"But you love your job—"

"I've traveled the globe because I had no reason to put down roots. I was trying to fill a void, an emptiness that you erased the moment I met you. I can limit myself to local assignments or consult on projects that won't keep me away from you for weeks on end."

He peeled off his gloves, then hers. When they were skin to skin, palm to palm with their fingers laced he squeezed her hands. "Be my reason for coming home."

He was offering everything she'd ever dreamed of. "I don't want you to feel as if you're giving up everything for me, for us. I don't want our child to feel like you resent his presence."

"I love you and I will love this child and any others we might have. I promise you, Sabrina, if you'll allow me to be a part of your life, I'll be losing nothing and gaining everything." He lifted her chin with his knuckle. "Tell me I haven't lost you, that you still love me."

A tear scalded its way down her cheek. Gavin brushed it away before it had a chance to cool. "I do love you, Gavin. And I want to spend the rest of my life showing you how much."

"I promise you won't regret it."

He pulled her into his arms and kissed her so tenderly Sabrina's tears overflowed, then he pulled back and tugged her down the path.

"Where are we going?"

"Into the mine. I want to carve my initials next to yours in that beam for all the future Jarrod generations to see. One of these days we'll be telling our grandkids it all started with a little hole in the ground…one filled with silver and dreams, but the riches weren't in the minerals."

* * * * *

INHERITING HIS SECRET CHRISTMAS BABY

BY
HEIDI BETTS

An avid romance reader since school, **Heidi Betts** knew early on that she wanted to write these wonderful stories of love and adventure. It wasn't until her first year of college, however, when she spent the entire night reading a romance novel instead of studying for finals, that she decided to take the road less traveled and follow her dream. In addition to reading, writing, and romance, she is the founder of her local Romance Writers of America chapter and has a tendency to take injured and homeless animals of every species into her Central Pennsylvania home.

Heidi loves to hear from readers. You can write to her at PO Box 99, Kylertown, PA 16847, USA , (an SAE is appreciated but not necessary) or e-mail heidi@ heidibetts.com. And be sure to visit www.heidibetts.com for news and information about upcoming books.

From the Last Will and Testament of Don Jarrod

...and to my youngest son, Trevor, I leave your mother's wedding band. It's unfortunate that you knew your mother the least amount of time. I wish you had been given the opportunity to share more experiences with the woman who loved you more than life itself. You may not have been aware, but the wedding ring she was buried with was not her original ring. This simple white gold band was all she wanted when we married. Only years later was I able to convince her to accept a more elaborate one. But she never got rid of her ring, and I think she would very much have wanted you, her precious baby boy, to keep and cherish it until you find the right woman to wear it. I hope that day comes soon for you, son.

One

Entering the expansive Jarrod Ridge Manor hotel through a private side entrance, Trevor Jarrod stomped the snow from his heavy ski boots and headed down the long hallway toward his office.

Thick oriental rugs lined the golden, highly glossed wooden floors as he passed his brothers' offices. Some of the doors were closed, others were open, voices and sounds of keyboards or ringing phones drifting out.

Opposite the row of office suites, tall, narrow tables dotted the fog-colored walls, each boasting a cobalt-blue vase that in summer would be stuffed with fresh roses and hydrangeas or other seasonal arrangements. Currently, however, they overflowed with bright red, burgeoning poinsettias to mark the upcoming Christmas holiday.

Stone and wood accents filled this wing of the Manor as well as the rest of the main hotel, which had been the original structure at Jarrod Ridge Resort more than a hundred years before. Since then, the resort had grown by leaps and bounds, with additions to the Manor, and separate lodges, shops and other accommodations being built on and around until the place looked for all the world like a quaint, isolated little village.

But the family's offices were still located here in the main building, and their private living quarters—for those who chose to stay there—still occupied the top floor of the Manor, keeping the Jarrods very tight-knit and in near constant contact, whether they liked it or not.

Reaching his own office, Trevor greeted Diana, personal assistant extraordinaire, before stashing his skis in the wide hidden closet behind her desk.

"How were the slopes this morning?" she asked, tipping her head to one side so that her long, black, curly hair fell over her shoulder.

"Could have been better," he replied, stripping out of his navy-blue ski clothes and switching to a pair of worn Timberlands to go with his jeans and tan cable-knit cashmere sweater.

Casual for office attire, sure, but then so was going to work straight from a run down the slopes. And this was, after all, a ski resort—as well as a spa, summer retreat and host location for one of Colorado's biggest events, the annual Food and Wine Gala. So it paid to have guests see the owners and employees enjoying all the activities and amenities Jarrod Ridge had to offer right along with them.

"I think I'm losing my mojo," he grumbled.

"Nah, you just haven't had as much time as usual to play…I mean, practice," she corrected with a wink.

Wasn't that the truth. In the five months since his

father had passed away, Trevor had been juggling two nearly full-time jobs. Donald Jarrod's will had forced all six of his children to return to Jarrod Ridge to manage the resort or risk losing their shares in the family dynasty.

But as much as he may have been forced to take over as president of marketing for Jarrod Ridge, it certainly hadn't been a hardship for him. After running his own very successful marketing firm in downtown Aspen, the job here came almost as naturally to him as breathing.

Unfortunately, it didn't leave him a lot of time for what he loved most—the outdoors and all the sporting activities it had to offer. In the summer, he spent nearly every minute of his free time hiking, climbing, kayaking or riding his mountain bike. In the winter, he loved to hit the slopes, usually on his skis, but occasionally snowboarding.

Nature was great, and he appreciated it as much as the next person, but for him, it was all about the adventure. The rush. There was nothing in the world like speeding down a snow-slick mountainside, dodging rocks and trees, feeling the cold sting of the wind on his face. Or jumping from a plane at thirteen thousand feet with nothing but a parachute and his own skills to break his fall.

Oh, yeah. He had to get on the ball and figure out what he was going to do about balancing his two vital positions, so he could get back to putting in *normal* workaholic hours and carve out a bit more time on the slopes. But until he found someone he trusted and could truly rely on to take over Jarrod Promotion and Marketing, he was just going to have to deal with it, he supposed.

"Any messages?" he asked Diana, running his

fingers through his dark hair to brush away any excess moisture.

Getting to her feet, she handed him a stack of pink papers. More than he was in the mood to deal with at the moment.

"Before you go into your office…" she began, only to let her words drift off, her bottom lip disappearing between her teeth as she worried it nervously.

"Yes?"

She took a breath and met his gaze. "There's a young woman waiting for you. She's been calling, and insisted on seeing you in person. I started to turn her away, but didn't have the heart, and…well, I just thought she was someone you should deal with personally."

He frowned. Diana might be pixie-petite, but he'd seen her in protective, full linebacker mode. The woman waiting in his office must indeed be brave to have gotten past Diana. Brave, or very convincing.

"Who is she?" he asked. "A company rep wanting us to use their products to supply the Ridge, or a possible client who hasn't been able to catch me at JPM?"

Diana shrugged. "You'll have to ask her yourself. She didn't say, she was just…very determined."

With a sigh, Trevor folded the stack of messages and stuffed them in his pants pocket. "Fine. I'll take care of it."

Pulling open both of the heavy oak doors that separated his office from the reception area, he paused to take in the sweep of his office. The thick Gulistan carpeting. The unlit fireplace built of smooth river stones lining the back wall. And in the center of the room, his heavy, ornately carved desk with its lamp at one corner, computer monitor at the other and stacks of paper at the center.

But no woman in either of the guest chairs waiting to see him.

Closing the doors behind him with a click, he stepped farther inside. As the sound echoed through the room, his espresso-dark leather desk chair tipped slightly before swiveling around to reveal a lovely woman with honey-blond hair and blue eyes. On her lap, leaning back against her chest, was an infant busily chewing on his own hand.

Trevor frowned. Well. The woman was no surprise; Diana had warned him one was waiting to see him. His so-called assistant had failed to mention, however, that said woman had a child with her.

What kind of woman came to a business meeting with a baby in tow? he wondered. Even an impromptu meeting that—judging by the way this one was starting—might not last long.

"My secretary said you needed to speak with me," he said, rounding the desk with every intention of taking her place and relegating her to one of the guest chairs.

If he'd expected her to hop up and bashfully bustle around to the other side of the desk, though, he was doomed to disappointment. She held her ground, remaining seated in *his* executive chair—the one he had special-ordered and waited nearly a month for it to arrive, the one that had taken another month to break in and now cushioned his body like a glove during each of the many long hours he put in here at Jarrod Manor—while she bounced the child up and down on her knees.

"I'm Trevor Jarrod," he offered when she didn't seem eager to fill the chilly silence.

"I know who you are. I've been trying to reach you for the past two months."

Her tone was flat with a trace of annoyance threading through, but also light and extremely feminine. Lifting a hand, she swept a chunk of her straight blond hair behind one ear, revealing a single ruby-red stud that matched the knit V-neck sweater she was wearing with a pair of sleek black slacks.

The baby on her lap was dressed in blue denim overalls with an embroidered train engine on the front pocket and a shirt underneath with dozens more trains covering the white cotton. A boy, Trevor assumed, otherwise he would be looking at a little denim jumper covered in pink butterflies or some such.

As though he sensed Trevor's perusal, the baby gave a smiling gurgle and kicked his legs out in front of him.

Dragging his attention back to the woman who'd fought so hard to gain an audience with him but suddenly seemed at a loss for words, Trevor crossed his arms over his chest and lifted a brow. "And you are…?"

That brought her to her feet, shifting the child in her arms until he was perched on one hip.

How did women do that? Were they born knowing how to hold babies, change diapers and distinguish between eighteen different types of cries?

Of the six Jarrod children, Melissa and Erica were his only younger siblings. Which meant he didn't have a lot of experience with babies. Even being this close to one, with his mother right here, ready, willing and able to react to the baby's every need, made Trevor more than a bit uncomfortable.

Clearing his throat to cover the fact that he'd nearly taken a step back, away from the woman and her child, Trevor waited. She still owed him a name and an explanation for her presence, and he had work to do.

"My name is Haylie Smith."

He blinked, waiting for her to elaborate. Instead, after several long seconds ticked by, she tipped her head and let her eyes go wide, as though she'd just delivered a punch line. But he didn't get the joke.

"Haylie Smith," she said again, more firmly this time, careful to enunciate each syllable. "From Denver."

"I heard you," he murmured, fighting the twitch at the corner of his lips as they threatened to lift in an amused grin.

It wasn't often that he was treated like the slow kid in school. Very few would dare. Because while he was known to be fairly laid-back and fun-loving, even flirty at times when it came to women, he was also a Jarrod. One of the heirs to Donald Jarrod's vast fortune, and a successful entrepreneur in his own right.

He was rich, and he was powerful. And while it might take a lot to shake him from his easygoing nature, he wasn't a man other men wanted to risk pissing off.

That this stranger—a woman, no less—seemed to have no compunction about going nose-to-nose with him was more arousing than it should have been.

Not that she wasn't an attractive woman. At what he estimated to be about five feet four or five inches to his six-two, she was tall enough, but not too tall. She was also far from reed-thin, but nowhere near fat, either. She had curves in all the right places, pressing against the front of her sweater and filling out the hips of her slacks. The kind of figure that would feel soft and warm against his hard chest and firm thighs.

Her long, straight hair was like bottled sunshine and framed a heart-shaped face that was a fascinating mix of innocence and sensuality. The rosy bow of her mouth, the sharp, crystal-blue of her eyes, the way she held that baby with both confidence and possessiveness…

None of it should be turning him on, since he was about three seconds away from booting her out of his office, but damned if he wasn't starting to feel a telltale warmth in his blood and tightening in his gut.

Unfortunately—or maybe fortunately—she didn't seem to be suffering the same physiological response to him.

"I've been calling you for the past two months," she charged impatiently. "Leaving messages that you apparently couldn't be bothered to return."

With a nod, he moved around her and took his rightful place behind his desk. "My secretary mentioned that. Although I can't understand what's so pressing if you weren't willing to leave details about why you wanted to speak with me."

Just as he'd intended, his near dismissal of her caused her to move back around to the front of his desk. She didn't sit, though, instead standing directly in front of him while she bounced her hip and wove back and forth in a calm, gentle motion he assumed was for the baby's benefit.

"Some things are better said in person. And I didn't think you would appreciate your secretary being privy to your personal business."

At that, his brows drew together and he dragged his attention from the folder on the desk in front of him to her glittering gaze.

"I'm sorry, but I've never seen or heard of you before. What kind of personal business could you possibly have with me?" He nearly scoffed, wondering if this woman might be slightly unhinged. Maybe she'd convinced herself she was yet another long-lost Jarrod heir. Or maybe she'd seen one too many photographs of him in the local and national tabloids, and had convinced herself that she was one of his many feminine conquests.

He was debating the wisdom of getting up to open the double doors again, and possibly even buzzing for hotel security, when she switched the baby from one hip to the other and began to round his desk again—in the opposite direction this time—with slow, determined steps.

"You're right, you don't know me. We've never met. But a year ago, you met my sister, and from what I've heard, the two of you had a heck of a good time."

She stopped in front of him, towering over him in a manner he *definitely* didn't appreciate. He sat back, prepared to launch to his feet and stare her down, if necessary, but her next words glued him in place.

"And maybe if you returned a phone call once in a while, it wouldn't have taken me two months to track you down and introduce you to your son."

With that, she plopped the baby unceremoniously on his lap before leaning back to cross her arms beneath her breasts and look down at him with what could only be described as a satisfied smirk.

Two

Haylie really shouldn't have taken so much pleasure in Trevor Jarrod's shocked reaction to her pronouncement, but she did. His eyes flashed wide, his mouth dropped open like a guppy's and his hands on either side of Bradley's pudgy little body made him look as if he were juggling a ticking time bomb instead of a four-month-old infant.

She had to give Trevor credit, though. The minute she'd plopped Bradley on his lap and stepped away, Trevor's arms had come up to balance the child on his lap and keep the baby from toppling over.

After a few seconds of dead silence, Trevor seemed to regain a bit of his equilibrium. Snapping his mouth shut, he licked his lips and pushed to his feet, holding Bradley out in front of him. Apparently sensing Trevor's discomfort and nerves, the baby's legs started to kick and his face started to scrunch up and turn red.

Haylie stepped forward immediately and took the baby back, her pseudo-maternal instincts kicking in at the first sign of Bradley's distress. Cradling him against her chest, she patted his back and bounced gently up and down. In seconds, he was once again calm and content.

Trevor, however, looked anything but. His face had fallen into a hard, angry mask, his mouth thinning into a tight, flat line.

"I don't know what kind of game you think you're playing," he told her, his tone as cold as his coffee-brown eyes, "but I'm not amused. I'm afraid I'm going to have to ask you to leave before I'm forced to call security."

He was already moving around his desk and toward the double oak doors, so he didn't see her roll her eyes at his overly dramatic he-man speech.

He certainly wasn't going to need security to get rid of her. She would be more than happy to leave under her own steam.

In fact, if she didn't feel so strongly that a man deserved to know he was a father, and that a child deserved to know his only remaining parent, she wouldn't be in Aspen at all. She would be back home in Denver, minding her own business and doing her best to raise her nephew.

Not for the first time, Haylie cursed her sister's carefree, irresponsible nature. It had been Heather's place to find Trevor after their one-night stand and tell him she was pregnant. Her place to inform him that he had a son after Bradley had been born.

But, of course, her sister hadn't done either of those things. Oh, no, that would have been responsible and mature and right, a sign that she was finally growing up and might actually be ready to raise a child.

Haylie honestly didn't know what had been going

through her sister's head those long months of her pregnancy. Most of the time, Haylie had gotten the impression that the fact that she was a soon-to-be mother hadn't really sunken in for Heather. She'd gone about her business almost as though nothing in her life had changed except her belt size.

To the best of Haylie's knowledge, Heather *had* stopped drinking and smoking, and she'd cut down on her penchant for partying once her growing belly had put a bit of a damper on the fun of that, but otherwise, Heather had gone through those nine months with her head in the clouds.

Boy, talk about the cold slap of reality. Haylie didn't think she'd ever seen anyone so surprised as her sister when she'd gone into labor. And for the first couple of weeks after Bradley's birth, Haylie had actually thought Heather was growing up. Was going to step up to the plate and be a good, loving, *reliable* parent.

As usual when it came to her younger sister, however, the show of sensibility had been as fleeting as a summer storm. Before Bradley was a month old, Heather had started falling into her predictable, selfish habits. Staying out all night and sleeping well into the afternoon…not paying her bills…and worst of all, ignoring Bradley.

Despite her many shortcomings, Haylie loved her sister, but as far as Haylie was concerned, the last had been nearly unforgivable.

Bradley wasn't Haylie's child, but from the moment he'd come into the world, she'd loved him with an intensity that made her understand a mama bear's fierce instinct to protect her young. It was inconceivable to her that her sister—Bradley's *biological mother*—didn't share the same deep, powerful feelings for her own son.

But the point was moot, Haylie supposed. It was

her job now to protect and care for Bradley, and if she didn't love the little boy so much, if she didn't think he deserved the very best of everything and believe to the depth of her soul that he had the right to know his father—and that his father had the right to know him—she wouldn't be at Jarrod Ridge right now, in Trevor Jarrod's office, facing down a man who could not only have her thrown out of his family's resort, but possibly barred from the entire state of Colorado.

"You can call anyone you like," she told him, her tone much more cool, calm and collected than she felt, "but it won't change my reason for being here."

Carrying Bradley to one of the guest chairs in front of the desk, she started rooting in her purse with her free hand, then straightened, holding a small sheaf of papers. She crossed to Trevor, who was clutching the curved gold door handle in his long, bronzed fingers, but hadn't yet opened the door. She offered him a photo from the top of the stack.

"This is my sister, Heather," she murmured, then had to swallow when her voice grew thick and tears threatened.

At least Trevor was looking at the photograph, actually studying her sister's features rather than dismissing her out of hand. But as he lifted his head and their eyes met, Haylie knew he had no recollection whatsoever of meeting and sleeping with Heather.

With a mental sigh, she swallowed again and licked her lips before continuing. "You apparently met her while in Denver on business, at one of the clubs downtown. Heather was a beautiful young woman, but she liked to party. And she *didn't* like to go home alone."

Something flickered in the depths of his dark sable eyes, and he said, "Was?"

Haylie's chest hitched as she gave a shaky nod and handed him the newspaper clipping she'd brought along with Heather's picture. "She was killed in a car accident two months ago."

Her chest tightened even more when a look of genuine sympathy passed over his features. He might not remember Heather, and he might suspect Haylie was up to no good with her *it's a boy!* announcement, but he didn't appear to be completely cold and heartless.

"I know you probably think I'm trying to work some elaborate scam on you. Or that I'm hoping to snag a bit of the Jarrod fortune for myself. But I assure you, that isn't the case."

Bradley started to fuss, and she jiggled him slightly, transferring him to her other hip. "I'm only here because Heather told me you're Bradley's father, and since she never got around to contacting you yourself, I felt it was my place to let you know she'd passed away, and that you have a child. More importantly, I think he—" she lifted Bradley, making it clear to whom she was referring "—deserves to know his father and where he comes from on his father's side."

When Trevor didn't respond, she slipped the photograph and obituary out of his loose grasp. "So check me out if you need to. Draw up whatever legal documents you feel are fair and will protect your assets. But don't punish your son for his mother's mistakes."

Trevor's grip tightened on the door handle while he studied the woman standing before him. He'd met his fair share of young ladies with dollar signs in their eyes and their sights set on the Jarrod millions, and had become adept at brushing them off.

But none of his usual gold digger alarm bells were

going off with Haylie Smith. Something about her told him she was sincere. Even if she was wrong about the baby's paternity, it was clear she *believed* what she was saying—or at least what her sister had apparently told her before her death.

Glancing down at the photograph clutched in Haylie's white-knuckled fingers, he once again racked his brain for any memory of the woman he'd supposedly spent a less-than-memorable night with. He remembered the trip to Denver, and even stopping in at one of the city's more popular nightclubs for a drink after a day filled with disappointing meetings and a potentially lucrative business venture that had fallen through. He'd been frustrated and annoyed, and had needed to blow off some steam.

The earsplitting techno music had rattled his brain, but he'd stuck around long enough to down a few drinks. And he remembered women…lots of women in short skirts and ice-pick stilettos, both out on the dance floor and crowded into booths the color of Hpnotiq vodka. Several had hit on him, but he hadn't been in the mood.

Or maybe, after a few more drinks, he had.

There was no recollection there, though. The only thing he found familiar about the woman in the picture came from her resemblance to the woman standing in front of him now. They had the same blue eyes and honey-blond hair, the same bow-tie mouth and long, thick lashes. But that's where the similarities ended.

Where Heather's hair was styled in a bold, spikey do, with a streak of magenta running down one side, Haylie's fell soft and naturally around her face and looked infinitely touchable.

Where Heather's lips were painted a bright, shocking

shade of pink, Haylie wore nothing but a layer of clear gloss.

And where Heather's eyes appeared hard and jaded, Haylie's were deep pools of warmth and earnestness.

How could two women—sisters—with so many of the same features look so very different? he wondered.

He also wondered how one sister could go nine-plus months without making a single effort to inform a man he was allegedly going to be a father, while the other had spent two months trying to track him down by phone and felt so strongly about her duty to inform him of his parenthood—again, *alleged* parenthood—that she'd driven nearly four hours from Denver to Aspen with a baby in tow and wheedled her way into his office just to confront him.

For that reason alone, he found himself wanting to know if her allegations were true. And if they were... Well, he wanted to know for himself if she was right about the child in her arms being his.

He wasn't sure how he felt about the possibility of being a father. The very thought made his stomach clench and his chest grow tight. But not with any innate paternal sentiments. No, what he was feeling was much more along the lines of dread and panic.

At only twenty-seven, the notion of getting married and starting a family had never crossed his mind. And the idea of having a child dropped in his lap out of the blue had been even further behind.

He was too busy enjoying his life, sowing wild oats and working to build his marketing company. Add to that the more recent turn of events that had made him the president of marketing at Jarrod Ridge, and he barely had time to hike, to ski, to *breathe,* let alone raise a child.

There was no point worrying about that or projecting into the future, though, until he knew for certain.

Releasing the door handle, he returned to his desk. Much more of this stalking back and forth and the carpet would need to be replaced.

As he lowered himself into his chair and reached for the phone, he gestured for Haylie to take a seat.

"Diana," he said the minute his secretary picked up. "Get Dr. Lazlo on the line for me, please."

Once she'd answered in the affirmative, he hung up and leaned his arms on the desk. He looked at the baby on Haylie's lap, searching for signs that this was, indeed, his child, but all he saw was…a baby.

He didn't see his eyes or his hair or his smile, didn't see *Jarrod bloodlines* stamped on every inch of that pale, pudgy baby skin.

Did that mean the child…Bradley, his name was Bradley. Did that mean Bradley *wasn't* his…or simply that a four-month-old's parentage couldn't be determined just by looking?

Lifting his gaze, Trevor pinned Haylie with a hard stare. "We'll have a paternity test run immediately. And God help you if your story is a lie."

He wasn't sure what he would do, exactly, but the very thought that she was trying to get one over on him made his jaw lock and his temperature rise. On the desk in front of him, his fists clenched until his knuckles cracked.

If this whole thing turned out to be some crazy fabrication in a bid to get money or besmirch his good name—his family's good name—he *was not* going to be happy. The Jarrods had Erica's fiancé and longtime family attorney Christian, as well as a bevy of other legal eagles on retainer, who would have no problem racking up billable hours devising new and creative ways to make Haylie Smith sorry she had ever come to Jarrod Ridge.

At his veiled threat, he'd half expected her to blink. To decide that maybe this charade wasn't the wisest plan of action, after all.

But once again, he'd underestimated her. Not only didn't she blink—figuratively or literally—but her expression remained just as firm and determined.

"If he's not your baby," she said softly, "it won't be my lie, it will be my sister's."

As the minutes crawled by, with Trevor Jarrod staring her down like an opponent in a boxing ring, the silence in the luxurious office was thick enough to carve with a knife. There was no fire crackling in the hearth behind him, and no office noises filtering in from the other side of the wide double doors. Only the rhythmic ticking of the clock on the far wall and Bradley's occasional contented gurgle and sucking on his tiny fist kept her from hearing her own heart pounding beneath her ribs.

She could certainly understand Trevor's anger and suspicions. In his shoes, she would be thinking and feeling the exact same way.

But she was not the bad guy here. In fact, she was being an excessively *good guy* by bringing Bradley to Jarrod Ridge at all. She could have just as easily remained in Denver and raised her sister's child as her own.

It wasn't as if Trevor would have known the difference. Up until now, he hadn't been aware of Bradley's existence, and she sincerely doubted he'd have been struck by a sudden twinge of conscience and returned to Denver to see if he'd left behind any stray, fatherless progeny as a result of his numerous one-night stands in the Mile High City.

And she didn't even have a deathbed promise to her sister hanging over her head, prompting her to do the right thing by both Bradley and Trevor. Given the fact that Heather had claimed several times that she would tell Trevor about the baby or had been trying to contact him to do just that…and that she very obviously hadn't done anything of the sort…Haylie was only following her own strict moral code, which dictated that a man had the right to know he'd fathered a child.

Whether or not he stepped up and took responsibility for that child was a different story, but he had the right to know, and Haylie's own conscience wouldn't have let her go much longer without making sure that he did.

If it turned out Trevor wasn't Bradley's father… Well, she couldn't very well go back in time and strangle her sister, but she sure would be tempted. The best she could do, she supposed, was apologize for the misunderstanding and any inconvenience she'd caused him and go back to Denver to do what she'd planned all along—raise Bradley on her own.

Before either of them could form words to break the Mexican standoff between their cool, targeted gazes, the phone on Trevor's desk buzzed. He grabbed the handset and listened, presumably to whatever his assistant had to say.

"Thank you," he murmured, and a moment later, "Dr. Lazlo, Trevor Jarrod. I've got a situation here that requires the utmost discretion."

After a pause in which the physician was likely raising a hand, swearing on both his Hippocratic oath and a stack of Bibles, Trevor continued, "How long will it take to get results on a paternity test?"

A small frown marred his brow, and Haylie raised one of her own. Obviously any response other than "instantaneously" didn't set well with Mr. Jarrod.

"Very well, although if there's any way to rush that and still maintain accuracy…" More silence while the person on the other end spoke, too low for her to hear. "We can be at your office in thirty minutes."

With a nod, Trevor thanked the doctor for his time and hung up before turning his dark stare back to her… and the baby on her lap.

"We're driving into the city to have blood tests done," he told her, as though she hadn't heard every word of his side of the conversation. And his tone left no room for argument, even if she'd cared to make one. "Now."

Pushing up from his desk, he came around, no doubt expecting her to hop up and follow him like a well-trained puppy. Instead, she pushed slowly to her feet, shifting Bradley around to her front as she strode slowly across the office to one of the soft-as-butter leather sofas lining the side walls.

"What are you doing?" Trevor asked crossly. In her peripheral vision, she saw him fold his arms over his wide chest and tap the toe of one fawn-colored boot in annoyance.

"I'm changing Bradley's diaper before I stuff him back into his snowsuit," she told Trevor calmly, laying the baby down and beginning to unsnap the legs of his denim overalls. But before she removed the soiled diaper, she tipped her head meaningfully in Trevor's direction. "Unless you'd prefer to drive all the way to the doctor's office with the windows down."

Mouth flattening into a thin, unhappy line, he

dropped his arms and stuffed his hands into the front pockets of his jeans instead. "No, go ahead."

Biting back a gloating chuckle, she returned her attention to Bradley and quickly finished cleaning him up, then got him tucked into his thick, baby-blue snowsuit. When she tightened the faux-fur-lined hood around his face, he grinned and kicked his little legs, and she couldn't resist leaning in to flick his nose and grin back.

Then, remembering that Trevor was still in the room, watching them like a hawk, she cleared her throat and straightened somewhat self-consciously.

"Almost ready," she said, standing to put on her own sage-green parka before gathering Bradley and reaching for the strap of his diaper bag.

Trevor was suddenly there, grabbing it for her. "I've got it."

She swallowed again, this time because the intensity of his dark gaze had her cheeks going hot and her stomach swooping like a roller coaster on the downslide.

"Thank you," she managed, following quietly behind him when he moved to the office door, opened it and stepped into the reception area.

His secretary lifted her head at her boss's approach, but her glance skated quickly past Trevor to eye Haylie and Bradley. Haylie didn't think the woman had heard anything that had been said behind the closed office doors, but it was obvious she was curious about who exactly Haylie was, what she'd needed to talk to Trevor about and why she'd brought a four-month-old along to do it. But like all good secretaries, she was discreet, keeping her mouth shut and waiting until her employer told her what he needed.

"Diana, I'm going to be out of the office for a while,"

Trevor informed her, not bothering to introduce Haylie, even though it was clear that wherever he was going, she was tagging along. "Possibly the rest of the day. Reschedule any meetings for me, please, and field anything else that comes up."

"Yes, sir," Diana responded, jotting a note on her desk blotter before taking to her keyboard to bring up what Haylie assumed was Trevor's daily schedule.

From a hidden closet behind the receptionist's desk, Trevor pulled out his coat and shrugged it on. Stuffing his hands into the pockets, he pulled out a cell phone, checked the display and put it back.

"My cell will be on if you need to reach me," he added, "but—"

"—Try not to need you," Diana finished for him.

He flashed a quick half smile. "Right."

Lifting his gaze to Haylie's, he met her eyes for a second, then said, "Ready?"

She nodded, passing the reception desk to once again trail after the man who was—for the moment, at least—in charge. But instead of taking the lead, this time he held the door and ushered her and Bradley ahead of him. An act of chivalry that for some reason had her tightening her grip on her nephew and reminding herself that she didn't fall into bed with every handsome man she met the way her sister always had. If anything, while she was in Trevor Jarrod's presence, she needed to be even more diligent about disengaging her female hormones and keeping her wits about her.

But if Haylie were honest with herself, she would have to admit that, not for the first time since meeting Bradley's father, she couldn't quite blame her sister any longer for having a one-night stand with this man. If Haylie were a bit more extroverted, a bit less timid when it came to flirting with the opposite sex and had a bit more time on her hands to actually meet people of the opposite sex, she suspected she'd be tempted to fall into bed with him, too.

Three

The trip to Dr. Lazlo's office took closer to forty-five minutes than thirty, mostly due to the fact that Trevor had never been around a child and had no idea how much paraphernalia they required just to get from point A to point B.

First, he'd led Haylie through one of the Manor's side exits to his fire-engine-red Hummer parked in a reserved spot in the employee parking lot. Only to have her arch a brow and refuse to get in on the passenger side until they'd collected Bradley's car seat from her vehicle.

So they'd tromped back to the Manor—because she wouldn't get in with the baby, even to let him drive them around to her car—and through the main hallways of the hotel until they'd reached one of the more public entrances closer to the guest parking area.

Trevor would have preferred to simply walk around

the giant building, finding the light fall of snow and chill in the air bracing. But in the short time they'd been outdoors, Haylie's and Bradley's cheeks had already turned pink with cold, and Trevor didn't want to risk either of them getting sick or frostbitten, so he'd opted for taking the partially heated shortcut past God knew how many inquiring eyes.

As if having a strange woman pop up in his office with a baby she claimed to be his wasn't bad enough, the idea that someone might find out about this latest wrench in the works and splash it across the front page of every rag tabloid in Colorado and beyond was enough to give him an ulcer *and* high blood pressure. All he could do was hope that the people they passed were mere tourists and not some form of despicable paparazzi disguised as guests in an effort to dig up dirt on the Jarrods yet again.

All he needed was for the three of them to wend their way through the buzzing center of the main hotel and out to the parking lot without being waylaid by anyone who might be curious about Haylie's identity.

At least it didn't look as though he and Haylie were together. She was walking off to the side two paces behind him, and they weren't doing anything telling like holding hands. For all onlookers knew, he was simply showing a VIP guest to her lodge personally.

Although, he had to admit that the urge to reach out and clasp her hand *was* there.

Not because he was attracted to her. He gave a mental snort. Nothing as ridiculous as that.

No, it was just that she wasn't exactly wearing the most sensible winter boots. He doubted they had much tread on them at all, and the ground was slippery.

For that matter, the parts of the resort's flooring that

weren't covered in rugs or carpeting could be slippery if they got wet, too. It wasn't worth the risk of a lawsuit to have *anyone* fall and hurt themselves on Jarrod Ridge property, and he certainly didn't want Haylie to lose her footing and chance dropping Bradley. Whether the baby turned out to be his or not, he would never want to see a child hurt.

They were halfway across the lobby, exit in sight, and he thought they might just make it.

And…no such luck. Trevor gave a low curse beneath his breath as he saw his brother Guy bearing down on them.

Guy was their other brother Blake's fraternal twin, as well as Jarrod Ridge's main restaurateur-slash-food guru. Or as the Jarrod boys liked to tease, their chief cook and bottle washer. The resort boasted four restaurants and six bars, all of which Guy helped to oversee.

Food might be Guy's specialty, but because Trevor was in charge of resort-wide marketing, most publicity related to the restaurants fell under his umbrella. And though their largest public affair—the Food and Wine Gala—was behind them for another year, that didn't mean they weren't constantly working on other events, tossing around other ideas.

At the moment, he and Guy were trying to organize specialty menus and advertising for a sort of "world tour" of the Manor's eateries. Chagall's would cover a taste of France, Emilio's would cover a taste of Italy, The Golden Palace would cover a taste of China, and so on.

Guy could have picked a better time to bother him about it, though.

Stopping in his tracks—in the middle of the damn lobby, no less—Trevor braced himself for Guy's approach and prayed Haylie would have the sense to keep her mouth shut.

"Hey," his brother greeted him.

Three years older than Trevor and only an inch or so shorter, he was dressed in black slacks and a plain white button-down shirt. Casual, and yet not quite as casual as Trevor's current post-ski-slope attire.

His brown hair, which he normally wore a bit long and unkempt, was cut short and neatly styled. Avery's doing, no doubt. As were the new clothes and the twinkle that never seemed to leave his brother's eyes these days. Trevor liked Guy's new fiancée, but the fact that she so obviously loved his brother and was having such a positive influence on him in every way only made Trevor respect her all the more.

"Hey," he murmured back. And just as he'd expected, Guy unrolled a sheaf of oversize papers he'd been carrying under his arm.

"I've been looking over the poster mock-ups, and there are a few changes I'd like to make. Especially to the proposed menus." One corner of his mouth lifted in a grin and he winked. "You know how I am when it comes to food. Do you have a minute to discuss it?"

"Actually, now isn't a good time," Trevor replied honestly. "Can I catch you later?"

Since Trevor was all about marketing and almost never unavailable when he was at the Ridge and in full business mode, his brother's raised brows came as no surprise. Then Guy happened to glance over his shoulder, to where Haylie was standing just behind him, still holding a powder-blue, near mummified Bradley. There was no denying that she was with Trevor, patiently waiting for him to finish his conversation so they could carry on.

"Oh, yeah," Guy muttered. "Sure."

From the expression on Guy's face, Trevor knew he was curious, that he was dying to ask about the pretty woman and her baby. Thankfully, he was wise enough to keep his mouth shut. At least for the moment. Of course, the family grapevine ran at the speed of light, so Trevor had no illusions that word of his mysterious companion wouldn't get around. Dammit.

And then Guy went and made matters even worse. Stretching an arm past Trevor's impeding bulk, he offered Haylie his hand.

"Guy Jarrod," he said by way of introduction. "Trevor's older brother. Older, smarter and more handsome, of course," he added with a wink. This time, it was meant to be charismatic, not self-deprecating.

Trevor rolled his eyes, as much at Guy's display of chivalry as at the fact that things seemed to be getting dicier for him by the second.

Haylie accepted Guy's hand and gave it a polite shake. "Haylie Smith," she offered. Nothing more, nothing less. Thank goodness.

While she was perfectly courteous, Trevor noticed she didn't seem the least impressed by his brother's attempt at charm. For some reason, that pleased him. Not that it mattered one way or the other—Guy was very happily and very firmly engaged, and Trevor wasn't interested in any woman who came with even a hint of strings attached.

And Haylie came with enough strings to knit an afghan.

"Look," Trevor said to his brother, doing his best to tamp down his growing impatience. "We're in kind of a hurry. I'll talk to you later, all right?"

With that, he tilted his head, silently gesturing for Haylie to move ahead of him toward the nearest exit.

"Right. Fine. Later," Guy mumbled as they stepped away.

Trevor felt his brother's gaze on his back the entire time, and knew his mind must be racing. Dammit, just what he needed—more attention drawn to Haylie's presence and his peculiar behavior.

Against his better judgment, as soon as they stepped outside into the brisk December chill, Trevor gave in to the voice in his head that kept telling him to reach out and touch her.

But he didn't take her hand. Too intimate and not his place. Instead, he took her elbow, just to steady her and avoid any accidents while they made their way to her car.

She didn't seem startled by the action, even shooting him a small smile over Bradley's fuzzy, hooded head.

"Your brother seems nice," she said, and he knew she was just trying to make small talk.

"Yeah" was his monosyllabic response.

Sure, Guy was nice. Nice and curious, no doubt.

Haylie's car, as it turned out, was another cause for concern. Though it was several years old and a model he was pretty sure had been taken off the market, it looked to be in good enough shape. Except for the tires.

How could anyone live in Colorado and not have snow tires on their vehicle by the time the weather turned icy? Or if they were snow tires, the tread was so worn that they might as well have been inner tubes.

None of his business, Trevor told himself while Haylie dug into her purse for her keys. Unless, of course, it turned out that Bradley *was* his son. In which case, it was very much his business, and he would see to it that all four of the woman's tires were replaced immediately. Or better yet, he would replace her car entirely…buy her something much safer and better suited to Aspen and Denver in the winter months. A Hummer like his. Or maybe a damn tank.

Juggling her purse and keys and the baby, Haylie struggled to get the driver's side door open, and Trevor stepped forward to help.

"Here, let me," he murmured, taking the keys from her hand.

Once he had the car unlocked, she opened the rear door, then turned to him and said, "Could you hold him for a minute?"

Without waiting for a response, she thrust Bradley against his chest and his arms came up automatically to grab the overstuffed bundle shoved in his direction. Catching the baby beneath the arms, Trevor held him out away from him like a bag of angry, venomous snakes.

Haylie was facing the opposite direction, fiddling with the child's safety seat and the belts that held it in place, so she didn't see what he was sure was an expression of sheer terror on his face.

He didn't know anything about babies. Not how to hold them or feed them or change a diaper. What if Bradley started crying? And didn't babies leak? Tears and drool and spit-up, and even worse things that, thank God, a diaper would likely catch.

But Bradley wasn't leaking. If anything, he looked positively delighted by his new handler. His cheeks were pudgy and pink, his eyes bright with amusement. He was kicking his little legs as though dancing to music only he could hear, and if Trevor wasn't mistaken, he thought the child might even be smiling.

Did babies this age smile, or did he just have gas?

Bradley gave an extra-exuberant kick and giggled. Intentionally. Definitely not gastrointestinal related.

With a silent chuckle of his own, Trevor's trepidation began to fade and he bent his arms, bringing Bradley back against his chest.

He was kind of a cute kid. Didn't mean he was a Jarrod, but he still had that whole irresistible baby thing going on that Trevor had heard so much about, especially where women and their biological clocks were concerned.

A minute or two later, when Haylie climbed out of the car with the safety seat, Trevor was making faces at Bradley and bouncing up and down the way he'd seen her do back in his office.

"I can take him now," she said.

Trevor shook his head. "That's okay, I've got him."

After all, this wasn't as tough as he'd thought, and if the baby turned out not to be his, it might be the only chance he got to do the new-dad thing for quite some time. And if Bradley *did* turn out to be his son…well, he could use all the practice he could get.

Sliding his glance to Haylie, he nodded at the car seat. "Can you get that, or do you want me to carry it?"

"I can get it, but…" She frowned a bit and sounded slightly worried. "Are you sure you wouldn't rather trade?"

"Nope, we're fine," he said, giving Bradley another little jiggle that had him giggling. "Make sure your car is locked and that you have everything you need before we take off."

Half an hour after *that,* Trevor pulled the Hummer into a spot in front of the doctor's office and cut the engine. Haylie was already out of the car and working to collect Bradley when he got around to her side to help.

Unlike while Trevor had been holding him, the little boy's nose was now wrinkled, his mouth pursed and his eyes squinted in displeasure. He was wiggling and whimpering, and the pink in his cheeks definitely didn't have anything to do with the cold.

"What's wrong with him?" Trevor asked, trying not to let his concern slip into his tone.

"He's just fussy," Haylie replied, lifting the child from the car seat and shouldering him at the same time she hefted the bulging diaper bag with its yellow giraffe and purple hippopotamus.

Trevor took the bag for her and closed the door before they started up the sidewalk in front of the tall redbrick building.

"Can you get a bottle out of there?" she asked, pointing to one of the bag's side pockets. "He's probably hungry, and after that he'll need a new diaper and then a nap. I hope this doesn't take too long, or we're going to have one very loud, unhappy baby on our hands. Unless he sleeps through the whole thing. That would be nice."

A loud, unhappy baby didn't sound like something Trevor cared to experience. Unfortunately, DNA tests tended to involve needles and poking, which he didn't think would do much to improve Bradley's current disposition.

Entering the office, he left Haylie to find a seat and give Bradley his bottle while he let the receptionist know in a whispered voice who he was and why they were here.

It didn't take long for the nurse to call them back and lead them to a private exam room, where the baby continued to empty his bottle, his lashes fluttering as his eyes grew heavier and heavier. Moments later, the doctor arrived, greeting Trevor and introducing himself to Haylie. After a brief examination of Bradley, who had finished his bottle and was now sound asleep in Haylie's arms, the doctor pushed his stool back and regarded both adults.

"It's my understanding that you'd like a paternity test to determine that the child is…"

Dr. Lazlo let the sentence trail off, and Haylie quickly supplied, "His," with a tilt of her head in Trevor's direction.

"Bradley is my sister's son," she continued to explain. "Heather passed away two months ago in an auto accident, without informing Mr. Jarrod that he was a father. Mr. Jarrod wants to be sure I'm telling him the truth about Bradley's parentage and didn't come to Jarrod Ridge to pan for gold with a baby and a well-constructed story."

Trevor shot her an annoyed glance, leaning back against the high countertop to cross his arms over his chest. "That's probably more than the good doctor needs to know," he pointed out.

The doctor gave a friendly chuckle. "Not to worry. I've conducted thousands of these tests, and I assure you, I'm very discreet. I'll handle your samples and the results personally, and send them to the lab under fictitious names."

Trevor inclined his head in approval, but he still wasn't happy. Bad enough they were here at all—he really didn't need the entire situation spelled out for him again, or for relative strangers.

"Now," the physician said, resting his hands on his knees. "There are two types of paternity tests. Both have long, hard-to-pronounce medical names that I'm sure you don't care about, but suffice to say that one, PCR, involves swabbing the inside of the cheek, the other, RFLP, drawing blood."

"Which is more accurate?" Trevor wanted to know.

"RFLP, the blood sample. We can do both, if you like. Each test is fairly accurate, but with both there would be very little doubt as to the child's paternity."

Cocking his head, Trevor turned to look at Haylie. She stared up at him, her eyes and face telling him nothing of her inner thoughts.

"Would you mind if we did both?" he asked. "To be certain."

She was silent for several seconds, then lifted one slim shoulder in a shrug. "It's all right with me, but the blood test is definitely going to wake Bradley, and he is *definitely* going to shatter some eardrums."

"We'll start with the buccal swab," the doctor told her, "and I'll be as gentle as possible."

Twenty minutes later, Bradley was once again sound asleep, this time in the backseat of Trevor's Hummer as they headed back to Jarrod Ridge. The needle prick had woken him, just as Haylie warned it would, and he'd shrieked at the top of his lungs for a good three minutes. But after that, he'd wound down to a few ragged whimpers before drifting off again against Haylie's shoulder.

Breaking the silence inside the car, Trevor murmured, "The doctor said the test results could take a couple of weeks, depending on how backed up the lab is."

She nodded, twisting in her seat to look at him rather than out the window. "I think he's right about not putting a rush on it. You want to keep this quiet until you know for sure whether Bradley is your son, and that would only rouse suspicions."

"I believe Dr. Lazlo will be as discreet as possible,"

he agreed, "but things have a way of getting out, anyway, especially if employees get curious and start poking around."

"I don't mind waiting, if you don't. And I promise to be just as circumspect as the doctor. No one back home knows anything about you. I don't think they're even particularly curious about who Bradley's father might be." Her mouth turned down at the corners, eyes narrowing. "Heather had that kind of reputation. No one was surprised when she turned up pregnant without a man hanging around to claim the baby."

To Trevor, she sounded slightly embarrassed by that fact, as well as disapproving, but also...defensive. As though she hadn't agreed with her sister's behavior, wouldn't have chosen that sort of lifestyle for either of them, but would stick up for Heather no matter what. Even now that she was gone.

He couldn't fault her for that. As it turned out, he had one sister more than he'd known about while growing up, but that didn't keep him from feeling protective of both his full sister, Melissa, and his recently discovered half sister, Erica.

For that matter, he felt protective of his entire family. The Jarrods were sort of like the Three Musketeers—all for one and one for all.

None of them were perfect, but despite their mistakes and the occasional flaw in their personalities, he would still defend any one of them to the death. That Haylie felt the same way about her sister—and her sister's child—didn't surprise him.

"That's something else we need to talk about, actually."

"What?" she asked, her brows drawing down in confusion.

"Where you'll be staying until the test results are in."

"Oh. That's no problem. As soon as we get back to your office, I'll give you my address and phone number, all the ways to reach me. You're welcome to visit Bradley anytime, if you like. Although, if you'd rather not until you know for sure…I'll understand," she finished quietly.

Understand, but not necessarily approve, he thought with some amusement.

Not that it mattered.

"That's not what I meant," he told her.

"I'm sorry. What did you mean then?"

"I've been giving it some thought, and until we know for sure whether or not Bradley is my son, I'd like the two of you to move in with me."

Four

For long minutes, Haylie was too stunned to respond. She sat there in the passenger seat of Trevor's SUV with her mouth hanging open. Catching flies, as her mother used to say. But she couldn't have been more surprised if he'd announced he wanted to give up his family's millions and go to work as a fry cook at a fast-food restaurant.

Shifting around to face him more fully, she wiggled inside of her overstuffed parka, loosening the zipper in an effort to cool down and breathe a bit more easily. The heating vents were blowing, but she didn't think they were the reason she was suddenly feeling flushed.

No, that would be confusion mixed with a fair dose of alarm.

After swallowing a couple of times and barely resisting the urge to squiggle her ears to make sure she hadn't misheard him, she managed to utter two rather strangled words. "Excuse me?"

Without taking his eyes off the road, he said, "I think it's best for everyone involved."

She *really* wanted to slap her ears and make sure she was hearing him correctly, because nothing he was saying seemed to make sense. Swallowing again, she cleared her throat and asked, "How so?"

He shrugged one broad shoulder, made even broader by the thickness of his coat. "If Bradley is mine, then I've got some lost time to make up for. I'd prefer to keep him close by, start getting to know him…and get used to being a father."

His voice tightened with his last few words, as though the thought that he might truly be the father of a little boy he'd known nothing about until a couple of hours ago was something he'd prefer not to think about.

Too bad said little boy was sleeping in the backseat at that very moment. And while Haylie certainly didn't have the kind of money to gamble with that Trevor Jarrod had, she'd have been willing to bet the DNA tests would come out with a glaring "Congratulations, Daddy!" message stamped all over them.

"I can understand that," she agreed, "but it won't take *that* long for the paternity results to come in. And Bradley is already four months old—surely another couple of weeks won't make that much difference. Besides, I have a life back in Denver. A business to run. I can't just pick up and disappear."

"Then leave the boy with me. You've had four months with him, I've had barely a day. And I have plenty of room, as well as the money to hire a round-the-clock nanny."

Haylie's eyes went wide. She'd never considered

herself a violent person, but right that second she was extremely tempted to reach out and slap the man sitting beside her. There were so many things wrong with what he'd just said, she didn't know where to begin.

The boy? A nanny?

Leave Bradley with Trevor?

"Absolutely not."

This time, it was her voice that came out strained, but not due to nerves. Oh, no, hers was all temper. She was skating past mere anger, headed deep into furious territory.

"I may not be Bradley's biological mother, but I'm the only mother he's known for the past two months—and quite a bit before that, if the truth be known. There is *no way* I would leave him *anywhere,* with *anyone.*"

The waterproof material of her jacket made a slick scratching sound as she crossed her arms. "I don't care if you are his father," she muttered with no small amount of aversion to the word.

What was that saying about no good deed going unpunished? Boy, was she being smacked in the face with its meaning now.

All she'd wanted was to do the right thing. To let a man know he'd fathered a child with a woman who never would have told him on her own, and whom he never would have run into again otherwise.

She'd wanted to do the right thing by Bradley. He was a Jarrod, after all. And even though she didn't need the family's millions, didn't believe a child needed that kind of money to grow up happy and healthy and well-loved, he still deserved to know where he came from, who his ancestors were.

But *no good deed…* And here she was, only a handful

of hours past her "good deed," and it was already biting her in the butt.

For several seconds, Trevor didn't reply. Then his low voice carried over the short distance separating them, his words stopping her heart and freezing her blood.

"I could take him from you, you know."

Okay, so that hadn't been Argument Number One in Trevor's big plan to convince Haylie to move in with him for the next couple of weeks. But something about the way she'd gotten up on her hind legs about not leaving Bradley with him put him on the defensive.

On the one hand, he liked how protective she was of the infant. If the kid really did turn out to be his, he suspected he was going to have a lot of moments of feeling very grateful toward her for caring for his son the way she had.

Sure, Bradley was her nephew, so he knew there had to be a strong bond there. But from the sounds of it, Bradley's mother—this now-deceased Heather he had no recollection of ever meeting—had been a bit of a troublemaker. Or rather, gotten into her fair share of trouble.

It would have been easy, even understandable, for Haylie to cut her sister off and say no more. No more cleaning up her messes, no more coming to her rescue.

But Haylie hadn't done that, had she? No, she had not only stuck by her sister through all of her screwups, but had taken over the role of mother to her infant son after Heather's unexpected death.

For that, Haylie deserved a whole row of gold stars. And if he turned out to be Bradley's father, she would also have Trevor's undying gratitude.

"I'll fight you for him," she said through gritted teeth, breaking into his thoughts.

She sounded completely outraged, on the verge of doing him bodily damage, and his opinion of her ratcheted up another dozen notches.

Of course, she wouldn't have a chance in hell. She could fight him from now until doomsday, but if he wanted to take primary physical custody of the little boy in the backseat, he had both the lawyers and the resources to see that it was done. Even before the DNA results came in, the argument could be made that *she* had come to *him* with claims of his paternity and, given that the child's mother had kept both her pregnancy and the infant a secret from him…well, he imagined the courts would be only too happy to rectify the circumstances in his favor.

That *wasn't* the route he wanted to take, however, and was already regretting bringing it up. Instead, he preferred to finesse the situation. Something he was normally much better at.

Considering the baby bomb that had been dropped on him only hours ago, Trevor decided to cut himself some slack. He was still reeling from the first moment the words "here's your son" had slipped from Haylie's mouth, let alone everything that had been spinning through his head since.

And the fact was, he needed Haylie on his side. It wasn't easy for him to admit that, even to himself, but he knew *nothing* about kids. Little ones, big ones; they might as well have been tiny green creatures from the planet Krypton.

If Bradley turned out to be his flesh and blood, then no matter what Trevor had said about hiring a nanny, he was going to need her to teach him everything he needed to know about his own son. A nanny could change diapers and heat up bottles, but she wouldn't know Bradley's favorite brand of baby food, or whether he was ticklish or what made him laugh and cry.

Haylie knew those things. She'd spent the last four months learning all there was to know about his son.

Maybe his son.

His possible son.

No sense getting ahead of himself—or the paternity tests.

Still, the Jarrods were big on family, which meant that if he ended up with the right to lay claim to the baby, he would never dream of shutting Haylie out of Bradley's life. Bradley would need an aunt on his mother's side, as much as a father and aunts and uncles on Trevor's side.

So it would be smart to make Haylie his ally rather than his enemy. And better to start down that path sooner rather than later.

"Let's try to avoid the threats and talk of a custody battle altogether, shall we? At least for the time being. I think if you consider what I'm suggesting, you'll realize it's best for everyone involved."

When he cast a quick glance in Haylie's direction, he found her staring at him, one brow raised.

"Really?" she asked, sarcasm heavy in her tone. "How do you figure that?"

With a shrug, he returned his attention to the road. "Like I said, it's only for a few weeks, and it will give Bradley and me a chance to get to know each other." No, that didn't sound quite right. What was a better word for getting acquainted with your possible progeny? "To bond."

From the corner of his eye, he saw her lips thin in

what he thought was reluctant approval. He'd gotten one right, then...and annoyed Haylie in the process.

"What about me?" she asked, her gaze focused straight ahead through the windshield, just like his.

He frowned. "What about you? I already said that you and Bradley can move into my home together. I've got plenty of space, if that's what you're worried about. The two of you can have your own room and have the run of the place during the day while I'm at the resort."

"And what about my life back home? I do have a job, you know. A business to run, employees to oversee, a schedule to keep."

He shook his head and readjusted his hands on the steering wheel. "I'm sorry," he said. "What is it that you do?"

He couldn't believe he hadn't wondered about that before now. Chalk it up to yet another sign of his complete and utter shock at having a four-month-old child dropped in his lap. Literally.

Now that the topic had been brought up, however, he realized a background check wouldn't be out of the question. As soon as he returned to the office, he would make some phone calls and find the best person to do a bit of very *quiet* digging into Haylie's life, both the professional and private sides.

As long as they were at it, he'd see what they could learn about the sister, too. She might be deceased, but a good investigator should at least be able to determine whether Heather had actually been in Denver at the same time as Trevor's visit. If she truly had frequented the club where Haylie claimed he and Heather had met, and if there were any other candidates for fatherhood lurking in the shadows.

And even before Dr. Lazlo called with the paternity

results, a background check would give him an idea of Haylie's financial situation. Whether it was more or less likely that she was using her dead sister's child to wring a few of the Jarrod family's millions from him.

"I'm an event planner," Haylie supplied, oblivious to the thoughts and plans spiraling silently through his head.

"And you own your own company?" he encouraged.

She nodded. "A small one. I only have a handful of helpers, but the holidays are a busy time for us. I can barely afford to be away overnight, let alone for a week or two."

Ignoring the last part of her statement—temporarily, at least—Trevor asked, "What's the business called?"

Apparently, he was being too nice all of a sudden, because she cast him a suspicious glance before answering.

"It's Your Party."

"Cute," he murmured, an idea springing to mind and starting to take shape.

"Thank you."

"Do you specialize in anything in particular?"

"Not really," she admitted. "Or not yet. It's only been three years since we opened our doors, so we're still finding our footing and working to build a reputation as Denver's go-to event-planning company."

"Bet you're dealing with a lot of upcoming Christmas party preparations, huh?"

"Definitely. November and December are very good months for us, thank goodness."

She smiled a little then, and something warm began to unfurl in his chest.

No doubt about it, Haylie Smith was a damned

attractive woman. If she were anyone else, and they'd met any other way, he was pretty sure he'd have put the moves on her already. Offered to buy her a drink. Flashed his famed Trevor Jarrod playboy grin…the one that came complete with dimples and teeth so white and sparkly he could pose for a toothpaste ad.

But Haylie was off-limits, wasn't she? Not only because of the big, bad paternity issue she'd tossed on his doorstep with all the grace of a heavyweight fighter going down for the count, but because he got the distinct feeling she wasn't a woman who could be easily seduced.

Unlike her sister. Which brought him right back around again to the brick wall of the paternity thing.

"Ever planned a wedding?" he asked, returning to the kernel of an idea that had sprung up earlier.

Her brows knit a bit at that, but she answered readily enough. "A few. Small ones on my own, especially when I was first starting out. A couple of bigger ones once I'd hired staff to help out."

He hit the blinker, making a left turn that would take them farther from Jarrod Ridge, not closer, and hoped she was distracted enough not to notice. "They're a lot of work, I take it."

She chuckled. "Oh, yeah. Especially if you're dealing with a high-strung bride or family members who turn the entire event into a 'too many cooks' situation."

"But you enjoy them?" he pressed. "Wouldn't mind doing another?"

The lines crinkling her nose deepened, and her confused gaze completely focused on him now. "Of course not. It's Your Party, remember? No event too big, no party too small."

"Neither snow nor rain nor gloom of night…" he paraphrased with a teasing note.

"Exactly," she agreed with a laugh. "Although I do recommend event insurance if a client is putting a lot of money into something or the weather forecast is bleak."

"Smart move—if folks take your advice."

For a second, she didn't respond. Then her eyes narrowed and she said, "Why are you asking so many questions about my business?"

"Can't I just be curious?" he tossed back as he turned off the main road and onto a much more narrow private drive. Haylie was so engrossed in their conversation, she didn't seem to take note of the complete lack of traffic and the rougher drive as the Hummer navigated the snow-covered dirt-and-stone path.

Making a noise halfway between a scoff and a snort, she said, "Somehow I doubt you're ever 'just curious.'"

He grinned, thinking that even though they'd met for the first time only that morning, she knew him fairly well already.

"You're probably right about that. I've got a sister, though. Half sister, actually, who's engaged to be married. She and her fiancé were talking about a Christmas wedding, but they've put things off for so long and spent so much time waffling back and forth that I don't think they know what they want to do anymore."

They were climbing now, the oversize vehicle doing its job of hugging the road and navigating the less than smooth terrain.

"Where are we?" Haylie asked, finally realizing

that he hadn't driven them back to the resort as he'd promised.

Sidestepping the question, he told her instead, "So I was thinking that maybe you could talk with Erica. Maybe give her some pointers or help to allay her wedding jitters."

"I would be happy to. She can call me anytime, but…" Frowning, she twisted around in her seat just as his house came into view. "This isn't part of Jarrod Ridge. Is it? Where are we?" she asked again.

He remained silent until they reached the large two-car garage several yards from the main house. Both buildings were done in a dark, almost black wood stain that both stood out and blended beautifully with the rugged mountain terrain surrounding the property.

She was wrong about it not being part of Jarrod Ridge, though. No, it wasn't connected to the resort, but the small parcel of land he owned privately directly bordered the extensive Jarrod Ridge holdings.

Hitting the remote for one of the wide garage doors, he shifted to look at Haylie while the door slowly rolled upward.

"This is my place," he told her. "I thought I'd show you around, let you get a feel for the house before you turn me down flat on my invitation."

He could tell by the flattening of her lips and flare of her nostrils that she was *this close* to ripping him a new one. His only chance at avoiding a total nuclear meltdown was the hope that, with Bradley asleep in the backseat, she would be reluctant to wake him by launching into a full-blown tirade.

Trevor's eyes continued to blaze, and Haylie's jaw

worked as though she were grinding her teeth to keep from shrieking.

"Invitation?" she repeated, her tone acid sharp. "Don't you mean *order?*"

Five

"So that's it, isn't it. You're *ordering* us to stay here."

They were in the living room, logs crackling in the fireplace, the afternoon sun casting a lovely rose glow over the snowcapped evergreens and sleek white mountain slopes through the floor-to-ceiling windows that lined the west side of the house.

After taking a drowsy Bradley from his car seat, Trevor had given them a quick tour of the first floor while Haylie continued to fume. The baby was settled on a blanket in the middle of the floor now, his diaper changed and another bottle emptied. He was taking turns playing with his feet and a plastic ring of toys Haylie had pulled from her bag of tricks.

Haylie, however, was standing on the other side of the room, fuming. Her arms were crossed at her waist and her toe was tapping, actually tapping, in time with her bottled-up frustration.

"It's not an order," Trevor told her, doing his best to mollify her. Yes, he could force her to go along with what he wanted, but he would prefer to have her stay with him willingly. Or at least not as an adversary.

Moving into the open kitchen, he lifted two wineglasses from the rack hanging over the center island and pulled a bottle of his favorite merlot from the island itself. Then he went in search of a corkscrew.

"I'm *asking* you to stay here for a while," he continued, keeping his voice mild and hopefully cajoling without sounding patronizing. "So that I can be closer to Bradley. So I can get to know him through you, as well as getting to know you and learn more about your sister."

As well, keeping an eye on them. If they were under his roof, he could be sure she didn't do anything stupid like going to the press or deciding to seek her fifteen minutes of fame, along with a hefty payoff from the Jarrod family coffers.

With the cork free, he poured two healthy portions of the rich red wine and carried them back to the living area. He handed one to Haylie and was surprised when she took it—without tossing it in his face.

"If Bradley really does turn out to be my son, then I'd appreciate this time with him. Private time, before the rest of the world finds out that I fathered a son with a woman I don't remember, and then didn't find out about him for two months *after* her death."

Haylie cringed a bit at the word *death,* and he immediately regretted his matter-of-fact tone. Regardless of how he might feel about the woman who presumably kept his child from him for four months...and nine months before that, if he counted the full term of her pregnancy…he needed to remember she was Haylie's sister and that Haylie had loved her.

He took a sip of wine, pleased when she followed suit, then said in a softer voice, "You have no idea how callous the media can be when it comes to a family like mine. They keep us in the crosshairs of their telephoto lenses twenty-four seven, leaving us very little privacy, and turning every tiny occurrence into a major publicity campaign—to their benefit, not ours. They're especially talented at taking everyday, average events and blowing them completely out of proportion."

Tunneling his fingers through his hair, he blew out an aggravated breath. "If word were to get out about why you're here, even before we hear back from the doctor, headlines will be splashed across every gossip rag in the country labeling me a deadbeat dad and your sister a gold digger who intentionally got pregnant with a Jarrod heir."

Haylie seemed to consider that, swirling the merlot absently in her glass. Firelight reflected off the dark red wine and flickered shadows over her slim form while the muted sunlight shining through the window at her back cast her in an almost angelic glow that brought out the myriad shades of gold and brown and copper in her honey-blond hair.

His fingers itched suddenly to reach out and touch the silky strands, to find out if they truly were as soft and warm as they looked.

"Won't my staying with you, living under your roof, bring about a media frenzy just as much as if I were to go back to Denver and someone inadvertently found out about Bradley's parentage?" she asked.

Valid point. "We would keep that under wraps as much as possible, but if the question comes up, you're a family friend. That's all. A family friend and her son, staying with me rather than at the resort. We can even make it look as though you're a paying guest and I'm staying in the family quarters at the Manor so that you have this place all to yourself."

She cocked her head, looking skeptical, so he glossed over that sticking point and moved on to another of her bigger concerns.

"As for you taking time away from work, I don't know how long you took off after your sister's death, but surely folks would understand if you needed a bit more of a mourning period. And as I mentioned before, my sister really is in the process of planning her wedding. I'm sure she'd love having the help of a professional, and we can arrange it so that your stay here is actually a working visit."

Glancing down into her glass before lifting her gaze back to his, she murmured, "Are you sure your sister hasn't already hired a wedding planner? I mean, she is a Jarrod, after all, and can afford the very best. I would think hiring a professional is the first thing she'd think to do."

"I can't be sure, but I haven't heard anything about a wedding planner being hired, so I sort of doubt it." With a shrug, he drained the last of his wine and set the glass on the low, glass-top coffee table in front of the sofa. "If it makes you feel better, I'll call her right now."

Haylie opened her mouth to stop him, but he was already headed for the cordless on the kitchen counter.

To be honest, he hadn't intended to tell even his family about Haylie's sudden appearance and disturbing claims just yet, but he supposed they would find out soon enough, anyway. It wasn't as if he could take a few days off work or drag her to the Manor with him without the rest of the Jarrods swooping in to pepper him with questions. Sometimes, he thought wryly, they were worse than the press.

Hitting one of his many speed-dial numbers, he listened to the rings and waited for Erica to pick up. When she did, he greeted her with an upbeat, "Hey, sis, it's Trevor. I've got a question for you."

A second later, he shot Haylie an enthusiastic thumbs-up. "So how would you like to hire one? I'd consider it a personal favor, actually."

"Please tell me you aren't asking me to hire one of your temporary bimbos to plan my wedding," Erica begged with a groan.

Trevor didn't know whether to chuckle or be offended by her low opinion of his usual female companions. Not that he hadn't earned the reputation, he supposed.

But while it had never bothered him before, he found himself suffering a twinge. Of guilt? Embarrassment? He wasn't quite sure, but he didn't like the sensation.

Letting his gaze drift over Haylie's straight blond hair, conservative sweater and slacks, and classy but sensible shoes, he knew Erica would never mistake her for a bimbo. Or one of his temporary distractions, either.

"No," he answered firmly. "She's a very talented professional event planner, and I need to give her a really solid reason to stick around Jarrod Ridge for a couple of weeks."

"Why?" his sister asked without a hint of finesse.

"It's a long story," he muttered, looking down at the floor. "I'll explain later. So are you interested? Will you at least talk to her?"

"Of course. Frankly, it would be a relief to have

someone else worry about the details for a change. And someone to talk to about the wedding other than Christian. I love that man, but I swear he'd fly me to Galapagos if I asked him to, just to be married and done with it already."

"Great," Trevor responded, relief washing through him. "You two can arrange a face-to-face later, but for now, will you mind telling her that yourself?"

He held the phone out to Haylie and waited for her to take it. She did, reluctantly putting it to her ear.

"Hello?"

He couldn't hear the other side of the conversation, but Haylie nodded and offered his sister her name. For the next minute there were a lot of affirmative sounds and more nodding, followed by, "All right. I'd like that, thank you."

Hitting the disconnect button, Haylie handed the phone back to him. He knew her chat with his sister had gone well, but her expression was curiously blank.

"So?" he prompted, raising a brow.

"I'm apparently having lunch with your sister tomorrow to discuss the planning of her wedding."

"Excellent."

Haylie watched Trevor return the phone to its cradle, then collect the open bottle of wine and cross to the low coffee table where he poured a couple more inches for himself. Her glass was still nearly full, so he didn't offer to top her off.

Excellent? For him, maybe. She wasn't so sure about herself. She'd come to Aspen looking for a father for her nephew, not a new job.

Should she even help his sister with her wedding preparations, or should she back out of the impromptu lunch meeting she'd just agreed to? She could definitely develop a decent argument for temporary insanity, since not only her day but her entire life was beginning to feel very surreal and out of control.

On the other hand, they were talking about a Jarrod wedding here. *A Jarrod wedding!*

Celebrity-event planners would beg, borrow, steal and commit bloody murder to land a Jarrod wedding, and she was standing in the middle of Trevor Jarrod's living room being handed one on a silver platter. Even if they didn't pay her a dime, having a Jarrod wedding in her portfolio could take It's Your Party to a whole new level. From putting together mostly children's birthday parties and bar mitzvahs, to garden parties, high-society anniversaries and even more high-profile weddings.

The thought was so overwhelming that for a second she couldn't breathe, and the lack of oxygen caused tiny starbursts to flare in front of her eyes.

Forcing herself to take a deep breath before she did something truly embarrassing like fainting dead away while Trevor stood less than a yard from her, sipping his merlot, she reminded herself that she was projecting, blowing the entire situation way out of proportion. At the moment, the only thing her business future held was a harmless lunch date with Trevor's sister…and a decision to make.

Steeling her spine and her nerves, she fixed him with a firm glance and said, "I'll stay the night and meet with your sister tomorrow, but I'm not promising anything more than that."

"Fair enough," he agreed with the shrug of one shoulder. "Though I think once you talk to Erica, you'll decide that sticking around Jarrod Ridge for a couple of weeks isn't the worst idea in the world. And in case you're worried about losing profits while you're away from Denver, rest assured that we'll pay you well for your services. Very well," he added, winking at her over the rim of his wineglass.

Agreeing to stay overnight at Trevor Jarrod's house and actually following through were two entirely different things, Haylie soon learned.

For one, she had packed the car and made arrangements for a day trip, nothing more. She had enough formula and diapers for Bradley to get through the next few hours. If they were lucky.

For another, she had nothing with her *for her*. No nightgown or toothbrush or makeup remover, and only the clothes on her back to wear to her lunch with Erica the next day.

It was enough to make her reconsider her decision, that was for sure.

"Maybe this wasn't the best idea," she whispered, standing in the doorway of one of Trevor's extra bedrooms, staring at a comfortably snoozing Bradley.

He'd fallen asleep while finishing his bottle, and hadn't stirred while she'd changed him into one of the only remaining diapers. Of course, Trevor didn't have a crib or anything else that even remotely resembled a proper child-care necessity, so they'd had to improvise.

A soft, thick comforter on the floor in one corner, surrounded by pillows and a couple of the cushions from Trevor's expensive leather sofa, and she didn't think Bradley was going anywhere, even if he did wake up in the next few hours, which was highly unlikely.

"It's not that bad, is it?" Trevor asked from directly behind her. "I mean, it doesn't look great, but he's safe enough, right?"

Turning from the doorway, she nodded. "He'll be

fine. He doesn't move around much at all when he sleeps. The important thing is just to make sure he can't roll anywhere and that there's nothing nearby that will hurt him if he does wake up."

Leading her back down to the first floor of the elegant, expansive log cabin, he said, "Then why are you worried this wasn't a good idea?"

"Not Bradley, staying here. I wasn't planning to be gone overnight. I'm not prepared to stay *anywhere,* let alone with you."

Heat suffused her cheeks when she realized how that sounded, and she rushed on with her explanation in hopes that he wouldn't catch the slip.

"Bradley is almost out of diapers and formula, I have no personal items with me.…" Slipping her hands into the front pockets of her slacks, she hunched her shoulders and looked down at her outfit. "Even if we get through the night, I'm going to end up looking like a bag lady when I meet your sister after having slept in my clothes and makeup."

One corner of Trevor's mouth tipped up in a grin. "You forget who you're talking to," he told her from across the kitchen island.

Sliding a pad and pen across the marble countertop, he said, "Write down everything you need. Be as detailed as possible—brand names, quantities, your clothing and shoe sizes. I'll have it all delivered tonight, along with your car."

"My car?" She tipped her head, watching his brown eyes and handsome face carefully. "Are you sure you want to have it brought here? Aren't you afraid I'll sneak off in the middle of the night with Bradley?"

"There may be exigent circumstances connected to your visit, but you're still a guest, not a prisoner. Besides, you gave me your word you'd stay through tomorrow, and I believe you."

"Why?" she wondered aloud. "You don't even know me." And she might very well be the gold digger she knew he suspected she was.

With a shrug, he said, "I think any woman who would take a day out of her life and drive four hours to tell me I have a child I knew nothing about—allegedly, anyway—just because she feels it's the right thing to do can be taken at her word."

Tossing back the last sip of his merlot, he set the glass down with a tiny clink before adding, "And you know what they say about keeping your friends close and your enemies closer."

Six

The next morning, Bradley had Haylie out of bed early, but he didn't wake her. She was already awake, having tossed and turned half the night before giving up on sleep altogether to simply lie there, letting her thoughts and anxieties run rampant.

Now, fresh from the shower and staring at the collection of clothing and accessories that littered the guest-room mattress, she decided that if this was an example of how Trevor treated his enemies, Haylie was sincerely considering becoming his nearest and dearest friend.

True to *his* word, not long after nightfall the evening before, a Jarrod Ridge employee had come to the door with everything from her list and more.

By the time the young man left, every inch of the marble island had been covered with fabric totes, a boxed dinner for two from one of the Ridge's exclusive restaurants waited on the counter near the stove and her car was parked in the drive. Trevor had thanked him with a nod and what looked to be a fifty-dollar tip, something Haylie quickly pretended she hadn't seen.

She'd known the Jarrods had money, of course. Which was sort of like saying the Sahara desert had sand. They were, in a word, loaded.

Yes, she understood that. And if she hadn't before driving down from Denver, the sight of the Jarrod Ridge Resort certainly would have clued her in. Trevor's demeanor of entitlement and the lavishness of his own private home were really just icing on the cake.

And though she considered herself a generous person, always tipping well at restaurants and after hotel stays, she didn't have a fifty-dollar bill in her wallet for emergencies, let alone floating around as extra change to give to a complete stranger in thanks for doing her a favor.

He hadn't been stingy when it came to supplying her with personal and baby items or a fresh outfit for her lunch with his sister, either. The vanity in the guest bathroom and the kitchen countertops all resembled a well-stocked drugstore, and the guest bed looked like the fitting-room floor of a woman trying to find the perfect dress for her high school reunion.

A new sweater and another pair of slacks would have been fine, but Trevor had apparently requested one of everything in her size from several of the resort boutiques. There were dresses and skirts and pants, blouses and pullovers and casual tops with both short and long sleeves. Even shoes and undergarments.

She couldn't decide whether to be impressed in a *Pretty Woman* sort of way or intimidated by the power Trevor so obviously wielded. He snapped his fingers and people jumped. He said, "Jump," and people asked, "How high?"

If the blood tests came back showing Bradley was his son—and she had no doubt they would, unless Heather had lied to her for the last year of her life—and Trevor got it into his head to fight for custody, she wouldn't stand a chance.

Haylie's heart seized in her chest at the thought, and her hands actually shook while she rushed to get dressed. She might not have money or power or even the biological rights that Trevor did, but she would still do whatever she had to in order to keep Bradley in her life.

She hadn't given it a lot of thought before making the trek to Aspen—something she was beginning to regret—but she realized now that it wouldn't be feasible for her to maintain full custody once the DNA results came in. The knowledge did nothing to loosen the low-level panic gripping her chest. But she would do anything and everything she could to make sure she was able to see the baby and spend time with him on a regular basis.

Surely Trevor would be open to visitation, right? He might be a Jarrod, used to getting his own way and ordering people around like pawns on a chessboard, but he wasn't cruel, was he? He wouldn't invoke his parental rights and cut her out of Bradley's life altogether. Would he?

Haylie wasn't sure what the symptoms of a full-blown panic attack felt like, but if her shallow breathing, sweaty palms and the ringing in her ears were any indication, she suspected she might be headed in that direction.

She needed to calm down. The test results wouldn't be in for weeks yet, so it wasn't as though Trevor was going to snatch Bradley out of her arms and run off with him. Considering the fact that he hadn't even held the baby yet—voluntarily, at any rate—she thought he was probably hoping the tests would come back negative so he could wash his hands of the whole situation and return to his fun-loving, playboy lifestyle with barely a ripple.

In the meantime, however, she had a business lunch to get ready for. One she was unaccountably nervous about.

Almost as nervous as she was about finally poking her head out of the bedroom and once again coming face-to-face with her host.

It had taken every ounce of composure she possessed just to get through last evening. Especially after half the bags from Jarrod Ridge had been unpacked and he'd carried plates of food to the dining area and invited her to eat with him.

What she'd really wanted to do was race upstairs and lock herself into the guest bedroom with Bradley. Bury her head under the quilted satin duvet and not come out until morning.

Playing ostrich seemed like such a good idea compared to remaining in Trevor's presence. She hated to admit it—*really* hated to admit it—but he intimidated her. In addition to his significant wealth, his towering height, broad shoulders and movie-star good looks were more than a little overwhelming.

Oh, she hadn't been the least bit overwhelmed or intimidated when she'd stuffed Bradley in his car seat and headed for Aspen to confront the man who'd unwittingly impregnated her sister and left a child fatherless.

Nor had she felt so much as a twinge of nerves while

she'd stared down Trevor's overprotective secretary, demanding an appointment with him, or sat in his office waiting for him to arrive so she could toss the cold bucket of reality in his face.

She hadn't even been worried when he insisted they go for blood tests immediately, even though it meant getting into a car with a man she'd never met before and letting him drive away from a public place crowded with witnesses.

Not the smartest thing she'd ever done, admittedly, but none of that had caused her a moment's hesitation.

Then somehow, somewhere along the way, the tables had turned and she'd gone from being a woman in control and on a mission, to a woman completely out of her element, maneuvered as easily as a remote-control airplane by her nephew's absentee father.

She felt completely at his mercy. Not only because she was staying under his roof, but because she knew how easy it would be for him to take Bradley from her if he really wanted to.

Which made her wonder if this luncheon with Trevor's sister was a good idea...or a mistake of epic proportions. Given how Haylie was feeling at the moment, she suspected it could go either way.

With a sigh, she took one last look around the room to be sure she had everything, then collected her purse and Bradley's diaper bag, and finally Bradley. The bedroom door swung open without a sound, and she moved just as quietly down the hall, down the stairs and into the main area of the house.

Trevor was already in the kitchen, awake and ready to start his day. Well, no surprise there, since it was past 10:00 a.m. He'd told her last night to take her time getting ready; that they would both go into the Manor just before she was supposed to meet Erica.

But unlike yesterday, he was quite obviously dressed for the office. Instead of a warm, thick sweater, comfortable jeans and Timberland boots, he wore a blue suit so dark it was nearly black, a bright red tie and dress shoes polished to a high shine.

She didn't know enough about designer clothes to properly place each item of his wardrobe, but she would have bet money none of them came off the rack, and that each bore some fancy, posh name like Gucci or Valentino or Armani.

Her own ensemble, provided by one of the exclusive Jarrod Ridge boutiques, had come with similar tags, but not by any designers she recognized. Just wearing them made her feel as though she was covered in something very fragile and valuable. Not the sort of clothes you wanted to snag or dirty or, God forbid, spill something on. And with a four-month-old whose favorite pastimes were chewing on her sleeve or spitting up on her shoulder, she was a walking bundle of nerves—for more reasons than one.

"Good morning," Trevor murmured as soon as he saw her.

He stepped forward, coffee cup in his hand, and she caught a sudden whiff of his cologne. Something crisp and clean and woodsy that reminded her of exactly where they were—a beautiful mountainside dotted with tall evergreens and sparkling with fresh snowfall.

She'd never before considered that the smell of trees could be sexy, but now the winter forest scent coming from the man in front of her had her knees going weak. His wavy, carefree hair, fresh-shaven face and Boss of the Year persona didn't hurt, either.

She swallowed hard, her grip on the baby tightening as her stomach did the slow roll of sexual attraction and...oh, so not good...longing.

"Coffee?" Trevor offered, completely unaware of the war currently being waged between her sensible mind and traitorous body.

She swallowed again, licking her dry lips before answering. "No, thank you."

She was already a writhing ball of anxiety, she didn't need to add caffeine to the mix.

With a nod, he finished the rest of his own coffee, then set his cup aside and headed for the door. Before she could pass through ahead of him, he slid both bags from her shoulder, leaving her with only Bradley to balance on her way to the garage.

When they arrived at his office, Trevor's secretary, Diana, was at her desk, as usual. And perched on the edge of that desk was a lovely, curvy woman. She wore a flowing, emerald-green blouse with tan pants, and her layered, silky brown hair just brushed her shoulders. The minute she saw them, she hopped to her espadrille-clad feet and smiled.

"Hi," she greeted them both. Then, bypassing Trevor, she held a hand out to Haylie. "You must be the wedding planner."

"Haylie Smith," she offered. "It's nice to meet you, Miss Jarrod."

"Actually, it's Prentice. I'm a newly discovered member of the Jarrod clan, but they love me, anyway. Right?" she said with a chuckle, slanting an amused glance in Trevor's direction.

"Do we have a choice?" he asked, deadpan. But while his face remained impassive, his brown eyes sparkled with affection.

Far from being offended, his sister grinned. "Nope."

Turning back to Haylie, she said, "But it doesn't matter, because you're going to call me Erica. And who is this adorable little guy?" she asked, zeroing in on Bradley.

Still bundled like a snowman at Haylie's hip, Bradley kicked his legs and giggled as Erica tickled one of his pudgy pink cheeks.

Clearing his throat, Trevor stepped forward and put a hand to the small of Haylie's back. The innocent touch shouldn't have sent currents of electricity rippling up and down her spine, but it did.

"Let's go into my office for a minute, shall we?" he murmured in a low voice, shooting his sister a meaningful glance.

Although her lungs didn't seem to be functioning properly in her chest and her feet felt like lead weights inside her shoes, Haylie managed to follow Trevor's prodding.

While he moved behind his desk and Erica took a seat in one of the guest chairs in front of it, Haylie went to the same sofa along the far wall that she'd used the day before. Laying Bradley on his back, she began stripping him of his snowsuit so he wouldn't get overheated now that they were indoors.

Leaning back in his chair, Trevor steepled his fingers and tapped them against his lips. "Normally, I'd prefer to keep this under wraps, but since it will probably come up during your lunch, and I don't want Haylie worrying about letting something slip, I think it's only fair that we tell you what's going on here."

Erica raised a brow, her gaze going from Trevor to Haylie and back again. "All right," she replied cautiously.

"And since you're my sister—a Jarrod now," he stressed, "I'll expect this to stay just between the three of us. We can't risk it getting out. The fallout would be astronomical."

His sister's mouth turned down in a frown. "You're starting to make me nervous. Just tell me already."

"There's a chance…" Glancing briefly at Haylie, who now had the baby balanced on her knees, he took a breath and gave voice to the words he hadn't even let himself truly consider yet. "There's a chance Bradley is my son."

For a second, his sister didn't respond. Then she blinked and did the owl thing again, looking from him to Haylie, him to Haylie…or possibly from him to the child on Haylie's lap.

"Oh, my goodness," she muttered, putting a hand to her heart.

"Yeah, I know," he agreed, wincing.

"You're my brother, and I love you, so forgive me for saying this, but…" She shook her head. "All that womanizing was bound to catch up with you eventually."

"I'm not a womanizer," he grumbled with a scowl.

Her eyes widened and she cocked her head to one side. "No, you're simply a connoisseur of the fairer sex and like to try a different flavor every week."

Which was merely a creative way of calling him a womanizer, he thought, his scowl deepening. But before he could argue the point further, Erica was out of her seat and crossing his office, making a beeline for the baby.

"You mean this might be my nephew? Why, he's just the cutest thing ever. May I?"

Haylie nodded and lifted the baby into Erica's waiting arms. "His name is Bradley."

"Hello, Bradley," Erica said in a high, baby-talk voice by way of introduction. "I'm your aunt Erica. Maybe."

Pushing to his feet, Trevor crossed to the two women, a frown still marring his brow.

"This is why I wanted you to know what's going on," he told his sister. Crossing his arms in front of his chest, he tapped the toe of one foot in irritation. "You can't let anyone hear you referring to him as your nephew. You can't link him to me or the rest of the Jarrod family at all, in any way, until we're sure."

Erica's head bobbed up and down in what could have been interpreted as a nod, but since she was busy cooing and laughing at Bradley, Trevor wasn't sure she was listening to a single word he had to say.

"This is important, Erica," he stressed in a firm voice, turning on his heel and beginning to pace. "We've already gone for blood tests, but the results won't be in for at least two weeks."

A dilemma his instincts were still screaming for him to throw money at. Cutting a generous check or paying for a new wing to be built at the local hospital had a way of speeding up test results, but that would only draw even more attention to a situation he was determined to keep strictly confidential.

"I've invited Haylie to stay with me until we find out for sure," he continued, uncrossing his arms from his chest and stuffing his hands into the pockets of his tailored slacks instead. "But she's concerned about being away from work for that long. She's a party planner, as you know, and has her own event firm in Denver. That's where you come in."

Stopping in front of his sister, he waited until she

met his gaze and he was sure he had her full attention. "I thought perhaps if we could *hire her* to plan an event for us, she wouldn't feel quite as uncomfortable about sticking around."

It was Haylie's turn to cross her arms. "I am in the room, you know," she chastised him. "And stop pressuring her. I won't have your sister or anyone else 'hiring me' for a job they don't need done just so you can keep me on a short leash until the tests come back."

Trevor opened his mouth, not sure whether he intended to apologize or strengthen his position and stand his ground, when Erica piped up.

"Actually, I'm glad you're here, Haylie. I really do have a wedding to plan, and just thinking about it is turning me into a nervous wreck. So let's go to lunch and have a nice, long chat, and if I end up hiring you, you can rest assured it will be because I want and *need* your help, not just because Trevor asked me to. Sound good?"

A beat passed while Haylie considered that. Then the tautness in her shoulders and spine seemed to wash away and she let her arms drop to her sides. Her gaze flicked to Trevor for a moment before settling back on Erica and Bradley.

"All right," she said softly.

Seven

As nervous as she'd been about going to lunch with Trevor's sister, Haylie couldn't believe how quickly the hours flew by. They'd talked about the weather, childhood memories and almost everything in between.

With a dreamy look in her eyes that told Haylie the woman was well and truly in love, while they'd picked at their salads Erica had shared the story of her whirlwind romance with her husband-to-be, Christian Hanford. She'd pulled a picture from her wallet of a very handsome, clean-cut, dark-haired man, showing it off in a manner that reminded Haylie of herself with pictures of baby Bradley.

As the Jarrod family attorney, the duty of telling Erica the truth about her parentage had fallen on Christian's shoulders after Donald Jarrod's death. Haylie couldn't imagine how shocking it must have been to have that sort of information dropped in her lap out of the blue.

To spend her entire life thinking one man was her father, only to be blindsided by the news that he wasn't, and that another man, now deceased, was.

Unless it felt a bit like having someone walk into your office and announce that you had a child you knew nothing about, she'd thought with a small sting of guilt.

And though she hadn't intended to spend any time at all talking about herself, before she'd even realized it, she was confiding in Erica about her rocky relationship with her sister. Their years growing up, when Heather had been the "pretty one," Haylie had been the "smart one" and it had seemed they were in constant competition— for their parents' affections, for attention, for friends and boyfriends.

She told Erica about her sister's apparent one-night stand with Trevor, and all the months that had followed leading up to Bradley's birth and Heather's tragic, unexpected death. And about Haylie's own almost pathological need to clean up after her sister, to try to do what was right one final time instead of what was easy and most often selfish.

By the time she'd finished, more than an hour had passed, and she was mortified at how much talking she'd done. How open and unguarded she'd been. She blamed it on the fact that she felt extremely comfortable in Erica's presence, as though they'd known each other all their lives.

Or rather, were becoming fast friends.

But while Haylie truly did like Erica, Haylie knew she couldn't get too close to the woman. For one thing, she was Trevor's sister, and Haylie wasn't even sure she would end up being friends with him, regardless of his biological ties to Bradley.

For another, Erica was about to become a client, and it was never smart to get too close or grow too comfortable with a client. Especially brides, since they had a tendency to be Pollyanna one minute and Bridezilla the next.

By the time they'd actually started to discuss potential wedding plans, their entrées were gone and they were sipping cups of strong, French roast coffee while waiting for dessert to arrive.

Even though she hadn't been at Jarrod Ridge long enough to try any of its other restaurants, Haylie had to admit that the Sky Lounge had been an excellent choice. And if this was merely a lounge, more of a bar with a limited menu, then the rest of the eateries the resort had to offer must be truly extraordinary. Of course, the fact that she was dining with one of the Jarrods probably had something to do with the level of service and amount of privacy they received.

After sharing more about their personal lives than either of them were probably used to revealing, and then finally getting down to the more vital topic of wedding plans, she returned to Trevor's office.

Erica was beside Haylie, having offered to walk with her so they could continue to chat. First, though, they'd had to retrieve Bradley from the colorful, bustling day-care center on the premises.

Haylie had balked at leaving the baby with anyone, especially out of her sight while she was technically in enemy territory. But Erica had assured her that they employed some of the best child-care providers in the state. Once Haylie had seen the facility and met some of the ladies watching over children of all ages, she'd decided turning Bradley over to someone else for a few short hours while she had a professional, adult conversation with Trevor's sister wasn't the worst idea in the world.

From there, the two women had strolled back to the main hotel and to Trevor's office. Haylie still couldn't believe how amazing Jarrod Ridge was. The more she saw of it, the more impressed she was by the many narrow streets and buildings of all shapes and sizes.

The main hotel—also known as the Manor—was the largest and the most important focal point of the resort. Apparently because—according to Erica's thirty-second recap of the Ridge's history—it was the first structure built by Trevor's great-great-great grandfather, and the rest of the resort had grown up around it. There were now private bungalows and shops and myriad activities available to keep visitors entertained.

Skiing was of course the main draw, at least during the winter months. But not everyone who vacationed at a ski resort was interested in actually hitting the slopes, so the Ridge also boasted a world-renowned spa, an ice skating rink, a bowling alley and an arcade for both the young and young at heart. The four restaurants spread throughout the resort served everything from quick deli sandwiches to fine dining and specialty cuisines.

It was like a tiny, self-contained village with everything guests could possibly want or need to make their stays more enjoyable. Even Haylie, who was here for reasons other than taking a holiday, was beginning to feel quite pampered and catered to.

As they entered the reception area of Trevor's office, Diana lifted her head and said, "You can go right in. He's expecting you."

Pausing in front of the double oak doors, Erica gave her a quick hug, Bradley and all. "Thank you so much for all your wonderful advice. I can't wait to tell

Christian that I'm not going to be such a raving lunatic about the wedding from now on. He'll be extremely grateful, believe me. He may even send you flowers," she added with a chuckle.

"I'm happy I can help," Haylie told her.

"You have all my numbers, right? And my email? And Christian's email, just in case?"

"Absolutely." Haylie tapped the side of her handbag. "My cell is loaded and ready to go. I'll be in touch soon."

"Excellent." With a wide smile, Erica leaned in and gave her another appreciative squeeze before spinning away and sauntering off.

As soon as she left, Haylie tapped on Trevor's door in warning, then let herself in. Turning from his computer, he leaned forward, resting his joined hands in the center of his desk.

"How did it go?" he asked.

She couldn't decide if he looked concerned or simply curious. Stepping forward, she lowered herself onto one of the guest chairs with Bradley on her lap.

"Fine. Well, even."

"Where did you eat?" he wanted to know.

"Sky Lounge. It was lovely."

The rooftop bar and sometimes grill had leather chairs and floor-to-ceiling windows that looked out over the sprawling resort, snow-covered mountains and miles of clear blue sky. She could only imagine how beautiful the view must be at night, all sparkling lights and black, star-filled sky.

Trevor inclined his head. "Good choice. It's a little less crowded up there during the day, especially at this time of year."

She nodded. "Except for a couple of people at the bar, we were the only ones there."

For several long minutes, the room was quiet, neither of them speaking. Then with a sigh, Trevor pushed back from his desk and stood.

"Why don't we head back to the house."

Haylie's eyes widened in surprise. "Can you do that? I mean, it's only three o'clock. Don't you need to stay until the end of the day?"

She wasn't sure exactly how she'd anticipated spending the rest of the afternoon now that her lunch with Erica was over, but she certainly hadn't expected Trevor to drop everything just to keep her company.

He flashed her a cocky grin that had her stomach doing somersaults.

"I can do whatever I want, I'm the boss. Well, one of the bosses, anyway. And while you were visiting with my sister, I made arrangements to be away from the office more than I'm here for a while."

Turning away from her, he began tossing files and papers into what looked like an expensive leather brief-case, standing open on a credenza beside the fireplace. "I can do a lot of work from home, and this way my schedule will be more open to spend time with you and Bradley."

For a second, she didn't say anything. She licked her lips, trying to get her racing pulse under control.

His offer made her uncomfortable, but she wasn't entirely sure why. Was it because she was coming to realize that she found Trevor attractive on more than simply the level of "gee, that guy's kind of hot"? Or because she was going to be spending *a lot* more time with him in the very near future than she'd originally intended?

"You didn't need to do that," she told him quietly.

With a shrug of one broad shoulder, he rounded the corner of his desk, coming to stand beside her. Or loom over, to be more accurate.

"It's done. Now let's go. You can fill me in on the details of your luncheon with Erica while I cook dinner."

She leaned back, her eyes once again going wide. "You cook?"

"I'm just full of surprises today, aren't I?" He flashed her that same cocky, amused grin before leaning over to pick up her purse and the diaper bag, adding them to the hand that held his briefcase. With a quick flick of his opposite wrist, he gestured for her to follow him to the door.

"Actually, I don't cook very often," he admitted as they crossed the office, "but I can hold my own with a pot of boiling water and a spatula."

At the door, he stopped and turned back to her.

"Tell me one thing before we leave," he murmured in a low voice.

Her chest tightened at the intensity in his dark-chocolate eyes and she swallowed in an attempt to dislodge the sudden lump growing at the base of her throat. When the lump didn't budge, she forced her chin down in a jerky nod.

"Are you sticking around for a while to help Erica with her wedding, or do I need to pack a bag and follow you back to Denver?"

She could tell by his expression that he found the latter option about as appealing as a full body wax—but that he would do it if that's what it took to keep her and Bradley close until the DNA results came in.

She still wasn't sure it was the smartest thing to do,

but at some point during her lunch with his sister, she'd made up her mind. Or perhaps had simply given up on trying to fight the innate stubbornness and determination that apparently ran in the Jarrod family.

"Erica wants a small, intimate Christmas Eve wedding right here at Jarrod Ridge, which only gives us a few weeks to pull everything together."

"So you'll stay?"

Please, God, don't make me regret this, she thought, even as a tiny voice in the back of her head ran through a laundry list of doubts.

"I'll stay."

A few hours later, Trevor carried two plates of pasta from the kitchen to the dining room. Rather than putting them at opposite ends of the long table, he'd created two place settings much closer together, at one corner. He told himself it was because Haylie hadn't yet filled him in on the details of her lunch meeting with Erica, and he didn't want to miss a word. But that wasn't entirely true, was it?

No, the truth was that Haylie smelled really good. Like citrus with a hint of wildflower. He'd noticed it when she'd first come downstairs that morning and he'd leaned in close to take her purse and the baby's diaper bag on their way out to the garage. It had stuck with him during the whole ride to the Ridge and seemed to fill his office long after she and Erica had left for their luncheon. It was as though the scent, her own unique fragrance, had crawled under his skin and taken root.

So, yes, he wanted to hear what she and his sister had talked about, reassure himself that she really would be sticking around until those test results came in. But he also found himself simply wanting to be closer to her. To that citrus-floral scent…to the silky blond hair that ran down her back and brushed the swells of her breasts… to the sparkle in her blue eyes and the lift of her rosy pink lips when she smiled.

Returning to the kitchen, he grabbed a bottle of wine and two glasses, letting his gaze trail to the stairs. She was up there now, giving Bradley a bath.

As soon as they'd gotten home, he'd changed from his suit into more comfortable jeans and a lightweight sweater, with the intention of impressing her with his culinary skills. Granted, they were limited, but he'd found that even the simple acts of boiling pasta and opening a jar of marinara sauce could be impressive to women as long as he did them with flair.

Unfortunately, instead of perching on a stool at the island to watch him work, the way his female guests had in the past, Haylie had decided to spend the last couple of hours upstairs with Bradley, feeding him, changing him and now getting him ready for bed.

Trevor suspected she was trying to avoid being alone with him, but that wouldn't last much longer. If she didn't come down on her own in the next thirty seconds, he fully intended to go up after her—and drag her to dinner, if he had to.

He was pouring the wine, hoping she would arrive before the pasta got cold, when he heard her padded footsteps on the stairwell. Tipping his head in that direction, he watched her take the last few steps and felt something strange tickle behind his rib cage.

She'd changed out of her blouse and slacks and was now wearing a pair of skintight black leggings with an equally snug short-sleeved top. The soft pink shirt had a faded floral design on the front, interspersed with tiny glittering rhinestones. She was wearing matching pink ballet flats on her feet and had pulled her hair back into a ponytail.

"Good timing," he said as she moved closer, rubbing the palms of her hands against her thighs nervously. He pulled out a chair and held it for her before taking his own.

"Did Bradley go down okay?"

She nodded, reaching for her glass of Barbaresco and taking a small sip. "I think being around all those other children at the day-care center wore him out."

"Is that a good thing or a bad thing?"

"Anytime a four-month-old child is happy or sleeping, it's a good thing, pretty much regardless of what made him that way."

Trevor chuckled, offering her some salad and fresh-grated Parmesan. "I'll remember that."

Shifting in her seat, she picked up her fork and started toying with the long strands of pasta on her plate, pointedly *not* meeting his gaze. "You didn't need to buy the crib and changing table and everything, though. We aren't going to be here that long and could have made do with just a bassinet or maybe a small playpen."

While they'd been gone that afternoon, he'd had the entire house fitted for Bradley and baby proofed. He hadn't known exactly what was needed, but thankfully there were professionals he could hire who did.

"Don't be silly," he told her, digging into his own meal. "You're a guest, and should have what you need to be comfortable. Besides, a baby shouldn't be sleeping on a pile of blankets on the floor, and if Bradley really is my son, then I'll be needing everything here, anyway."

The plastic locks on the cupboards and the playpen in the center of the living room were going to take some getting used to, and considering that Bradley wasn't even crawling yet, a lot of the precautionary measures leaned toward overkill. But just like the furniture, if Bradley was his, it would all be necessary eventually.

"Well, thank you," Haylie said quietly. "This is delicious, by the way."

"I'm sure your lunch at Sky Lounge was much better, but it's passable. And I'll tell you a secret." He paused, sipping his light red wine until she looked in his direction. "The sauce came from Emilio's."

"Really?"

"Mmm-hmm. If you like Italian, it is *the* place to eat at the Ridge—or in all of Aspen, frankly. The food there is much better than anything I could pull off, believe me," he offered with a self-deprecating wink. "If you like French cuisine, though, you really should try the main restaurant, Chagall's. I'll have to take you there sometime."

"I thought you didn't want anyone to know about our visit until you're sure about Bradley," she reminded him, taking a bite and chewing slowly. "Especially your family."

"Well, you've already met Guy. And I have a feeling Erica will make sure the rest of the family all knows that you're here and why. She'll swear them to secrecy, and they'll respect our privacy, but I wouldn't be surprised if several of them make up excuses to drop by over the next few days to check out you and Bradley."

"I'll keep that in mind."

"Speaking of Erica," he said between bites, "you haven't told me yet what the two of you discussed at lunch."

Tilting her head, her ponytail swung behind her. Her long lashes fluttered as she lowered her gaze. "It was just boring girl talk. Why do you want to know?"

"Call me curious. I feel a bit like a matchmaker waiting to hear how a blind date turned out. I'm the one who set the two of you up, now I want to make sure everything went okay."

Raising those cornflower-blue eyes back to his, her tone tightened. "I already told you I'd stay, if that's what you're worried about."

"I'm not worried." His teeth made a tiny clinking noise against his fork as he bit down harder than he'd intended.

He wasn't used to having to work this hard to get information. With women, he usually just smiled at them, maybe brushed his fingertips down the side of their arm, and they became either flustered enough or enamored enough to open their mouths and tell him anything he wanted to know. With men, a stern glance and subtle reminder of exactly who he was and of his family name had them delivering whatever he needed.

Haylie was different, though. She was a woman, so he suspected she was naturally attracted to him on some feminine level; they all were. But she was also stubborn and determined, which meant she wasn't going to let her hormones override her common sense.

And even though she'd agreed to his bargain of sticking around for the DNA results, he knew she wasn't entirely pleased about the decision. Something he couldn't blame her for, he supposed. After all, he got to stay right where he was, in his own home, working in his own office. She, however, had to adapt to a new environment, moving in with a man she'd just met, taking time away from her business and her friends and everything she was used to.

The complete upheaval of her life couldn't be easy

for her. Which was why he was determined to see that her stay remained as painless as possible.

Picking up his wineglass, he brought it to his lips. "I do want to be sure you and Erica are both content with whatever decisions you made, though. She's my sister, and I love her. I don't want her to feel pressured into working with you if the two of you didn't hit it off. And although I realize there are probably a hundred other things you'd rather do than stay here with me—"

"A thousand," she cut in shamelessly.

One corner of his mouth twitched. "A thousand others, then. I want to make sure you'll be at least relatively happy during your visit."

A few seconds ticked by while she seemed to consider that. He sipped his wine, watching as she twirled her fork over and over again through the long strands of pasta still on her plate.

"I like your sister very much," she finally replied. "And I think she must have liked me, as well as my ideas for her wedding, because she..."

She trailed off, her voice going soft, her head bowed.

"She hired you, I assume," he put in. "Otherwise, I doubt you would have agreed to stick around."

Dragging her gaze up to his, she nodded. And then she whispered, "She offered to pay me twice my usual rate."

She seemed embarrassed by the admission, though he couldn't fathom why.

"Excellent," he said. "You're worth it, I'm sure."

Haylie's brows drew together. "You can't know that. Neither can Erica. I could be the worst event planner in the world, ready to put her in orange taffeta and the groom in a powder-blue tuxedo."

He gave a low chuckle. "That would be quite the sight."

Shaking her head, she dropped her fork and leaned back in her chair, arms going across her chest in a clear sign of annoyance. "It's not funny. You're both putting an awful lot of faith in someone you don't even know. This is her *wedding,* for heaven's sake. One of the most important days of her life. She should be hiring someone she knows. Someone who's been recommended to her by all of her friends. Someone she has utter faith in."

Setting aside his own utensils, Trevor leaned back, mirroring her rigid posture. "First, I only asked Erica to meet with you, I didn't tie her up and order her to hire you—not that she would have, even if I had. And I trust my sister's judgment. If you hadn't impressed her with your knowledge and ideas while the two of you were together, she wouldn't have hired you."

Uncrossing his arms, he leaned forward, draping them on the edge of the table instead. "Second, she—and I, and the rest of the family—can afford to be generous with you. Erica could hire an army of stylists, if she wanted to, but I think the notion of a smaller wedding appeals to her, as does fewer people to help her organize the event."

Lowering his voice, he moved in even closer, making sure she understood the importance of his next words and just how serious he was about them. "Third, I want you here. You and Bradley both. If Erica hadn't hired you to plan her wedding, I'd have found another reason for you to stay. Believe me, Haylie, when it comes to you and that baby sleeping upstairs, money is the least of my concerns. I'll pay you triple, even quadruple your usual rate, if that's what it takes to keep you here until I can be sure I'm Bradley's father."

Eight

Haylie sat, stunned. The silence filling the dining room, and in fact the entire house, was thick and heavy, making her feel as though she'd been physically battered by Trevor's words.

She might not be comfortable with the situation, or thrilled with the way he'd maneuvered her into moving in with him, but one thing she could no longer doubt was his determination to see this through.

It impressed her, actually, as painful as that was to admit. Most men would be doing everything they could think of to avoid laying claim to some random woman's child, scrambling for excuses *not* to take a blood test.

But Trevor had not only insisted on a paternity test first thing, he wanted to keep Bradley under close watch until the results came in and he could know for sure that he was—or was not—Bradley's father.

Not only that, but Trevor was willing to take her in,

too, as the child's aunt, guardian and the closest thing Bradley had to a mother. Take them in, transform his house from a luxurious bachelor pad to one step up from a day-care center, and manufacture a job for her out of thin air to keep her from losing business or income while she was away from home.

Granted, she didn't *need* any of those things. She had her own apartment back in Denver, as well as a successful business. But the fact that he was willing to move heaven and earth to ensure their presence over the next couple of weeks raised her opinion of Trevor by several notches, at least.

Forcing herself to loosen her rigid posture, Haylie let her arms fall to her lap and gave a soft sigh. She preferred to categorize it as a tired sigh, not a defeated one, but there was a small part of her that had decided to wave the white flag of surrender.

She'd come here to let Trevor know about his son. It wasn't her fault that things had snowballed in a manner she hadn't anticipated, but since she'd already agreed to help Erica plan her wedding, already agreed to move into Trevor's house…was there really any point in battling over the fine points now? Wasn't it better to simply relax and let the unstoppable tide that was Trevor Jarrod sweep her away?

She gave a mental wince at that thought. All right, perhaps not entirely. She was too darned stubborn herself to simply roll over and let another human being dictate her actions or her life.

But a little acquiescence wouldn't kill her. And, in fact, if she gave Trevor's sister the wedding of her dreams, it might even prove quite beneficial to her livelihood down the road.

With that in mind, she picked up her fork, keeping

her attention on her plate as she said, "Erica told me that she and her fiancé had originally planned a big, summer wedding. But they've been so busy, and things have gotten so out of control that now they just want to be married already, without all the hoopla of a large reception."

Her willingness to talk seemed to relax Trevor as well. Sitting back in his chair, he reached for his glass, taking a drink of wine before returning to his meal.

"I'm not sure exactly how it came about, but she loves the idea of a Christmas Eve wedding. Something private and low-key, held at the resort, though we haven't decided yet on exactly where."

Trevor nodded, swallowing a bite of pasta before replying, "She'll have plenty of choices. We tend to have a nice handful of guests over the holidays, but aren't as full as usual. It shouldn't be hard to reserve a ballroom or two and keep most of the public from even knowing what's going on until after the fact."

"That's what Erica said. Pulling something like this together in only two weeks' time won't be easy, though. I'm going to need a place to work. A telephone, fax machine… It would really help to have my laptop and Rolodex," she murmured distractedly as an unending list of necessities and to-dos started scrolling through her head.

"Whatever you need. You can use my office here at the house, if you'd like, or we'll set up another room for you. I'll even run you back to Denver to collect some of your things," he told her. Then added with a wink, "As long as you promise not to abandon ship."

The wink sent her heart rate skittering, effectively hitting the brakes on the runaway train of her work-related thoughts. Seconds ticked by while her mind went blank and her temperature climbed degree by slow degree into the red.

What had they been talking about? Oh, right, a wedding. His sister's wedding. All the plans she had to put in motion in the rush to get everything done by December twenty-fourth.

Needing something to cool her down and hopefully get her brain cells functioning again, she tossed back the last few swallows of wine in her glass. It didn't help. What she needed was water. Ice-cold water, preferably in bucket form, being tossed right in her face.

Before she could even finish that nice little cooling-off fantasy, however, Trevor was stretching an arm in front of her to refill her glass with the lovely, brick-red liquid. As tempting as it was, Haylie refrained from emptying that glass, too, instead keeping one hand on her utensils and the other tucked away beneath the table.

Clearing her throat, she hoped her voice wouldn't squeak when she tried to speak. "Would you mind if I used the resort's child-care facility for Bradley? Not all the time...I don't like to be away from him for long stretches."

Even back home, she kept him with her at work and only left him with someone else for a few hours if she absolutely had to. Jittery brides tended to get annoyed with wedding planners who spend half their time bouncing and burping a fussy baby.

"But I know I'll need to do some running around, and also some touring of the Jarrod Ridge property, so it would probably be better to have someone else watching him then."

"Of course," Trevor readily agreed. Finished with his dinner, he crossed his legs and leaned back in his chair, the picture of quiet ease. "In fact, let me be very clear—you've got carte blanche while you're here, Haylie. Anything you need, it's yours."

Uncrossing his legs, he pushed away from the table and stood, collecting their empty plates. Gathering the cutlery and glasses, she followed him through the house to the kitchen.

"I'll see that you're set up with a winter-safe vehicle and a place to work, both here and at the Manor," he continued. "I can even arrange for you to have as many assistants as you'd like from the temp agency we use for the Ridge, and you can come to me or Diana for anything else you might need."

She helped him load the dishwasher, then leaned back against one of the counters to study him. It felt odd to her to see a man like Trevor doing such mundane chores. She would have expected him to have a cook and housekeeper, to be catered to rather than catering to her.

And he did exude that air of power and privilege at times. Especially when he wore a suit and tie and looked like he should be posing for the cover of *Forbes* or *GQ*.

The very thought made her knees go weak, and she dug her nails into the edge of the countertop to keep from sliding to the floor in a heap.

Oh, yes. He was handsome enough and impressive enough to make James Bond look like a vagrant. But he also possessed a very wide independent streak. She'd recognized that the minute he'd brought her to his house.

No family mausoleum or giant mansion with round-the-clock servants to satisfy his every whim. And though she was sure he had someone come in to clean at least once a week and could have anything he desired delivered within hours at the snap of his fingers, it was obvious he valued his privacy.

Probably because he liked to bring women home with him, and live-in staff would have cramped his style.

Her mouth twisted. That thought didn't sit very well. And then it twisted even more because she shouldn't have cared one way or another who he brought home or what he did with them once they were here.

But, oh, how she hated picturing him here with other women. In this same room, this same house... and upstairs in his bedroom.

She'd only gotten a glimpse of it during his initial tour, but she could well imagine the feel of those soft, hunter-green sheets beneath her bare skin. His hard, muscled body above her as they stretched out on the wide, king-size bed. His mouth and his hands and...

A wave of longing swept through her, followed by a blast of warmth that lit her up like a Christmas candle, she was sure. She swallowed hard and tried not to look conspicuously aroused as Trevor finished what he was doing and turned back to face her.

"Maybe you could even let me watch him some of the time."

Haylie blinked, praying he wouldn't notice the blush tingeing her cheeks, or the fact that she was panting ever so slightly.

God, she was such a sap. She should be keeping him at arm's length. Two or three arms' lengths. Not daydreaming about how amazing he probably looked without clothes on.

Shaking her head, she tried to clear the haze of lust fogging her brain and focus on his words.

"I'm sorry, what?"

"I said maybe I can keep Bradley once in a while when you're busy with Erica or whatever. It will give us a chance to get to know each other—man to man."

He offered a lopsided smile that had her heart flip-flopping inside her chest.

"Are you sure that's a good idea?" she asked with a mental wince. "Babies are a lot of work."

Instead of backing down, his expression hardened. "According to you, Bradley is my son. Which means I might as well start learning the ropes now."

Dark eyes flashing, he stalked toward her, closing the distance between them and making her shrink back.

Placing his hands against the marble countertop on either side of her waist, he leaned in, crowding her. She fought the urge to squirm as his warm breath danced across her face and his chest brushed the tips of her breasts. They might both be fully clothed, but she felt the touch right down to her soul, her nipples budding inside the cups of her bra.

"And I thought you could teach me what I need to know," he whispered, his gaze locked on her lips. "In the evenings, when you're not busy with plans for Erica."

She opened her mouth, wanting to tell him that in order to be ready for a Christmas Eve wedding, she would likely be working mornings, evenings and every minute in between. Sleep would be a luxury, never mind taking the time to give him child-care lessons.

But having him close enough that she could see the gold flecks in his chocolate-brown eyes and smell his cologne like it was a part of herself sent logical thought flying right out the window.

"All right," she agreed, almost as though someone else were speaking for her.

His head dipped in what she thought was a nod, and

then he lifted his gaze to hers. The heat and intensity there made her want to rear back…but she couldn't seem to move.

"I'm going to kiss you now, Haylie Smith," he murmured in a low, mesmerizing voice.

"Why?"

He grinned. "Because I've been thinking about it all night. I want to feel your lips, know what you taste like."

Oh, he should write greeting cards. His assertion melted her insides until she could barely hold herself upright.

She knew she should say no, push him away, but darned if her body would listen to reason. Instead, her lips parted and she whispered the only two words she could manage.

"All right."

Haylie's acquiescence was nice, but he didn't need it. At that moment, a herd of wild horses couldn't have stopped him from kissing her.

But even as Trevor covered Haylie's mouth with his own, he knew he shouldn't be doing this. The obstacles between them were enough to add an extra mile or two to the Great Wall of China. He couldn't have picked a more complicated woman to be attracted to if he'd walked into a psychiatric ward and announced he would pay a million dollars for a willing bride.

She was practically a stranger. She'd shown up in his office with a baby she claimed was his—and her dead sister's, no less.

And that was just the tip of the iceberg. If Bradley really did turn out to be his, then there was the whole custody issue to deal with. Custody, and the fact that he didn't know the first thing about being a father.

Trevor would never be able to turn his back on his own child. Say *thanks for letting me know about my kid, but I'm not interested in being a dad* and be content with sending a support check every month to assuage his guilt.

But he knew, with every fiber of his being, that if he voiced his desire to keep Bradley and be a true father to the little boy, Haylie would fight him every step of the way. She was bonded to the baby like nothing he'd ever seen before. Of course, given what he knew about her sister, he had no doubt that Haylie had stepped in to mother Bradley from the moment he was born.

He admired the hell out of her for that. But it was definitely going to complicate matters if the tests came back positive and he asserted his parental rights.

And still he kissed her. A soft brushing of lips at first, followed by a firmer pressing.

She felt exactly as he'd imagined she would—like rose petals or plush velvet. And she tasted even better. Like the Barbaresco they'd had with dinner—spicy and tart, but with an extra-sweet tang that was uniquely her own.

Leaning in a few brief inches, he let his body rest against hers. From chest to thigh, they touched, heat swirling between them and sending their temperatures—or his, at any rate—skyrocketing.

He brought his hands up, cupping her face and deepening the kiss. Running his tongue along the seam of her mouth, he urged her to open for him. When she did, he delved in, groaning at the explosion of sensation that rocked him.

Why did this feel so good? So right?

Haylie was not the first pretty girl he'd ever kissed. Far from it; he'd been with dozens—dare he say hundreds?—of women.

She wasn't even his type. Oh, he liked blondes well enough—as well as brunettes, redheads and everything in between. But where he normally didn't give much thought to a woman's hair one way or another, he had to admit that *hers* was spectacular, all honey highlights, like a ray of sunshine trapped inside a glass jar.

She was tall enough, about five-five to his six foot two. Slightly shorter than his usual arm candy preferences, but the top of her head came to his chin, which he thought was pretty much perfect. He liked looking down at her, and the idea of having her fit against him just right when he tucked her close.

Her fuller, more rounded figure was also an unexpected turn-on. He was used to the stick-thin model sort…high heels, high hair and size-zero bodies squeezed into belts that doubled as dresses that barely covered their rear ends.

And always before, that had gotten his motor running. Or maybe he'd simply had it in his head that those were the type of women he was supposed to be with—super-photogenic party girls who enjoyed being seen with a Jarrod heir almost as much as they enjoyed actually being with him as a man.

But therein lay the difference: They were girls and Haylie was a woman.

Haylie possessed none of the qualities he normally looked for in the opposite sex, yet he loved the feel of her soft curves pressed against his harder frame. Loved the way she looked and smelled and let him ravish her mouth without pulling away.

Threading his fingers into the hair at the nape of

her neck, he let his other hand stroke down the side of her throat, the curve of her breast, her waist. Then he reached the hem of her shirt, tunneling beneath to touch warm, smooth skin. A low, primal groan rolled up from his diaphragm, and he leaned closer, deepening the kiss.

This wasn't what he'd intended when he'd first decided to taste her. He'd only wanted a tiny nibble, something to satisfy his curiosity and maybe put her a little off guard.

Instead, it felt as though a brushfire had broken out just under his skin. Pinpricks of heat and sensation that urged him to keep going.

Forget about the *just a taste* thing. Forget about a quick kiss to assuage his interest. He wanted to lift her onto the counter right then and there and have his way with her. Wanted to pick her up and carry her upstairs to his bedroom where he could undress her slowly, lay her out on the satin sheets covering his king-size mattress and explore every inch of her luscious body. Slowly.

He wondered what Haylie would think of the erotic images suddenly flitting through his mind. She certainly hadn't pulled away when he'd told her he was going to kiss her. And since she still wasn't resisting—was in fact kissing him back with a passion and fervor that had his blood heading due south at a rapid pace—he thought there was a chance she might be willing to act out a few of them.

A scratchy, whimpering sound reached his ears, and he wondered if it originated from his own throat or from hers. But when it came again, even more persistently and from across the room, he knew neither of them was the source of the strange noise. Something else was.

When Haylie cocked her head and pulled away, he

knew he was right. He also had the satisfaction of seeing that her eyes were glazed and she was breathing hard.

A second later, before he had time to really enjoy it, she whispered "Bradley," and slipped past him before he had a chance to react. He watched in confused silence as she darted out of the kitchen and up the stairs, belatedly realizing that the scratchy whimper that had interrupted one of the best kisses of his life had come from the baby monitor in the living room.

Trevor couldn't say he was thrilled with this turn of events, but in an odd way, he was amused. Having the four-month-old ruin a perfectly good kiss that may very well have led to even more intimacies was his very first experience with fatherhood. And if Bradley turned out to be his son, it was something he should probably get used to.

Nine

The week and a half following "The Kiss," as Haylie had come to think of it, was a busy one. Partly because she really did have a million and one things to do to keep up with Erica's wedding plans, and partly because she was actively avoiding Trevor.

Unfortunately, making a point to avoid him physically didn't mean she could do the same mentally.

For some strange reason, he seemed to be deeply embedded in her brain. Whether she was on the phone ordering flowers and linens, or running around the Ridge trying to organize people and plans and locations, there was always a moment when his face or voice or the memory of his seductive cologne would pop into her head.

She blamed it on "The Kiss." Before that, she might have found him attractive, but not distracting.

The Kiss... Boy, howdy, had anything ever curled her toes like that before?

Sure, she'd been feeling mellow from the delicious meal he'd prepared for her and the exceptional bottle of wine they'd shared. And she could admit to more than a bit of curiosity, too. He'd told her in that low, mesmerizing voice of his that he was going to kiss her, and her inner fairy-tale princess had gone aflutter, thinking, "Yes, please." After all, one little kiss had never hurt anybody.

But that kiss had been about as far from a fairy tale as one could get. Oh, no. Fairy tales were sweet and soft and romantic, while what she'd experienced at Trevor's hands had been closer to a scene from a disaster movie. Oceans churning, volcanoes erupting, palm trees being whipped to and fro under gale-force winds.

The minute his lips had touched hers, the world as she knew it had ceased to exist. If it hadn't been for Bradley's sleepy whimpers echoing from the baby monitor, and the well-honed maternal instincts she'd developed over the past months that wouldn't allow her to ignore his needs, she would probably still be propped up against the kitchen counter, wearing Trevor like a warm fleece blanket. Letting him kiss her stupid...and oh, so much more.

She was very much afraid that if the opportunity presented itself again, they wouldn't stop at just a kiss, which was why she was determined to keep her distance.

In the mornings, she made sure to be dressed and ready and to have Bradley with her from the time she left the guest room, because she knew Trevor wouldn't make a move while she had the baby in her arms.

During the day, she stayed busy, busy, busy, whether she was working from Trevor's home office—which he'd generously let her take over—or running errands both around the resort and in downtown Aspen.

Evenings, though…those were tough. Even if all she wanted to do was put Bradley down for the night, then soak for a couple hours in a hot bubble bath, or fix a nice dinner for one and put her feet up while she watched a bit of TV, more often than not she found herself taking food to her room and hiding out there until she was sure Trevor had gone to bed.

Though the house was large and spacious, there was too much danger of running into him, too much chance of dim lighting and sleepy brain cells telling her it wasn't a bad idea to kiss him again, after all. Kiss him and touch him and let him take her to his bed.

Oh, no. She most definitely had to stay away from Trevor Jarrod. Although she was starting to understand how her sister had fallen for him so quickly. They might have shared only a less-than-memorable—at least on his part—one-night stand, but Haylie could see how his handsome features and charming personality would sweep any woman off her feet.

Pushing through the front door, she kicked it closed behind her, juggling the baby and her bags until she could unload some of them. It had been another busy day, but thanks to the Ridge's day-care center and the completely over-the-top, champagne-colored four-wheel-drive Cadillac Escalade Trevor had gotten for her to tool around in, things were going very smoothly indeed.

The first time she'd been behind the wheel, she'd felt completely ridiculous. It was like driving a tractor trailer. And she knew how much something like that cost—more than she could afford, and more than someone like Trevor should be spending on someone like her.

But as usual, he'd been resolute. Hidden the keys to her car, she suspected, since she hadn't been able to find them since the Escalade had been delivered. And she had to admit, it was a nice ride. Comfortable and much safer than her little sedan, she supposed, for both Bradley and herself.

So with Erica's help, she had menus completed for both the rehearsal dinner and wedding reception… rooms reserved…flowers ordered…linens, silverware, and glassware lined up… Invitations had gone out the week before to the small group of guests Erica and Christian had decided to include in their special day— mostly family and a few close friends—and RSVPs were already flooding in.

All in all, she was very proud of the progress they'd made in such a short amount of time. Of course, she suspected that as soon as the happy couple left the reception for their honeymoon, she would crash and burn, sleeping for a month straight.

In fact, just last week, when Erica has insisted she take an afternoon to relax and enjoy a full spa day with her, she'd fallen asleep on the table during her massage. Erica and Trevor's sister Melissa, as well as their brothers' significant others, Sabrina, Samantha and Avery, had all joined them. It had been a Girls' Day of sorts, something Haylie didn't get to experience very often given her hectic schedule and, yes, lack of close female friends back in Denver.

The women had kept up a constant stream of chatter and laughter, and though she'd managed to stay awake during their manicures, pedicures and cucumber face wraps, Haylie had simply drifted off during the massage.

Not surprising, considering how amazingly relaxing it had been, but still.

She had to admit that it had been both fun and informative to meet so many other members of the Jarrod clan. In addition to being gracious and friendly, they'd treated her just like "one of the girls," and she'd genuinely enjoyed herself.

As curious as she knew they must be about her sudden appearance in Aspen and her living arrangements with Trevor, they hadn't asked a single awkward question or given her even one piece of unsolicited advice about Erica's wedding. Something she had definitely been on guard about from the very beginning.

Dropping some of her things near the oak-and-marble island with a tired sigh, she started to shrug out of her heavy winter coat while simultaneously loosening Bradley's warm snowsuit.

"Hey."

Trevor's low voice startled her, and she jerked around to find him coming down the stairs. As usual when at home, he was dressed in jeans and a thick sweater. Today's choice was khaki-green and did amazing things for both his chest and eyes.

Not that she had any business noticing the mouth-watering appeal of either.

"Hi," she greeted him, still tugging and unzipping.

Moving through the house's open-design living area, he crossed to the kitchen and took Bradley right out of her arms. "Here, let me."

For a second, she froze, used to doing pretty much everything herself, and unused to having assistance with much of anything, especially the baby.

No, that wasn't quite true, was it? Ever since moving in with him, Trevor had been quite helpful. He'd supplied her with everything she'd needed to be comfortable and do her job for Erica, and then some. He was courteous and accommodating and was almost obsessively single-minded about lending a hand with Bradley.

As unnerving as it was on a lot of levels, he got definite brownie points for how involved he'd been in Bradley's care. He'd asked her early on to show him everything he needed to know about babies, adamant about learning how to prepare bottles and formula, change a diaper, give Bradley a bath.

He seemed to have a million questions—which was understandable, she supposed, from a man who didn't have much experience with young children, but suddenly found himself faced with the possibility of fatherhood. And more than once in the middle of the night, when she hadn't hopped out of bed quickly enough in response to Bradley's cries, Trevor had come to her door, tapping softly and offering to help with whatever the baby needed.

Given that they didn't even know for sure yet that Bradley *was* his son, he was certainly doing everything that could be expected of a new father.

On the one hand, having Trevor around to take care of everyday obligations that she was normally responsible for all on her own was nice. It relieved a modicum of her personal stress and gave her a little extra time each day to focus on the preparations for Erica's wedding.

On the other, she wasn't sure she liked somebody else playing parent to Bradley, even if that person most likely *was* his biological parent. But she was so used to caring for her infant nephew by herself, she didn't want anyone usurping that position, pushing her out of Bradley's life. And if someone else *could* care for him as well as she did, then that was a real possibility.

Oh, who was she kidding? When those DNA results came back and showed that Trevor was Bradley's father—which she fully believed would be the case—chances were he would take the baby away from her. Or try to, anyway.

Lord, why had she come here in the first place? It had seemed like the right thing to do at the time, but now... The thought of losing custody of Bradley made her blood go cold, and she wished she could go back in time and do the wrong thing by keeping the baby to herself.

Stripping Bradley down to his brown corduroy pants and long-sleeved duckie shirt, Trevor set the bulky snowsuit aside, then arranged the infant on his hip as if he'd been doing it half his life.

"Have you had dinner yet?" he asked.

She shook her head, still feeling slightly uneasy as she shrugged out of her own outerwear.

"You look tired. Why don't you go upstairs, change clothes, maybe take a long, hot bath. I'll get Bradley fed, and you can decide what you'd like to eat later."

It was as if he'd read her mind. She was tired and more than a little worn out simply from the schedule she'd been keeping lately, but while she knew she needed to eat at some point, what she *wanted* was to sink beneath about a foot of bubbles for an hour or two and let the hot water and steam-filled room wash away the stress and exhaustion of the day.

But she hated that he knew that...or could read her so easily. Or maybe she hated how reliant she'd become on him, knowing that he intended to take Bradley away from her once it was proven he was the baby's father—and how comfortable she was with that reliance.

The truth was, she *liked* living here, under Trevor's

roof. She liked coming home at the end of the day to find him here, or being here when he walked in the door. She liked talking to him, and looking at him, and smelling the faint scent of his cologne in a room long after he'd left it. And she liked having someone to help her with Bradley, to care *about* Bradley, after doing everything alone for so long and being the only person in her nephew's life who gave a damn about him.

But all of that also made her feel threatened, insecure. When it came to Bradley, the more Trevor learned to do on his own and the more confident he became in his ability to care for an infant, the less she would be needed. And when those tests finally came back, showing that he was the baby's father...well, she would be pretty much expendable, wouldn't she?

She pressed the heel of her hand to the center of her forehead, where a headache that hadn't been there five minutes ago began to pound right between her eyes.

"Go ahead," Trevor told her, moving around her statue-like form to the cupboard, where he began to collect assorted baby food jars for Bradley's dinner. "We'll be fine."

Yeah, that was the problem.

But without a word, she dragged herself upstairs, too tired and suddenly out of sorts to pass on the offer of a nice, hot bubble bath, even if it had been suggested by the man who'd put her out of sorts in the first place.

Resisting the urge to reach around and pat himself on the back, Trevor walked quietly into Haylie's room and laid Bradley down in the crib in the corner. He put the baby on his back, just as Haylie had instructed the first time she'd shown him how to put the boy down for a nap, and wound the timer on the jungle animals mobile hanging overhead.

He was pretty sure he'd remembered everything. After feeding Bradley, he'd given the baby a bath in his bathroom because Haylie was still locked in hers, then put him in a new diaper and Onesie. He'd even brought along a pacifier, which Bradley was busily sucking while his eyelids grew heavier and heavier.

Trevor was getting pretty good at this, if he did say so himself. As unhappy as he'd been when Haylie had first dropped Bradley in his lap, and as nervous as he'd been when he'd first decided to step up to the plate and learn his way around the care and feeding of an infant, he was now confident that if the paternity test came back naming him Bradley's biological father, he would be fully capable of caring for the child on his own. It would mean some rearranging of his life and normal routine, but he could do it.

Just as the baby's eyes drifted closed one last time and the suction on the pacifier slowed to only an occasional twitch of his soft, round cheeks, Trevor heard the bathroom door click open.

Raising his arms to the side like someone being held at gunpoint, he kept his back to that side of the room, hoping against hope that Haylie wouldn't be startled enough by his presence in her bedroom to shriek and wake the baby.

Not sure whether or not she'd noticed him yet, he took a step away from the crib and whispered, "Sorry. I was just putting Bradley down for the night."

He waited a beat, wondering if he was standing in the middle of an empty bedroom, talking to himself. But a second later, she whispered back.

"It's okay. You can turn around, I'm dressed."

Dressed, Trevor decided, when he'd done what she suggested, was a gross understatement.

Haylie stood just outside the bathroom in a pale peach robe that looked as if it was made of some kind of satin or silk that—unless his eyes were playing tricks on him—he could see straight through. At the very least, the diaphanous material was clinging to her damp skin in all the right places, making his mouth go bone dry and his groin tighten with want.

Her hair was twisted up and covered with a towel, but while he stood there trying to catch his breath, she tilted her head, swung her hair free and used the towel to continue to dry the long, damp strands.

He knew there was a four-month-old in the room with him, but all Trevor could think about was tossing Haylie down on the bed and making love to her. She was rosy-pink from her bath, some flowery fragrance wafting from the open doorway, and she was naked beneath that robe. It made him itchy, twitchy and hard.

"Did he get his dinner?" she asked, apparently heedless of the erotic thoughts racing through his brain.

He nodded, slipping his hands into his pockets to keep from doing something truly stupid like reaching for her, and rocking back on his heels. "And a bath and a fresh diaper."

Her eyes widened slightly and her movements slowed. She didn't say as much, but he knew she was surprised he'd managed so well all on his own. He half expected her to cross to the crib and double check that he hadn't taped Bradley's diaper on backward or stuck his head through the Onesie's leg hole.

He bit down on a grin when instead she only murmured a half-approving, "Good."

She twisted around to drape the wet towel over the bathroom doorknob, and her robe parted, the V at her neck opening just enough to flash the swell of one pale breast.

Sweat broke out along the nape of his neck and he could feel his flesh prickle as it grew taut around his muscles and bones. If he didn't get out of there soon, he was going to do something they would probably both regret, sleeping baby or no sleeping baby.

"I had the resort deliver dinner while you were in the tub," he said, because it was the first nonsexual thought that popped into his head. "There's a plate waiting for you downstairs. I'll heat it up while you get changed."

Without waiting for a response, he strode to the door and yanked it open harder than he'd intended. Once in the hall, he stood stock still, trying to catch his breath and regain his equilibrium.

Dammit, how could one woman shake him up so badly? He'd been with models, actresses, beauty queens... He'd dodged gold diggers and marriage-minded misses, extricated himself from women on the verge of becoming obsessive.

Then there was Haylie, who showed no interest in him whatsoever, asked nothing of him and maintained that she'd only sought him out in the first place to let him know he'd fathered a child.

Yet *she* was the woman that his libido apparently wanted more than any of the others. *She* was the one he couldn't stop thinking about, who kept him up nights for all the wrong reasons.

He'd kissed her once already, purely to satisfy his curiosity, but promised himself he wouldn't do it again.

Behind him, the door clicked, and he straightened,

feeling like a deer caught in headlights. He was supposed to be downstairs, busying himself as though he were completely unaffected by her presence. Instead, he'd gotten all of six inches from her room before overheating and stalling out.

Turning, he found her still in that sheer, lust-inducing robe and fisted his hands at his sides to keep from tearing it off her.

"I changed my mind," she said before lifting her head all the way. Before meeting his eyes. "I'm not hungry. I think I'll just go to bed."

With a curse, he reached around her, pulling the door closed, then backed her up against the hard, flat panel and boxed her in.

"To hell with it," he growled. "I changed my mind, too. I *am* going to kiss you again."

Ten

Trevor's mouth was warm and firm and just as spine-melting as the first time he'd kissed her.

Haylie knew, far in the back of her mind, that she should push him away. Kissing this man—or letting him kiss her, rather—was not a good idea. After the last time they'd done this, she'd made a long, long list of reasons why, mentally repeating them to herself often and sternly.

At the moment, however, she couldn't think of a single one. Not when only items from the "Pro" column seemed to be jumping up and making themselves known.

Like how the winter-fresh scent of his cologne wrapped around her, clinging to her nearly as tightly as his arms wrapped around her waist. Or how intoxicating his lips were. Both soft and unyielding, they brushed and pressed and nipped, commanding her to respond like to a snake charmer's flute.

Of their own volition, her arms lifted to circle his neck, and she leaned even more heavily against the closed door. Her legs were the consistency of rubber bands, only the door and Trevor keeping her upright.

A million reasons not to let this happen, and only one in favor of dropping her reservations and going with the tidal wave of passion threatening to bowl her over: She wanted him.

Pushing every other thought, every other caution aside, she let go and threw herself into the kiss. As though he sensed her capitulation, Trevor moved closer and deepened the pressure of his mouth. She moaned, tangling her tongue with his and threading her fingers into his hair.

When her leg came up to bracket his hip, her bare foot teasing the back of his knee, she knew she was in trouble…and knew he knew it, too.

Pulling his mouth from hers, Trevor rested his brow against hers, his chest rising and falling with his ragged breathing.

"Come to my room with me," he whispered, the pad of his thumb rubbing back and forth, back and forth across her cheek. "Let me take you to bed."

Could he possibly believe she was going to say no? After two of the most amazing kisses of her life and the way she was draped around him now, in the middle of the hall?

Of course, at this very second, she couldn't form much of a response either way. Words failed her because her lungs were still straining for oxygen, her throat still thick with longing.

So she nodded and tightened her leg where it wound around his hip, which she hoped was answer enough.

It was. Blowing out a pent-up breath, Trevor grabbed

her by the waist and lifted her, pulling her against his body. She brought her other leg up and crossed her ankles at the small of his back, meeting him halfway when he leaned in to kiss her again.

Then they were moving. Trevor spun to the left and stalked down the hall, carrying her as though she weighed no more than little Bradley.

With barely a pause, he pushed the door of his room open, then kicked it closed behind them with the heel of his foot. A moment later, she found herself falling backward, bouncing as she hit the firm king-size mattress.

Trevor followed her down, covering her with his long, hard body even as his hands began to explore her own. They slipped beneath her robe, touching her bare skin as he brushed the material away.

First he uncovered her thighs, taking the time to stroke them outside and in as he went. Then he moved past her hips to her waist, where he unknotted the robe's sash and spread the two sides apart to reveal her breasts and torso.

Swallowing hard, Haylie resisted the need to pull the robe back together or cover herself with her hands. Trevor was staring down at her like an explorer who'd just discovered the Lost World. It was both disconcerting and flattering—and the only thing that kept her from squirming under his blazing hot gaze.

She couldn't remember the last time a man had looked at her with such blatant intensity. Or the last time she'd wanted one to…or wanted one just as much.

Eyes twinkling, dark hair tousled and falling carelessly around his handsome face, Trevor lowered his head and kissed the hollow of her throat, then trailed his lips down the center of her chest. Between her breasts and over her stomach, his touch made her burn.

When he reached the apex of her thighs and placed his mouth right at the heart of her, she nearly shot off the bed. But Trevor was having none of that. He flattened one large, rough-palmed hand over her abdomen, holding her in place, while he shifted between her legs, parting them even farther and making himself comfortable.

She had to admit, this wasn't what she'd expected. From the minute she'd decided to throw caution to the wind, she'd expected something fast and furious. A flash fire of passion, scalding hot, but quickly burned to embers. And, yes, more than a bit of selfishness on Trevor's part.

He was a Jarrod, for heaven's sake. One of the Jarrod Ridge Jarrods of Aspen, Colorado. Rich beyond her wildest imaginings, able to buy and do whatever he liked. A man used to getting his way in all things. She knew *that* from personal experience.

She also knew from all the newspapers and magazines he'd appeared in over the years that he was used to dating extremely glamorous, extremely beautiful women. Two characteristics Haylie could never claim for herself.

Oh, she was attractive enough. Not movie-star gorgeous, but not in line at the grocery store for a bag to put over her head, either. Of course, the ten or fifteen pounds that made her a little more lush than society's image of womanly perfection would definitely push her to the other side of Trevor's penchant for chopstick-thin model types.

As far as being glamorous went... She was too busy building her business and taking care of Bradley to worry about keeping her hair flawlessly coifed or making sure to wear the latest designer fashions. Some days, she was lucky if she remembered to put in earrings or got her shoes on the right feet.

Yet here she was, sprawled naked on the bed of a man she was sure would never have looked twice at her if they hadn't been thrown together through bizarre circumstances, and he was being extremely...anything but selfish. Incredibly *un*selfish, in fact.

Her hands clawed at the quilted duvet as he increased the pressure of his mouth. When he hit a particularly sweet spot, she nearly shrieked, hips shooting off the bed. Trevor's hands flexed where they framed her thighs, and she could have sworn she felt him smile.

Smiling was the furthest thing from her mind, though. He was creating entirely too many amazing, mind-boggling sensations for Haylie to even form a coherent thought, let alone control her facial expressions.

All she knew was that her entire body was on fire. She was writhing, panting, straining for a completion only he could give her.

"Trevor, please." The words slipped out before she could stop them. She hated to sound so desperate, even though she was, and bit the inside of her lip to keep from saying anything more. Saying, moaning, begging...

Thankfully, he didn't make her speak. Kneading her thighs like a hungry kitten while she clutched at his thick, wavy hair, he redoubled his efforts, using his tongue and teeth to tease the tiny bundle of nerves hidden between her folds. Before she could manage a full inhalation of short, broken breaths, pleasure swamped her, hitting her like a bolt of lightning and sending her arching up from the mattress with a keening cry.

She hadn't quite come down to earth yet when Trevor slid up the length of her body. Her lashes fluttered as she opened her eyes. No easy feat.

This time, she did smile. A small, wavering smile, but a smile all the same.

He was naked. Deliciously so. Though she had no idea when he'd stripped out of his sweater and jeans. Had her eyes been closed for that long? Or had she actually lost consciousness there for a minute after that orgasm?

It had been an incredible orgasm, so her guess was loss of consciousness.

Returning her grin with a very self-satisfied one of his own, he lowered himself on his forearms, covering her from breast to ankle. The heat of his skin seeped into hers, warming her like a bonfire, and she took a deep breath to inhale his wonderful scent.

Against her better judgment, she lifted her arms and draped them around his neck. She was surprised, really, that she could move at all; her bones and muscles were the consistency of runny gravy.

"That was awfully nice of you," she murmured by way of a thank-you.

The corners of his mouth twitched. "Glad you liked it."

"'Like' *sooooo* doesn't cover it," she said with an unladylike snort.

If possible, his grin turned even cockier. She could practically feel his ego growing by leaps and bounds.

"I'm a gentleman," he told her, leaning in to nuzzle her throat. "And gentlemen always make sure ladies come first."

She chuckled, the sound weak and still slightly breathless. "I don't think that's how the saying is supposed to go."

"My bed, my rules."

"Really?" She tilted her head, giving him better

access. "Do those rules include pleasuring a woman so thoroughly, she falls asleep immediately afterward, leaving you to your own devices?"

He raised his head, brow arched. "Definitely not."

"Well, you're in trouble, then. Because that one did me in. I'm ready for a nap." Stretching her arms up over her head, she gave a wide, theatrical yawn.

"Hmm." The sound rolled up his throat, low and thoughtful. "Guess I'll just have to change your mind about that."

With an exaggerated sigh, she arched her back and let her eyes drift closed. "I suppose you can try."

Amusement flashed across his features while determination sparked in his espresso-dark eyes. "I do love a challenge."

Oh, so did she. But where this one was concerned, she didn't think she'd last very long.

Returning his mouth to the side of her neck, he kissed her pulse point, then let his tongue dart out to lick the spot, followed by gentle sucking. That alone sent her heart racing…a fact she was sure he could feel beneath his lips.

He kissed a trail up the line of her throat, over her jaw and to her mouth. That was when she discovered what a kiss really was. Not counting that first scorcher in the kitchen. Or the second scorcher outside her bedroom door.

When their lips met, it was as if all the oxygen had been sucked out of the room in one giant gulp. And when his tongue delved inside to tangle with hers, everything around them burst into flame.

Tiny explosions went off in her bloodstream, making her wrap both her arms and legs around him even more tightly. She stroked his hair, his shoulders, his back.

Moaned when he began to do the same at her breasts. Soon his mouth followed, licking, circling, gently suckling until her nipples were stiff, pebbled peaks, so sensitive, she could hardly stand it.

She'd known from the start that Trevor was a man used to getting his way, one who didn't like to lose. Now she also knew never to challenge him or doubt his determination. Because even though she'd only been teasing when she'd mentioned leaving him to his own devices, she was now very interested and very much involved, whether she liked it or not.

Which didn't mean she was going to let him be in control—at least not entirely. Working her hands between their bodies, she used her thumbs to toy with his own tiny, flat nipples…and earned herself a deep groan.

Given Trevor's love of outdoor sports and his level of activity, it shouldn't have surprised her that he had an amazing physique. But truly, she thought, he was *amazing*.

Almost everything about him was rock solid—biceps, pectorals, six-pack abs. He should be the poster boy for the local gym, or even for Jarrod Ridge.

Put a tanned, sweaty, half-naked Trevor on a few posters advertising the best skiing, rock climbing, white-water rafting in the state, and men and women alike would flock to Aspen in droves. The men in hopes of getting a bit of his adventurous streak to rub off, the women in hopes of tracking down Trevor and checking out all of those sinewy male muscles for themselves.

Yet for now, at least, they were all hers.

Letting her fingertips slide down the center of his chest, she stroked her way to another hard, impressive muscle. She brushed the backs of her knuckles up and down his velvety length, smiling when he released her mouth in order to draw in some much-needed air.

"You're killing me," he panted, a lock of dark hair falling forward over his brow.

"Not yet," she murmured in her best sultry, Marilyn Monroe voice, "but soon. If you're lucky."

He gave a breathy chuckle, then startled a small yip out of her when he rolled and shifted until he was sitting in the middle of the bed and she was perched above him, her bottom perched on his knees.

"Do your worst," he told her. "I can take it."

"Do you have a condom?"

Trevor stretched out an arm, patting the top of the comforter until he found the foil packet he'd dropped within reach earlier. Holding it between two fingers, he offered it to Haylie, a punch of longing slamming into his solar plexus when she took the square from him and tore it open with her teeth.

Oh, yeah. Taking her to bed was *definitely* one of his better ideas. Maybe not smart in the long run, but at the moment, he considered it freaking brilliant.

He sucked in a breath and clutched the bedspread in his fists to keep from shooting off like a rocket when she covered him with the thin layer of latex. She was barely touching him, and it certainly wasn't the first time a woman had put a condom on him, but for some reason, having Haylie do it—*watching* her do it—was one of the most erotic experiences of his life.

And if he survived the rest of the night—which, at this point, was doubtful, very doubtful—he swore to repay her for every little bit of torture she was doling out on him. What was good for the goose, tit for tat, and all that.

Once the protection was in place, Haylie lifted up

on her knees, hovering over him as she ran her fingers through his hair, tipped his head back and kissed him. Softly, sweetly, and arousing as hell. As though he needed any more fuel thrown on his fire.

While their mouths were still locked together, she reached between them to wrap a hand around his straining erection…a move that had him gripping her waist and thrusting his tongue even deeper. Positioning herself just right, she sank down, inch by agonizing inch, until she was fully seated, taking him to the hilt.

Sensation swamped him, and from the digging of her nails into the meat of his shoulders, he suspected she was feeling the same.

As promised, he let her set the pace. For several long minutes, all they did was kiss, which was just fine with him. He thought he could probably spend from now until eternity kissing this woman and never get bored. Her taste and texture were just too damn intoxicating.

When she was ready, though, she began to move. Carefully at first, lifting herself only an inch or two. Then sliding back down. Again and again until his teeth ached from the delicious friction and his muscles twitched from holding back.

Just as his already thready control was about to snap, she broke their kiss, gasping for air and arching so that her breasts were right in front of his face. And how could he resist such a delectable offering? Flicking his tongue over one raspberry tip, he urged her on, wanting to increase the burn of satisfaction for her the way she was for him.

He watched her cheeks flush and the pale curve of her lashes flutter as her eyes closed. His own eyes were wide open, and he intended to keep them that way. He wanted to see every shift of color across her skin, every hitch of her chest with her rapid breaths, every degree of pleasure that showed on her face.

And when she came again—very soon, if he had anything to say about it—he wanted to see that, too.

Wrapping his arms around her waist, he pulled her closer. Her breasts flattened against his chest, sweat-slick skin to sweat-slick skin. She rearranged her legs to circle his hips, ankles locking and riding the small of his back, and he let his hands float along the small indentation of her spine until his fingers could twist in her hair, bring her mouth closer to his own.

Lips and tongues met, twined, fought for dominance, while at the same time, their lower bodies moved in tandem. His back and forth, hers up and down, creating ripples of bone-melting sensation that brought them closer and closer to the edge.

And then they were over. Haylie gasped, shuddering and spasming around him. The feel of her body tightening, clenching on his rocked him to his core and straight to a climax of epic proportions.

Squeezing her hard enough to break something, he gave one more high, powerful thrust before his body stiffened and he spilled inside her.

Eleven

Hours later, Haylie shifted in her sleep, bobbing toward consciousness. She was warm and cozy and more comfortable than she could remember being in a long, long time.

And then she realized why. A heavy arm draped her waist, a heavy male body framing her from behind.

She was in Trevor's bed. In Trevor's arms.

A stab of something… Fear? Regret? Clutched her heart even as she admitted to herself that making love with him was one of, if not *the,* most amazing sexual experiences of her life. It complicated things, without a doubt, but it had also made her eyes roll back in her head.

Before she could decide whether to stay and drift back to sleep or extricate herself from Trevor's firm hold and sneak back to her own room, she heard a squeak.

Bradley. That must have been what had awakened her in the first place.

Doing her best not to wake Trevor, she lifted his arm from her waist and slowly rolled out of bed. Her robe was a mass of wrinkled material on the floor, where it had gotten tossed hours earlier, but she picked it up, shook it out to find which end was up, and quickly covered herself, tying the sash as she tiptoed out the door.

Her bare feet padded on the cool hardwood floor as she crossed the hall to her room. Inside, Bradley was lying on his back in the crib, face crinkled and arms and legs flailing as he fussed.

She scooped him up, patting his back as she carried him downstairs to the kitchen to fix a quick bottle. Taking the baby and the bottle back upstairs, while Bradley drank she sat in the beautiful, hand-carved rocking chair Trevor had insisted she have.

Once Bradley's belly was full and he'd fallen asleep again, she put him in a clean diaper and returned him to the crib, hopefully for the rest of the night. She didn't even know what time it was and had to check the clock when she returned the dirty bottle to the kitchen.

Five after two. She had to be up again in only four more hours. But the question now became, did she go to her room and spend those hours alone...or return to Trevor's bed and curl up next to his warm, firm body?

Oh, she so wanted to do the latter. The thought was almost irresistible. But that didn't mean it was smart. Sleeping with him once had been stupid enough; better not to compound that by making Bad Decision Number Two.

Rinsing the baby bottle, she left it in the sink to be dealt with in the morning, and turned to head back upstairs. A shadow fell across the tiled floor, rising over her and sending her back a step. She opened her mouth to scream, then quickly caught herself as her eyes adjusted and she realized she wasn't about to be swallowed whole by the abominable snow monster.

"Good lord," she breathed, slapping a hand over her chest to stop the rapid pounding of her heart, "you scared the life out of me."

Rather than offer an apology, Trevor's dark eyes blinked sleepily and he rubbed a hand through his tousled hair. He'd pulled on a pair of blue-and-white-striped flannel pajama bottoms, but both his feet and chest were still bare.

She'd never noticed before how sexy his feet were. Of course, the last time he'd been wearing so few clothes she hadn't exactly been interested in his toes.

"I woke up and you were gone," he said in a tired, gravelly voice.

"The baby woke me," she told him. Not that she owed him an explanation. If she'd been smart, she would have sneaked out of bed even without Bradley's prompting and locked herself in the guest room, well away from roving hands and tempting lips.

"Is he okay?"

She nodded. "Needed a bottle and a new diaper. He's back to sleep now."

Trevor tipped his head, which she took as a sign of approval. Then he took a step forward. And another. And another.

Haylie retreated, not sure what his intentions were, until the counter stopped her. But it didn't stop Trevor. He continued stalking her until his chest brushed the tips of her breasts. She wondered if he could feel her nipples budding through the thin satin of her robe.

"Trevor," she whispered as he leaned in, began nuzzling a spot just beneath her ear.

"Mmm-hmm."

"What happened before…" She trailed off. It was so hard to concentrate while he was doing that with his mouth.

"Mmm-hmm."

"It was…"

He licked the lobe of her ear, then nipped gently with his teeth, and her knees nearly buckled.

"A mistake," she forced out breathlessly. "It was a mistake."

"Definitely," he agreed, though the fact that he was now kissing a hot, wet path to the hollow of her throat made her think he didn't agree, not really. "A terrible mistake."

She swallowed, determined to keep her mind on track and *not* let him distract her, no matter how hard he was trying.

"Then why are you…doing this?"

His fingers slipped under the belt of her robe, untying the knot and letting the garment fall open. Cool air hit her overheated skin and she shivered.

"The way I see it," he murmured, sliding his hands inside her robe and pushing it open wider, "the mistake's already been made. Can't undo it."

He made a good point. Maybe only because his hands on her breasts and his mouth on her collarbone were as intoxicating as a bottle of fine wine, but still…

"We're both consenting adults," he continued, kissing a path down the center of her chest. "I don't see any reason why we shouldn't continue to enjoy one another for as long as you're here. No strings, no promises. Just—" his tongue darted out to sweep across one tight, sensitive nipple "—pleasure."

Her head fell back on a shudder, her eyes slipping

closed. He made another very good point. The man was clearly a genius, his skills obviously wasted at a menial marketing job for Jarrod Ridge when he could be curing dreaded diseases, negotiating world peace and discovering life forms on other planets.

A tiny voice sounded inside her head, a faraway echo offering a small semblance of sanity. It forced her to open her mouth and say, "But…"

That's all, just "but…" She knew there should be more, knew there was some kind of argument she should be posing, but darned if she could think of a single one.

So Trevor finished the thought for her. He straightened enough to reach her mouth, kissing her until the only thing taxing her brain was a flurry of stars in swirling colors.

He broke away, giving her a chance to catch her breath, but only for a second before grasping her waist and hoisting her onto the countertop.

"It's only for a week or so more," he told her, nudging the robe from her shoulders and letting it float down her arms to pool at her hips. "As soon as those test results come in, everything is going to change. But until then, we've got nothing but time."

He kissed the curve of her breast. "To spend together."

Her collarbone. "Alone."

The line of her jaw. "Just the two of us."

And finally, her mouth. "Enjoying ourselves—" his hands cupped her knees, prying her legs apart so that he could step closer and fill the space; the flannel of his pajama bottoms was soft and highly erotic against her inner thighs "—in increasingly pleasurable ways."

There was only one thing she could think to say to

that, while his lips ravished hers and his thumbs circled closer and closer to her center.

"Okay."

Two days later, Haylie returned from the Ridge earlier than usual. She shouldn't be doing this. She had a mile-long list of things to do, and contrary to her fondest wishes, the time leading up to Christmas Eve and Erica's wedding seemed to be speeding up rather than slowing down.

But Trevor had finally convinced her to let him take her to dinner at Chagall's. Even if they requested a private booth, tried to slip in under the radar, they were bound to be noticed. By the staff, by other guests, and eventually word would reach the kitchen. Trevor didn't seem to mind, so she was trying not to worry about it, either, but that didn't mean she was looking forward to being fodder for the Jarrod Ridge gossip mill.

Then again, maybe no one would even notice them. It was possible. It was also possible that Trevor had prepared for any such scrutiny and had a perfectly plausible story in mind to explain what the two of them were doing together.

The problem was that while they'd agreed to act as though they were merely business acquaintances and weren't on a date, a date was exactly what this evening's dinner would be. At least she assumed so, given the fact that she was living under Trevor's roof and currently sharing his bed.

She knew she should be feeling guilty about the last, but heaven forgive her, she didn't. Not yet, at any rate. And she promised herself that when the end came—which, of course, it would—she would handle it in a mature fashion. No tears or histrionics, because she and Trevor had agreed that there were no strings or expectations to this affair. They were simply two consenting adults enjoying each other's company for as long as it lasted.

But an affair, by definition, was supposed to be kept under wraps, wasn't it? Full of clandestine meetings and secret rendezvous. Not going out to a crowded restaurant in a very public resort where anyone could see them and speculate about their relationship, begin all manner of ugly rumors.

It was Trevor's call, though, and he'd insisted they do this now, before she got too much more swept up in Erica's wedding preparations. She suspected, too, that it had something to do with wanting her to experience the five-star opulence of Chagall's before those DNA test results came in.

Maybe he wanted to impress her. Though she didn't know how she could be any *more* impressed, given everything she'd already seen of both his personal home and the family's holdings.

Or maybe he was simply trying to be nice, to give her a bit of a break from all the hard work and long hours she'd been putting in on his sister's behalf. Of course, such a large job had been his idea in the first place, and his way of keeping her close until he found out Bradley's paternity.

But still, Trevor was being kind and romantic, and she was just weak enough to go along with it, to let herself be swept up in the fantasy, however short-lived it would turn out to be.

Bradley was still at the resort's day-care center, so she didn't need to worry about him. And she had a good hour to shower, change clothes and redo her hair and makeup before meeting Trevor back at the resort, at his office, as they'd agreed.

Kicking off her shoes just inside the door, she shook off her coat and hurried upstairs. Twenty minutes later, she hopped out of the shower and began the ritual of drying and styling her hair, applying a few dabs of her favorite perfume and touching up her makeup to something a bit heavier and more appropriate for evening than work.

From there, she walked barefoot to the guest-room closet and pulled out the little black dress she'd been thinking about all day. When she'd first noticed it among the wardrobe offerings Trevor had had supplied for her, she'd thought it was entirely too fancy for anything she'd be doing during her stay in Aspen.

But the moment he'd convinced her to dine with him at Chagall's, she'd known she would finally put the velvet sheath to good use. She'd also known exactly what shoes and jewelry she would wear with it—a pair of steep, nearly four-inch open-toe stilettos with tiny white bows on the sides and a triple strand of ivory pearls with matching earrings.

When she was pretty much ready, she grabbed a small black clutch large enough to hold a few necessary items such as her cell phone and lipstick, then realized she didn't have a watch. She must have left it in Trevor's bedroom.

She really tried not to leave her things in his room, because even though they were *technically* living together and *technically* now sharing a bed, moving anything into his room felt too personal, too much like true cohabitation or like this was all leading somewhere. But considering the number of times he'd lured her in there fully dressed, then stripped her down...a shiver

skated down her spine at the warm, intimate memories…
it was no wonder she'd managed to leave something
behind.

Crossing the hall, she pushed open his door and
moved toward the nightstand, where she most expected
her watch to be. Halfway there, she noticed a lump in
the center of Trevor's bed.

Odd, since she remembered straightening the
covers herself that very morning. She might not have
managed hospital corners or done as good a job as his
housekeeper, but she definitely hadn't left a big, messy
lump in the middle of the mattress.

It took a moment for her brain to process what she was
seeing, but then she started to wonder if something had
happened. She'd spoken to Trevor that morning before
they'd parted ways outside his office at the Manor, but
not since. There hadn't been a need, since their plans
for dinner had been ironed out the night before.

But what if he hadn't been feeling well? What if he'd
eaten some bad sushi for lunch or some such, and had
come home sick? She'd like to think he would have
called or texted her about that sort of thing, or even had
Diana contact her, but perhaps he'd been *too* sick even
for that.

Stepping forward, she reached for the covers, slowly
drawing them back as she whispered his name. "Trevor?
Are you all right?"

But it wasn't Trevor beneath the bunched up sheets.
At least not unless he'd grown three feet of extra hair
and dyed it a bright copper-red over the last six hours.

Dropping the covers like they were a nest of wriggling
vipers, she jerked back, eyes wide.

Behind her, she heard a creak and turned to find
Trevor waltzing through the open bedroom door. His

hair was still short and brown, and he was wearing the same suit he'd left the house in earlier that morning.

He grinned at her, sweeping up to press a quick, hard kiss to her lips. His hand at the base of her spine was firm and possessive, and even with the cold reality of what was lying in the bed beside them, it warmed her.

"I thought I'd pick you up for dinner instead of making you drive back to the Ridge by yourself. Besides, it's easier to drop off my briefcase now than remember to pick it up later on our way out."

Licking her lips and removing probably half of the lip gloss she'd just painstakingly applied, she did her best to find her voice.

"Really?" she asked. "You didn't come home early for a little afternoon delight?"

His grin turned into a full-blown leer. "I hadn't, but if you're offering…" He tipped his left wrist to check the time. "Our reservations aren't until seven, and one of the many perks of being a Jarrod *is* that we can be late and still get a table."

He leaned in, going for another kiss, but she quickly sidestepped, moving farther away from him. His hand dropped from her back and his smile slipped, sliding downward into the beginnings of a frown.

"What's wrong?" he asked, sounding genuinely concerned.

"I wasn't talking about me." She cocked her head toward the bed. "I meant Goldilocks over there."

His eyes darted to the lump under the covers that was just starting to wiggle around and wake up. In three long strides, he reached the bed and stretched out an arm to whip back the sheets and spread.

A long, lithe form with curly red hair and wearing only a matching hot-pink bra and high-cut underwear blinked thick lashes and rolled from her side to her back. Her lips curved when she spotted Trevor.

"Hi, baby. Hope you don't mind that I let myself in."

That was all Haylie needed to hear. Or maybe all she could stand to hear without becoming ill or violent, or both.

Spinning on her heel, she marched from the room. Of course, by the time she got downstairs, she wasn't sure what to do.

She could have stormed out, climbed back into the Escalade that didn't belong to her and drive away...but where would she go? Jarrod Ridge? Home to Denver? A local hotel? Any of those options would require returning to the resort to pick up Bradley, at the very least.

But deep down she knew she wasn't going to do any of those things. She also knew she didn't really have a right to be upset at all.

What business was it of hers if Trevor had another woman in his bed? If he had a dozen Playboy bunny girlfriends on the side?

She and Trevor might be sleeping together—a decision she'd known from the outset wasn't the wisest move of her life—but no one had ever said their relationship was an exclusive one. In fact, they hadn't called it a relationship at all.

And she'd known his reputation with women, known he had a girl in every port, so to speak. Could she even be surprised that one had popped up out of the blue? Although, it would have been nice if this particular flavor of the month hadn't popped up in his *bed* while Haylie was still sharing it with him, but that was the risk one ran, she supposed, when one chose to take up with Colorado's most notorious ladies' man.

Which meant Haylie needed to get over it. Stop acting like a jilted lover, a jealous spouse.

But just because logic was winning out over raw, knee-jerk emotion didn't mean she could shed the physical effects of her upset quite as easily. Her heels click-clacked on the polished hardwood floors as she stalked to the giant stone fireplace. It was cold now, empty, but she didn't care.

Crossing her arms beneath her breasts, she slowly began to pace. Not out of anger, exactly, but more to burn off the excess energy still thrumming through her bloodstream and give her something to do while she waited for…whatever she was waiting for.

Though she doubted she and Trevor would end up going to dinner now, she was overdressed for anything else. And even going back upstairs to hide in her room wasn't an option because she was too afraid of running into Trevor and his copper-haired bimbo along the way.

So she stayed where she was, wearing a path in front of the fireplace until she heard footsteps upstairs, moving closer. Bracing herself for what was to come, she dropped her arms and tried to look as casual and unruffled as possible.

The woman was fully dressed again, though parts of her silver lamé jumpsuit looked like it was painted on. Her hair was piled on top of her head like a giant, flame-red crown, and big, chunky jewelry graced her neck and wrists. Haylie was sure the outfit was the height of fashion, but she looked a bit like a stowaway from the disco era. Her makeup was also smudged in places, and every few steps she would sniff, then wipe at her nose as though she'd been crying.

Trevor, on the other hand, was the picture of stoicism as they made their way down the stairs, single file. He kept one hand on the railing, the other in his trouser pocket and his gaze firmly on Haylie.

Haylie watched them move through the house to the front door, watched the woman turn on her go-go booted toe to flash doe eyes at Trevor and run a manicured fingertip down the center of his chest over his navy-blue tie.

"Are you sure, Trev-Trev?" the redhead murmured in a clear pout. Her lips were pursed in a deep frown, her lashes batting fast enough to cause a draft.

To his credit, Trevor didn't respond to the woman's flirtations, except to grasp her hand and very firmly move it back to her side. "I'm sure. Have a safe flight, Isabelle."

With that, he opened the door and saw her out.

Haylie didn't want to believe that the woman's departure could affect her one way or another, but as soon as the door closed behind Isabelle with a click, a wave of relief washed over Haylie. But only because it meant there would be no ugly arguments, no petty confrontations. Right? Certainly not for any other reason.

Pushing away from the front door, Trevor started walking slowly in her direction.

"I'm sorry," he said. "That definitely wasn't how I intended this evening to begin."

"That's all right," Haylie responded, ever so proud that her voice came out steady and sure. "It's none of my business who you invite into your bed."

Okay, so that didn't sound quite as detached and aloof as she might have hoped.

Halting in front of her, he cocked his head, lifting a hand to the side of her face. "I didn't invite her," he said softly. "At least not recently. We dated a while back, and I guess she was hoping we could strike things up again."

"Since she had a key to your house, I guess she wasn't far off the mark."

His lips quirked up in an indulgent half smile, and Haylie locked her jaw, telling herself to keep her mouth shut before he started to take her comments as a sign of jealousy.

"She knows where I keep a spare, though I'm thinking I should probably change that now. And she only climbed into my bed to wait for me because she was tired. She's a model and just flew in from her last shoot in Paris."

A model. Of course. Haylie should have guessed as much from the woman's perfect body, perfect hair, and how perfect she'd looked standing next to Trevor, all tall and lovely and photo-ready.

Haylie's aversion must have shown on her face because Trevor gave a low chuckle and brushed his knuckles across the line of her jaw. "Don't worry, I sent her away. For good. She won't be bothering us again."

Haylie would have been lying if she hadn't felt a small thrill at his words. But the reality of the situation was close behind, reminding her that she didn't belong here, and that today's Sleeping Beauty was only the first in a long string of women Trevor had wrapped around his pinky and was dangling like marionettes from his fingertips.

Licking her lips, Haylie whispered, "There is no us. Not really."

Rather than draw away, as she'd expected, a tiny, bittersweet smile tugged at his lips. "At the moment, there is. And I'm not going to let a surprise visit from a presumptuous runway model ruin that *or* our plans for the evening. Now," he said in a firmer tone, retreating a step, "are you still interested in dinner at Chagall's or would you prefer to stay in?"

Haylie's first instinct was to say "neither." His uninvited guest had been like a splash of cold water, startling her out of her warm but misleading cocoon.

Even though she'd warned herself not to, she'd grown comfortable under Trevor's roof. Sharing his bed. Moving through his world as though she belonged there. Sticking her head in the sand and letting the fantasy of living in Aspen, with all that it encompassed, carry her away.

On the other hand, maybe Isabelle's impromptu arrival was exactly what Haylie needed to remind her *not* to get too comfortable with her current circumstances.

She couldn't leave, because she'd promised Trevor she would stick around until the paternity results came through. And by agreeing to arrange Erica's wedding, she'd sort of inadvertently agreed to stay through the Christmas holiday, hadn't she?

It certainly wouldn't do for the wedding planner to up and run off before the actual nuptials. Especially over something as unreasonable as discovering that her temporary (and accidental, really) lover had other girlfriends. Not when she'd known from the very beginning that he was the playboy type. How hypocritical it would be of her to get upset now simply because she'd been slapped in the face by the flesh-and-blood evidence of his true nature.

So she couldn't leave Aspen because she'd given her word, and she couldn't stomp off in a snit because she didn't have a right to *be* in a snit. And either way, Bradley still needed to be picked up from the resort's day-care center.

Taking a deep breath, Haylie forced her mouth to curve in a smile. And, really, it wasn't that difficult. Not once she'd put things into proper perspective.

Her current situation might not be ideal, not the fairy-tale romance she might have created for herself if she were the author of this story, but it was one she'd walked into with eyes at least moderately wide open. She'd made her bed, so to speak, and until he kicked her out of it or something more significant happened to change her mind, she was going to share that bed with Trevor.

Twelve

Haylie was unaccountably nervous. It was the Friday before Christmas Eve and a week before Erica and Christian's Christmas Eve wedding. But more importantly, it was Erica and Christian's rehearsal dinner, all planned and prepared by Haylie herself.

Which meant it needed to go off without a hitch. Not only because she wanted everything to be perfect for Erica, but also because she took immense pride in the events she organized.

But being in the same room with so many Jarrods was more nerve-racking than she'd anticipated. Especially considering her ongoing affair with Trevor.

Did they know? Had he told any of them, maybe let it slip? Had someone seen them standing a little too close? Speaking a bit too intimately? Acting too familiarly with one another?

What if they could tell, just by looking at Haylie, that

she spent her nights in his bed, making love with him in a thousand different ways? Wonderful, amazing ways. Ways that she was going to miss and long for once she left Aspen and went back to Denver.

Did her cheeks flush when she glanced in his direction? Did she stammer in response when someone asked her how she was enjoying her time at Jarrod Ridge?

Her only hope was that even though everyone in the room knew Trevor quite well, they didn't really know her, and would perhaps excuse any odd behavior on her part as the simple anxieties of an event planner coming up on *the* big event.

Although Trevor's brother Guy had volunteered chefs from the various restaurants to prepare the evening's meal, the dinner itself was being held on the Manor's rooftop, at the Sky Lounge, which they'd temporarily closed to guests.

Tables had been arranged and place settings laid out. Soft, romantic instrumental music filtered through the air, wine flowed liberally and members of both the family and wedding party had been mingling for the past half hour.

Haylie was pretty sure she'd met all of the Jarrods now, as well as their significant others. Erica, of course, she was starting to know rather well just from the amount of time they'd spent together the past few weeks. And she'd been introduced to most of the ladies during the spa day Erica had organized.

Now she was also becoming acquainted with more of the men. She'd interacted with Christian and Guy occasionally because of the wedding plans. Then there were Trevor's brothers Gavin and Blake, and Melissa's fiancé, Shane McDermott.

Thankfully, she was good with faces and names—it was sort of a necessity in her line of work—otherwise, she suspected it would have all been very confusing.

At a signal from the kitchen staff, she started strolling through the room, asking everyone to please make their way to the table, where dinner was about to be served. Normally, once that was done, she would quietly slip into the background again, keeping an eye on the party, but also coordinating with the kitchen to make sure everything was running smoothly.

Tonight, however, she was pulling double duty as both hostess and guest. At Erica's insistence that she join them, and Trevor's reassurance that her presence was more than welcome, there was a place set for her near the end of the long, cloth-draped table, directly on Trevor's left. This would allow her to be involved in the dinner party, but also to jump up and make a quick escape if she was needed elsewhere.

For the first time all evening, Haylie let herself take a deep breath and relax as napkins were placed on laps and the waitstaff began to serve the salad course. So far, the party had gone off without a hitch. Everyone seemed happy, and everything was going exactly as planned.

To her right, Trevor was dressed in a stylish, dark blue suit with a lighter blue tie that made him once again look as if he should be posing for the covers of magazines. Of course, that was true no matter what he wore—a business suit, jeans and sweater or worn flannel pajama bottoms.

Not when he was naked, though. When he was naked, she thought he could grace the cover of a much sexier, much more adult women's magazine. Just thinking about that—and accidentally letting herself picture him as she'd last seen him gloriously naked—made her breath catch in her lungs.

Since the night one of his model ex-girlfriends had decided to play Goldilocks by climbing into his bed uninvited, Haylie had done a much better job of compartmentalizing her responsibilities and her feelings. She'd let him take her to dinner at Chagall's, taken pleasure in the evening as though it were a real date, and put thoughts of all his other women out of her head.

Not the smartest choice, perhaps, but it was the one she'd made and the one she'd come to terms with. Despite the Goldilocks incident, Trevor had done nothing, said nothing, to make her think he was seeing another woman—or women—while she was sharing his bed and his home.

She had no illusions that she and Trevor had a future together, but she'd given herself permission to pretend, just for a little while, that the future didn't exist. To enjoy the short time she did have with him and push everything else away.

Call it denial. Call it delusional. She preferred to think of it as walking on the wild side for once in her otherwise very prim and proper life.

Heather had always been the carefree one in their family. The happy-go-lucky risk taker, while Haylie was the careful, staid sister. Heather had gone through men like cold sufferers go through tissues. Haylie had dated maybe ten different men in her entire adult life… and some of those had been one-time encounters over nothing more than coffee.

Trevor was like her get-out-of-jail free card. Letting herself get involved with him wasn't smart, it wasn't practical…but it *was* going to be a memory she pulled out on all of those cold, lonely, dateless winter nights to come.

So she was going to enjoy him, dammit. Without feeling guilty, without second-guessing herself. And hopefully, when the fantasy came to a screeching halt, she wouldn't end up too damaged, either physically or emotionally.

Beside her, Trevor smiled and reached beneath the table to pat her knee. Which would have been fine, except he left his hand there, his thumb gently rubbing her stocking-clad thigh.

So much for relaxing. His touch made her the very opposite of relaxed, causing all of her nerve endings to buzz like live wires.

If they weren't careful, someone was going to notice that something was going on between them. Or more to the point, if *she* wasn't careful. Trevor was completely calm, completely unruffled, looking no different than at any other time, while she felt as though her face was a kaleidoscope of emotions for the whole world to see.

She was so wrapped up in the uneven beat of her heart and the pounding of her pulse in her veins that she missed the first several minutes of conversation at the table. It wasn't until she heard the word *wedding* that her brain kicked in and began functioning properly, reminding her that she was on the clock and needed to be awake and alert to her clients every whim.

Whoever had mentioned the wedding, though, wasn't talking about Christian and Erica's upcoming nuptials. They were grilling Trevor's brother Guy and his fiancée, Avery, about their plans. From what Haylie gathered, the two of them had been involved for quite some time, and the family was beginning to wonder why they hadn't tied the knot yet. Or perhaps pressuring them to get the show on the road already.

Across from her, Haylie noticed a rosy flush climbing toward Avery's hairline.

"Actually, we haven't gotten around to making any wedding plans yet," Guy responded in a low tone, pointedly taking Avery's hand and twining his fingers with hers on the table between them. "And...well, we've been keeping it under wraps, but now that we've discovered we're expecting, we may have to put it off a while longer."

It took a brief second for Guy's words to sink in, a moment in which the entire lounge was eerily silent, given the number of people occupying the room. But a second after that, chaos erupted. Cheers and high-pitched feminine shrieks of joy mixed together as several family members rose from their chairs and circled the table to surround the happy couple, offering hugs and hearty handshakes.

Haylie stayed in her seat, part of the dinner party, but not really part of the family revelry. Once everyone had returned to their spots, she offered her congratulations and said, "If there's anything I can do to help with the wedding plans—when you *are* ready to plan something, that is—I hope you'll let me know."

"Oh, that would be wonderful." Avery breathed in what could only be described as acute relief, lifting her free hand to her chest. "I have to admit, I really would like to be married before this pregnancy becomes too obvious, but the whole idea is so overwhelming, I don't even know where to begin."

"I felt the same way," Erica put in from her place beside Christian at the head of the table. "But Haylie is amazing. She thought of everything, and then took care of it all before I even had a chance to get stressed. It's been so nice to be able to sit back and relax, letting someone else do the work and the worrying for me."

With a chuckle, she added, "Sorry, Haylie, but it's true. You've been a lifesaver."

Haylie offered the bride-to-be a genuine smile. "My pleasure. That's what I'm here for, after all."

Well, that and determining Bradley's paternity, but sometimes the less said in front of two dozen witnesses, the better.

"Do you think…" Avery paused, biting her lower lip nervously. "Maybe after Erica and Christian's big day, and you've had a chance to take a bit of a breather, could we sit down and chat? You've done so much for them on short notice, if you're not too worn out by then, maybe we could discuss another small, private ceremony for just after the New Year."

Avery looked to her fiancé for his opinion on the matter, and Guy nodded in agreement. Haylie had a feeling Avery could suggest a speedy elopement and he would have them halfway to Las Vegas before she finished her sentence.

"We won't rain on your parade, though," Avery added, leaning forward to glance down the full length of the table at Melissa and Shane, who were also expecting and scheduled to tie the knot on New Year's Eve.

Haylie wasn't even sure she would be around after the New Year, but since she'd gotten involved in Erica's wedding mainly to build her portfolio and hopefully garner even more wealthy clients in the future, it seemed silly not to agree to Avery's request.

Besides, Haylie was enjoying working with the staff at Jarrod Ridge, and would be happy to do so for a second event. She would even help Trevor's sister Melissa with her upcoming wedding, if she needed any assistance, but Haylie suspected the plans were pretty well ironed out by now.

"I'd love to," Haylie said. Then, belatedly realizing she probably should have checked with Trevor before offering her services to yet another member of his immediate family, she added, "If that's all right with you."

After all, regardless of what they shared in the wee hours of night, in the privacy of his bedroom, he might not want her around once the DNA tests came back and he knew whether or not he was Bradley's father.

If he was, he might even want her gone—as in, *give me my child and never darken my doorstep again.* And if he wasn't…well, he might feel the same either way.

But his response was quick enough and sure enough that she thought he must be sincere.

"Of course," Trevor murmured a moment before swinging his attention to his brother and soon-to-be sister-in-law. "Just be sure you're not stingy when it comes to her fee. I've been telling her all month how generous we Jarrods are, and I'd hate to have you ruin our reputation in her eyes by getting married on the cheap."

The statement was made in a jesting tone, but she suspected there was a note of seriousness underscoring the words as well. She didn't know whether to be flattered that he was watching out for her…or embarrassed by the attention he was drawing. To her, to him—to them.

"If she makes my Avery happy and does as impressive a job for us as she has for those two," Guy said, tipping his head in Christian and Erica's direction, "she can have a blank check. Hell, she can have the whole check-book."

Trevor nodded in approval at his brother's quick, magnanimous response. Leaning toward Haylie, he murmured, "See, I told you we'd make it worth your while to stick around."

Then he winked and squeezed her knee under the table, making her feel as though a neon sign was hanging over her head flashing the words *Sleeping with Trevor Jarrod* for the whole world to see. Surely everyone in the room must be thinking that very thing about her.

But before she could burst into flames of mortification, to Haylie's immense relief, conversation picked up and moved in an entirely different direction. The main course was served, followed by a truly decadent chocolate-caramel-mocha dessert created by Guy himself, and then coffee.

Before she knew it—possibly because she was used to staying behind the scenes rather than being smack in the middle of them—Erica and Christian were standing, thanking everyone for coming and for being a part of their very special day, and then the guests began to leave.

Trevor collected their coats and waited patiently while she ran around making sure everything was cleared away properly and that nothing was left undone. She'd told him he could go home without her, or down to his office to catch up on some of the work she knew he'd fallen behind on ever since she'd shown up and thrown his life into turmoil. But he'd refused, telling her not to be silly, and then promptly seated himself at the bar to finish the glass of scotch he'd nursed all through dinner.

When she was finally ready, they made their way out of the lounge and through the hotel to the rear parking lot. Some resort guests were still milling about, but it was late enough that the halls were less busy and crowded than usual.

To Haylie's surprise, as they neared the exit, Trevor took her hand, holding it tightly all the way to his car. His touch warmed her. Not only her bare, chilled fingers, but his heat seeped through her skin to her bones, chasing the cold away, from the tips of her toes to the top of her head.

He must have been confident, though, that no one would see them, otherwise she knew he wouldn't have risked such an intimate gesture.

She didn't want to consider too closely how it made her feel, either. Mostly because she was very afraid she would feel *too much*.

As often as she told herself their involvement was *just* a convenient affair, just a fun way to pass a few hours during her stay in Aspen, lately that reasoning had become more and more difficult to believe.

Trevor was a great guy. Handsome, smart, successful. Rich, partly due to the family he came from, but also in his own right because of the business he'd built from the ground up. He was thoughtful and kind, wonderful with the baby....

If she did an internet search for "The Perfect Man," she was pretty sure his picture would pop right up. If she were filling out a questionnaire for one of those matchmaking services, everything she was looking for in a Mr. Right would describe him to a T.

Yet, ironically, he was the one man in the known universe she needed to be most wary of. The one she should have been smart enough to stay away from.

Coming to Aspen to confront him probably hadn't been the brightest idea to begin with. Letting him talk her into sticking around to await paternity results had been only slightly less intelligent. But going to bed with him…*continuing* to sleep with him even though she knew better, was downright dangerous.

So she couldn't be falling in love with him. It didn't matter that her heart flipped over in her chest the minute he walked in a room. Or that her insides turned all warm and mushy at the first hint of his cologne.

It didn't matter that she found herself wanting to spend more and more time with him, even if it was only to share a meal or kick back and watch a bit of television. Or that making love with him was the single most amazing experience of her life—over and over and over again. And it just seemed to get better every time they were together.

No, none of that mattered, because falling in love with him would not only be foolish…it was pointless.

Even if she was beginning to develop questionable feelings for Trevor…and she wasn't, not really…she had no doubt he was still completely feeling free. He was enjoying their time together—and what red-blooded American man suddenly presented with the luxury of a no-strings live-in lover wouldn't? But she was sure that for him, it didn't go beyond sex. Sex, and finding out if he was Bradley's father; that was the extent of his involvement.

Which was fine with her. She would be going back to Denver soon, anyway, so she needed to keep the very same mind-set.

Of course, reminding herself that she and Trevor were sharing "just good sex" didn't stop her from looking forward to it. As he pulled slowly up his drive and into the garage, she wondered if Bradley would be asleep already, and how quickly they could get rid of the sitter

Trevor had arranged to have watch the baby while they were at Erica's rehearsal dinner.

They exited the Hummer, and he took her arm as they climbed the porch steps and opened the front door. The babysitter—a college student who worked as a part-time server at one of the Ridge restaurants, was on the sofa. Her bare feet were propped on the coffee table, Bradley cradled in her lap, gumming the long, floppy ear of a stuffed bunny.

After shrugging out of their coats, Haylie took Bradley while Trevor paid the girl and saw her safely to her car.

"I'm going to take Bradley upstairs," Haylie told Trevor when he returned. "See if I can get him to sleep."

Trevor nodded. "I'll be up in a few minutes."

Standing at the landing, he watched Haylie climb the stairs. It was too attractive a sight to miss.

Once she disappeared around the corner, he loosened his tie and turned toward his office—or what used to be his office, at any rate. At his urging, Haylie had turned the spacious den into Wedding Central, but he was still allowed to enter as long as he promised not to touch anything.

Surprisingly, that particular order had come from his sister rather than Haylie. As comfortable as she'd become with living in his house, Haylie still acted like a guest instead of a live-in...whatever she was, exactly. But Trevor couldn't seem to break her of the habit of asking if she could use his fax machine or spread her paperwork out on the kitchen island. And that bothered him, more than he would have expected.

Erica, however, possessed no such qualms. And God help anyone who misplaced a sample menu or put so much as a finger on the ten-thousand-dollar designer gown Haylie had picked up for her earlier that week.

Careful not to disturb anything, he took a seat behind the desk and turned on the computer. While he waited for the system to boot so he could check his personal email, he picked up the phone and checked for voice-mail messages.

There was only one, but hearing Dr. Lazlo identify himself had Trevor's heart and stomach plummeting. He didn't even know what the doctor's message was going to be yet, and already his muscles were tensing, his chest growing tight with a mix of anticipation and dread.

"Mr. Jarrod, this is Dr. Lazlo," the other man's voice intoned. "I realize it's late, but the results of your tests have come in, and I know you're eager to hear them. I'll be in the office for a while yet, and after that, you can reach me on my cell phone. I'll be at your disposal all weekend, in case you don't get this message right away." He recited both numbers, and Trevor quickly jotted them down.

Heart still pounding in his chest, Trevor disconnected, then began to dial. This was it—the moment of truth. In the next couple of minutes, he would know one way or the other whether Bradley was his son.

A few weeks ago, he had known exactly which side of the fence he hoped the results would fall. *No match. Ninety-nine percent chance this is not your child.*

But that was before Haylie and Bradley had moved in with him. Before he'd learned how to change a diaper and mix formula and give a baby a bath. All things he never could have imagined he'd enjoy…but realized now he did.

He looked forward to them, even. Looked forward to

waking up in the morning and seeing Bradley's bright eyes and adorably pudgy baby cheeks. Looked forward to holding him while he drank a bottle or dodging splatters of carrot puree while he attempted to feed him his lunch.

And then there was Haylie. He *really* hadn't anticipated becoming attached to her, but damned if he didn't look forward to seeing her first thing each morning, too. Preferably right beside him in his bed, naked and drowsily welcoming.

Not only was she beautiful and headstrong, but she had no trouble standing up to him, which was in itself an unusual and admirable trait. He also admired how hard she'd worked to give Erica a perfect wedding day, with all that entailed. Add to that the incredible love and care she showed for Bradley, and it was possible she was as close to being the ideal woman as one could get.

Not something Trevor ever would have thought he'd catch himself considering. He was much more familiar with women of the flashy-but-flawed variety. And that had been fine, because he was never with any of them for very long.

But Haylie was different, and had him thinking outside the "temporary amusement" box.

Before he could contemplate *that* notion too closely, the doctor picked up the other end of the line.

"Dr. Lazlo, it's Trevor Jarrod," he identified himself. He didn't have to say anything more; they both knew why he was calling.

A minute later, he thanked the doctor for his time, then returned the phone to its cradle and sat back in his chair, letting the breath he'd been holding for what seemed like forever slide slowly from his lungs.

"Hey," Haylie said from the doorway. "Is everything all right?"

He lifted his head to look at her, saying nothing for a moment as he took in her long blond hair, bow-shaped mouth and gently rounded curves. Then he pushed himself up and moved across the crowded office space.

"I have some news," he said softly.

She tipped her head to the side. "Good news, I hope."

"I think so," he replied honestly. "The doctor called while we were away. The paternity results came in, and I *am* Bradley's father."

He wasn't sure what he'd expected—cheers or a cocky *I told you so,* maybe? Instead, a look of near panic passed over Haylie's features, quickly tamped down and replaced by stoic indifference.

"That's great. Wonderful. I'm happy for you."

The high pitch and speed of the words belied her sincerity, and for some reason that bothered the hell out of him. Hadn't she been the one to show up in his office without warning, bluntly informing him that he was the father of her sister's child? She should be delighted to have been proved right, rubbing his nose in it, even.

But as quickly as annoyance flashed, it was gone as he realized how she must be feeling. Yes, she'd been proven right in her belief that he was Bradley's father, but where did that leave her? Was he going to fight for full custody? Would he take the baby and cut her out of her nephew's life forever?

He wasn't sure yet about the first, but to the second, the answer was a big, fat, unequivocal *NO!* He wouldn't do that to Haylie *or* to Bradley. And out of the blue, he knew exactly what needed to be done.

"So now that we're sure, I think I know what our next step should be."

He watched her lips thin and her cheeks pale. But he didn't want to make her nervous, didn't want horrible, frightening scenarios running through her head when he could bring an immediate end to her unwarranted anxieties.

"I think we should get married."

Thirteen

Haylie felt like a Ping-Pong ball, being paddled from one end of a table to the other and back again. She'd gone from wanting to get the baby to sleep so she could come back downstairs and work at seducing Trevor into bed, to being panicked that there was no question about his paternity any longer and that he might try for full custody, to having the rug yanked out from under her with a shocking and unexpected proposal.

For a long, oxygen-deprived minute, all she could do was stand there, staring at Trevor. Blinking stupidly while her brain struggled to make sense of the sudden awkward tilt to her world.

"I—I—" Her mouth was open, but only stammered, stumbling sounds came out.

"It makes sense," Trevor supplied, looking about as moved and romantic as a wet sponge. "You're Bradley's legal guardian. We now know that Bradley is my biological child. And I think it's become clear over the past week that we're more than compatible physically."

He reached out to grasp her wrist, letting the pad of his thumb play over the inside pulse, as a hint of a smile played at one corner of his mouth.

"Getting married seems like the perfect solution to all of our problems. It will alleviate any concerns about custody, keep the press from turning into a pack of rabid wolves the minute they catch wind that I fathered a child with a complete stranger, and give Bradley what he needs most—a loving father *and* mother."

Haylie swallowed hard, trying to get a hold on her runaway emotions and put some kind of order to her scrambled thoughts.

On the one hand, she was happy they finally had their answer, that they—Trevor, especially—knew without a doubt that Bradley was his son. She hadn't been lying, hadn't come to him with some crazy, made-up story and dollar signs dancing in her head.

On the other hand, this news put a giant, ragged hole in the little bubble she'd allowed herself to live in these past few weeks. The one that let her believe everything was fine, that let her enjoy her time with Trevor, being under his roof, pretending that the fictitious happily-ever-after fantasy she'd invented would last forever.

But she'd always known it wouldn't, she just hadn't expected it to end quite this abruptly or in quite this way.

And she certainly hadn't expected Trevor to propose marriage.

Great sex was *not* a good enough reason to get married. Neither was primary physical custody of a child they both loved and wanted desperately. The fact that he was suggesting they tie the knot in such a cold, calculated manner told her that much.

He made it sound like a business proposition. A deal that would benefit them both.

And maybe it would. On paper, it all sounded very logical.

They both wanted Bradley, and by marrying, they could both keep him.

She worked well with his sisters, and had proven she could plan grand parties and events at Jarrod Ridge, as well as anywhere else in Aspen, Denver or beyond.

They suited each other well in bed, so even if their marriage was a loveless one, there would be no lack of passion.

But that was the problem, wasn't it? Any union between them would be completely lacking in what it needed most—*love*.

Worse, she was very much afraid that would only be true from his point of view, because she'd already fallen a little bit in love with him, hadn't she? It didn't seem possible, given that they'd only known each other for three weeks, but it was true, all the same.

She didn't think she could agree to a business arrangement marriage with him, and then go through the rest of her life loving him even though she knew he would never love her in return. And if he went back to his old habits of being a smooth, suave ladies' man, sleeping with other women on the side… *That* would surely kill her.

"I—I—" She caught herself stammering again and made herself stop, take a deep breath and start over.

"No," she said more firmly. With conviction. "No, I don't think that would be a very good idea at all. I don't need a marriage certificate to provide for Bradley—or your money. I'm perfectly capable of caring for him on my own, back in Denver, just as I have since the day he was born. You can see him, of course. Anytime. I won't ever try to keep you from him, and I'm sure we can work out a reasonable visitation schedule. But I'm not going to marry you simply because you think it would be an amusing convenience."

For a minute, Haylie didn't think he was going to respond, but she knew from the narrowing of his eyes and tightening of his mouth that he wasn't happy with her answer. Then he released her wrist and crossed his arms in front of his chest, regarding her with cold, dark eyes.

"I'm afraid that's unacceptable," he told her in no uncertain terms. "A child should know *both* of his parents. I'm Bradley's father, and for all intents and purposes, you're his mother. I don't want him shuffled back and forth between the two of us like a piece of luggage. After only recently discovering I have a half sister, and just now getting to know my own son, there's no way I'm going to let him out of my sight again."

"And that's the only reason you want to get married?" she asked quietly.

She didn't mean to, but she found herself holding her breath, waiting for his reply. Maybe he did have feelings for her. Even if it wasn't head-over-heels, undying love, maybe there was *something* there. Something they could build on, that would give her hope for the future.

"Of course," he answered. "Marriage is the best plan of action I can think of that will give us both what we want."

So much for rose petals and arias and heartfelt declarations of love.

"I'm sorry," she said, shaking her head and feeling the sadness of the words all the way to her soul. "I can't."

She felt Trevor's emotional withdrawal even before he stepped back, distancing himself physically.

"I'm sorry, too," he told her in a hard, flat voice. "And I'd urge you to reconsider. If you push me on this, I'm afraid I'll have to play hardball. I'll file for custody, Haylie, and you know that as Bradley's biological father, the courts will give him to me."

Not to mention his power and money and influence. He was right; if it came down to a court battle over Bradley, she would lose every time.

Careful not to touch her in any way, he moved around her and out of the office, leaving her alone to reflect upon his less than veiled threat.

For the first time since Haylie had started sharing his bed, Trevor woke up alone. He was sure it was only his imagination that led him to believe the room was quieter, the sheets cooler and less welcoming than when she was there.

With any luck, though, it wouldn't last.

They'd both gone to bed angry last night. After being turned down flat by the only woman he'd ever proposed marriage to, he'd let his temper get the better of him and stormed off to nurse his bruised ego.

He was sure Haylie hadn't felt much like singing after he'd left her in the den, either. He shouldn't have threatened her, and saying he would file for custody in order to take Bradley from her had been just that.

Surely there was a compromise to be made, some middle ground where they could agree on what was best for Bradley and how their relationship should proceed. He still thought marriage was the smartest way to go.

And there were worse situations he could think of than having Haylie in his bed every night and every morning, of sharing his home with her, of raising Bradley with her.

The more he thought about it, the more he liked the idea, and decided to bring it up to her one more time. Maybe in the bright light of day, she would be more agreeable to seeing sense.

After grabbing a quick shower, he dressed for work, then went downstairs, expecting to find Haylie there, fussing with Bradley and getting ready to go with him to the Ridge. Instead, he found the first level eerily quiet, the kitchen empty and exactly as they'd left it last evening.

With a frown beginning to mar his brow, he checked the other rooms just to be sure she wasn't tucked away somewhere, working on more wedding plans. When he didn't find Haylie or the baby, he climbed back upstairs, stopping in front of her bedroom door. Her *closed* bedroom door, which she normally left open during the day when she or the baby weren't in there.

Tapping gently, he waited for a reply. When he didn't get one, he tapped again and called her name. Nothing.

Trying the handle, he found the door unlocked and slowly pushed it open...only to find the room just as empty as the rest of the house. The bed was made, the baby's things missing from the crib and changing table, Haylie's belongings gone from the closet and bathroom vanity.

A slick feeling of dread began to trickle down his spine, tightening his chest and gut. If their things were gone, then that meant ...

Taking the steps two at a time, he hurried back

downstairs to search again. Everything. Every room, every broom closet, and finally the garage. The Escalade was still there, but her older, less roadworthy hunk of junk was not. It was gone, and so, he feared, were Haylie and Bradley.

She'd left him. Packed up in the middle of the night and taken off. Back to Denver, no doubt. Without a word. Without even leaving a note.

Dammit. He didn't know who he was more upset with: Haylie for running away—with his son, no less—or himself for royally messing up last night's difference of opinion.

Not quite sure what to do or how to handle the situation, he climbed behind the wheel of his Hummer and headed for Jarrod Ridge. He would go to the office, just as he'd planned. Work out his anger and frustrations at the computer, and maybe later on the slopes.

He certainly wasn't going to go racing off to Denver, chasing after her like a lovesick fool. At least not until he knew what his next plan of action—with Haylie, with Bradley, with both of them—should be.

Hours later, Trevor had several tabs open on his computer screen, several files spread across his desk... and didn't feel as though he'd gotten a damn thing done since he'd walked in the office.

A rap on the door caught his attention and increased his level of annoyance, which had been steadily growing as the day progressed.

"What?" he snapped, not bothering to look up from what he was doing. Part of the convenience of working weekends was fewer interruptions. In theory.

When he raised his head, he found himself staring into the eyes of his older brother Blake.

Looking tall and commanding, as usual, Blake wore his role as leader of the Jarrod family and Jarrod Ridge as well as he wore his tailored, gray Armani suit. He also looked as though he knew Trevor was out of sorts and wondering at the cause.

Not waiting for an invitation, his brother strode forward and took a seat opposite Trevor's.

"Word has it you're in a lousy mood today and taking it out on your lovely and talented receptionist. Much more, and I'm afraid she might walk."

With a sigh, Trevor dropped his pen and rubbed his eyes. "I know. I'll send her flowers and increase her Christmas bonus by way of an apology."

"An actual apology might help, too," Blake suggested.

Trevor nodded. "Before I leave for the day."

"Good." His brother smoothed the crease in his slacks, obviously searching for his next words. "So what's the cause of this suddenly sour disposition? Care to share?" he asked.

Leaning back in his chair, Trevor rested his hands on his stomach and decided that his older brother might not be the worst person to confide in at the moment.

"Haylie's gone," Trevor admitted. Even voicing that fact hurt, let alone picturing his house as he'd last seen it—empty, empty, empty.

"Gone?" Blake repeated. "As in gone-gone?"

"As in packed up her belongings and the baby and went back to Denver," he bit out, every word stinging like a paper cut.

"Any reason why she'd just up and take off like that?"

Trevor took a deep breath, then slowly let it out. "Paternity results came back. Bradley is mine."

Blake's eyes flashed wide. "That's terrific." Then after a second, he said, "It is good news, isn't it?"

"Hell, yes," Trevor responded without a qualm. He might not have planned to become a parent at this point in his life, if ever, but now that Bradley was here, and he knew for certain that the boy was his son… Well, he was just about bursting with love and pride for the kid. And he missed him, dammit. Already.

"I take it Haylie doesn't feel the same," Blake said carefully. "Is she going to fight you for custody?"

"I don't know," Trevor replied honestly. "We didn't quite get that far."

"So why did she leave?"

That caused Trevor's lips to twist. "I guess she didn't feel comfortable living with me any longer after I asked her to marry me and she turned me down flat."

Blowing out a surprised breath, Blake sat back. "Wow. I have to tell you, that surprises me. The way you two have been getting along these past few weeks, I would have expected her to accept. Or at least stick around long enough to see where things between you could lead."

"Tell me about it," Trevor muttered.

"Never thought I'd see the day a woman turned you down for anything, little brother," Blake teased. "Especially once you told her you loved her."

Trevor's eyes widened. "Whoa," he said, rocking uncomfortably in his chair. "Who said anything about love?"

For a minute, dead silence echoed through the room. And then Blake said, "Please tell me you didn't propose without telling her you love her."

When Trevor didn't respond, Blake added in a tone

part disbelieving, part chastising, "What were you thinking?"

Sitting up straight, Trevor moved to rest his forearms on his desk. "It isn't about love," he told his brother, "it's about what's best for Bradley."

"And what would that be?"

"Having two loving parents in his life, full time. Not being passed back and forth between caretakers and residences like an afterthought."

If anyone should have been able to understand Trevor's feelings on the subject of caring for and raising Bradley, it was Blake, who had a child of his own on the way now. One he at least knew about and could prepare for, Trevor thought wryly.

"Agreed. One hundred percent," his brother agreed. "But that's not what you're talking about, are you? You're talking about using a marriage certificate so you can have a live-in nanny. One who will also warm your bed."

Trevor blinked in surprise. Where did Blake get off making such a crass remark? One that was completely off base, no less.

"Don't be ridiculous," he scoffed. "If I wanted a nanny, live-in or otherwise, I'd simply hire one."

"Then why marry Haylie?"

"Because she's Bradley's aunt and has raised him his whole life. She might as well be his mother, she loves him so much and has taken such good care of him."

"Right," Blake said slowly. "And you want to marry her because…"

Trevor's brow crinkled in a frown. "I just told you—"

"No," his brother corrected, "you told me you want to keep Haylie in Bradley's life, and having her move to

Aspen to live with you would make that more convenient for you. What you *haven't* told me is why you want to make her your wife. To have and to hold, in sickness and in health... I'm sure you've heard the vows before."

Growing aggravated with Blake's obscure riddles, Trevor sighed and rubbed the bridge of his nose where a headache was forming. "What's your point?" he asked.

"Given your dating history, I'd think you'd have picked up on this by now. But my *point,* little brother, is that no woman wants to be asked for her hand in marriage because you're interested in full-time child care. They want flowers and candy and romance. A diamond the size of a walnut wouldn't hurt, either, but you can't just say, 'Hey, I think we should get married so we can both live under the same roof and raise my son together.' Especially not to a successful, independent woman like Haylie."

Well, when he put it that way...

A sinking feeling filled Trevor's stomach at the knowledge that that's exactly how he'd proposed to Haylie. Blunt, straightforward, unemotional.

He realized, too, that he hadn't even *asked* her to marry him, but had simply told her that's what he thought they should do. He'd proposed business deals with more enthusiasm than he'd proposed marriage to a woman he honest-to-goodness cared for.

In his defense, though, this was all new to him. He'd never even considered asking a woman to marry him before. Never thought about what it would be like to spend the rest of his life with someone. "Love" was still off his radar and a bit too disconcerting to contemplate, but he was willing to admit he felt *something* for Haylie.

More than he'd feel for just a live-in nanny, thank you very much, he nearly blurted out to Blake. But since he'd apparently already made enough of an ass of himself where his brother was concerned, he decided to keep his mouth shut.

"Will you take a word of advice from your big brother?" Blake asked when Trevor remained oddly quiet.

"Sure." At this point, he'd take anything he could get.

"Figure out how you feel about her. *Really* feel about her. And if the idea of going through the rest of your life without her in it makes you want to crawl into a hole and die, don't waste another minute on the *whys* or *what-ifs*. Go to her and tell her how you feel. Use the L-word—repeatedly and with great enthusiasm. As someone else who let his pride get in the way of love for far too long, I'm here to tell you you'll never be sorry."

With that, Blake pushed to his feet, straightened his suit jacket and moved toward the door. Grasping the handle, he turned back and fixed Trevor with a sober glance.

"For the record," Blake said quietly, "we all really like Haylie. She's good for you. And personally, I think you'd be an idiot if you let her get away."

Without waiting for a response—not that Trevor had one to offer—Blake left the office, closing the door behind him.

So his brothers and sisters and their significant others all liked Haylie, and had obviously been speculating about their relationship behind his back. He should be annoyed, but surprisingly, he wasn't. He wanted the family to like her.

What he had to figure out, as Blake had suggested, was how *he* felt about her. And what he was going to do about it once he did.

Fourteen

Why was it that when she was in a hurry, everything including the kitchen sink seemed to fall in her path?

The last thing Haylie needed—because she *was* in a hurry—was another interruption eating up her time and throwing her even more off schedule. But that's exactly what she got with a knock on her door bright and early Monday morning.

Thanks to being up half the night with Bradley, who had decided to develop colic and been too cranky to sleep, she was already running dreadfully late. For her first day back at the office after her extended absence, too. Her employees were quite capable and reliable, but still she knew she would be walking into a beehive of activity and returning to a giant game of catch-up.

She wished now that she'd given herself more than just one short weekend of being back in Denver before once again jumping into the fray. She should have simply stayed home without letting anyone know she was actually back. A few days tucked into bed with a gallon of Rocky Road and a stack of tearjerker DVDs sounded better than jumping immediately back into the fray, that was for sure.

Not only that, but in addition to trying to juggle her return to It's Your Party, she would also be making the long trek back to Aspen tomorrow already…and probably several more times this week because Erica's wedding was on Friday. Because regardless of her feelings for Trevor at the moment—or the fact that she'd let herself develop feelings for him *at all*—she would never leave his sister in the lurch.

Admittedly, she'd picked up and taken off without warning and without thinking through every detail of her sudden disappearance. But as soon as she'd gotten home, she'd done the responsible thing by picking up the phone and calling Erica.

She hadn't mentioned Trevor's name at all, even though it hadn't been easy. But she'd been afraid that if she spoke about him, if she so much as *thought* about him while talking with his sister, she would burst into tears.

So she'd stuck to the facts, or the facts as she was making them up for Erica's benefit, telling her that she'd been called back to Denver on a business "emergency," but assuring her that she would return to Aspen as often as necessary, and that everything connected to her Christmas Eve wedding would go off without a hitch.

And she intended to follow through on her promise. She only hoped she would be able to navigate the ins and outs of Jarrod Ridge—especially the Manor—without running into Trevor.

It wouldn't be easy, that was for sure. She might even

have to hire a few extra assistants to run errands for her so that she could hole up in one of the back conference rooms or ballrooms where no one was likely to find her. And she would definitely need to ask someone to run to Trevor's house to collect all of her and Erica's things from his office.

With a groan, she once again bemoaned her hasty decision to pack up and leave rather than sticking around and simply dealing with the up-front knowledge that Trevor wanted her in his bed, wanted her as a caretaker for Bradley, but didn't want *her*. Not really.

The doorbell rang again, making her want to tear her hair out. She chose instead to mutter a strained curse beneath her breath. The baby was still fussy, she'd spilled formula on the first outfit she'd put on, she couldn't seem to find her keys, and now—*now*—someone was on her doorstep, beckoning her to become even more frazzled and late.

It had better be something important, like her landlord reporting a gas leak or a firefighter needing to rescue her from a five-alarm blaze. Because if it was just an annoying salesperson or a neighbor wanting to borrow a cup of sugar, she wouldn't be responsible for her actions.

With Bradley whimpering from his baby seat in the kitchen, she raced for the front of the apartment, searching for her keys as she went. Yanking the door open with every intention of blurting out, "I don't want any," no matter what the person standing on the other side was selling, she stopped short.

The first thing she saw was flowers—a gigantic bouquet of soft pink lilies and roses filling nearly the entire space of the open door. Then a gold-wrapped box the size of a small continent appeared. And higher, as her gaze traveled beyond the outlandish offerings, she found Trevor.

He was dressed in one of his elegant, tailored suits, face smooth and freshly shaven, his dark hair stylishly tousled. He looked like a million bucks—which was probably how much he'd spent on the flowers and what she assumed were gourmet chocolates. But it was Trevor himself, not the gifts, that made her mouth go dry and her head spin like a top.

Then she remembered their last interaction, and his threats to take Bradley from her by any means necessary. Grip tightening on the knob, she was ready to slam the door in his face, ready to grab the baby and jump out a rear window if she had to.

"What are you doing here?" she asked, keeping her voice carefully controlled, and trying not to let her anger or fear seep into her tone.

"I had a rough weekend after you left," he told her, not mincing words. His dark brown gaze was steady, the corners of his mouth drawn tight.

"Wandered around the house without answering the phone or checking my email. Didn't even hit the slopes or get any work done, which is what I usually do when I need to think. I also had a bit of a heart-to-heart with my brother Blake. Among other things, he pointed out that women don't get swept away by being told they should get married for practical reasons. They want flowers and candy and grand romantic gestures. So here I am, with the first two, at least."

He thrust the flowers and box of chocolates at her, catching her off guard enough that she released her hold on the door and took them, clutching them to her chest.

"As for the grand romantic gesture…"

Reaching into his pocket, he took out a small, heart-shaped box of black velvet—one that looked disturbingly like a ring box—and dropped to one knee.

Oh, my God. Was this really happening, or was she dreaming it? Haylie's eyes widened as the room began to spin around her, her brain struggling to process what she was seeing, to make sense, not only of Trevor's sudden appearance on her doorstep, but of his words and actions, as well.

"As much as I hate to admit it, Blake is kind of a smart guy. He also mentioned that if I just want someone to love and take care of Bradley, I can hire a nanny. But that if I cared for *you,* I needed to stop being such an idiot and tell you so."

Her heart was pounding so hard, it made a knocking sound inside her chest that echoed in her ears. Was this going where she thought it was? Maybe she wasn't hearing him correctly. Maybe he was here to tell her he'd hired that nanny to take care of Bradley and had only brought the candy and flowers in an attempt to soften the blow.

"That's where the restless weekend comes in. Once I sat down—or rather, paced a hole in the floor—and really thought about it, I realized my brother was right. I don't love only Bradley," he continued from his half-kneeling position. "And if the tests had shown he wasn't my son, I wouldn't have cared. I would still have wanted you to stick around. I figured it out, Haylie. The two nights of soul-searching worked."

She watched his Adam's apple do a slow drop and climb as he swallowed, feeling the same rush of nerves low in her own belly. Her heart *thu-thump thu-thump thu-thump*ed like a herd of wild horses in her chest, making it harder and harder for her to breathe.

"I love you. I love *you,* Haylie," he blurted out just before the rigidity in his perfectly squared shoulders eased a little.

"I've been with a lot of women," he admitted, "but I've never been in love. I guess that explains why I didn't recognize it when it finally happened to me. Why it took the sucker punch of you taking off in the middle of the night for me to wise up." His mouth curved up in one of her favorite wry, self-deprecating smiles.

"But here's what I do know. I know I've been happier and more content in the brief month I've known you than in all the rest of my adult life. I know the house is empty and lonely as hell without you and Bradley there to fill the space with warmth and laughter. And I know that when I think about never seeing you again, it feels as though someone is reaching into my chest cavity and ripping out not only my heart, but my soul."

Of their own volition, tears flooded her eyes. She didn't think she'd ever heard anything so beautiful, except maybe in her own head when she thought about him.

But did he mean it? Did he really and truly feel this way about her, or would he change his mind the minute some cute little twenty-four-year-old with a short skirt and surgically enhanced bosom crossed his path?

"So I'm here to propose again." He soldiered on. "This time, though, I'm going to *ask* instead of tell. And if you say yes, it won't be a marriage of convenience. I'll love you with every fiber of my being, and expect the same from you. I'll expect you to live with me, till death do us part, whether that means you relocating to Aspen or me moving here—I honestly don't care which."

Taking a deep breath, his voice softened only a fraction when he said, "And if you say no… Well, that's okay, too. I mean, I don't want you to say no, of course, but I'd understand. *Understanding* doesn't mean giving up, though. It just means I'll have to start from scratch and work twice as hard at convincing you that my feelings are genuine."

His eyes glittered with conviction as he added, "And no matter what, I won't try to take Bradley away from you. Ever. I don't want you to worry about that. I want him, don't get me wrong, but we'll work out a visitation schedule that we can both live with, I promise."

Popping the lid of the velvet box, he held it out to her, revealing a bright gold band and stunning, marquise-cut diamond that had to be three or four carats, at least. Every facet winked and sparkled, making her almost dizzy.

"Will you marry me, Haylie? Be my wife, my lover, the mother of my children—Bradley, as well as any more we decide to have together?"

Her chest was so tight, her lungs refused to function. Her heart, which had been racing at full speed only seconds before, seemed to screech to a halt.

She wanted so much to believe him, to throw herself into his arms and shout *yes, yes, yes!* Nothing would make her happier than to be with him. Forever. Even if it meant moving to Aspen, starting over in a whole new city, a whole new element. Or maybe not starting over, but branching out.

Could she? Should she?

Taking a shuddering breath, she looked deep into Trevor's eyes, and what she saw there warmed her more than any amount of flowers or candy or pretty words could. Love. And longing. And determination.

He loved her, he wanted her, and if she turned him down, he really would dig in his heels and fight for her.

For a moment, she considered saying no, just to see what he would do. Would there be more flowers, actual dates, attempts at wining and dining her in ways that only a millionaire Jarrod heir could?

But she didn't care about Trevor's money, did she? Or about being wooed. She only cared about him.

Letting go of the flowers and chocolates she'd been clutching to her chest, she fell to her knees in front of him and gave the only answer she could. The only one that made sense both in her head and in her heart.

"Yes," she whispered, throwing her arms around his neck and hugging him tight. His arms circled her waist, squeezing her just as tightly, and then his mouth covered hers, kissing away any further response.

For long minutes, they knelt there, simply kissing, holding, loving. When they finally came up for air, Trevor was grinning, and she could feel a damp smile of her own spreading across her face.

Wiping the tears from her cheeks with the pads of his thumbs, he kissed her one last time before producing the ring box and cocking his head to one side. "May I?"

"Please," she said, extending her left hand. Her *shaking* left hand.

He took it by the wrist and slid the diamond on her finger. As large as it was, she was surprised to find it didn't weigh more. But still, she couldn't resist lifting it up to the light, turning it this way and that, admiring the symbol of her love for Trevor, and his for her.

That he had picked it out just for her and come here to declare his feelings for her on bended knee… She would never forget this day, as long as she lived.

Climbing to his feet, Trevor pulled her up with him, still holding her close to his chest.

"I know we have a lot to discuss," he murmured, "and

you look like you were on your way out, but there are only two things I want right now—to say hello to my son, and then to put him down for a nap so I can make love to my beautiful fiancée."

His wolfish grin as he walked her backward into her apartment and kicked the door closed behind him made her chuckle.

"It's a little early for his nap, but he was up half the night, so you might get lucky." Kissing his ear, she whispered, "And just in case you do, I'd be happy to call in sick to work so you can get lucky with me, too."

Leaning back, he met her gaze, his expression serious. "I already have," he told her in a low voice. "I already have."

Epilogue

It was Christmas Eve.

Snow was falling softly outside the windows of one of the Manor's gorgeous ballrooms. Strands of tiny lights were strung along the walls and ceiling like a starry sky, and a humongous Douglas fir decorated with gold ribbons and ivory bulbs stood at the far end of the room.

Round tables draped in white linens spread out all around, leaving only the center dance floor bare, and guests mingled at both, dancing to a mix of romantic and holiday music played by a string quartet, or enjoying the last bites of wedding cake.

The guests of honor, the newly united Mr. and Mrs. Christian Hanford, were seated at a long, rectangular table reserved for the wedding party, but they had eyes only for each other. In fact, the longer the reception went on, the more they looked as though they couldn't wait to thank everyone for sharing in their special day, then take off for more enjoyable honeymoon pursuits.

Not that Haylie could blame them. She imagined that when her turn came to tie the knot, she would be just as eager to shed the formalities of the official event and get Trevor alone and out of his tuxedo.

A ripple of excitement ran beneath her skin, letting her know just how much she was anticipating her own wedding day. They'd barely discussed plans of any sort since he'd shown up at her door and proposed to her on bended knee, mostly because there were just too many other things going on at the moment.

She'd still needed to see to last-minute preparations for Erica and Christian's wedding. Then there was Melissa and Shane's New Year's Eve wedding, which she would be attending only as a guest, thank goodness. And immediately after, Avery and Guy's nuptials to contend with.

She still didn't know exactly when that would be taking place, but Avery had assured Haylie that she wanted her help with everything from setting a date to deciding on centerpieces.

Which was fine. Better than fine, actually, since one of the things she and Trevor *had* discussed was her carrying on her work here at the Ridge. Rather than closing down or relocating It's Your Party, they'd agreed that it would probably be smarter to leave the Denver business open and put one of her senior employees in charge.

Trevor had suggested that she then branch out and turn the company into a bit of a franchise, opening a second location—at the Ridge itself, if she preferred. He'd promised to help her find the perfect site on the premises to set up shop, but also wanted her to take over as the resort's event coordinator. It would mean getting involved in more than just weddings—it would mean anniversaries, birthdays, engagements, bachelorette parties, and she would certainly be available for any family celebrations.

She liked that idea. She liked the idea of working at the Ridge, being able to keep Bradley with her much of the time or leave him with very reliable day care when she couldn't, and of being able to walk down the hall or across the street whenever she felt compelled to see her soon-to-be husband. Maybe distract him from his computer screen or latest marketing plans.

When a pair of strong male hands slid around her waist and pulled her back against an equally strong male chest, she grinned, thinking that someone else's thoughts must have been running along the same lines as her own.

"You know," Trevor whispered in her ear, "I may have to change my mind about you becoming the event coordinator for Jarrod Ridge."

She jerked her head back, shocked and hurt.

"You're a little too good at this, and I'm afraid you'll be in such high demand once people figure that out that I'll never get to have you all to myself."

As the rest of his words sank in, she released a relieved breath, the cold chill of his perceived criticism replaced by a pleasurable warmth.

Of all the weddings she'd taken part in, she thought she was probably most proud of this one. Not only because she'd pulled it all together in such a short amount of time—and no matter how "simple" Erica had assured her she wanted her special day to be, there wasn't really anything simple about a wedding unless the couple eloped to Las Vegas. And even that involved booking airline tickets and finding a chapel.

But in addition to the food and decor, and keeping everything and everyone on schedule, the entire immediate Jarrod family was in attendance this evening. All the brothers and sisters, husbands and wives. And most surprising of all, Erica's father and stepmother were not only there to help celebrate their daughter's big day, but seemed to be getting along well with all of the Jarrods.

During their time together, Erica had told her about the shock and hurt of discovering that Walter Prentice, the man who'd raised her from birth, wasn't her biological father and that Donald Jarrod was. A fact she hadn't become aware of until after Donald's death. Given that the Prentices and Jarrods apparently hadn't gotten along all that well to begin with, it had taken all these months for the two families to overcome their differences.

Haylie was glad. Erica deserved to enjoy her wedding day without the stress of worrying about how the people she loved most in the world were going to act once they were in the same room together.

Turning her attention back to the man who was holding her snuggly against his chest, swaying back and forth to the airy notes of Chopin, Haylie said, "I was just thinking about that myself. Mostly about how convenient it would be to work here, knowing we could drop in on each other throughout the day."

"And why would we want to do that?" he murmured, feigning puzzlement even as his tone rang with amusement.

"Oh, I don't know. In case we need to discuss some pressing matter where Bradley is concerned. Or for the occasional office quickie. I've always had a fantasy about making love on a desk in the middle of the workday."

Her head spun as he whipped her around to face him. The tea-length skirt of her emerald-green gown swirled around her legs before rustling to a stop.

"You never told me that," Trevor ground out, his coffee-brown eyes narrowed and intense, one brow raised in keen interest.

She cocked her head to the side. "It's never come up before now. And you never asked," she replied primly.

His other brow went up in what she could only perceive as a challenging expression. "I've got a desk. Downstairs. And that's one fantasy I'd be happy to realize right now."

"But how would that look," she began, reaching up to straighten his already perfectly straight black tie, "for the wedding planner to go missing in the middle of the wedding reception? And you're the bride's brother. Your disappearance would look even worse."

Sliding a hand to the small of her back, he tugged her close, letting her feel the proof of his interest.

"You're assuming I care what anyone thinks. Let me assure you, I don't."

"I know you don't," she murmured softly.

That poise and self-confidence was one of the reasons she loved him. And it was going to come in handy once the media found out he was marrying her, the aunt of his nearly five-month-old illegitimate son.

She couldn't *wait* until that hit the fan. But as Trevor said and had assured her numerous times before, it didn't matter what others thought or how many crazy headlines the national tabloids invented. Only the truth mattered, and the truth was that she loved him to distraction, just as he loved her.

They had each other and Bradley, and maybe one day more children to add to their happy family. As far as Haylie was concerned, that made her life just about perfect.

"An hour," she told him, leaning her face into his. "One more hour, and whether the bride and groom have left or not, I'll let you whisk me down to your office and seduce me on top of your desk."

To her delight, Trevor responded with a low growl. The sound made her shiver, and she couldn't help but laugh.

"Sixty minutes," he agreed, synchronizing his watch, "and not a second more."

She nodded.

"In the meantime, how about a dance?"

Taking slow steps backward, he pulled her with him, and she went willingly, following him onto the dance floor and into the rest of her wonderful, happy-ever-after life.

* * * * *